**"I've read a dozen accounts of the Tower.
I've never heard of the Skirts."**

"Maybe your books are out of date." The youth straightened his expression when Senlin didn't return his smile. "My name is Adamos Boreas. Call me Adam." Senlin shook the youth's strong hand and introduced himself. The youth's mature tone and self-confidence were a little disarming. Though his beard was still a patchwork of youthful fuzz and tougher bristle, he seemed entirely adult in his address. "I take it you're in the silk trade." Adam nodded at the bindle of women's garments, still sitting atop the morbid boulder. Black silk stockings dangled from the mouth of it.

Gathering up the bundle, Senlin felt momentarily flustered, and his embarrassment was only made worse by the statement, "They're for my wife."

"Where's your wife?" Adam asked, craning his neck about searchingly.

Senlin's tongue felt as dry and stiff as a leather belt. He thought he might gag if he tried to swallow. He would've given a king's ransom for a drink of anything, and yet worse than his thirst was the confession that stood lodged in his swollen throat. He felt as he had on his first day in front of a class: like a fraud. What sort of husband loses a wife?

Tugging the parcel of silks down from the boulder and clamping it under his arm, he squared Adam with a singular, miserable smile and said, "It's odd you should mention my wife. I seem to have lost her."

Praise for
Senlin Ascends

"*Senlin Ascends* is one of the best reads I've had in ages...I was dragged in and didn't escape until I'd finished two or three days later."
—Mark Lawrence, author of *Prince of Thorns*

"*Senlin Ascends* crosses the everyday strangeness and lyrical prose of Borges and Gogol with all the action and adventure of high fantasy. I loved it, and grabbed the next one as soon as I turned the last page."
—Django Wexler, author of *The Thousand Names*

"Bancroft succeeds amazingly in creating a baffling world that offers little tenderness or hope, but in which the pursuit of instinct and love, dedication and shared sacrifice can overcome barriers...the reader will find much to applaud." —*Publishers Weekly* (starred review)

"*Senlin Ascends* starts off with a bang, and it never slows down. With its breathtaking pace, this book will appeal to a wide variety of readers." —*San Francisco Book Review*

"A great fantasy!" —*Portland Book Review*

"This is an exceedingly rich book. A depth of imagination married with a poetic turn of phrase and an engaging cast of characters conspire to deliver an epic story soaring high above the clouds."
—*Fantasy Faction*

Senlin Ascends

By Josiah Bancroft

THE BOOKS OF BABEL

Senlin Ascends
Arm of the Sphinx

The Books of Babel
Book I:
Senlin Ascends

JOSIAH BANCROFT

www.orbitbooks.net

Copyright © 2013 by Josiah Bancroft
Excerpt from *Arm of the Sphinx* copyright © 2015 by Josiah Bancroft
Excerpt from *Soul of the World* copyright © 2017 by David Mealing

Author photograph by Kim Bricker
Cover illustration by Ian Leino
Cover copyright © 2017 by Hachette Book Group, Inc.
Maps by Josiah Bancroft

Orbit
Hachette Book Group
1290 Avenue of the Americas
New York, NY 10104
orbitbooks.net

Originally self-published in 2013
First Orbit Digital Original Edition: August 2017
First Trade Paperback Edition: January 2018

Orbit is an imprint of Hachette Book Group.
The Orbit name and logo are trademarks of Little, Brown Book Group Limited.

The publisher is not responsible for websites (or their content) that are not owned by the publisher.

The Hachette Speakers Bureau provides a wide range of authors for speaking events. To find out more, go to www.hachettespeakersbureau.com or call (866) 376-6591.

Library of Congress Cataloging-in-Publication Data:

Names: Bancroft, Josiah, author.
Title: Senlin ascends / Josiah Bancroft.
Description: First Trade Paperback edition. | New York : Orbit, 2018. |
  Series: The books of Babel ; 1
Identifiers: LCCN 2017040301| ISBN 9780316517911 (softcover) |
  ISBN 9780316517904 (ebook) | ISBN 9781549140877 (audio book cd)
Subjects: LCSH: Babel, Tower of—Fiction. | Missing persons—Fiction. |
  BISAC: FICTION / Fantasy / Epic. | FICTION / Fantasy / Historical. | GSAFD:
  Fantasy fiction.
Classification: LCC PS3602.A63518 S46 2018 | DDC 813/.6—dc23
LC record available at https://lccn.loc.gov/2017040301

ISBNs: 978-0-316-51791-1 (trade paperback), 978-0-316-51790-4 (ebook)

Printed in the United States of America

LSC-C

10 9 8 7 6 5 4 3 2 1

For Sharon, who never gets lost in the crowd.

SILK GARDENS

PELPHIA

NEW BABEL

THE BATHS

THE PARLOR

THE BASEMENT

THE SKIRTS

THE MARKET

THE TOWER *of* BABEL

a Map of the Lower Ringdoms

The Tower of Babel is sometimes called the Sink of Humanity. Its immensity, the variety of its ringdoms, its mysterious and luxurious heights are irresistible to all comers. We are drawn to it like water to a drain.

—Introduction to *Everyman's Guide to the Tower of Babel* (Fourteenth Edition)

Part I
The Basement & the Parlor

Chapter One

The Tower of Babel is most famous for the silk fineries and marvelous airships it produces, but visitors will discover other intangible exports. Whimsy, adventure, and romance are the Tower's real trade.

—*Everyman's Guide to the Tower of Babel*, I. V

It was a four-day journey by train from the coast to the desert where the Tower of Babel rose like a tusk from the jaw of the earth. First, they had crossed pastureland, spotted with fattening cattle and charmless hamlets, and then their train had climbed through a range of snow-veined mountains where condors roosted in nests large as haystacks. Already, they were farther from home than they had ever been. They descended through shale foothills, which he said reminded him of a field of shattered blackboards, through cypress trees, which she said looked like open parasols, and finally they came upon the arid basin. The ground was the color of rusted chains, and the dust of it clung to everything. The desert was far from deserted. Their train shared a direction with a host of caravans, each a slithering line of wheels, hooves, and feet. Over the course of the morning, the bands of traffic thickened until they converged into a great mass so dense that their train was forced to slow to a crawl. Their cabin seemed to wade through the boisterous tide of stagecoaches and ox-drawn wagons, through the tourists, pilgrims, migrants, and merchants from every state in the vast nation of Ur.

Thomas Senlin and Marya, his new bride, peered at the human menagerie through the open window of their sunny sleeper car. Her china-white hand lay weightlessly atop his long fingers. A little troop of red-breasted soldiers slouched by on palominos, parting a family in checkered headscarves on camelback. The trumpet of elephants sounded over the clack of the train, and here and there in the hot winds high above them, airships lazed, drifting inexorably toward the Tower of Babel. The balloons that held the ships aloft were as colorful as maypoles.

Since turning toward the Tower, they had been unable to see the grand spire from their cabin window. But this did not discourage Senlin's description of it. "There is a lot of debate over how many levels there are. Some scholars say there are fifty-two, others say as many as sixty. It's impossible to judge from the ground," Senlin said, continuing the litany of facts he'd brought to his young wife's attention over the course of their journey. "A number of men, mostly aeronauts and mystics, say that they have seen the top of it. Of course, none of them have any evidence to back up their boasts. Some of those explorers even claim that the Tower is still being raised, if you can believe that." These trivial facts comforted him, as all facts did. Thomas Senlin was a reserved and naturally timid man who took confidence in schedules and regimens and written accounts.

Marya nodded dutifully but was obviously distracted by the parade of humanity outside. Her wide, green eyes darted excitedly from one exotic diversion to the next: What Senlin merely observed, she absorbed. Senlin knew that, unlike him, Marya found spectacles and crowds exhilarating, though she saw little of either back home. The pageant outside her window was nothing like Isaugh, a salt-scoured fishing village, now many hundreds of miles behind them. Isaugh was the only real home she'd known, apart from the young women's musical conservatory she'd attended for four years. Isaugh had two pubs, a Whist Club, and a city hall that doubled as a ballroom when occasion called for it. But it was hardly a metropolis.

Marya jumped in her seat when a camel's head swung unexpectedly near. Senlin tried to calm her by example but couldn't stop himself from yelping when the camel snorted, spraying them with warm spit. Frustrated by this lapse in decorum, Senlin cleared his throat and shooed the camel out with his handkerchief.

The tea set that had come with their breakfast rattled now, spoons shivering in their empty cups, as the engineer applied the brakes and the train all but stopped. Thomas Senlin had saved and planned for this journey his entire career. He wanted to see the wonders he'd read so much about, and though it would be a trial for his nerves, he hoped his poise and intellect would carry the day. Climbing the Tower of Babel, even if only a little way, was his greatest ambition, and he was quite excited. Not that anyone would know it to look at him: He affected a cool detachment as a rule, concealing the inner flights of his emotions. It was how he conducted himself in the classroom. He didn't know how else to behave anymore.

Outside, an airship passed low enough to the ground that its tethering lines began to snap against heads in the crowd. Senlin wondered why it had dropped so low, or if it had only recently launched. Marya let out a laughing cry and covered her mouth with her hand. He gaped as the ship's captain gestured wildly at the crew to fire the furnace and pull in the tethers, which was quickly done amid a general panic, but not before a young man from the crowd had caught hold of one of the loose cords. The adventuresome lad was quickly lifted above the throng, his feet just clearing the box of a carriage before he was swung up and out of view.

The scene seemed almost comical from the ground, but Senlin's stomach churned when he thought of how the youth must feel flying on the strength of his grip high over the sprawling mob. Indeed, the entire brief scene had been so bizarre that he decided to simply put it out of his mind. The *Guide* had called the Market a raucous place. It seemed, perhaps, an understatement.

He'd never expected to make the journey as a honeymooner. More to the point, he never imagined he'd find a woman who'd have him. Marya was his junior by a dozen years, but being in his midthirties himself, Senlin did not think their recent marriage very remarkable. It had raised a few eyebrows in Isaugh, though. Perched on rock bluffs by the Niro Ocean, the townsfolk of Isaugh were suspicious of anything that fell outside the regular rhythms of tides and fishing seasons. But as the headmaster, and the only teacher, of Isaugh's school, Senlin was generally indifferent to gossip. He'd certainly heard enough of it. To his thinking, gossip was the theater of the uneducated, and he hadn't gotten married to enliven anyone's breakfast-table conversation.

He'd married for entirely practical reasons.

Marya was a good match. She was good tempered and well read; thoughtful, though not brooding; and mannered without being aloof. She tolerated his long hours of study and his general quiet, which others often mistook for stoicism. He imagined she had married him because he was kind, even tempered, and securely employed. He made fifteen shekels a week, for an annual salary of thirteen minas; it wasn't a fortune by any means, but it was sufficient for a comfortable life. She certainly hadn't married him for his looks. While his features were separately handsome enough, taken altogether they seemed a little stretched and misplaced. His nickname among his pupils was "the Sturgeon" because he was thin and long and bony.

Of course, Marya had a few unusual habits of her own. She read books while she walked to town—and had many torn skirts and skinned knees to show for it. She was fearless of heights and would sometimes get on the roof just to watch the sails of inbound ships rise over the horizon. She played the piano beautifully but also brutally. She'd sing like a mad mermaid while banging out ballads and reels, leaving detuned pianos in her wake. And even still, her oddness inspired admiration in most. The townsfolk thought she was charming, and her playing was often requested at the local public houses. Not even the bitter gray of Isaugh's winters could temper her vivacity. Everyone was a little baffled by her marriage to the Sturgeon.

Today, Marya wore her traveling clothes: a knee-length khaki skirt and plain white blouse with a somewhat eccentric pith helmet covering her rolling auburn hair. She had dyed the helmet red, which Senlin didn't particularly like, but she'd sold him on the fashion by saying it would make her easier to spot in a crowd. Senlin wore a gray suit of thin corduroy, which he felt was too casual, even for traveling, but which she had said was fashionable and a little frolicsome, and wasn't that the whole point of a honeymoon, after all?

A dexterous child in a rough goatskin vest climbed along the side of the train with rings of bread hooped on one arm. Senlin bought a ring from the boy, and he and Marya sat sharing the warm, yeasty crust as the train crept toward Babel Central Station, where so many tracks ended.

Their honeymoon had been delayed by the natural course of the school year. He could've opted for a more convenient and frugal destination, a seaside hotel or country cottage in which they might've secluded themselves for a weekend, but the Tower of Babel was so much more than a vacation spot. A whole world stood balanced on a bedrock foundation. As a young man, he'd read about the Tower's cultural contributions to theater and art, its advances in the sciences, and its profound technologies. Even electricity, still an unheard-of commodity in all but the largest cities of Ur, was rumored to flow freely in the Tower's higher levels. It was the lighthouse of civilization. The old saying went, "The earth doesn't shake the Tower; the Tower shakes the earth."

The train came to a final stop, though they saw no station outside their window. The conductor came by and told them that they'd have to disembark; the tracks were too clogged for the train to continue. No one seemed to think it unusual. After days of sitting and swaying on the rails, the prospect of a walk appealed to them both. Senlin gathered their two pieces of luggage: a stitched leather satchel for his effects, and for hers, a modest steamer trunk with large casters on one end and a push handle on the other. He insisted on managing them both.

Before they left their car and while she tugged at the tops of her brown leather boots and smoothed her skirt, Senlin recited the three vital pieces of advice he'd gleaned from his copy of *Everyman's Guide to the Tower of Babel*. Firstly, keep your money close. (Before they'd departed, he'd had their local tailor sew secret pockets inside the waists of his pants and the hem of her skirt.) Secondly, don't give in to beggars. (It only emboldens them.) And finally, keep your companions always in view. Senlin asked Marya to recite these points as they bustled down the gold-carpeted hall connecting train cars. She obliged, though with some humor.

"Rule four: Don't kiss the camels."

"That is not rule four."

"Tell that to the camels!" she said, her gait bouncing.

And still neither of them was prepared for the scene that met them as they descended the train's steps. The crowd was like a jelly that congealed all around them. At first they could hardly move. A bald man with an enormous hemp sack humped on his shoulder and an iron collar about his neck knocked Senlin into a red-eyed woman; she repulsed him with an alcoholic laugh and then shrank back into the swamp of bodies. A cage of agitated canaries was passed over their heads, shedding foul-smelling feathers on their shoulders. The hips of a dozen black-robed women, pilgrims of some esoteric faith, rolled against them like enormous ball bearings. Unwashed children loaded with trays of scented tissue flowers, toy pinwheels, and candied fruit wriggled about them, each child leashed to another by a length of rope. Other than the path of the train tracks, there were no clear roads, no cobblestones, no curbs, only the rust-red hardpan of the earth beneath them.

It was all so overwhelming, and for a moment Senlin stiffened like a corpse. The bark of vendors, the snap of tarps, the jangle of harnesses, and the dither of ten thousand alien voices set a baseline of noise that could only be yelled over. Marya took hold of her husband's belt just at his spine, startling him from his daze and goading him onward. He knew they couldn't very well just stand there. He gathered a breath and took the first step.

They were drawn into a labyrinth of merchant tents, vendor carts, and rickety tables. The alleys between stands were as tangled as a child's scribble. Temporary bamboo rafters protruded everywhere over them, bowing under jute rugs, strings of onions, punched tin lanterns, and braided leather belts. Brightly striped shade sails blotted out much of the sky, though even in the shade, the sun's presence was never in doubt. The dry air was as hot as fresh ashes.

Senlin plodded on, hoping to find a road or signpost. Neither appeared. He allowed the throng to offer a path rather than forge one himself. When a gap opened, he leapt into it. After progressing perhaps a hundred paces in this manner, he had no idea which direction the tracks lay. He regretted wandering away from the tracks. They could've followed them to the Babel Central Station. It was unsettling how quickly he'd become disoriented.

Still, he was careful to occasionally turn and construct a smile for Marya. The beam of her smile never wavered. There was no reason to worry her with the minor setback.

Ahead, a bare-chested boy fanned the hanging carcasses of lambs and rabbits to keep a cloud of flies from settling. The flies and sweet stench wafting from the butcher's stall drove the crowd back, creating a little space for them to pause a moment, though the stench was nauseating. Placing Marya's trunk between them, Senlin dried his neck with his handkerchief.

"It certainly is busy," Senlin said, trying not to seem as flustered as he felt, though Marya hardly noticed; she was staring over his head, a bemused expression lighting her pretty face.

"It's wonderful," she said.

A gap in the awnings above them exposed the sky, and there, like a pillar holding up the heavens, stood the Tower of Babel.

The face of the Tower was patched with white, gray, rust, tan, and black, betraying the many types of stone and brick used in its construction. The irregular coloration reminded Senlin of a calico cat. The Tower's silhouette was architecturally bland, evoking a dented and ribbed cannon barrel, but it was ornamented with grand friezes, each band taller than a house. A dense cloudbank obscured the Tower's pinnacle. The *Everyman's Guide* noted that the upper echelons were permanently befogged, though whether the ancient structure produced the clouds or attracted them remained a popular point of speculation. However it was, the peak was never visible from the ground.

The *Everyman's* description of the Tower of Babel hadn't really prepared Senlin for the enormity of the structure. It made the ziggurats of South Ur and the citadels of the Western Plains seem like models, the sort of thing children built out of sugar cubes. The Tower had taken a thousand years to erect. More, according to some historians. Overwhelmed with wonder and the intense teeming of the Market, Senlin shivered. Marya squeezed his hand reassuringly, and his back straightened. He was a headmaster, after all, a leader of a modest community. Yes, there was a crowd to push through, but once they reached the Tower, the throng would thin. They would be able to stretch a little and would, almost certainly, find themselves among more pleasant company. In a few hours, they would be drinking a glass of port in a reasonable but hospitable lodging on the third level of the Tower—the Baths, locals called it—just as they had planned. They would calmly survey this same human swarm, but from a more comfortable distance.

Now, at least, they had a bearing, a direction to push toward.

Senlin was also discovering a more efficient means of advancing through the crowds. If he stopped, he found, it was difficult to start again, but progress could be made if one was a little more firm and determined. After a few minutes of following, Marya felt comfortable enough to release his belt, which made walking much easier for them both.

Soon, they found themselves in one of the many clothing bazaars within the Market. Laced dresses, embroidered pinafores, and cuffed shirts hung on a forest of hooks and lines. A suit could be had in any color, from peacock blue to jonquil yellow; women's intimate apparel dangled from bamboo ladders like the skins of exotic snakes. Square-folded handkerchiefs covered the nearest table in a heap like a snowdrift.

"Let me buy you a dress. The evenings here are warmer than we're used to." He had to speak close to her ear.

"I'd like a little frock," she said, removing her pith helmet and revealing her somewhat deflated bronzy hair. "Something scandalous."

He gave her a thoughtful frown to disguise his own surprise. He knew that this was the kind of flirtation that even decent couples probably indulged in on their honeymoon. Still, he was unprepared and couldn't reflect her playful tone. "Scandalous?"

"Nothing your pupils will need to know about. Just a little something to disgrace our clothesline back home," she said, running her finger down his arm as if she were striking a match.

He felt uneasy. Ahead of them, acres of stalls cascaded with women's undergarments. There wasn't a man in sight.

Fifteen years spent living as a bachelor hadn't prepared him for the addition of Marya's undergarments to the landscape of his bedroom. Finding her delicates draped on the bedposts and doorknobs of his old sanctuary had come as something of a shock. But this mass of nightgowns, camisoles, corsets, stockings, and brassieres being combed through by thousands of unfamiliar women seemed exponentially more humiliating. "I think I'll stay by the luggage."

"What about your rules?"

"Well, if you'll keep that red bowl on your head, I'll be able to spot you just fine from here."

"If you wander off, we'll meet again at the top of the Tower," she said with exaggerated dramatic emphasis.

"We will not. I'll meet you right here beside this cart of socks."

"Such a romantic!" she said, passing around two heavy-set women who wore the blue-and-white apron dresses popular many years earlier. Senlin noticed with amusement that they were connected at the waist by a thick jute rope.

He asked them if they were from the east, and they responded with the name of a fishing village that was not far from Isaugh. They exchanged the usual nostalgia common to coastal folk: sunrises, starfish, and the pleasant muttering of the surf at night, and then he asked, "You've come on holiday?"

They responded with slight maternal smiles that made him feel belittled. "We're far past our holidays," one said.

"Do you go everywhere lashed together?" A note of mockery crept into his voice now.

"Yes, of course," replied the older of the two. "Ever since we lost our little sister."

"I'm sorry. Did she pass away recently?" Senlin asked, recovering his sincere tone.

"I certainly hope not. But it has been three years. Maybe she has."

"Or maybe she found some way to get back home?" the younger sister said.

"She wouldn't abandon us," the older replied in a tone that suggested this was a well-tread argument between them.

"It is intrepid of you to come alone," the younger spinster said to him.

"Oh, thank you, but I'm not alone." Tiring of the conversation, Senlin moved to grip the handle of the trunk only to find it had moved.

Confused, he turned in circles, searching first the ground and then the crowd of blank, unperturbed faces snaking about him. Marya's trunk was gone. "I've lost my luggage," he said.

"Get yourself a good rope," the eldest said, and reached up to pat his pale cheek.

Chapter Two

Savvy shoppers will revel in the Market that coils about the foot of the Tower. Don't be afraid to walk away while haggling; a little retreat may win a great bargain.

—*Everyman's Guide to the Tower of Babel*, I. IV

enlin sat atop a sandstone boulder near the foot of the Tower, eating the pistachios he'd bought for breakfast. His chapped lips stung. Small brown birds scavenged through the shells he dropped, picking at the flakes of germ. He didn't recognize the species. A few hours earlier, he'd bought a drink, a single ladle of water that cost as much as a dram of good brandy back in Isaugh. Already, he was thirsty again.

He'd brought a little notebook to record his impressions, as any amateur anthropologist might, but he hadn't cracked it since disembarking from the train. He didn't wish to record any of this. His copy of the *Everyman's Guide* dangled open in his hand. An untidy bundle of women's undergarments sat at his side. He felt dizzy with exhaustion; his fingers quaked from it. If he laid back on the sun-warmed rock and closed his eyes, he would fall asleep in an instant. He was afraid of doing just that.

It was now two days since they'd climbed down from the train, two days since he'd first glimpsed the Tower through the tattered awning, two days since she'd turned away and gone laughing in search of a frock. Something scandalous.

The Tower of Babel swelled before him like the step of a great plateau, a rock face that surged without apparent end. Except for the arched entrance that yawned about a deeply shaded tunnel a hundred yards away, the lower span of the Tower was unbroken by windows or ledges. Higher up, Senlin could discern a few structures jutting from the Tower like thorns from the trunk of an old rosebush. Airships clung to these thorns, their gondolas made as small as aphids by the distance. Skyports, Senlin supposed. He'd read that most levels of the Tower, or ringdoms, had several such ports. If only he had come with Marya by airship! But traveling by air was prohibitively expensive; two tickets would cost nearly a year's salary. Worse yet, he was prone to seasickness. The locals of Isaugh often teased him for it: The headmaster of Fishtown can ring his bell, but he can't ride a swell. He hadn't wanted to spend their honeymoon voyage dangling over the rail of an airship, seeding the landscape with the contents of his stomach. Besides, the walk up to their eventual destination, the Baths, had been part of the adventure, and Marya had looked forward to it.

A sudden realization made him jump and nearly tumble from the rock he sat perched on. The paper sack of pistachios slid from his hand and bounced down the boulder to the ground, the pale shells skittering every which way across the red hardpan.

He knew it would be there before he looked, and yet he tore into his satchel, rummaging through the side pocket, past spare pens, his coat brush, and blank postcards until, at last, his hand closed around the cause of his alarm. He pulled free the pair of train tickets.

He had her ticket home.

He had been only momentarily distracted by the loss of her luggage and had gone charging off through the press of hagglers and tourists without any sense of which direction the thieves had gone. It wasn't long before he conceded that the luggage was lost. He returned to the stall, nearly certain it was the same display of socks they'd stood by just minutes before, and there he spent the first afternoon and then the first night of their honeymoon in Babel, rocking on his heels, all alone. He was certain she would find her way back. He focused himself on being level and rational and even occasionally optimistic. This wasn't a very great inconvenience. Perhaps it was an adventure, the kind that made vacation stories enjoyable to recount. She would return.

But over the course of that night, he'd watched as first one stall and then another was packed up, their stock dragged away by camel and mule, on sleds and in wagons. New merchants arrived. New awnings and tables were raised, changing the topography of the alleys between vendors, changing even the cutout shape of the sky above him. Now it made sense why the *Everyman's Guide* didn't include any maps of the Market. One might as well try to draw a diagram of tomorrow's sunset. The Market's evolution never ceased. When the sock stall where he'd promised to wait was transformed into a vendor of oil lamps, he realized that she would never find her way back to him. He couldn't stand idle any longer.

The next day he undertook a systematic search, beginning with what remained of the silk district of the Market where she had disappeared. He searched in an expanding spiral as best he could manage, buying from every few merchants a silk slip or a pair of stockings, some trifle sufficient to get their attention long enough for him to ask if they'd seen a woman in a red helmet in the past day. He was glad, at least, to have an easy way to describe her: a woman in a red helmet. She'd been more clever and prudent than he'd given her credit for. After a day of this, he had accrued an embarrassing bindle of women's clothes. But there was no news of Marya. The clothiers began to turn into potters, and the tables of silks were replaced with galleries of crockery and stoneware.

Where the awnings and tents were sparsest, he clambered up on kegs and crates to scan the crowd for her, certain she would stand out, vivid as a cardinal in a tree. But it was impossible to really see anyone distinctly amid the throng. Almost unconsciously, his search began to take him closer to the Tower, which turned out to be farther away than it had first seemed. Or perhaps he had only wandered farther from it. He couldn't be sure.

As the hours of the second night swam by, he became less organized, less restrained. He wandered about heedlessly, calling her name. When he saw even a glimpse of red, he'd crash over stalls and vendors, shove aside milling shoppers, shouting breathlessly, "Marya, Marya!" only to find a man in a red fez, or a boy carrying a red paper lantern on a pole, or a red blanket peeking from under a horse's saddle...

He wasn't accustomed to feeling panic, nor did he know how to console himself when despair descended upon him. Their honeymoon was ruined, that much seemed certain. They would have to fabricate some fable of luxury to tell their friends, and he would, of course, make it all up to her with a quiet weekend in a pastoral cottage, but for the rest of their marriage she would remember what a terrible trial their honeymoon had been. It was an inauspicious start.

Everywhere he looked now he saw groups of people roped together. Any movement through the crowd was made more difficult by the web of leashes. Why had the *Guide* neglected to mention that little nugget of wisdom? Bring a good rope.

Senlin tucked the train tickets into the pages of his *Everyman's Guide*, cursing himself for having been so shortsighted as to carry both of their fares. He wondered if she had enough to buy a new ticket and did the quick sum in his head. He had seven minas, sixteen shekels, and eleven pence to his name, and unless she had been robbed, she would have about the same. A ticket to Isaugh, even third class, would cost ten minas at least. No, she hadn't nearly enough. Marya was stranded here.

A wishbone of an old man, bald and naked to the waist, staggered past Senlin's boulder lookout, bent double under a sack. Blackened rivers ran down his back from where sweat mingled with the coal he carried. The old slave, goose-necked and tottering, watched only the boot heels of the well-dressed tourist ahead of him. Both were part of a column of travelers streaming toward the entrance at the Tower's base. Otherwise, the ground that collared the Tower was noticeably empty. This no-man's land extended a hundred paces out from the foot of the Tower. Senlin couldn't imagine why this space should be left empty while the Market behind him was choked with people.

"Are you lost?" asked a young man standing near his feet at the base of the boulder.

"Why do you ask?" Senlin said. The youth winked in the sunlight, his thick, dark hair glowing with the luster of oil. He had the broad shoulders, short stature, and narrow waist of an acrobat, and his complexion was a rich olive color that drew out the gold flecks in his eyes.

"Most people don't lounge about in the Skirts. That stone you're sitting on..."

"Is it sacred?"

"No more than a headstone. It fell a few days ago and landed on a tourist."

"Fell from where?" Senlin asked, appalled. The youth only pointed up in reply.

Feeling conspicuous now, Senlin clambered down the smooth face of the boulder. "I don't understand," Senlin said, dusting his hunkers and straightening his jacket. "The Tower of Babel is the surest construction in the world. It's built on deep bedrock. It doesn't shed boulders like an oak drops acorns. It's a miracle of engineering!" Senlin wagged his *Everyman's Guide* at the youth as if the book proved his point.

"Oh, it's a miracle for sure. But sometimes it dumps a little miracle on us," the youth said. "It doesn't matter if something falls from the second or the twenty-second ring. It all crashes on the same ground: the Skirts. I wouldn't pitch my tent here if I were you."

This discovery did not jibe at all with Senlin's studies, nor with what he had taught his students about the Tower, which were always his favorite lectures. He'd draw schematics of the Tower and the network of railroads that radiated out from it. He'd introduce the Tower's murky history and the venerable historians who debated its age, original architects, its internal machinations, and its purpose. He even taught them about the Baths, famous for its therapeutic spas, where he'd promised to take Marya. "I've read a dozen accounts of the Tower. I've never heard of the Skirts."

"Maybe your books are out of date." The youth straightened his expression when Senlin didn't return his smile. "My name is Adamos Boreas. Call me Adam." Senlin shook the youth's strong hand and introduced himself. The youth's mature tone and self-confidence were

17

a little disarming. Though his beard was still a patchwork of youthful fuzz and tougher bristle, he seemed entirely adult in his address. "I take it you're in the silk trade." Adam nodded at the bindle of women's garments, still sitting atop the morbid boulder. Black silk stockings dangled from the mouth of it.

Gathering up the bundle, Senlin felt momentarily flustered, and his embarrassment was only made worse by the statement, "They're for my wife."

"Where's your wife?" Adam asked, craning his neck about searchingly.

Senlin's tongue felt as dry and stiff as a leather belt. He thought he might gag if he tried to swallow. He would've given a king's ransom for a drink of anything, and yet worse than his thirst was the confession that stood lodged in his swollen throat. He felt as he had on his first day in front of a class: like a fraud. What sort of husband loses a wife?

Tugging the parcel of silks down from the boulder and clamping it under his arm, he squared Adam with a singular, miserable smile and said, "It's odd you should mention my wife. I seem to have lost her."

Chapter Three

The happy traveler will look for the broadest, most beaten path, will look to his fellow traveler for behavioral cues, will be an echo but will not raise his voice. It is dangerous to blaze a trail when one is already so clearly cut.

—*Everyman's Guide to the Tower of Babel*, I. VI

The berth in their sleeper car had hardly been wide enough for the two of them to occupy at once. They had to lie, shoulder to shoulder, with the ceiling not an arm's length away. The mountain pines made the moon flicker through their window like a stroboscope, and the car swayed as tenderly as a cradle.

Senlin was unprepared for marriage in every way. He possessed neither the imagination nor emotional warmth that intimacy required. So he lay there on his back like a fish stranded by the tide, a sturgeon gasping out of water. Here was the moon and the rocking crib and the far from prying eyes and every romantic thing a man could request, and what did he do with it? He was drowning in opportunity.

Marya lay propped on her elbow watching him appear to sleep with his eyes open. She pressed the flat of her finger against his cheek, lifting up a smile like a fishhook, trying to tease some life from him. She tugged at his earlobe, bit lightly at his shoulder, and blew on his neck. Still he lay, sometimes flinching but not responding.

"Tell me, Tom, how deep is the well beneath the Tower?"

Senlin swallowed, his throat ribbiting like a frog. "Six thousand feet, as I recall."

"Six thousand feet! If the well was wide enough to drop the Tower into—"

Senlin interrupted, stuttering. "Impossible. The well would collapse if it—"

Marya pressed on in a voice hardly above a whisper, "If it were wide enough, would the Tower be tall enough to fill the well?"

He considered it. "It's possible, I suppose, if there are sixty levels at a hundred feet apiece..."

"It's possible?" she said, her mouth nearer his blushing ear.

"Possible," he confirmed. And the moon flickered through the aspens, and the car sawed from side to side, carrying them further from familiar things.

The dark-haired youth dipped his head out of respect or abashment at Senlin's obvious straining. The headmaster's neck was stretched so drastically that the ribs of his throat showed. "If it makes you feel any better, you aren't the first to lose someone."

Senlin took Adam for a local, or perhaps a visitor of such long standing that he'd become an émigré. He knew too much to be a tourist. "I was hoping she would pass by here. I don't suppose you've seen a woman wearing a red sun helmet?"

"That's not much of a description."

This was the first time he'd been encouraged to say more about his lost wife. All his other inquiries had been met with dismissive gestures: a waved hand or a shallow shrug. Though he felt a little uneasy, hope overrode his preference for discretion. He forced himself to describe her more fully. "She's about your height. Slender with auburn hair and pale skin. Pretty."

"No luggage?" Adam asked, and Senlin shook his head. "About your age?"

Senlin hesitated. "More youthful." A small bird with a dark tail swooped between them and began picking, unperturbed by their presence, at the spilled pistachios. "That is a blackstart," Senlin said, identifying the bird.

He was relieved to have a momentary distraction. "They're a determined species, from what I've read. Aren't afraid of much."

As if to test the bird, Adam moved his toe nearer it. The bird hopped pertly on the top of his boot and rebounded into the red sand. Adam snorted his amusement. "You a bird-watcher?"

Senlin shook his head. "Just an armchair naturalist. I'd never seen one in person before today." Senlin had the distinct impression that the young man was looking him up and down, measuring him in some way.

"I suppose you've already visited our little Lost and Found," Adam Boreas said, and taking Senlin's blank expression as answer, offered an explanation. "Where the lost post notes."

Senlin brightened. Of course! Surely hundreds of people had wandered away from their companions before. He wasn't the first to lose someone in the Market. It made perfect sense that there existed a forum for reuniting people. "Would you take me to it?"

"I will," Adam said. "But it won't help."

"Let me be the judge. Please," Senlin said, stowing the guidebook in his satchel. "Lead the way."

Following Boreas toward the base of the mountainous Tower, Senlin felt momentarily hopeful. The willingness with which Adam had responded to his direction reminded him of how his commands were received in his classroom. Perhaps he wasn't entirely incapable after all.

The Skirts were as barren as a salt pan, flat as an iron, and almost as hot. The sun seemed to shine from both the sky and the earth at once.

When he'd first spotted the Tower through the shaking frame of their cabin window, many miles removed, it had appeared like a dark scratch on the blue lens of the sky. Now it seemed like a sheer corner in the earth, as if the ground and gravity and every natural thing had been folded upward. The Market experienced two nights: the natural night of the earth and the strange gloom of the Tower's shadow. They were fortunate now to be approaching the Tower while it was still sunlit, though the Tower's umbra crept nearer like the hand of a monstrous sundial. In a few minutes, the Tower's night would fall on them.

Boreas led him to one side of the gate where the flow of traffic naturally thinned. All along the curved length of the Tower's base, figures leaned and kneeled against the wall, their faces pressed close. They seemed like pilgrims praying to a shrine. The facade was papered with sheets and scraps of paper as far up as Senlin's arm could reach. These weathered, discolored tatters were layers deep, wrapping the enormous blocks of granite in a shell of papier-mâché.

"Aren't they afraid of being hit by falling rocks?" Senlin asked, indicating the readers to either side of them.

"Some urges are more immediate than fear," Boreas replied.

It was a moment more before it dawned on Senlin that this endless tatter of paper was the Lost and Found. He suspected Boreas was watching him for a response, so even as he felt hope leave him, he formed his shoulders and chin into the posture he used for lecturing. "It only makes sense that there would be so many. I suppose it is like this all the way around?"

"I haven't walked it myself, but I imagine so," Adam said.

"Of course. And these people risking death from above are searching for notes from lost loved ones." Senlin leaned in and read one of the fresher scraps of paper. The fine cursive suggested that the author was well educated. It read, "Robert, I will find my way home. Come after me. Love, Mrs. K. Proffet." This note led him to the next, more crudely drawn and in pencil: "My Dear Lizzy. I wait for you every day at noon at Owl's Gate. I'm under your yellow umbrella. Your loving husband, Abraham Weiss." The neighboring note simply read, "Hu Lo, I give you up to your new life. Don't look for me. Jie Lo."

He read another and another, sliding his nose from one announcement of heartbreak or hope to the next. He felt the beginning of a compulsion growing within him, felt the urge to read just one letter more. The next might be in her handwriting. Or the next.

But he quickly realized that he could fritter the rest of his life reading his way around the Tower and still never find a note from Marya. One might not even exist, or might have existed but been buried under another's desperate post.

The contents of the notes he'd read brought on a more unsettling revelation. It occurred to him for the first time that their parting might be more than an inconvenience. He might never find her. Marya might be lost for good, might perish from exposure or illness or violence. She might be absorbed into another's life, become another man's love, a younger man...a man who wouldn't lose her so quickly. "Useless," he said.

Assuming that he referred to the overwhelming breadth of the Lost and Found, Boreas said, "I've spent my fair share of hours crossing my eyes at this wall."

"You've lost someone?"

"My sister, Voleta."

"How long ago?"

"Two years and a month."

"Oh, my word." Senlin felt faint. His knees gave without warning, and he dropped into an awkward crouch with his back to the Tower. "What about the local authorities, the magistrates? Who polices the bazaar?"

"There are a few roaming constables. You'll occasionally see a man in a khaki uniform. But half of the time they aren't really officials of any kind. They're thugs who stole the uniform or bought it. Even the real constables can be treacherous. I've known more than a few men who've been beaten and robbed by them." Adam rubbed his neck, exposing a circular scar on his forearm. The wound was so perfectly round it could've been drawn with a compass.

"Is the Tower entirely ungoverned?"

"It's a little better inside, and even better higher up. There are many ringdoms where one power or another has taken up the law."

A woman with bruised, hooded eyes who had been scrutinizing the wall beside Senlin now began to read over his head as if he was not there. He had to crawl around her to return to his feet. The woman's blank expression could've been the work of a hypnotist. But what began as pity for her quickly turned to private resolve. He had to shake himself free of the stupor that had claimed him since

Marya had vanished. He'd spent the last days running around with an uncharacteristic lack of consideration. He hadn't taken the situation seriously enough at first, and then he'd allowed panic to direct him. If he expected to find Marya, he would have to rely on his reasoning, his ability to observe and analyze. He was not as helpless as this poor wretch, inching her life away, perusing the scroll of the doomed. He had his wits. The courage would come. For now, he had to think.

After her initial shock had faded, how would Marya have reacted? Without a ticket to take her home, she would have to navigate the common mire of vendors and thieves on her own. She would naturally seek a safer refuge. She was not without resources: She had some money of her own secreted in her waistband—not an extravagant amount, but enough to keep her in room and board for a while. There were no permanent accommodations in the Market, and he doubted that she would hire a tent to sleep in. It made sense, then, that she would enter the Tower, knowing of course that they had intended to lodge on the third level in the Baths. They had not settled on a particular hotel because it was impossible to make reservations from such a distant town as Isaugh, but she would have no problem securing a room. What had she said just before they parted? We'll meet again at the top of the Tower. Wasn't the Baths their pinnacle? Wasn't that the limit of their resources? Adam's promise of improved law and order gave him further confidence in the idea.

There was really only one thing to do: go after his wife who had gone on ahead.

"Mr. Boreas, you seem familiar with the Market. How familiar are you with the ringdoms of the Tower?"

"I know the lower four very well."

"That's all I need. Would you be willing to share your experience for a day or two? I would compensate you for your time."

"I could use the work, I must admit."

"Can you begin at once?"

"Give me one moment," Boreas said, and unfolded a brilliantly white piece of stationery.

As he tacked it to the wall, Senlin could not help but read the clearly blocked words, which read, "Voleta: A rescue is coming. Adam." Boreas caught him looking and responded with an ironic smirk. "A superstitious habit."

Senlin tried to keep his smile from seeming condescending, but he couldn't help thinking of it as an indulgence, a compulsion that Boreas had mistaken for hope. Senlin was preparing to make some remarks on the virtues of pragmatism when they were interrupted by a smattering of distant screams. The cries, as if contagious, quickly spread to a chorus. Senlin turned just in time to see the blur of something plunging down, something that was as big as a barn. It crashed against the packed earth with a thunderous boom.

Chapter Four

The camaraderie between travelers becomes more palpable the closer one draws to the Tower. Do not be surprised if you find yourself swept up in a spontaneous parade.

—*Everyman's Guide to the Tower of Babel,* II. XIV

The cloud of red dust surged at them so rapidly it was as if they were falling into it. Senlin shielded his face a split second before splinters and pebbles began to pelt him. A piece of shrapnel passed through his splayed fingers and stung his cheek. He clapped his hand over the flash of pain. The debris pinged and ricocheted everywhere, needling his skin and crackling against the Tower. A series of hollow whumps reverberated through the ground, drumming the earth like meteors.

When he dared to squint again into the billowing, blotting storm of red grit, he couldn't see any farther than his hand. He watched the blood on his fingers quickly turn to mud. A moment later, the hail changed direction. Instead of coming in sideways, the ejecta began to rain dryly on their shoulders and the tops of their heads.

Adam, coughing into the crook of his arm, emerged from the dusky haze at Senlin's side, looking unsteady but uninjured. Senlin pulled the lapel of his corduroy jacket over his mouth and nose and tried to draw a clear breath amid the scattering fog. The initial screams of shock, briefly silenced by the crash, now began to rise again. The tone

26

of the cries had changed. The fear and surprise were gone, replaced by excitement, eagerness... delight. A breeze swept the red cloud away, unveiling the wreckage, hardly a stone's throw distant from them.

Much of the wreck was draped and snagged with tattered silk that billowed like cobwebs in the wind. As the air cleared further, he began to make out the tangled limbs of bodies amid the wreckage: a limp hand dangling from a broken wrist, a knee bent unnaturally under a turned foot, a man cracked like a broken book with the back of his head between his heels. The separate whumps he'd heard had not been falling stars, but tumbling, doomed aeronauts.

Senlin loved nothing more in the world than a warm hearth to set his feet upon and a good book to pour his whole mind into. While an evening storm rattled the shutters and a glass of port wine warmed in his hand, Senlin would read into the wee hours of the night. He especially delighted in the old tales, the epics in which heroes set out on some impossible and noble errand, confronting the dangers in their path with fatalistic bravery. Men often died along the way, killed in brutal and unnatural ways; they were gored by war machines, trampled by steeds, and dismembered by their heartless enemies. Their deaths were boastful and lyrical and always, always more romantic than real. Death was not an end. It was an ellipsis.

There was no romance in the scene before him. There were no ellipses here. The bodies lay upon the ground like broken exclamation points.

It had been an airship. The enmeshed corpses had been her crew. What or who had brought it down, Senlin couldn't guess, but he knew with absolute certainty that just minutes before it had been a graceful machine of flight bobbing in the blue sky.

Even as this morbid realization dawned on him, the wreck was swamped by Market-goers. Corpulent merchants and stiff-legged soldiers scrabbled through the cracked ribs of the hull, turning through the shambles of crates and cargo. Well-dressed men in brushed bowlers and women in holiday bonnets followed near behind, lured into the Skirts by the promise of loot. The cries Senlin heard were not of rescue or of mourning, but of laying claim: "Mine! I saw it first! I had it in my hand before you!" They scoured the ship's wreckage with the efficiency of crabs cleaning the bones of a beached fish. Some ran off clutching armfuls of silk, the bottom half of a keg of grain, a coil of rope, an iron cannonball, a bent brass monkey, a pair of cuffed boots. Then men with crowbars came and salvaged planks, rails, hatches, and even one miraculously preserved pane of stained glass.

Senlin couldn't look away, though the sight sickened him. He was shocked to see such barbarism at the foot of the Tower of Babel. Such desperation! He wanted to gather all the looters up, sit them in rows, face them forward, and remind them of their civility. Desperate times were never improved by the surrendering of ideals!

In a very few minutes, the only thing that remained of the disaster was a crater, a fine confetti of debris, and the nearly stripped bodies of the crew.

And then, as if a curtain had been drawn over the whole shameful scene, the shadow of the Tower passed over them.

The semigloom of the Tower's nightfall made Senlin shiver. He cleared his throat and turned toward Adam, silhouetted by the rapidly fleeing line of sunlight. "Who will bury them?" Senlin rubbed tenderly at the dust-clotted gash in his cheek.

"The vultures," Adam said grimly. "We should go. The passage into the Basement is a little long." He loosed his leather belt from his canvas trousers, forming a loop with the buckle on one end. He pulled the loop around his wrist and offered the other end to Senlin. Though a little chagrined, Senlin took the leash. "Hold to it. The passage gets a little pinched."

He followed after Adamos like a sleepy dog walker, or, conversely, like a sleepy dog. Glancing over his shoulder, he saw the woman with darkly ringed eyes pull a candle stub from her dress pocket. She struck a match, set it to the wick, and continued reading the letters of the lost by the candle's jaundiced light.

Three months earlier Senlin had stood at the head of his classroom, pinching a diamond of chalk and sketching the last angle in a diagram of the Tower of Babel.

A windowless house with large gables, the school sat on blocks at the end of Isaugh's main avenue. Each spring, the schoolhouse was painted white as a bride, and every year the oceanic elements slowly undressed it. Senlin loved every knot in every board of that leaky, drafty house.

He wore the long black coat and slender black trousers that were his uniform and preference. His voice filled the room to the high, bare rafters. The tufts of a bird's nest showed on the central beam. "At its base, the Tower of Babel's wall is a quarter mile thick," Senlin said. "Which means the entrances to the Tower—there are eight—must carry visitors through a quarter mile of solid stone." He turned on his boot heel, square coattails flaring at his hip, and regarded the four rows of ancient cedar desks. His current students were the usual crop: straight-backed, sleepy-eyed boys and girls, ranging in age from eight to sixteen. He tapped the chalk diamond to his temple. "Imagine that. You go home and open the front door to your house, and then have to walk five hundred paces before you're even inside the mudroom. That's quite a threshold! And then you'll have only arrived in the first ringdom of the Tower."

When they didn't respond with the astonished looks he thought the subject deserved, he called upon the lad in the back row, Colin Weeks, who had gone nearly walleyed from daydreaming. "Mr. Weeks, remind the class what a ringdom is?"

Startled out of his reverie, Mr. Weeks lurched forward in his seat, pegging his stomach on the lip of the desk and inducing a little grunt. "Oof," he said. Seats creaked as the heads of other students turned toward him. The barn swallow in the rafters let out a poorly timed warble.

"Miss Stubbs, I trust that you completed the assigned reading. Can you come to Mr. Weeks's assistance?" Senlin said, turning to a sharp-nosed girl who occupied the front row like the proud figurehead of a ship.

"Yes, Headmaster. The levels of the Tower are called ringdoms because they are like little round kingdoms," she said in a piercing but intelligent tone. "They're like the thirty-six states of Ur, each unique in their way, but instead of being spread out across the map, the ringdoms are stacked up like a birthday cake." The class tittered at her spontaneous analogy, amused to think of the great Tower of Babel as a layered cake.

"Quite so. And does the Tower of Babel have a king?" Senlin curtly clapped chalk from his palms.

"It has many monarchies and democracies and bureaucracies, too," she said. "It's like a mincemeat pie. It's full of all sorts of exotic ingredients." The class laughed again, and this time Senlin smiled a little, which made the eager Ms. Stubbs blush.

"Very good, though your analogies make me wonder if you aren't a little hungry." Squaring his mouth, Senlin marched along the length of the board, canvased with equations and corrected lines of doggerel, to the bisected sketch of the Tower's lower levels: the Basement, Parlor, and Baths. "Of course, we don't know how many ringdoms there are in all because they have not been reliably documented. The permanent clouds about its pinnacle make ground observations impossible."

"Why not just fly an airship to the top of it and stake a flag for Isaugh?" a voice from the middle row asked.

"A good question"—Senlin craned about to see who had asked the question, and found him—"Mr. Gregor. But think of it this way... I know you have a little rowboat. I've seen you oaring it around the cove all weekend. Now, what would happen if you pulled your boat into the best slip in the marina? You know the one, right front and center and wide as the schoolyard."

"Old Captain Cuthbert would drop his anchor on it."

"Why?"

"It's his slip!" the boy cried, with an exasperated flourish of his hands.

"Exactly so. And if you rowed your boat across the Niro Ocean, to some exotic port that was guarded by forts and long guns and a fleet of warships, how well would you be received? What if they didn't like the look of a young scamper like yourself plowing along in your dingy?" Mr. Gregor smiled and snorted at this, folding his arms. "It's

just so with the Tower, I suspect, Mr. Gregor. You can't expect every
port to welcome you with open arms."

He dismissed the class for the day. In the coatroom, they pulled
on their boots, their voices giddy. It was raining outside, as it often
did throughout the spring. The water gurgled under the floorboards
of the schoolhouse, filling the classroom with the aroma of earth. His
students knew well enough not to bang the door on their way out,
but their escape was boisterous in every other way. Not even the cold
drizzle could dull their relief at being freed for the day.

Little did they know, he enjoyed the momentary liberty, too.

Drawing the chalk duster dreamily across the blackboard, carv-
ing away at the diagram of the Tower, Senlin imagined himself on the
deck of an airship, circling the Tower, a spyglass to his eye...

He couldn't help but scowl at the image. No, the Sturgeon would
never turn into a bird.

The hard leather of Adam's belt blistered his hand, and still he gripped
it tighter.

The passage was indeed a quarter mile long, but otherwise, it bore
no resemblance to Senlin's fantasy. He'd expected graceful surfaces
and an orderly thoroughfare. Instead he found a tunnel like a mineshaft. There were no lanes or rails. Inbound traffic battered against the
outbound traffic like rams on a bridge.

Tourists, merchants, rogues, and wanderers buffeted him on every
side. His toes were stamped, his heels shaved, and his elbows knocked
numb. Smoke and soot from infrequent oil sconces burned his eyes
like black pepper. He couldn't catch a solid breath. The smoke undu-
lated like an upside-down river along the iron rafters above them. The
distressed bray of pack animals, the stubborn barking of the man that
drove them, and the rattling sob of an overcome young woman were
all amplified by the horn of the tunnel walls until Senlin felt he might
scream and break into a run.

But there was no room to run and no good air to scream with.

The experience was so terrible and so at odds with his impression
of the Tower that, even amid that chaotic slog, he convinced himself

that it must be some anomaly, a fluke. Perhaps he was caught in the rush of an annual festival, or it might be that some regular mechanical device, a fan or regulator, had temporarily failed. For all he knew, he had blundered upon the servants' entrance.

After two days of sleepless panic, the march and the bad air quickly exhausted him. When the press of bodies abruptly relaxed and the air sweetened a little, Senlin knew they were at last inside the first cavernous ringdom of the Tower, though he could not see it for the smoke in his eyes. He stumbled on tear-blurred cobblestones, half-blind, and landed on one trembling knee. Still, he gripped the lifeline of Adam's belt like a mountaineer who, having crested the final summit, could not believe he had arrived at the top.

But of course, he hadn't reached the top. He had only groped his way to the foot of the Tower. And here, the trail began.

Chapter Five

The Tower's well produces a water that is famously crisp and pure. It is this untainted source that gives the local beer its ballyhooed flavor.

—*Everyman's Guide to the Tower of Babel*, III. II

Senlin woke in a dusky chamber to a terrible scream. Frightened and disoriented, he leapt from the rickety cot he lay sprawled upon. The pine boards creaked and bounced beneath him like the slats of an old pier, and the air was rank with rot and mold. Above him, in a gloomy corner of the room, a blood-colored shadow suddenly flapped. Senlin threw up his arms to defend himself against the red wraith descending upon him and let out a hoarse yelp.

The large parrot hopped down from its roost, landed on an edge of Senlin's disheveled cot, and cawed again, its voice piercing in the small room. The bird cocked its head at Senlin, its small black-and-white eyes shuttering curiously.

The only light came from an oil lamp with a low flame that lapped the air like a cat's tongue. It cast an orange glow on walls that seemed as thin as the mildewed wallpaper that covered them. A dented zinc sink caught the drips from a primitive faucet. The only other furniture, a three-legged stool, seemed as likely to throw a person on the floor as not. The majestic bird, completely out of place in the shabby room, picked at the brown blanket tangled on the cot with its hooked beak.

How long had he been asleep? He didn't feel well rested. In fact, the nausea of exhaustion was still turning his stomach like a winch. It felt like two hours had passed. Or four, perhaps. It was impossible to say for sure.

It was a moment more before Senlin remembered how he had come to the room.

By the time he and Adam had broken from the smoggy burrow into the cavern of the Basement, Senlin was an absolute wreck. His eyes were nearly swollen shut from the fumes of the tunnel. His arms and legs felt unnaturally heavy, as if he'd fallen into water while wearing all of his clothes. He was hungry and exhausted and couldn't catch his breath without choking on soot.

Adamos Boreas had helped him into the first lodging they'd come upon, which had been little more than a row of tar-paper flophouses. There was no lobby or central hallway. The doors of the rooms exited onto the street where a thick-necked innkeeper sat on an upturned crate shaving bits of ahle wurst into his mouth. The smell of that pork sausage had seemed as rich as frankincense to Senlin, and his mouth watered like a dog's.

If Senlin had been in any better shape, he would've argued against taking the room. He thought the whole row of shanties should be burned down and the ashes deloused. But weary beyond argument, Senlin let Adam check them into a room where he could sleep for a few hours while his young guide looked after his belongings. Senlin sprawled himself upon the cot like a spill, his limbs pouring over the sides limply. He'd been too spent to even notice the parrot perched above him. He'd slept deeply.

He wondered where Adam was.

He turned on the faucet. The connecting pipes shuddered, and water sprayed briefly from a rag-repaired joint in the plumbing, and then the basin began to fill. The murky water smelled vaguely of sulfur, and had Senlin been more awake, he might not have plunged his face into it so eagerly. The water felt wonderful on the wounds on his cheek and hand, but as thirsty as he was, he still couldn't bring himself to drink it. The *Guide* had recommended caution when confronted with suspicious plumbing; a single sip of bad water had ruined many a holiday.

When he straightened again, he realized he was soaking his coat's lapels and there was no towel, only a rag on a peg hardly large enough to dry a mouse. His corduroy suit, pink from the desert clay, now began to redden as the embedded dirt turned to mud. Recalling the change of clothes in his satchel, he turned to locate his luggage.

While his back had been turned, the parrot had managed to make up the bed. The clever bird screeched again, and then in a roughly human voice, said, "Time to go! Time to go!"

"Give me a moment!" Senlin replied, flustered. His hair drenched his collar as he hunted about for his bag.

It didn't take long for him to realize that his satchel and the parcel of women's silks were gone. When he reached for the pockets of his trousers, he found them turned out. His small change, the pence and halfpence, was gone. He had been robbed. His razor and soap, his journal, his comb and coat brush, his linen gloves and handkerchiefs, his vest, trousers, socks, his guidebook, and the tickets that were tucked inside. All gone.

In a panic, he felt the waistband of his trousers. The telltale lump of bills was still there. He let out a rueful laugh. How clever he had been to insist on the secret pockets! Though, really, how clever could he be? This marked the second time in as many days that he had been robbed.

"Time to go!" the parrot repeated in its coarse voice. With its tidying complete, it leapt back to its perch in the corner and began to preen.

Senlin's hand was on the doorknob when he spotted the book in the shadows under the cot. Dropping to his hands and knees, he fished it out, tapping loose a tagalong ball of dust. It was his *Everyman's Guide*. To his great relief, the train tickets were still wedged inside, snug as a bookmark.

He still had most of his money, and he had his passage home. For a man who'd just been robbed, he felt very fortunate.

How could he have been so wrong about Adam? He'd always

thought himself a good judge of character. Years of experience had taught him how to distinguish the liars and cheaters from the merely nervous students. He should've been suspicious of anyone who still posted notes to the Lost and Found after two years of futility. Boreas was irrational, superstitious, and desperate. Such men couldn't be trusted, no matter how sympathetic they seemed. Adam wasn't even sensible enough to steal the guide!

Angered by this further setback, which would only make his reunion with Marya all the more humiliating, and embarrassed by his lapse in judgment, Senlin dropped the guidebook in his coat pocket. He moved the tickets to his secret pocket, withdrew a few shekels, and exited the room. With a parting squawk, the parrot reminded him of the relative time.

The streets and blocks of the Basement city were all contained within a single, vast cavern. Senlin supposed that all of Isaugh, from the schoolhouse to the spits of the cove, could have easily fit inside. Sweating pipes, patched with yellow moss, were girded to the chamber walls and domed ceiling where they ran like a maze in every direction. A slow rain of condensation splattered his shoulders, the slate pavers, and the clay tiles of cottage roofs. Thousands of snails, some as large as cows, clung to the waterworks above, their shells the color of dark, unpolished jade. The trails of these giant shells glistened like cracks in glass.

As strange as the scene was, it wasn't the bottled city or the bull snails that first captivated him. It was the hulking, iron merry-go-round turning in the public arcade. He'd been drawn to the arcade by the aroma of shish kebabs. He bought two of the skewered morsels, and as he paid, he asked almost automatically if the vendor had recently seen a woman in a red helmet. His question was shaken off, as it had been a hundred times in recent days. The goat tasted good but probably benefitted from the seasoning of starvation.

As he chewed, he watched the dozen grown men who rode the black merry-go-round before him. They seemed as joyful as his students when he dismissed them for the day.

The merry-go-round clanked and whirred and rumbled the ground. It seemed as ancient as a millstone. Twelve stools stood welded to the iron wheel, and beneath each were foot pedals that might've been taken from a bicycle. If one rider slowed his pedaling, the others cheered and jeered him back up to speed. They seemed, working all together, to be powering the merry-go-round, though its plodding speed didn't seem to match the frenzied efforts of the riders. It seemed a strange pastime for grown men, and then he saw the fountain spurting from the conical hub of the machine. The water cascaded down the slope of the cone toward a trough that frothed at chin-level with the seated men. Ivory stems curled up from the trough to their mouths, and they drank from these fixed straws with great relish while they pedaled.

Senlin licked the grease of the goat meat from his lips. He couldn't remember the last time he had been so thirsty.

And just when he thought he might be desperate enough to chase along and try to jump aboard the spinning fountain, a loud clunk shook the whole machine and it came to a stop. The men aboard hardly had time to whoop in anticipation before the whole disc began to turn back the other way. It spun so rapidly in reverse that the hunched backs of the men blurred together. The troughs threw out a sideways rain. Some spectators scurried to keep from getting drenched, while others opened their mouths and tried to catch some of the fountain's wake. A single lash of the stuff splashed Senlin across the face. He tasted the pungent liquid running down his cheeks. It was not water. It was beer.

Without warning, one rider lost his grip and was ejected from his seat. He first flew and then rolled across the flagstones of the arcade. A passing tourist had to leap to keep from being bowled over. The merry-go-round, seeming to have exhausted its coiled energy, clicked to a dead halt like an unwound clock. The remaining eleven riders dismounted unsteadily. They went away on wobbling knees and crossing feet, and the seats they left behind were soon refilled.

Overcome with empathy, Senlin ran to the thrown rider. Even before he turned the man over, he could tell by his tattered collar and rank odor that the man was a pauper. When Senlin rolled him onto his back, the man's eyes were closed; his jaw hung loose, showing a largely toothless maw. Senlin wondered if he hadn't been killed by his tumble.

But then the man's eyes popped open, and he expelled into Senlin's closely drawn face a wind that smelled as sour as a spittoon. He wasn't dead, only drunk. The man's initial burst lengthened into an uproarious cackle. He grasped Senlin's coat to pull himself up but only succeeded in ripping one entire lapel free. They both gaped at the shred of corduroy that the man held in his fist. The drunk made a pitiful attempt to reattach the strip.

Senlin realized with sudden clarity that he was in no position to rescue this man, or anyone else for that matter. If they stood side by side on the street, he doubted anyone would be able to tell them apart. A mere three days off the train and he already looked like a beggar.

His wife was missing. He had to get ahold of himself. He was a headmaster, after all.

Beneath the snails and the plumbing sprawled a city of public houses, shops, hostels, and cottages. Most were built out of hob or clay or crumbly black cement, and their walls were warped and dimpled. Gas lamps cast the city in a dusky twilight. The crowds were not as stifling as they had been in the bazaar outside, but they were every bit as motley. At one moment, a woman in frills might pass by on the arm of a fancy gentleman, the two of them smelling like potpourri and hair wax. The next moment, a pilgrim in colorless rags might hobble by, reeking like a fishmonger in August. What Senlin wouldn't give for a good scouring sea breeze! Here and there, a reliable structure stood like a tree among reeds. The red brick facades of shops and guild houses gave the streets some semblance of civility; otherwise, the architecture was rather pitiful.

He couldn't help but feel disappointed: This was not the glittering center of culture he expected. The Basement might've been, for all its lackluster, a port town where sailors came to lose their sea legs. There were fountains of beer everywhere, for heaven's sake! He'd passed six more since the first. The *Everyman's Guide* was a little vague in its description of the Basement's atmosphere, casting it as something of an amiable gateway to the greater attractions above, but even this seemed an exaggeration. It was more comforting to think of the Basement as the Tower's mudroom. It was the place where one knocked the road from their boots before entering the hallowed halls above.

In the distance, rising from the exact center of the Basement, a white column stretched from the streets to the domed ceiling. The marble spire reminded him of a lighthouse—not only in its imposing size, but also in the secure feeling it gave him. It was the first bit of architecture that seemed appropriately grand. Even the snails left it alone. He recognized the column from the description in his guide; it was the stairway to the second level of the Tower of Babel.

Marya was so much better at taking the flaws of the world in stride, which was why she was indomitable and difficult to disappoint. She probably found the bull snails and drunken merry-go-round charming.

Senlin caught a glimpse of himself in a shop window. His usually carefully combed hair now stood out like a frayed rope; his suit looked like a dishrag with pockets. He doubted Marya would find him charming.

It couldn't be helped. He needed a new suit.

A half hour later, Senlin was in a clothier's changing room observing himself in a wall mirror in his new clothes. He'd chosen a suit that felt practical, though in fact it looked a great deal like his headmaster's uniform: a thigh-length, square-bottomed coat, a matching black waistcoat and trousers, a white collared shirt, and black square-toed boots. After pocketing enough money to cover the cost of his new clothes and a little extra for the day, Senlin secreted the remainder of his finances in his boots. He was confident that not even the most agile of pickpockets would be able to get at it there. He left his ruined clothes in a tidy pile in the changing stall.

He was somewhat surprised to see someone else had come into the clothier, which other than the elderly, bespectacled tailor, had stood

empty a minute before. This newcomer was very short, a dwarf perhaps, and had a crooked nose and a tangled thicket of black hair. The
gold threading in his vest suggested that he was some sort of merchant. Whoever he was, he was quite an animated talker. He was
arguing with the tailor over a parcel of clothes. Not wishing to interrupt their haggling, Senlin began browsing the handkerchiefs. He'd
need three, at least.

"But I don't sell to ladies," the clerk said with finality.

"Think of it as an opportunity to expand your market. I'm not
coming to you with tatters. These are quality silks!" The wild-haired,
diminutive man had to tug to get a single slip of clothing free of the
parcel. He waved it like a flag. "See, they won't even hold a wrinkle."

"Excuse me," the tailor said curtly and turned to Senlin, who'd
selected three white, utilitarian handkerchiefs. They shifted to the
counter where a brass-edged register stood. Senlin paid for his suit,
boots, and new handkerchiefs. All the while, the merchant watched
the exchange of money like a cat tracks a bird. "Look," he pattered
on, "these silks are so sturdy, you could take this camisole, sew up the
ends, fill it with gas, and lift a barge with it!"

Shoving the register drawer closed so sharply that the bell rang, the
tailor removed his spectacles and began rubbing the lenses vigorously.
"I don't sell to barge captains, either."

The merchant clucked his tongue. "I love a man with a sense of
humor."

It was only when Senlin turned to leave that he caught sight of the
luggage dangling from the merchant's shoulder. The stitching was
unmistakable. It was his satchel.

Perhaps Senlin was inspired by his new suit and crisp shirt, which
felt satisfyingly sharp against his wrists and neck, or perhaps it was
the merchant's short stature, which reminded him of his students and
filled him with a sense of authority, or perhaps it was Adam's recent
betrayal of his trust and his subsequent thievery. Whatever the cause,
Senlin felt a surge of confidence, verging on rashness. He would not let
this thief go unchallenged! He would go against his usual restraint and

take action. Fearing that the man might be armed, Senlin decided the safest course was to take the dwarfish thief by surprise.

Senlin stood with his back pressed to the shop's facade beside the door; he would catch the thief entirely unprepared as soon as he exited the shop. Senlin felt an altogether unfamiliar thrill of anticipation warm him. When the shop door opened and the thief passed through, Senlin grabbed him by the collar and wrenched the dwarf from his feet.

"Ha ha, I've got you!" Senlin cried triumphantly. His triumph was swiftly subdued by a heel to his groin.

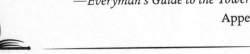

Chapter Six

The handkerchief is the universal utensil of the seasoned traveler. It can be a sanitizing device, a seat cover, a dust mask, a garrote, a bandage, a gag, or a white flag. One may feel well prepared with nothing but a pocket square.

—*Everyman's Guide to the Tower of Babel,*
Appendix, i.iv

H is engagement to Marya had been brief. Two weeks after Senlin put his knee in the clover and took up Marya's flourwhite hand, they were married.

The townsfolk of Isaugh knew of only one reason to rush a wedding like that.

It was an incredible scandal. It was incredible not because it was uncommon (many women had raced to the altar so they could present a bridal figure before it became a maternal one); rather, it was incredible because of who the scandal involved. They could hardly believe their Sturgeon was capable of such a thing. It struck the deckhands, captains, and fishmongers as a magnificent accomplishment, at least on Senlin's part. It seemed less magnificent to the ladies of the town, who felt they had been robbed in some way; they loved a proper public courting, and there had been none. The children thought their teacher's marriage a natural oddity, like lightning in winter or a two-headed snake. It seemed plausible, but unlikely.

Not that there was anything really the matter with their head-master. He was merely prudish and distant—traits that seemed to suit his profession. The townsfolk loved him because his students (their children) typically became productive, functioning, and stoic adults.

But he was peculiar.

Marya worked in the Berks's General Store, stocking the shelves and stretching lines of credit, to Ms. Olivet Berks's patient consternation. "Our customers aren't fish, my dear," Ms. Berks once remarked. "Lengthening the line doesn't make it any easier to reel them in."

Ms. Olivet Berks, a good-natured, never-spurned spinster, was Marya's older second cousin. They shared the apartment rooms over the store, rarely quarreled, and were both regulars at the Blue Tattoo public house. Olivet Berks patronized the Blue Tattoo because she loved gossip and pear brandy, and Marya accompanied her because the pub, at the time, housed the only piano in town.

Marya battered the black and yellow keys of the pub's piano four or five nights a week. She sang as she played, her voice strong and strange as a mockingbird's, leading rounds of popular songs. It was, everyone agreed, the best entertainment anywhere around.

Marya was charming to the men and frank with the women. Everyone adored her. And yet, as much as the town doted on Marya, they never detected her secret affair with Senlin, though apparently it had been going on for some months. Not even Olivet suspected it.

Marya finally told Olivet of her engagement while the two of them sat dividing a fifty-pound sack of rice into one-pound bags. Marya measured and poured the rice, and Olivet sewed the mouths closed. "But why him? Why now? Are you in some trouble? Is there some rush? Why not wait until next winter? They say winter weddings make a marriage more resilient."

"He asked me to marry him, and I love him, and he gave me a wonderful gift." Marya looked down at the scoop of rice she was pouring, an unreadable little smile lifting her cheeks.

Olivet snipped a thread with her teeth and winced. "Oh, don't go around calling it a gift, Marya. People will think you're as naive as him."

*   *   *

Senlin dropped, but did not release, the struggling thief. The pain shot through him like a crack in a pane of glass, sprawling and forking as it ran down his legs and up his spine.

It had been a mistake for him to attempt a physical confrontation. He had never been in a fight, had never raised a hand to a student. He depended entirely on his severe manner to keep him out of pub brawls and to preserve order in the classroom. It took a mule kick from a dwarf to teach him that his poise would not protect him in the ringdoms of the Tower.

Overcoming the urge to curl up from the radiant ache in the pit of his stomach, Senlin asked, "How is it that you have my luggage?"

"Your luggage? I bought this bag two hours ago," the thief said, his voice surprisingly resonant and carrying a lyrical accent Senlin didn't recognize. "I paid a lad four shekels for it."

"Where is he now?"

"Turning in the wind, for all I know. Let me go!" His collar twisted in Senlin's grip.

Senlin wrestled his satchel from the man's shoulder and released him. The buckles of the satchel clapped about loosely. The bag was empty. Far overhead, a corner of plumbing rattled and shook loose a brief shower. The rain dampened their tempers. "What is your name?"

"Finn Goll."

"Mr. Fingol, where are my things?"

"It's Finn Goll." He spoke the names more distinctly. "And your things, if they were yours, are sold." He held up the bundle of women's silks. "Unless you want to claim these as well?"

"Yes, thank you." Senlin snatched the bundle. In truth, he hardly wanted the parcel, had nearly forgotten about it. His frustration was making him peevish. "Is everyone here a thief?"

Goll straightened his shirt and smoothed his purple vest, primping with a little indignation. "Sir, I am not a thief. No more than you— who, as far as I know, has just robbed me."

"My name is Thomas Senlin. And what initials do we find stamped on the inside of my satchel?" Senlin showed Goll the monogram impressed on the leather lip of the bag.

"My luck!" Overcome with self-pity, Goll tugged at his wild black hair, making it wilder. He seemed a theatrical little man. "Take it, Tom. Just take it! It was an honest mistake. I should've known that boy was trouble. Never trust an Ostrich!"

"An ostrich?"

"An Ostrich, an Ostrich!" he said as if the repetition would make Senlin remember. "Someone who's been booted from the Parlor. They're banned, ostracized, cast back to the Basement. They brand their arms so they can't sneak in again." Senlin recalled the circular scar on Adamos's forearm. "If they do and they're caught a second time"—Goll made as if to pop his eye from its socket—"they take an eye. Come back for thirds"—he clucked his tongue—"they take the other eye. You ever see someone walking around with two eyes gone, you're looking at a slow learner. That scamp that robbed you, he'll be tapping around with a cane and a beggar's bowl soon enough."

"I hardly believe they're as barbarous as to be snatching out eyes." Senlin intended to give a dismissive chuckle, but instead he began to cough, his parched throat burning.

"Look, if we're going to debate, let's find a drink before one of us chokes," Finn Goll said.

Soon, Senlin was sitting on the scalloped metal seat of what Finn Goll called a "beer-me-go-round," or more succinctly, a "beer-me." It was a duplicate of the man-powered fountain he'd observed before, right down to the ivory straw and cleated pedals. According to Goll, there were dozens of the beer-mes spread regularly throughout the Basement. Senlin, who'd never been particularly fond of beer, had been convinced only by Goll's insistence that the beer was cleaner and safer to drink than pump water. Alehouses were as numerous and common as lampposts—and all seemed to be doing swift business—but the beer-mes had the distinct advantage of being free so long as one didn't mind a little work.

If the patrons of the Blue Tattoo (who thought the broom in the corner livelier than their headmaster) had seen Senlin seated at a mechanical fountain of beer in a public square, they would've rubbed their eyes, slapped their cheeks, and ordered three oysters to sober themselves.

The remaining ten rust-rimmed seats were quickly filled, and the work was begun. With the bundle of women's underwear balanced lightly on his lap, Senlin grasped the curled rim of the empty trough and began pumping his legs. Goll stood entirely upon his pedals, his stature making it impossible to sit and pump at the same time. Though his lurching progress seemed awkward to Senlin, Goll did not seem inconvenienced by it.

It was as if he were trying to ride a bike up a hill in the mud, and it was a few moments before their straining efforts began to eke the great wheel around. "Why are the gears so stubborn?" Senlin complained. "I've never seen a barkeeper pump a keg so furiously!" He had begun to huff from the effort, which made his throat burn all the more.

"What are you, an engineer? Who cares! It's free beer," Goll said loudly and was met with a general hurrah from the other riders. The man to Goll's right wore a leather apron, smudged with the muddy prints of horseshoes. He roared at them like a foreman to pump harder. The mouth of the fountain had only just begun to gurgle.

Senlin's eyes fell on a brass placard, green from age and regular dousing, which was bolted to the conical watershed before him. He read the trademark aloud: "The Dozen-Handled Pump of the Sphinx."

"So, you can read," Goll said. His dark locks had begun to mat with sweat upon his brow.

"Of course. I'm a headmaster," Senlin said with reflexive pride. When Goll asked what subjects he taught, Senlin could hardly keep from glowing. "Writing, art, geography, physics..."

"Math?"

"How could I teach physics without mathematics?" The sprocket beneath him rattled. For a moment he thought the chain might jump loose, and then it caught again.

"And you have to keep records, I'm sure. Grades and attendance and school fees and tuition, am I right? Maybe find a good home for the occasional mislaid shekel." He released the rail long enough to pat his vest pockets conspiratorially.

Senlin was about to say something indignant and virtuous when the fountain foamed up with volcanic suds, and a sheet of beer began to flow down the cone and splash into the trough. Every rider craned their necks forward, straining to get their lips around the ivory straw. The cool beer felt like velvet on Senlin's raw throat. Never had anything tasted so sweet. Out of the corner of his eye, he saw Goll sitting with his knees on the seat, the pedals abandoned but still spinning, drinking from his straw at an angle and smirking back at him. The blacksmith with the horseshoe prints on his apron barked at Goll to get back to pedaling. Goll threw up his arm in an obscene gesture Senlin knew but had never used. Goll might be half Senlin's size, but he had twice the nerve.

By the time Senlin came up from his straw, gasping for breath, his head had already begun to swim a little from the effects of the alcohol.

Pedaling again, Goll observed Senlin almost serenely, smiling like a man who was holding on to a joke. "You're a natural. You should stick around for the evening races. Those will really make your head spin."

"I can't. I am in a hurry. I'm looking for someone."

"Oh, muddit." Goll spat the word like a curse, though Senlin wasn't familiar with its usage. "This old, sad song again! Let me guess: You have lost someone sincere and dear to your heart. You are driven by the purest devotion to them. You will stop at nothing to find this mother-brother-aunt-child-or-miss you're looking for, and I don't want to know who it—"

"She's my wife. Marya Senlin. She wore a red helmet."

Goll made a fist and beat the lip of the trough until it rang. "Why do I speak?" He consoled himself with a long draw on his straw. Senlin smiled at the man's theatrics. When Goll came up gasping for air, he said, "Don't tell anyone you're looking for your wife."

"Then how will I find her?" Senlin's tone was incredulous, almost patronizing. He took to his own straw, still chugging away at the pedals.

47

"With your eyes and your wits and all on your own. Most likely, you won't find her at all. Women get sucked up the Tower like embers up a flue." He flapped one hand and gave a buzzing whistle. "Anything in a skirt floats! Did you tell the boy who robbed you about your dear old dame?"

"I did."

"And how did that go? He said kind things, hopeful things, I bet. He made you a babe in arms. He rocked you to sleep, and then he robbed you." Goll shook his head until sweat whipped off his dark curls. "Not a solitary soul will help you here. The good souls don't have the means or mind for it, and the bad souls will only bleed you dry. They'll sell you rumors, maps, guidebooks, things more suited for wrapping fish than finding wives! You'll get so much help you won't have a shekel left. Assuming that you aren't poor as a hod already..." He belched.

"Assuming," Senlin said evasively. As disreputable as Goll seemed, his warnings made sense. It might take more than a guide and a handkerchief to navigate the Tower. "What's a hod?"

"You've seen them, I'm sure. Bald, bone-thin, barebacked wretches with the iron jewelry. Slaves. Hods are slaves. They hump bags of sand, coal, and stone up and up and up! The construction continues. The Tower isn't done with us yet. Ah, muddit, I sound like a mystic!"

Just moments ago, Senlin had felt superior to this unpolished, unscrupulous man. Now, he thought there might be some benefit to keeping his company. "Look, Mr. Goll, I apologize for how I handled you earlier. And I appreciate what you've said. Perhaps you would consider being hired on as a guide..."

"Why do I speak?" he said again, raising his hands. "You may appreciate, but you haven't heard. No one can help you. You have to go it alone."

Abruptly, all the pedals under their feet jammed to a stop. The shock of it ran up Senlin's legs and made his kneecaps pop painfully. A gasp escaped through his teeth. Glancing about, he realized he was the only one surprised by their halt. They had reached the invisible summit they'd been pedaling after. The beer-me-go-round had come to the limit of its mighty internal spring, which lay coiled now, tighter than a threatened viper, at the center of the great wheel.

A new gear engaged, clanging like a bell underwater, and the pedals under his feet lost all resistance. Finn Goll hooted and cried, "Hold on," though his words were swept up by the beer-me's rapid acceleration as the tightened coil began to unwind. Spinning counterclockwise now, faster and faster, Senlin felt like he was hurtling back down the mountain he had just conquered. The public square turned into a smudge of wet stone and a shuttering of gaslights; the faces of the crowd all stretched out like taffy. Senlin set his eyes on the serene tip of the cone at the center of the wheel and clung to the trough, even as it lashed his face with beer.

In that moment of nausea and disorientation, he recalled Marya's description of how it felt to play the piano at the Blue Tattoo. She said, "I play and we sing until the room spins. It feels lovely to be at the center of that merry little circle."

"But, my dear," he replied, mistaking this as an appropriate time for a lecture on geometry, "the center of a circle is an infinitesimally small point. It hardly exists at all."

"Suits me. I'd rather be a nothing at the center of everything than a puffed-up somebody at the edge of it all." She said this in her usual unguarded way. And without meaning to, she had described him exactly: a puffed-up somebody at the edge of it all.

The bundle of women's underwear that had been resting on his lap fluttered open. Hosiery, bloomers, and camisoles flew into the crowd of the public square, alighting everywhere like doves in a park.

Chapter Seven

Newcomers may expect the ringdoms of the Tower to be like the layers of a cake, where each layer is much like the last. But this is not the case. Not at all. Each ringdom is unique and bewildering. The ringdoms of the Tower share only two things in common: the shape of their outermost walls, which are roughly circular, and the price of beef, which is outrageous. The rest is novel.

—*Everyman's Guide to the Tower of Babel*, I. X

Senlin mopped his neck with a damp handkerchief. Two guards in sooty red coats and tattered gold epaulets stood before the foot of the marble pillar. At their backs, the glass door into the pillar glowed with inviting golden light.

The guards looked suspiciously shabby. The scabbards at their hips did not match each other, as one would expect of standard-issue weapons, nor did they seem to exactly match the hilts of the sabers that filled them. The buttons of one guard's coat strained over his gut, and the other's pant cuffs bunched on his boots as if his trousers were too long. Senlin believed they were frauds, thuggish opportunists like those Adam had warned him about, ironic as that was.

But this was the only stairway to the Parlor. This was the only way Marya could've come, assuming that she had decided to carry on with their itinerary . . .

What else could she do but carry on? What else could he do but assume?

He'd lost track of Finn Goll after dizzily dismounting the beer-me-go-round. He stumbled through the mob that had been attracted by the strewn undergarments. Swerving into the first alley, Senlin was horribly and violently ill. When both his stomach and head were sufficiently clear, he emerged and searched out a hand pump by a watering trough. He wet his handkerchief and attempted to revive himself.

Feeling a little abashed, he beat a path to the white pillar as soon as he was steady enough to walk. He clutched his satchel much as a man lost at sea clings to a piece of driftwood. He couldn't afford to be robbed again.

The imposter gatekeepers were, at that moment, harassing a beggaring monk in a gray smock. The agitated old monk was trying to proselytize to the guards, saying, "The Tower must be saved! It sickens at the root. We are the rot! It must come down before the blight of man spreads to the clouds and the stars!" His voice carried a shrill edge of madness. Senlin had read a little about the mystics who professed the Tower's divinity, though the literature had suggested the order was all but extinct.

The larger of the two guards, whose dark beard stubble spread nearly to the sockets of his eyes, placed his boot on the monk's sunken chest and propelled him onto his back. "Get out of the lane, you lunatic, before I bob your ears." This seemed sufficient to discourage the mystic, who slunk off muttering and rubbing his bruised hunkers.

Before Senlin could begin his own approach, he was cut off by a swinging bustle of stiff crinoline. The bustle cage was attached to a young woman with rouged cheeks and bouncing ringlets of blond hair. She was pretty enough but seemed cold and conceited. In response to her approach, the imposters stepped aside from the door, both bowing and scraping with dubious grace. Senlin recalled Finn Goll's words: Anything in a skirt floats.

Soon as the pretty miss had passed through the warmly glowing glass doors, Senlin undertook what he hoped was a confident and resolute march toward the space between the guards, his head cocked high as a lord. But even as he approached, the gap closed, and he had to finally stop and recognize the imposters blocking him.

"Not so quick, there, Master Long Shanks," the larger guard said wryly. "There's a two-shekel safe passage fee to proceed into the Parlor."

In his most reasonable tone, Senlin said, "I noted the lady ahead of me was not taxed for her safety. It seems hardly fair that she be given an exception while I—" His argument met a quick end as the shorter of the imposters drove his fist into Senlin's stomach. As Senlin doubled forward, a second rabbit punch followed the first.

He had been naive to think that such obvious thugs would respond to a rational discussion. There was nothing to do but learn the lesson, pay the two shekels, and carry on.

"There is a four-shekel safe passage fee to proceed into the Parlor," the larger guard said with mechanical grimness. The shorter guard smiled at Senlin greasily, as if he hoped Senlin might protest a second time.

Senlin pulled himself straight and reached for his pockets. At that moment he would've emptied his boots if it meant getting free of that dank, beer-washed, and violent ground floor. The whole of the Tower yawned above him, and there he stood wallowing in the mudroom with the thieves and beggars. Muddit, indeed.

The glass doors of the pillar opened onto a carpeted corridor that spiraled upward. It was like passing from night into day. The clean and empty passage was railed with brass and well lit by winking gas lamps. It reminded Senlin of the decor of an opera house he'd once visited while at college. The sweet-smelling air carried a deep, regular thrum that was almost womb-like.

After a few minutes of ascending the carpeted helix, Senlin heard the murmur of a nearing crowd. Rounding a bend, he found himself joining a queue of travelers progressing at a shuffling pace. They were better dressed and more recently washed than most of the bedraggled people he'd encountered downstairs and outside. He was relieved he'd had the sense to buy a new suit.

He noted that the woman in the crinoline bustle was nowhere to be seen, and he voiced this observation to the man queued ahead of him. The man, naturally gregarious, was quick to answer that she had been allowed to cut ahead. "Apparently," the man explained, "there is a shortage of women for the scheduled play." Senlin didn't entirely understand this but chose to carry on as if he did; there seemed little benefit to announcing his ignorance.

Senlin's new acquaintance was primly arrayed in a navy three-piece suit. His thin mustache was well groomed and waxed. He would've been a fashion plate if he ever appeared on the streets of Isaugh. He introduced himself as Mr. Edsel Pining. Senlin took him for a minor aristocrat.

Pining inquired if this was Senlin's first visit to the Parlor. And when Senlin attempted a reply, he swallowed at the wrong moment so that his words came out as a small grunt. He'd always been especially awkward around socialites. Their breezy manner only made him more nervous: Their confidence sapped his own.

"I only ask because you seem entirely too composed," Pining said good-naturedly. "A man at peace, as it were. And here I am with my nerves in a knot, ready to run up the wall." He bobbed forward when he spoke, his hands clasped behind his back.

"I'd think a novice would be more excited than a veteran," Senlin said, recovering his voice.

"Not at all. You have no idea what you're in for. It's just a word to you: the Parlor. A paragraph in a book. A dot on a map. But once you visit the Parlor, you spend the rest of your life plotting a return." Pining swept his hand along the greased temples of his dark hair. Senlin guessed Pining was about his age, though his years hadn't translated into the same maturity. "Look at me. I'm giddy! I am not naturally so. In my home, I am a boorish, sullen invalid. I am an accountant. I have calluses on my fingertips from my abacus and pen. No, you can't imagine how the Parlor transforms you, or allows you to transform yourself. This will be my fourth visit."

Senlin felt disoriented by their conversation, which was cordial and carefree. It seemed at odds with everything that had come before: the wretches at the Lost and Found, the crashed airship, Adam's betrayal, and Finn Goll's dire warnings about the Tower's appetites and the ease with which it absorbed women. His gut still ached from the sucker punch he'd recently been dealt. Yet here he was, making small talk with a dandy. "Doesn't it begin to bore?"

"I promise, Mr. Senlin, it never bores. The plots are rewritten every month, the rooms redecorated, and the players, of course, are swapped about. I could visit the Parlor a hundred times and never get my fill. It takes only a little imagination. Having some wit certainly helps, but even a farmer would be entertained. It's only a shame that the performances are so brief, generally a week. Then the play is over, and we must return to ourselves." He affected a pitiful look.

Senlin wasn't entirely sure what Pining meant. The *Everyman's Guide* referred to the second floor of the Tower, the Parlor, as a theater district, one that had produced many fine acting troupes over the years. He and Marya had discussed taking in a show before retiring to the third level, the Baths, with its affordable rooms and numerous spas. The *Guide* provided suggestions for analyzing plays and pointers on audience etiquette, but to save it from becoming immediately out of date, the *Guide* offered very little by way of schedules or specific detail. Not for the first time since arriving at the Tower, Senlin felt unprepared. Yet, remembering Goll's advice to try to blend in, to seek without being conspicuous, Senlin decided to do his best to appear unperturbed.

Though he couldn't imagine any play, not even the most sprawling epic, lasting a week. Surely, that was an exaggeration.

The line inched onward. Pining prattled through his repertoire of humorous observations and uncolored philosophies, and Senlin, relieved to find that his companion required little assistance in the creation of small talk, was content to offer occasional encouragement by way of a smile. Before long, the upward spiral plateaued at the mouth of a curtained archway, and they found themselves in a level room that reminded Senlin of a theater's lobby. They faced four ornately carved box offices, and beyond each stood a gleaming turnstile. Men in white coats and ash-gray vests staffed the booths, which weren't much larger than a casket. This was fitting because the ushers inside were as pale and waxy as corpses.

Behind the uniformed men were four doors, the first marked with a brass letter *K*, the second an *S*, the third an *A*, and the final door with the letter *I*.

"Those are the ushers of the Parlor. They tell you what part you'll play and explain the rules of the stage. Pay attention to the rules, Mr. Senlin. These things are tedious, but every cog has its purpose, right?" Pining said without a shred of real earnestness. He pulled on the stays of his collar and was called forward by an usher. Pining gave the man a cordial, but causeless, laugh. It was his way of lubricating the cogs, though it had little effect. The man's expression was as dour as a bailiff's. For all of Pining's enthusiasm for the Parlor's charms, there was very little welcoming about the scene.

Senlin was waved forward by another usher, who had a well-groomed skirt of white hair and furrow lines that seemed to begin at the bald egg-point of his head.

The usher handed him a pocket-sized printed booklet. The book reminded Senlin of the basic primers his students used: rugged and unhandsomely bound with a serrated fore edge. "You will be playing the butler, sir," the usher announced without disturbing the latitudes of his wrinkles. The front of Senlin's booklet was stamped with the character's name: Isaac.

"I don't understand. I'm not an actor. I would like a seat, perhaps something near the back..." Senlin said. The usher's gaze was so blank Senlin couldn't tell if the lengthy pause was meant to infer disbelief or loathing. The man was as expressive as a doorknocker. Senlin swallowed noisily.

"You are both actor and audience, sir," the usher said. "You can sit down, if you like. The rules of the Parlor are included in the back of the program; I suggest you familiarize yourself with them. Most important, sir, is that you only go through the doors that are marked with an *I*. *I*, for Isaac. Entering another character's door will result in your removal from the Parlor."

"Could I just be removed now? I'm in something of a hurry to get to the Baths." He wasn't of a mind to attend the theater, no matter how novel and modern, while Marya was missing. Surely there would be some corridor for tourists passing through . . .

"No one is removed to the upper floors, sir, only to the Basement. If you wanted to circumvent our entertainment, you should've booked passage on an airship," the usher said dryly. "Secondly, we ask that you stoke the fires of the rooms you enter. Fuel has been provided, and I can assure you, all characters are required to tend the fires, not just those who've been given the role of the butler. Failure to keep the fires burning will result in your removal."

The usher asked for twelve shekels, which would've paid for a hotel room for three nights. Senlin was surprised and unhappy with the sum, but he didn't see that he had any choice. He'd recently learned what dickering over entry fees won a person. He could turn back and return to the Basement, or he could pay and forge ahead.

Paying required Senlin to remove his boot. His embarrassment would've been more pronounced if he hadn't caught sight of his new acquaintance, Pining, removing his carefully polished slipper for the same reason. It seemed Senlin wasn't the first to walk around on his bank. The discovery made him feel less clever.

Senlin passed through the polished turnstile, but before he could open the door emblazoned with a brass *I*, Pining touched his elbow and said, "In a week, you'll be pulled from this adventure, and it will be like an alarm clock ejecting you from a wonderful dream!"

Chapter Eight

Never let a rigid itinerary discourage you from an unexpected adventure.

—*Everyman's Guide to the Tower of Babel*, III. II

Despite the usher's mysterious recitations and Pining's enthusiasms, Senlin still expected to find rows of seats, upholstered in velvet, a stage, a proscenium, and a curtain: In short, he expected a playhouse.

Instead, he found himself standing at the threshold of a white-tiled hall that reminded him of the locker rooms at the boarding school he'd attended long ago. Cedar benches and stalls ran the length of the changing room. Dozens of humorless attendants in white strode about pushing racks of suits, carrying stacks of towels, rolling hampers full of polished shoes. Unlike the usher he'd just paid, these men's suits held the rumple of labor. The air was heavy with steam and the aggressive camouflage of colognes, soaps, and hair tonics. He recognized the space for what it was: the backstage. He was backstage. But where was the stage? And who was on it?

Senlin was adopted by an attendant who carried a neatly folded white towel with a pink soap cake squared atop it. His attendant had combed, stone-colored hair and gaunt cheeks shaved to pinkness; otherwise, he exuded all the gentility of a bait man. Senlin was a little alarmed to discover that the man was armed. A single-shot pistol hung at his hip. A further glance at the other attendants in the room revealed that most were armed. Unaccustomed to seeing guns publicly displayed (not even Isaugh's constable regularly carried one), Senlin took it as a sign that he was entering a more lawful section of the Tower.

Senlin gave his unpolished attendant a cordial smile. The attendant did not so much guide Senlin as shove him toward an open bathing stall.

Despite his anxiety, Senlin enjoyed the hot blast of the shower and the rough, sandalwood-scented soap. It seemed the first bit of genuine luxury the Tower had offered him. He would've lingered under the steaming spray longer if his gruff attendant had not roused him.

The attendant measured Senlin with a tailor's tape while Senlin stood in his towel, then left and soon returned with a change of clothes: a butler's tails and white starched dickey. Both fit, but neither flattered Senlin's lanky build. He was an unconvincing butler. The red bow tie looked so absurd on him that Senlin immediately removed it. His attendant, however, quickly took up the discarded tie and returned it without gentleness to Senlin's neck.

"No changes to your costume, sir," the steel-haired usher said. "Look to the rules in your program." Slowly, the full implication of the usher's words dawned on him: He was the actor and the audience. This wasn't theater. This was a charade. This was a child's game of make-believe. Of course there was no real audience. Who would want to watch?

The attendant directed Senlin to pack his clothes and valuables into his satchel, which he did apprehensively. He loathed the idea of being separated from his money, train tickets, and guidebook, but he seemed to have no option in the matter. The fact that the operation was so efficiently run and included so much security gave him some hope. Besides, it seemed he wasn't the only one to keep his money in his shoe, so how safe could it be?

His satchel was then locked inside a heavy, rolling locker alongside the personal items of other men, all of whom seemed much more at ease with relinquishing their possessions. And why not?

No one sitting in a theater worried that their coat was being stolen from the coatroom. These men had come to escape, to play, to act! They bantered and cackled and carried on like schoolboys, even though much of their hair was gray or gone. Younger men were present, too, but they were generally a little fat, or awkward, or unattractive. It seemed that men who lacked a certain presence were selected by the ushers to play the butler. How fitting, he thought sourly, that he be among them.

As he was dressed and primped by his attendant, Senlin read the program he'd been given. The program outlined the plot they'd be embellishing. The play took place in a mansion, so the set spanned multiple rooms and included a dining hall, a study, a kitchen, and a dozen other domestic spaces. There were only four characters in the play: a wealthy husband and wife named Kerrick and Alice Mayfair, a young business apprentice named Oscar Shaw, and Isaac, the butler—his role in the farce.

The players were expected to improvise a dialogue around the provided plot. The story was trite enough. The husband, Mr. Mayfair, is consumed with his business affairs. He thinks of his young partner, Mr. Shaw, as the son he never had and spends much of his time grooming him for the business world. Meanwhile, Mrs. Mayfair, feeling neglected by her husband, has begun to flirt with Mr. Shaw. Mr. Shaw is forced to choose between his future as a businessman and the burgeoning feelings he has for Mrs. Shaw, a lovely, if not flawed, woman of many moods.

Senlin was dismayed to discover that Isaac the butler would eventually have to decide whether to support the mercurial mistress in her indiscretion or to reveal the potential affair to his employer, Mr. Mayfair. It was a nightmare. The plot was exactly the sort of tart melodrama he discouraged his students from reading. The subtext was obvious: Love, pure and eternal, reigned supreme. Senlin did not believe in that sort of love: sudden and selfish and insatiable. Love, as the poets so often painted it, was just bald lust wearing a pompous wig. He believed true love was more like an education: It was deep and subtle and never complete.

The usher grasped Senlin's shoulder with a calloused hand, stirring him from his snit, and escorted him through the far end of the changing chamber into a carpeted hall. The passageway before him was reminiscent of something from a lavish hotel. Whitewashed doors were spaced regularly on either side of the hall, though unlike any hotel he'd ever visited, this hall had no corners. Rather, it stretched on and on until it gradually curved out of sight. The passage was filled with hundreds of men of varying shapes, but all dressed in the same black tails and starched bib that Senlin wore. The ubiquity of the red bow tie that itched at his neck made him feel less conspicuous but only more absurd.

It was as if he had stepped between two mirrors and was now watching himself doubled and redoubled into a dimming infinity. The scene made him dizzy.

His brusque attendant handed him a key and said, "Find an unlocked door in the hall. If it's unlocked, the play inside still needs someone to play Isaac, the butler. The other players may already have begun the play. Lock the door behind you. Your key will open all the interior doors that are unmarked and the door you entered by. If you exit to the hall, you cannot reenter the play. If you exit through another character's door, you'll be removed from the Parlor. Do you have any questions?"

A little stunned, but feeling in no position to quiz his handler, who seemed in no mood to answer anyway, Senlin shook his head.

"Enjoy your performance."

Get through the Parlor. Get to the Baths. She will be there, Senlin told himself again.

He felt the familiar cinching of his throat, the throbbing in his fingertips, the telescopic vision that announced the arrival of panic. There were too many people in the constricted corridor. He had to escape. He shouldered his way through the hall of milling, palavering butlers, none of whom seemed in much of a rush to find an open door. This was, after all, their holiday adventure! They experimented with theatrical accents and stage gestures; they blustered over which side they'd support once the play began. Love must win out! No, marriage is a sacred thing!

He wanted to scream.

The thought of bursting into some strange room unnerved him, but not so badly as the hall of butlers. He tried a door at random and found it locked. He rattled another; it snubbed him, too. The next was no different. The sweat on his palm became a lubricant, and the doorknobs began to slip under his grip. His distress worsened with each rebuff. For a moment, he stood outside himself, watching as this frenzied, willowy fool wrenched doorknob after doorknob.

His doppelgangers grumbled and threw their chins at him as he squeezed past. He bumped them against the wainscot and the gold-leafed wallpaper without apology. He couldn't help himself. He was being driven mad, not just by the familiar spasms of anxiety, but by the thought that Marya might be behind any one of these doors, acting in a play where she was one man's wife and another man's lover. He grasped the next doorknob as if he meant to strangle it.

It turned. He rushed inside and swiftly locked the door behind him. The silence was wonderful.

He stood at the threshold of a kitchen. It was as if he had walked through the back door of someone's house. Split logs lay in a neat pyramid beside a potbelly stove. Nets filled with gourds and onions dangled from exposed square rafters overhead. Jarred preserves glowed brightly in the light of an unshaded oil lamp. The lamp also lit an oddly placed brass nub fixed high on the wall. Senlin was quickly distracted from this oddity by the ham. The ham, pinned with bright cherries, sat on an ornate platter on the servant's table. The aroma of wood smoke, cloves, pork, and seasoned iron warmed the air. It was undeniably delightful. And peaceful. He could hardly believe he was still in the Tower of Babel.

He stoked the fire and refilled the cast iron kettle from a sturdy, green faucet. It was an automatic act; water was always on the boil in his cottage back home, ready at a moment's notice for a cup of tea. The pipes gurgled and coughed like an old asthmatic. The domestic chore comforted him. The splatters of grease on the stove made him think of breakfast: griddle cakes, stewed apples, and greasy kippers snapping in the pan. He was hungry. No, he was more than hungry; he was ravenous. He abandoned his manners and pulled a thick piece of greasy bark from the bronze ham. Eating the strip in one crude bite, he returned for another, then a third. He chewed and panted and chewed again. He gorged himself, standing over the ham like a vulture, so happy to be alone. The salted meat stung his lips, which were cracked from thirst. He took a teacup from a hook and filled it from the faucet, drinking and moaning with relief. Once he'd scarfed down as much meat as he could stomach, he wrapped a few more pieces in a cloth napkin and slipped the parcel into his pocket.

The porcelain teacup in his hands caught his attention, though it took him a moment to realize why. Its lip was painted with a quaint garland of dogwood blossoms. Just a few months earlier, Marya, in the process of melding their homes, had unpacked a straw-filled crate of china painted with a similar pattern. Her set was a family heirloom, a gift handed down from her grandmother on their wedding day. At the time, Senlin had observed several pieces of her set were missing, and, inspired by a desire to please and also by a preference for completeness, he had offered to locate replacements.

Marya had thanked him and tugged at his neck to kiss some softness into his expression. (He wondered now: Did he always scowl, even when they were alone?)

"The gaps are a part of the set, too," she'd said. "You can't replace them. I know how each piece was broken or lost. I broke a plate myself when I was nine. Now I'm an immortal part of the pattern. I'll take my gaps, thank you." She winked and pressed her tongue behind her upper lip. It was a face she had sometimes pulled in the classroom, many years earlier, and recalling it made him smile fondly.

No, he did not always scowl.

Senlin slumped into a chair in the warm sham-kitchen and buried his face in his hands.

Chapter Nine

Inevitably, invariably, eventually you will discover you are unprepared to make an informed choice. When in doubt, say, *Yes. Yes* is the eternal passport. *Yes* is the everlasting coin.

—*Everyman's Guide to the Tower of Babel*, I. XII

The obnoxious clanging of a bell woke him. He was surprised to discover he'd fallen asleep. One bell, in a bank of many mounted over the stove, jerked up and down, pulled by a cord that disappeared into the wall. Reflexively, he leapt toward the door beneath the bells, still clutching the teacup he'd been meditating upon.

He entered a long dining hall, which, except for a complete lack of windows, could've been transplanted from a provincial mansion. A parliament's worth of high-back chairs ran the length of a dining table that gleamed from a recent polish. Brightly painted shields hung in the spaces between tapestries on the wall. Several more of the brass nubbins were set high on the walls. Perhaps they were some sort of air valve? A wide fireplace seethed with enough coals to roast a boar. Though the room was empty, Senlin heard the muffled echo of voices in an adjoining room.

Deciding to avoid the other actors in the farce as long as possible, Senlin went to the rack of firewood, selected two quartered logs of wood, and angled them carefully upon the grate. He couldn't tell which direction the voices came from. Whoever it was, they sounded passionate, though whether the voices were raised in amusement or anger, he couldn't say. He was still groggy from his nap. He wondered how long he'd slept. Had the play already begun? He had expected some sort of introduction or preamble. He pulled at the bow tie unconsciously and wondered if he shouldn't just hole up in the kitchen and wait for the melodrama to run its course.

One of the dining hall's many doors flew open, and a woman in a formal hoop-gown dashed in with her teeth bared in frustration or disgust; he couldn't tell which. At first, she seemed unaware of Senlin, who stood frozen like a rabbit. When she spotted him, she covered her gritted teeth with an unconvincing smile.

"Isaac, where is our tea?" she asked. Beyond the open door, two men's voices volleyed back and forth intensely. "Didn't you hear me ring for you?"

It took Senlin a moment to remember he was Isaac. "Yes," he said, feeling a little galled. He was used to being the one who rang the bell to call the children in. He'd not spent six years at university only to become some stranger's imaginary manservant. But, wishing to avoid an argument, he forced himself to respond in character, though without a shred of enthusiasm for the part. "It's not ready."

She closed the space between them, and he saw her cheeks were flushed. Her hair, dark as a wet slate, was styled high on her head. Her complexion was the caramel color common in the south of Ur. Her charcoal eyes and thick eyebrows were striking, but not in a way that suited the frilliness of her peach-colored dress. She looked like an overfrosted cake. The effect reminded him of how easily a pleasant work of art could be overwhelmed by a glamorous frame. The neckline of her dress was low and crowded.

She took the teacup from him, peered into it, and then turned it upside down since it was empty. She gave him a disappointed look and foisted the cup back on him. "Leave the tea for the moment. My husband and Mr. Shaw are arguing in the study. I think it would help to have a calming presence in the room."

Senlin was confused by her theatrics. She seemed physically upset,

frightened almost, yet she referred to the other men by their characters' names. Perhaps she was just a talented actress. It occurred to him
that not everyone in the Parlor was the amateur he was. "What should
I do?"

She flung her hands out in a shooing gesture; it seemed more appropriate for steering a wayward chicken than a man. "Just go skulk in
the study!" She had slipped out of character; her accent was suddenly
rural. Recovering quickly, she concluded with a more staid, "Please."

Snatching the empty teacup from him, she began using it as a prop,
drinking air from it with her pinky finger thrown out. If the act was
meant to compose her or convince him that she was composed, it
failed. The cup clattered noisily upon the saucer when she lowered it.

He felt sorry for her; she seemed almost as out of place as he was.

With a resolute little sigh, Senlin dipped at the waist and said,
"After you, madam."

The chamber seemed more a trophy room than a study: Old bugles,
helmets, and sabers hung as decoration on the walls. An unwieldy
musket, some six feet in length, stretched between pegs over the fireplace. He doubted it was real. An imposing stuffed animal dominated
one corner of the room, its long, brown fur a little matted with age
but still thick. It took Senlin a moment to identify the beast: It was a
giant anteater. The black shock of fur at its throat, its splayed clawed
fingers, and rivet-small eyes were made more dramatic by its sheer
size—reared on its haunches, it stood nearly seven feet tall. The heads
of deer, elk, and moose were featured on another wall. The low firelight made them appear as if they were leering at him.

Two men in dinner jackets argued and paced about a mahogany
bar, sometimes stopping to tip the contents of a crystal decanter into
their tumblers.

Senlin was surprised to recognize the slighter and younger of the
two men. It was Mr. Edsel Pining, still with his hands behind his
back, bobbing forward as he spoke like a pecking hen. Pining, obviously cast as Oscar Shaw, the young and romantic apprentice, was
having a wonderful time waxing lyrical about the illogic of love and

the sterility of business. Apparently, he hadn't delayed initiating the crisis at the heart of the play. He had dived right in.

The larger man, playing Mr. Mayfair, was red faced, gray bearded, and, Senlin thought, alarmingly drunk.

Hardly noticed by either man, Senlin moved to the hearth and began shifting the embers with a poker, adding a brighter, more theatrical light to the two men's argument. The woman in the crinoline dress did not stray far from him. She settled her skirts over an ottoman by the fire.

"I took you into my home, exposed my accounts to you, and how do you repay me? By pawing my wife?" The man playing Mayfair barked and jerked his arm in punctuation, splashing liquor on the fiercely posed anteater.

"I repay your confidence by taking you into my own. I have shown you the ledgers of my heart. And just as a man of business cannot make the price of goods rise or fall as he pleases, a man of the heart cannot dictate how it swings. The stock market of the heart is a fickle thing. Mrs. Mayfair—"

"Is mine! This is not business; this is theft," he said, and surprised everyone in the room by dashing his glass on the floor.

"Perhaps we'll continue our conversation when your head has had a chance to clear," Pining said, hardly containing his delight at the passion of the scene. He turned to the woman whose skirts overwhelmed the footstool and half the rug it sat upon. Pining dipped to kiss her hand. "My dear, I leave you now to sweeten our reunion! Is not the sun most splendid in its exits and entrances? May our setting and rising, our dusks and dawns, be every bit as colorful!"

When Pining straightened again, a crystal decanter exploded against the back of his head. The halo of flying glass caught the firelight, causing Pining to appear, Senlin thought, briefly angelic.

Pining crumpled to the floor at Mrs. Mayfair's feet, a red spray freckling the front of her peach skirt. She reared back in horror, overturning the ottoman and crashing against Senlin, who stood frozen by the mantel, still holding the poker.

Mr. Mayfair, his jaw slack and his chin glinting with spit, stood over Pining. "She wants me," he murmured, dropping the jagged neck of the decanter. Then more fiercely, he cried, "She wants me!" He pointed at the unmoving sprawl of Pining. "You are a fraud, a little boy fraud. You couldn't satisfy this woman, you foppish, mouthy fraud. She needs a man! She wants me!" Overcome by drink and fury, Mayfair pulled at his face and careened toward the door Senlin had entered by.

Sensing his opportunity, Senlin went to Pining. He had to press his ear to the carpet to see a sliver of Pining's face between the bars of his flowing blood. Through one open eye, Pining focused on him, managing a fragile and unguarded smile. He was alive. The revelation filled Senlin with hope. He was alive! Of course he was; this was only theater. It was crude theater, perhaps, but they hadn't stripped off their humanity while pulling on their costumes. The main thing now was to suspend the play and tend to Pining's wound. Senlin had seen many a boy crack his head in the schoolyard, and despite the great streams of blood, none were ever mortally hurt.

The floor shook under heavy feet, and the woman screamed.

Senlin looked up to find Mayfair charging across the room. He had pulled a saber from the wall and held it in two hands like a man carrying a flag onto a battlefield. But there was no flag, no battlefield. There was only a wounded accountant in a costume, splayed on a paisley rug.

Mayfair staked Pining between the shoulders with a brutal grunt.

Arching as if he meant to crawl away, Pining showed that the saber had passed through him and bitten into the floor. He swatted the air twice, then slid back down the length of the blade. Floating on his own blood, Pining drew a breath that rattled like a snore, one that would've woken even the heaviest sleeper. But Pining did not stir.

Senlin backed against Mrs. Mayfair, who stood clutching her throat and mouth. Mayfair set his boot on Pining's back and yanked the saber free. The blade shone darkly with gore. Trembling behind the poker, Senlin felt a tugging at his coattails; the woman was pulling him toward a door set beside the hearth. It wasn't the door he'd come by, and he had no sense of where it led.

Senlin resisted the woman's pull and instead moved nearer Mayfair, who stood heaving like an enraged bull in the middle of the room. Senlin was rattled; perhaps he was even in shock. But something had to be said. He drew himself up to his full lecturer's height and spoke in his most scolding tone. "Are you insane? He was acting! You have killed a man for his dialogue! You are not her husband. You are not Mr. Mayfair." Senlin pointed vehemently at the ground: a man commanding a dog to heel. "This is a play, and you have ended it."

Mayfair dug his tongue about the corners of his mouth, as if clearing a bad taste, and then spat on the floor between them. He had the lumbering, apathetic posture of someone who has just risen from a bath. He swung the sword through the air almost languidly; a stripe of blood appeared on the rug. His eyes were red and haunted and dry as coals.

"Get away from my wife, Isaac," Mayfair said, and leveled his sword at Senlin.

Chapter Ten

Anything that distracts from the play becomes the play itself.

— *Everyman's Guide to the Tower of Babel*, III. V

Senlin wasn't exactly sure when the change had transpired, but at some point in the last dozen years spent as headmaster of Isaugh's school, he'd begun to think of the entire village as his classroom.

It hadn't been out of snobbery; at least, he hoped it hadn't. He did not think himself superior to the fishermen or their wives who dried, salted, and crated the cod and tusk. He did not tip his nose at the handful of sooty rail workers who operated their little station, or at the tradesmen who furnished the town with bread, clothes, and ale. Yet, he couldn't stop himself from supplying them with little tidbits of knowledge: an explanation of the uniformity of salt crystals, or a note on the evolution of the steam valve gear, or the exotic cousins of domestic yeast. The locals were tolerant of his impromptu lessons but did not enjoy them. They found such minutiae useless because it made their immediate work no easier. Even so, Senlin persisted, driven by the ideal that knowledge was the great antiseptic; the more educated a society was, the more clean, safe, equal, and prosperous it would be.

Of course, the standard of enlightenment by which all else was judged was the Tower of Babel. The Tower was, he had been so certain, the great refuge of learning, the very seat of civilization. He preached its gospel, and the villagers rolled their eyes.

And perhaps they had been right to roll their eyes. Here he stood, caught in the throat of the Tower, preparing for his own violent death. He hadn't a fact left in his head.

Mayfair lunged forward. Even in that glimpsing second, Senlin saw no trace of conscience in the man's expression: His rage had purged him of all reason. Instinctively, Senlin flung himself backward through the open doorway, crashing off balance against a loaded book cart. The woman leapt around him as he fell and hurled herself against the heavy door. The latch caught just as the door was battered from the other side.

"Alice, darling, open the door!" Mayfair shouted.

"My name's Edith, you lunatic, and if you come in here, I'll claw your eyes out!" she cried back. Senlin was relieved that she had finally dropped the act, but he was taken aback by the ferocity in her voice.

The door jolted on its hinges. "It's not locked," she hissed at Senlin. "Key! Where is your key?" When he took too long to respond, the gears of his mind frozen with shock, Edith began snatching up her petticoat. The voluminous underskirts bunched about her waist. The revealed leg looked like it belonged on a porcelain ballerina tucked inside a music box. The display did nothing to mitigate Senlin's shock. She pulled a key from the top band of her white stocking, and with her back pressed against the door, tried to fit the key by feel.

Before she could seat the key, the knob turned and Mayfair's arm shot into the room through a widening gap. His hand groped after her furiously, snatching at her hair. "Do as I say, woman!" he bellowed.

Her heels began to slide. She was losing the battle over the door. She screamed at Senlin for help, and the alarm in her voice was enough to break his petrification. He grabbed the nearest thing at hand, the librarian's cart, racked full of books, and barreled toward the opening door, the cart leading him like a plow.

Edith sprang out of the way, and Mayfair cast the door wide just as Senlin launched the cart. The rolling missile struck Mayfair and hurtled him back against the bar.

For a moment, Senlin thought he'd knocked the man unconscious, but even as he turned toward Edith he heard the dashing of glass behind him and an irate, animal cry. Again, she threw herself at the door, nearly catching Senlin against the jamb in the process. She set the key and turned the lock.

The pounding resumed. The doorknob jerked violently. They listened to Mayfair scraping his own key against the keyhole, but her key, still turned in the lock, kept his from engaging the mechanism.

A quick scan of the room revealed they were in the library. Crowded shelves spanned the walls from floorboard to molding. A round card table and four chairs sat on the medallion of a large rug. A fire smoldered in a fan-shaped hearth. Senlin, in an adrenaline fog, picked up one of the books that had fallen from the cart. He opened it. Sheaf after sheaf of blank paper passed under his thumb. It was a prop. The realization brought his emotions back into relief. He realized he was indignant. No, not indignant; he was angry. He threw the blank into the fireplace. It flared brightly, as if in self-disgust.

"Why couldn't we be the ones locked in the armory?" Edith asked. Her dark hair had fallen from its arrangement and lay in ribbons over her face.

They saw the other door in the room at the same moment. It stood open.

"We have to block it off," Senlin said.

"We'll be trapped," she said. Mayfair's drumming on the door quickened. "I don't want to be backed in a corner. There was a gun in there. You saw it. If it's loaded, we're finished."

"Then we must find an exit." Senlin retrieved the fire iron he'd dropped. He couldn't imagine wielding it, but it comforted him to have it. "You'll have to leave your key in the lock."

"Wait a minute," she said, and then more loudly and toward the door she called, "Don't break your hip, you old cuckold!"

Her taunt had the intended effect: Mayfair redoubled his efforts. While he thundered on, they snuck from the room through the unassailed door.

There was no time for social niceties or introductions. If they were going to escape the berserk Mayfair, it would be by their wits and vigilance. They would sort out the formalities later if they survived. For now, all that mattered was getting away. They reviewed their options as they slunk through the house.

It couldn't have been helped, but they soon realized they'd made a tactical error by leaving Edith's key behind. If they'd had her key, they might've fled directly to her character's bedroom, where she'd originally entered the play, and made their exit. Her chamber was on the opposite end of the staged mansion and far removed from the trophy room. With only Senlin's key, which unlocked the exit in the kitchen, they'd have to double back through the trophy room or the dining hall that adjoined it. With only two paths, they had a fifty-fifty chance of running into Mayfair again. To better those odds, Edith suggested that they lead Mayfair as far into the house as possible, back to where the bedrooms were numerous and the halls were tangled. Once they'd drawn him away from the trophy room, they would return to the dining hall and make a break for the kitchen. If they could reach the hall of Isaacs, surely they would find help.

Senlin suggested that they lock every door they encountered. Doing so would confuse and slow Mayfair: If every door was locked, there'd be no obvious trail to follow. Edith agreed and voiced her hope that Mayfair would keep making a racket. As long as he was drumming, they would know where he was.

The noise receded a little when they entered a dimly lit conservatory with a harpsichord. Velvet-backed chairs encircled the gleaming instrument. More of the strange brass valves protruded from the walls here. They seemed to be in every room. Hoping to light a candle he'd found, Senlin banked the fire that had dwindled nearly to ashes. But when he applied a lit piece of kindling to the candle, he discovered it had no wick at its center. He threw the wax stake into the fresh logs, bewildered by the ruse. What possible reason could anyone have for pulling the vein out of a candle? It was absurd.

He was about to try a second candle when the distant pounding abruptly stopped. They stood alert as startled deer for a moment and then hurried wordlessly into the adjacent sunroom.

The sunroom was a ghastly mockery. The walls had been painted to resemble windows that framed cauliflower clouds and an egg-yolk sun. A robin, painted in midflight, looked more like a smashed bug on a wall than a living bird. Many of the rooms were like this: just clumsy sets. Most of the objects were shells or props. The house was a stage in every way except that where there should've been an audience, there was only another wall. Senlin found himself wishing for the light of eyes to drive the shadows from the set. For once, he wanted to be the center of attention.

They crept onward through chambers and halls. Senlin's heart stopped whenever his key rasped inside a lock. The sound was excruciating, like sand rubbed upon glass. Even their breathing and the rustle of her voluminous skirts seemed to boom. When he came about a corner and was confronted by the raised specter of a saber, Senlin yelped and swatted at it with the fire iron.

The empty coatrack bounced against the wall and clattered to the floor.

Edith gritted her teeth at him in horror. He gave a helpless, apologetic shrug. What could he do? He was not equipped for this sort of intrigue. He started to explain, but she shushed him and hurried on.

After locking the door to a short, drab hallway, they entered a bedroom that was dominated by an enormous four-post bed, canopied with amber-colored silks. The door to the left of the bed was marked with a polished *K*.

"*K*, for Kerrick Mayfair. We're in his room," Senlin said, stoking up the coals in the green-tiled fireplace to light the room.

Edith began wrestling with her crinoline skirts. "This is ridiculous." She turned her back toward Senlin. "Unfasten me."

The request startled him. What sort of lady asked such a thing? He gawked at the nape of her neck, her caramel skin, a dark spatter of freckles. He realized that since the moment they'd been thrown together by grim circumstance, he had avoided considering who she was, or how she'd come to be here. Initially, he'd assumed she was a lady because she was playing one, and now he was critiquing her behavior because it wasn't ladylike. It was absurd! He wasn't a butler, after all. No, she was a person, like him, with a past and a home. For all he knew, she was lost or had lost someone, too. Perhaps somewhere at that moment a man longed for this exact intimate view of her neck. These thoughts surprised him and revived memories of Marya and the honeymoon he had spoiled.

Frustrated by this inconvenient jumble of thoughts, Senlin blurted out, "Why?"

"Really? Why do I want to remove ten pounds of stuffing and frills while being chased by an armed lunatic?" She watched him over her shoulder, her hand cupping her hair, dark as loam. "It took two women a half hour to get me into this thing. I can't get out alone."

He glanced about nervously and suffered a pang of shame when he saw the bed.

She sighed. "Are you a monk?"

"No."

"Then undo my dress!"

A slight creak, the briefest complaint of wood beams, interrupted them. The sound seemed to come from the hallway, though really it could have just as easily come from the ceiling or the floor beneath them. In fact, Senlin had the odd impression that the creak had originated from the corner of the room that was farthest from any door and which was empty except for the nub of a brass valve.

The hairs stood up on his arms as they did, sometimes, in the classroom when he had his back to the students. The hairs would rise, and he would know something was amiss behind him: Someone was out of their seat, or an arm was being raised to throw a paper ball, or . . .

He turned twice all the way around, searching for what had raised his hair. But there was nothing, just their shadows writhing upon the wall.

Chapter Eleven

If the actors are any good, or the script is, or the director, then the audience will be as quiet as a sigh. Unless, of course, the play is a comedy. Then quiet is a terrible and tormenting thing.

—*Everyman's Guide to the Tower of Babel*, III. XI

When they came upon Edith's bedroom, they found it dark. Senlin retreated to the previous room, lit a length of kindling, and carried it back like a torch. He rushed the sputtering stick to the ash-heaped grate and built up the fire from the wood pail. As he did, Edith tried the sturdy door emblazoned with an *A*. She didn't seem surprised to find it locked. "Why did I leave my key?"

"It couldn't be helped. I could try to force the door." Even as he made the offer, he thought back to the door he'd originally entered by. It had been as solid as a dyke.

"Are you sure?" she said with a doubtful turn of her head. It was a reasonable assessment, but he still felt the need to defend himself. He was a scholar, not a brute, after all. Perhaps if there were more scholars and fewer brutes in the world, they wouldn't be running for their lives! But he said nothing. "Because he'd certainly hear you banging away, and we'd be cornered."

He couldn't argue otherwise.

"I know where I am now," she said. "The foyer's this way."

A broad staircase with a green runner ascended to the ceiling, ending abruptly against the flat plaster where a second floor should've begun. The entranceway facing the bottom of the stair was painted on.

"For all its doors, this house is full of dead ends," Senlin said.

"The dining hall is through there. We're almost to the kitchen," she said, picking up her heavy skirts with dramatized effort. "If he's out there, and I get caught because of these stupid skirts, I'm holding you responsible." She gave a fleeting, nervous smile, then glanced anxiously at the poker dangling from Senlin's hand. "I wish we had a sword."

"I've never picked up a sword in my life," Senlin said.

Seeming disarmed by his candor, she smiled again. "Me neither." She saw that the fire iron trembled in his hand, and her smile waned. "I remember there were things on the walls that looked like shields. Is that right?" Senlin nodded. "I say we pull one down, and if it comes to it, we'll use it as a ram. The two of us together should be able to run over one old drunk."

"What if they're fakes?"

"The sword was real enough," she replied. He wondered why that was. Why have dummy candles and blank books but sharpened swords? He wished the stern attendant who'd dressed him had warned him of such things; better yet, he wished the attendant would dash in with his pistol out and put an end to the whole terrible ordeal.

He unlocked the door to the dining hall with Edith's skirts bunched against him. She craned over his shoulder, peering through the expanding crack. He half expected to see the barrel-chested Mayfair sitting at the head of the dining table, theatrical as a king. But the only life in the room was the fire, snapping inside the deep flagstone hearth.

The shields on the wall were enameled with bright crests. They appeared real enough. Senlin took down a nearby kite shield, faced with a blue cross. It was all he could do to hold the thick iron plate in front of them. He would sooner die than complain about its weight.

"All right, quietly now," she said, her knees bumping against the backs of his legs.

The hall seemed to telescope before him. The kitchen door receded as they began to move toward it, hunkered low behind the shield. Six doors led off from the dining hall. It was impossible to guess what direction Mayfair might attack from. Or he could just as easily be passed out on the floor. Senlin wasn't even certain that all the doors were real. The hair on his arms bristled. Not knowing which way to point their backs, he swung the shield back and forth.

They passed the study where Pining had been murdered. The door stood ajar—not enough for them to see into the room, but enough to allow a crack of light to shine into the dining hall. Senlin turned the shield toward the glowing seam, terrified that the light might flicker, fall into shadow, and then explode as Mayfair burst from the room. The image was so vivid that it felt like a premonition, but of course he did not believe in such things...

The squeak of old hinges interrupted his thoughts. Senlin squinted at the study door and was confused to find that the crack had not grown at all.

"The kitchen!" Edith screamed, and Senlin spun around.

Mayfair filled the doorway to the kitchen. He seemed as startled as them. A ham hung under one bulky arm. In his free hand, he gripped the musket.

"What is instinct?" Senlin stood rigid as a totem pole at the fore of the classroom. "Instinct is an inherited response to a particular circumstance." His gaze drifted over the rows of tired but attentive children. "The osprey instinctively knows how to build a nest. The mackerel instinctively swims in a school. Bears hibernate, rabbits dig warrens, and the tree frog sings. They do not know why they do these things, but all of these behaviors benefit the creature and help it to survive."

He strode quickly down an aisle between desks and snatched a folded slip of paper from the fingers of a startled boy. He ripped the note into a palm-full of confetti as he returned to the head of the class. The action hardly disturbed his lecture. "Instinct can be roughly divided into two urges: the urge to survive and the urge to reproduce. In humans, the conscious mind is aware of these urges. We built a society to manage our instincts. In fact, society so thoroughly mitigates our instincts, it is easy to forget that we have them at all."

He turned to the blackboard and began jotting a frenzied list. "We have customs, manners, governance, the constabulary, traditions, education, fashion, commerce, creative invention, sports, and on and on. All of these expressions of our society work to the same goal of suppressing and managing our instinctual response." The blackboard rattled and rocked on its feet, shaken by Senlin's emphatic jots. "Instinct is the fuel that fires the engine of civilization. Generations have labored to build and perfect the engine. Each of you, I hope, will spend your life working to preserve it. Because without it, we would be dangerous beasts."

He ran behind the shield. It seemed lighter now. Adrenaline fizzed in his blood as he charged at Mayfair. The brute stood like a steer frozen by the light of an approaching train. He seemed older and more vulnerable than he had before. Senlin saw and absorbed this information, though it made no impression on him. It stirred no shred of mercy. He wasn't thinking; he had transcended all thought.

And it felt good. He'd never felt such wild abandon in his life. He sensed Edith rushing along behind him, her own instincts tuned to his as they barreled down the dining hall. They were going to catch Mayfair flat-footed. They were going to survive.

Then Mayfair dropped the ham, drew the barrel of the musket level, and fired.

He sat at the bottom of a well. There was a point of light far above him. At the bottom of the well, a piercing note rang in his ears. It reminded him vaguely of a finger playing a wineglass.

His limbs felt as if they had been replaced with wet rope. He was confused but strangely unafraid. Slowly, he began to rise from the bottom of the well, his useless limbs slapping at the sides of the dark. The light grew. He emerged on the floor of the dining hall.

He stared at the side of his pale hand that lay by his face.

He rolled onto his ribs and felt each one as a distinct band of pain.

The shield, dog-eared at one corner, lay nearby. Through the ringing in his ears, he heard moaning and the clatter of wood. Toppled chairs splayed on the floor. Through the bramble of chair legs, he watched retreating boots. Another chair crashed to the floor.

It was Mayfair striding alongside the table, his hip to the edge in a manner Senlin found confusing. The brute kicked chairs from his path as he went, musket still in hand. The sight of the gun fanned the fog from Senlin's mind. He realized that Edith was no longer at his side. He had to get up.

Gripping the table edge, he pulled himself upright. He grabbed his head to keep it from exploding. Mayfair's shot had struck the shield and driven it back into the side of his skull. He feared he might black out again. Then he saw her sliding down the burnished tabletop. Mayfair dragged her down the table by her skirts. Mayfair's back was to Senlin when he paused to paw drunkenly at the whalebone ribs of her bodice and the shelf of vulnerable flesh. Edith appeared half-conscious. She groaned and rolled her head, her hair unraveling as Mayfair began dragging her again.

Senlin found the poker lying amid the toppled chairs. He raised it high over his head and charged at Mayfair's back, running on the edges of his boots. Edith emerged from semiconsciousness a split second before he arrived and began kicking through the piles of her skirts. Mayfair had time to cock his fist over her before Senlin brought the poker down, striking him in the muscled notch between neck and shoulder.

Mayfair collapsed, bowling through the last chairs as he fell. Senlin lost his grip on the poker, and it flew clattering end over end across the floor. He didn't try to retrieve it. He tugged at Edith's gown even as she scrambled to the table's edge and onto her feet. She bounced against his chest, her legs still weak from the blow. A ribbon of blood ran down her forehead and over one eye. Senlin saw the gash at her hairline. Though it bled profusely, it didn't seem dangerously deep.

They hobbled toward the kitchen door, their four legs crossing and knocking, clumsy as a calf. They managed the two steps down into the kitchen, still aromatic and quaint, though the sham had lost its appeal.

The letter *I* beamed from the door panel before them. Senlin felt the return of his rational mind, and the first thought to emerge from the dark of his instinct was as clear as it was heartbreaking: *Marya will never know if I die. If I die, she'll think I abandoned her.*

They were nearly free. Despite the quaking of his hand, Senlin fit his key into the lock on the first jab. The heavy door swung back, and they tumbled between worlds.

A score of black-coated butlers gawked with uncomprehending shock at the hyperventilating couple. Senlin and Edith's appearance was gruesome. Blood painted one side of her face and spattered her hoopskirts. Gory smudges stained Senlin's starched bib. Eyes shining with the clear polish of fear, they loped down the hall together as if they were running a three-legged race, her arm thrown over his shoulder and neck.

The butlers' initial shock erupted into bedlam. Some men responded in character, bowing as the two of them passed, the gesture inconvenient in the crowded hall. Some berated them for ruining the illusion. Others recoiled in distress, sure that the bloody man and woman were murderers on a spree. Senlin wedged through the black shoulders and split coattails with Edith at his hip. He thought again: *She'll never know if I die.*

A shout cut through the din. The voice came, not from the roof of a throat, but from the pit of a stomach. It was the unmistakable trumpeting of rage.

Senlin turned and found the center of the hall cleared. Butlers scrambled at either wall like beetles in a jar. At the end of the parted mob stood Mayfair with one eye closed behind the bead of the musket.

She'll think I abandoned her.

A shot thundered. The banks of butlers thrashed and fainted.

Chapter Twelve

Bribery wins more arguments than reason.
—*Everyman's Guide to the Tower of Babel*, I. IX

Mayfair fell like the house curtain of a theater. The singed hole in the back of his shirt welled with dark blood. His lungs rattled, empty.

A phalanx of white-coated men stood behind him. The attendant at the fore of the troop still held up a flintlock pistol. Smoke curled from the muzzle. Senlin recognized the man behind the gun: It was the attendant who'd escorted him through the backstage. The attendant's face was stony; if he had any compunction about shooting a man, he showed no sign of it now.

Mayfair had been transformed from a vital, ruddy man into a heap of common refuse. His gray head could've passed for a wrung-out mop; his hands lay flaccid as hot water bottles; his back suggested an overstuffed pillow... Senlin tried not to look at him, at it. If the attendants had arrived a moment later, Senlin would've been the pile of rubbish lying on the floor. Even though it was the second violent death he'd witnessed in as many hours, instead of horror, he felt relief: great, swelling relief. He was not dead.

Arm still hooked around his neck, Edith let out a shuddering sigh that blossomed into laughter. She squeezed him in an awkward, side-long hug. Senlin's posture straightened; his expression tightened. No one would guess that a moment before, this same man had been running wildly on instinct alone. Even amid her giddiness, Edith felt the change in his manner and recoiled a little from him. Senlin gave her a thin, appreciative smile.

But their relief was short-lived. Soon, it became apparent that he and Edith were going to be detained by the armed attendant and his company. They were grabbed just above their elbows and marched forward, their surprise making them as graceless as marionettes. It was a humiliating parade. After a few dozen paces down the seemingly infinite corridor, they arrived at a door that was only remarkable because it was unlettered. They were bullied through into a hall that was kinked with blind corners. The closing of the unmarked door abruptly killed the cacophony of the hallway.

The quiet did not last long. Edith saw to that. She complained about having been locked in with a lunatic and described how narrowly they had escaped. Someone had to be responsible for such a disastrous blunder! She demanded that she be released and jerked her elbows experimentally; it only made her escorts tighten their grip.

Despite Edith's increasingly irate protests, the reason for their speedy removal from the halls of the Parlor wasn't explained. Indeed, nothing was explained because nothing was said. Their escorts weren't hostile exactly, but the severity of their silence was unnerving. Senlin recalled Goll's warnings about the sort of punishments that were meted out in the Parlor—the branding and eye-gouging. Still, he couldn't bring himself to believe that such brutality really existed here amid the starched cotton uniforms, brushed carpets, and well-lit corridors. Surely, only the criminally deranged were ever tortured. And, he kept reminding himself, they had done nothing wrong.

Still, he wished he had his purse. Perhaps the man expected a gratuity for saving their lives. But, then, how could he reasonably expect a tip? He'd confiscated Senlin's possessions at the outset.

The halls they passed through were only remarkable for the many alcoves and inlets that jutted off from the main passage. Glancing to the ends of these dimmer cubbies, Senlin saw young men and women dressed in the dark navy uniforms of bank clerks. These clerks generally sat on stools, stenography pads open on their laps, pencils ready or scribbling away. All of them pressed an eye to something in the wall. Senlin had to pass several alcoves before he glimpsed the object of their attention. It was a brass eyepiece of the sort one might find on a telescope.

The implication was almost immediately clear. The brass nubs in the walls of the staged mansion weren't valves. They were peepholes.

It took him a moment more to realize that this was good news. One man's spy is another man's witness! There had to be a witness to the ordeal. Someone witnessed Pining's murder. Someone saw Mayfair fire at them and then drag Edith away with what must've been, Senlin shuddered to think, the vilest of intentions. Their play hadn't been without an audience after all. He and Edith would be vindicated!

Realizing this, Senlin caught her eye, even as she continued to deride their escorts, and flared his eyebrows in a way that said: *There's no reason to fight. Don't worry.* She squinted at him hotly but left off with her attacks. The muscular ball of her jaw continued to work restlessly. She hadn't liked his intervention, but he hoped she would be sufficiently consoled when she heard the reason for it.

Their procession was longer than either of them was prepared for, exhausted and injured as they were. The blood on Edith's brow and cheek had turned brittle and dark, the wound finally having clotted. Her face reminded him of the waning moon. Senlin's own head throbbed from the concussion of the gunshot. And still they marched through the doglegging hallways, past hundreds of alcoves, for an hour without any signs of progress or change.

Finally, the white plaster corridor opened into a space that could easily have been confused for the foyer of a state capitol. Chair rails and ornate black walnut doors, oil paintings and name plaques filled the walls. The air smelled of table wax and leather. Dozens of clerks in navy blazers filed into the vaulted foyer. They hurried between doors like mice between holes. As if in deference to the civility of their new surroundings, their escorts let go of their arms.

There were no dummy candles or painted-on birds here, no false doors or empty books. The shams had given way to substance. They seemed to have passed backstage again, but this time they were not in the dressing rooms. These seemed to be the offices of the Parlor, or so Senlin supposed. Where else could they be?

He would've liked to share this modest revelation with Edith, but she didn't seem ready to want to speak to him. She seemed to have been offended by his earlier signal for quiet and decorum. Perhaps she had thought he was being patronizing. Perhaps he had been. It didn't matter. He was already preparing to forget the whole misadventure. He decided that when he described the events to Marya, he would characterize Edith as "headstrong" and "forward." Though, to be fair, she had been better suited to the crisis than him.

Cringing, he recalled Edith's request to undo her dress. Perhaps he would avoid recalling the subject to Marya at all.

They were finally halted before an elevated desk. An embedded plaque read GENERAL RECEPTIONIST, though the lectern reminded Senlin more of a judge's bench than something a secretary might occupy. He imagined the title of "receptionist" meant something grander in the vernacular of the Parlor.

The general receptionist seemed a little harried, overworked even, though he still managed a professional cordiality, which Senlin admired. His desktop was forested with stacks of files, carbon papers, steno pads, and leather-bound ledgers. If there was a system, it was likely his alone. His dark hair suggested that his youth was not so far behind him, but his ears and nose seemed more suited to a man twice his age. Three monocles dangled on jewelry chains from his vest pockets, and he changed them frequently depending on how far away his subject was.

The receptionist dismissed their escorts quickly, located a fresh sheet of foolscap, and said, "Judging by your appearance, I could spend the afternoon apologizing and not finish the job. But instead of delivering the groveling performance I'm sure you both deserve, let me instead hurry this whole formality along and get you both back on your way."

Senlin glanced at Edith and saw, to his relief, that her expression had been softened by the receptionist's introduction.

The receptionist changed monocles, located a pen, and said, "You're married?"

Senlin said "Yes" at the same moment Edith said "No." This amused the receptionist, though he covered it by coughing into his hand.

"I am married, but not to the good lady here," Senlin explained.

"Of course." The receptionist pulled at the pronounced bulb of his nose. "Obviously, I know nothing of you or your ordeal. So, if you'll indulge me, I'm going to run through a few questions, which are quite tedious, I'm afraid, but which all will ensure that after today, you are appropriately compensated for your troubles." Regarding them both through a single-glazed eyepiece, he smiled. "Please, bear with me."

Edith, for her part, was frank in her answers, though the questions struck Senlin as being far afield from the matter at hand. She was thirty-four; she was from the farmlands of southern Ur, near the town of Niece. She had spent two years at a women's finishing school, which she quit to return to work on her father's farmland, where she oversaw two hundred of the family's three hundred acres. She could ride a horse, repair a fence, and follow the rolling of the land to find water even in an arid valley. She was also recently divorced after nine months of marriage.

"And have you been to the Parlor before?" the receptionist asked, still scribbling her answers down on his pad.

For the first time, she seemed a little self-conscious. "I've spent the past two months here, going from one performance to the next. Six shows in all, I think."

"I hope those prior outings were happier than the present one," the receptionist said kindly, and she gave a demure shrug.

And then it was Senlin's turn. He wished he didn't have to recite his personal details while standing in a public hall. He tried to be stoic, but it wasn't long before he was mumbling and stuttering his answers. He felt the blood come to his face. He was an only child; his parents were deceased; he was well educated and gainfully employed; he was married; he had no children. Confessing himself so succinctly embarrassed him in a manner he could hardly express. In short form, he seemed so unremarkable, so unaccomplished. Perhaps he was unremarkable. But he didn't feel that way.

With the general interview complete, the receptionist thanked them for their patience. "Now, as to today's events... Your case has been assigned to an assistant to the chief registrar, a Mr. Anen Ceph. Mr. Ceph is one of our most accomplished and thorough investigators. In a word, he is bright. You'll be temporarily, briefly, almost momentarily placed in a private room while Mr. Ceph has a chance to gather up all the evidence of the case." The receptionist blinked the monocle from his eye, and it swung down to his chest front. He signaled over a tall, bald clerk who seemed to have been sewn into his navy jacket. One could almost count the knobs of his spine. "The clerk here will show you through to your room. And I thank you both for your patience. You've been absolutely wonderful. I hope you recall me as fondly when you review your time here in the Parlor."

The gangly clerk led them from the grand hall, and after passing through another tangle of corridors, they entered a bustling hospital ward. It was familiar in every way except, of course, for the lack of windows, which Senlin always associated with contemporary hospitals. Sun and fresh air were, after all, essential to recovery. They passed two carts, the first of which was filled with steaming bowls of porridge, and the second of which held six copper cylinders that were about the size of a milking pail. These might've passed for helmets, except that where one expected to find the faceplate, there was only a valve wheel that was nearly as wide as the rest of the apparatus. Senlin couldn't guess what medical service the device performed.

Nurses padded around in soft, white leather shoes while patients with bandaged limbs and heads lay on cots in narrow, curtained spaces. The prospect of a clean bed and a nurse to wash their wounds filled Senlin with hope. He was shaken and exhausted and bruised; if he were at home, he would've gone to bed for a week and done nothing but read books and drink tea and listen to the waves recite their endless rhyme.

But he was soon disappointed when the clerk ushered them on

and out the other end of the ward, into a narrow, warm, lime-washed chamber. Opposite them stood an iron hatch, four feet high. Rust flaked from the hinges.

"Assistant Ceph will be by soon," the clerk said, unlocking the hatch with a heavy skeleton key.

Senlin and Edith looked at each other. She seemed apprehensive. He gave her a reassuring smile. It was a genuine and generous expression, and one that was quite rare on Senlin's face. The receptionist had charmed away his nervousness. Already, the whole terrorizing episode was beginning to soften and fade. The murders, the running, the hiding and breath-holding, all seemed to have happened to someone else.

And yet, something was just the tiniest bit unsettling about the warmth of the room and the sudden vigilant expression of the clerk behind them. Senlin shoved these thoughts aside as the usual residuals of panic and fear.

The hatch opened before them. They had to stoop to go through and were confronted by a light so dazzling neither could see into it. The air felt hot as a breath on their faces. The clerk prodded Senlin forward with the heel of his hand. Senlin was about to turn and complain when the floor creaked and bowed like a rusted bedspring beneath him, throwing him off balance, confusing him. The hatch slammed shut. They listened as the bolt bit back into the strike plate.

Still blind, Senlin struck his head when he tried to stand. He groped at the wire mesh above him, quickly discovered the corner, and there found the same wire links forming a wall. Squinting, he peered around; it seemed they were in something like a chicken coop or a rabbit hutch suspended in a blue room.

Then he realized he was looking at the sky. Not a painted sky, but the real blue heavens.

They sat in a cage that was bolted to the face of the Tower.

Chapter Thirteen

Ask anyone you meet, Don't you miss the sun? Don't you miss the moon? They'll reply, *Do you miss the heatstroke? Do you miss the howling wolves?*
—Everyman's Guide to the Tower of Babel, III. XII

A hundred feet below, the Market sprawled, colorful and intricate as a patchwork quilt.

Senlin beat fiercely on the black iron door. His commotion rattled the cage violently. Every joint creaked, and rust snowed down upon them. A wire link beneath them snapped. Edith urged him to stop, finally wrapping her arms around his neck. He could hardly hear her over his drumming. He chose not to hear her.

The receptionist had promised them a speedy result and a private room. After everything he'd suffered through, he had to believe this was an oversight. A mistake had been made! Why would anyone ever come to the Parlor? Was everyone a sadist? It was a madhouse!

He banged on the door once more, panting his mouth dry. He let Edith pull him from the door. He collapsed almost on top of her and clung weakly to the wire wall to calm his vertigo.

"Has this ever happened to you before?" he asked.

"Do you really think I would come back if it had?" She seemed slightly more composed than him, though her voice still quavered. She looked down through the lattice of the floor. "How old is this cage? It looks like it could go at any moment."

Senlin recalled in vivid detail the sickening sound the airship crew had made when they struck the earth. "Let's talk about something else," Senlin replied through his teeth. He didn't want to think about who would pick through his pockets if he crashed to the ground.

Their coop was wire mesh on all sides and about the size of a child's bed. There was sufficient headroom for them to sit with their backs to the linked wall, but not enough to stand. They had no choice but to crowd each other, which only added to Senlin's distress. He swallowed dryly and said, "I don't understand. They know full well we did nothing wrong."

"All the witnesses are dead. How could they know?" Edith asked. Senlin explained his theory about the brass peepholes in the mansion walls and the spying clerks he'd seen in the backstage corridor. She tugged up the neckline of her dress, which had an awkward habit of slipping, and said, "It never occurred to me that anyone was watching . . . Oh." She seemed to review a number of instances in her memory. "Those peepholes were in every room."

"If it makes you feel any better, I don't think anyone is spying on us now," Senlin said, wiping at the sweat that streamed down his face.

The sun bullied them mercilessly. He fashioned a little awning from his butler's coat by looping the sleeves through the ceiling mesh and pinning them on the exposed ends of wires. Edith spread out her thick skirts for him to sit on, which took some of the bite from the wire floor. He thanked her as he might thank someone for making room on a park bench. They listened to the cacophony of the Market, the camel brays and barker cries. The songs of distant train whistles were lifted up and then taken away by the arid wind.

The sun's glare moved behind the Tower, bringing on the artificial night. Senlin was better able to see the facade about them, and he found that studying it gave his mind a much-needed distraction. The walls were unpolished limestone. Here and there, old birds' nests tufted from the cracks between blocks. The nests appeared uninhabited. Other cages, similar to theirs and also uninhabited, were affixed some distance to their left and right. Looking up the Tower through a gap in his coat-awning produced such a strong feeling of vertigo in him that he could do little more than peek and look away. It didn't matter. There was little to see. Distant platforms protruded from the tower like thorns from a stem. He postulated that these might be airports, but it was only a guess. Otherwise, the facade appeared as vast and uninhabited as a desert.

Except for the clockwork spider. The machine was the size of a large dog and was at once frightening and marvelous when it crawled above the curvature of the Tower. Steam gassed from the joints of its eight steel legs. Its internal gears were visible through its copper skeleton. It was the most intricate and elegant clockwork Senlin had ever seen. As it drew nearer, he saw a red light, piercing as a ruby, glowing steadily at the heart of the machine.

Senlin was too awed to be afraid of the chattering machine, but he was careful to remain silent when he pointed it out to Edith. She took in a quick breath and gripped his arm, but it was soon apparent that the clockwork spider was indifferent to them. It stalked with the surety of a fly on a wall, its feet shoed with dark rubber pads. Just when Senlin began to wonder if the thing wasn't some sort of grand toy, its function became clear. It was repairing the Tower. It scoured the facade for flaws that it repaired by spraying some sort of gel. The gel appeared to harden quickly and soon glistened like quartz. Senlin watched the machine move from crack to crack, ripping out birds' nests and patching the gaps, until it had passed again out of sight.

It was an ingenious little automaton: practical and efficient. Seeing it gave him a little hope. The Tower was not all terror and confusion. There were wonders here.

Though all the wonders felt small and far away.

Neither of them speculated aloud about how long they would be kept, or whether they would be brought food or water, or whether this birdcage was to be their coffin. Voicing such thoughts would only make the wait more unbearable. But after another half hour of silence, Edith gave a sudden exasperated groan and said, "My imagination is driving me mad! I have now reviewed every embarrassment that might've been watched by spies, and every possible manner that we could die in this coop."

Senlin cleared his throat. "Me too. I just began to wonder how many vultures would have to perch on this cage before their weight combined with ours would be enough—"

"We have to talk about something else," she interrupted, clapping her hands on the tops of her legs. "So, your name is Thomas Senlin, you're a headmaster, and you are married." This had come out during the receptionist's inquisition, of course. "For many years?"

"No." Normally, his answer would have concluded there, but something pushed him now to confess more. Perhaps it was only out of camaraderie that naturally arises from shared trauma. Or perhaps, and he could hardly admit the possibility, he was dimly aware that the moment wasn't without...intimacy, and that with intimacy came temptation. To stave off the whole guilty train of thought, he blurted out, "I'm on our honeymoon; we're on my honeymoon."

He wouldn't have blamed her if she'd laughed. But she didn't, and her response was slow in coming. She stroked her cheek, scrubbing off dried blood. She seemed to be trying to decide whether to ask the obvious question: *Where is your wife?*

He was a little surprised, but relieved, when she instead began to speak of her own past. Since there was nothing else to do, her anecdotes quickly evolved into a history. It became apparent to him that she meant to not just summarize but also to embellish her story with all manner of small detail. He'd always been troubled by long-winded confessions. He never knew what to say. And yet, as she went on, he began to relax a little. She wasn't at all what he'd expected when he had first met her in her peach dress and she had ordered him about like a footman. She wasn't melodramatic or vain. She was quite likable, in fact. He liked her.

She told him more about her family's farmland and the acreage she had been responsible for sowing. There was pride in her voice as she described her talent for farming. She knew when to sacrifice blighted rows; she knew how to manage buffer yields and droughts, how to ferret out the dishonest foremen, the drunks, and where to recruit replacements. She had two brothers, both older, neither of whom had any talent for, or interest in, the family business. Both managed small plots and did so poorly. Her yields were always superior. Her father, who wanted to spend his twilight years hunting and pressing the fruits of his orchards into cider, was proudest of her. He called her the Generaless of the Garden.

Then, a little more than a year ago, her father had talked her into marrying a family friend, a man named Franklin Winters, who owned a modestly productive vineyard. She, the Generaless who needed no husband, had agreed only because her father pressed the point they both had tried for years to avoid: Her brothers were feckless, lazy, and worse yet, they were disloyal. If he left the land to them, they would only sell it and squander the profits. But he could not bequeath his fortune to an unmarried woman; she would be vulnerable to lawsuits, not least of all from her brothers. But if she were married, she would be safe from such attacks; she could continue to run the farm as she pleased.

Mr. Franklin Winters was an inoffensive enough mate. He was a little gaunt of feature and bland of character, but he hadn't any debts and his employees thought he was fair, which she took as good signs. Most importantly, he was amenable to her conditions for the marriage: Her role in the operations of the farm would not change. She would remain the Generaless. He agreed but had a caveat of his own. She could run the farm so long as it posed no risk to her health.

Edith wasn't a fool. She knew that Winters expected her to become pregnant and for that to be excuse enough to pull her from the field. Her father, too, held out hope that she would have children and continue the bloodline. She found the whole thing ridiculous. It was plain from her expression that motherhood held no charms for her. She agreed to Winters's request only because she knew it would never be an issue. She was hearty and stolid but also barren, the result of a riding accident years earlier. It was a fact only she and the county doctor knew.

The conditions were formalized, an agreement was signed, and they were married.

But soon after she became Mrs. Franklin Winters (in a ceremony that she described as "unsentimental"), Franklin found an excuse to exploit their contract. She developed a slight allergy to a weed that grew everywhere in the spring along the lanes and the caps of rows. It was the same long weed that she had once habitually chewed on when roaming the freshly plowed fields, checking the vitality of the soil. Now, the weed's blooming made her wheeze. It was excuse enough for Winters to pull her from her horse. Never mind that half the foremen had one ailment or another: gout or syphilis or cataracts. She had to hang up her reins, shelve her clod stompers, tie a ribbon around her straw hat, and accept that she was too delicate to manage a farm. She suspected the whole thing was to punish her for not bringing forth a son. To be fair, Winters himself had been unable to offer much support to that venture.

Senlin might've blushed if he hadn't already been so flush from the heat. "So you divorced him?"

"I did," she said. "Though he hasn't returned the courtesy."

"I don't understand."

"I don't either!" She laughed, and a warm burst of wind tangled her dark hair about her face. "He refused to give me a divorce, so I refused to stay."

"And so you came here..."

"To fritter his money, my money."

"And play a socialite's wife," Senlin said merrily but saw her expression turn stormy. He grimaced apologetically.

"It was a stupid play." She again forced down her ballooning crinoline skirts. "I had to play dress-stuffer while those two twits talked about business. Neither of them knew a thing about business. The stock market of the heart! Please! If it's not quantifiable, it's not stock. That is the basic characteristic of stock. And, as far as I know, no one knows how much love weighs, how voluminous it is, whether it can be divided or compounded... How many units of love does it take to make a romance? Five love units? Twenty? Stock market of the heart! If the one twit hadn't gone berserk, I would've." She was nearly raving, but there was a welcome edge of comedy to it.

Before he could respond, the hatch in the iron door opened.

They both crowded to it and were met by a young man's face, smiling broadly under a carefully waxed mustache.

"My God, it's warm," the face said, and a handkerchief briefly obscured it as he patted the frilly square across his forehead.

"You must let us in! This is ludicrous; we're in danger out here!" Senlin couldn't keep the desperation entirely from his voice. "We've done nothing wrong."

"Yes, no, I understand, but I have to investigate your case first, or they'll just heave you right back in here."

"Then investigate faster," Edith said.

The youth cleared his throat. "I am the assistant to the registrar. My name is Anen Ceph, and I will be assisting you today." The pattern of his speech was full of halts and gulps, and Senlin recognized in his manner a rank amateur.

"Faster," Edith repeated.

"I have concluded my inquiry, and I have reported my findings to the registrar, and he has returned with his decision—"

"Who is the registrar? What is his authority?" Senlin interrupted.

Ceph smiled, the lines about his mouth rippling out. "What wonderful humor!" Then, just as quickly, his expression flattened like a swamp closing over a footprint. "You, Mr. Thomas Senlin, will be escorted to the third floor, which is really very lovely. Do you like peacocks?"

"I have no opinion of them."

"The Baths are filled with peacocks and spas and warm springs."

"It sounds wonderful. Take us there," Edith said.

"Ah. Well." The grin wrinkled his nose, making him seem more juvenile, and he again cleared his throat. "Ms. Edith Winters is not going to the third floor. She is being expelled to the first floor."

"Expelled? Why?" Edith said. "You locked me in with a murderer, and I was attacked."

"Not me. I didn't lock you in any room, and you, as I understand, had a key and went into that particular stage house of the Parlor voluntarily." Senlin recognized in Ceph's answer the slithering cowardice of an administrator. The boy was a blooming bureaucrat. "There are two matters at issue. First, there is the issue of your exit, which was illegal. As you were told, characters must each exit into their original halls."

"We were being chased by a lunatic with a gun!" Edith reiterated, jabbing her finger too near the youth's nose for his liking. He again waved his handkerchief over his face.

"Yes. But, there remains the second issue of the fires, Ms. Winters," he continued. "You agreed when you entered the Parlor to stoke the fires of the rooms you entered. We have much evidence of Mr. Senlin doing this small chore, but it appears that you, Ms. Winters, were irresponsible with this charge. As a result, several fires went out."

"What does it matter? Get me a match, and I will restart them," she said.

"The damage is done, I'm afraid. You will be removed, and you will not be allowed to reenter the Parlor. That is the registrar's decision, and it—"

"Excuse me," Senlin interrupted, and using his lecturing voice said, "Young man, we are injured. We are perilously suspended over a great height. We are hungry and thirsty and frightened. I adjure you to return to your superior, your registrar, with a clear message: We will be freed, and we will continue, the both of us, to the Baths. We insist that we be given a chance to account for ourselves in your courts, whatever they might be, and we insist that we be removed from this inhuman birdcage you've unjustly imprisoned us in." He spoke with force and confidence he did not feel.

This seemed to momentarily dash Ceph's mask of officiousness, but he quickly gathered himself and recovered his smile. "I will speak to him and return. In the meantime, I have supper." Ceph passed through the hatch a tin flask and a small sack of toughly crusted bread.

"Will you please let us wait inside?" Edith said, restraining her anger for the moment. But Ceph had already closed the hatch. She struck the closed plate with the heel of her hand. "Numskull!"

They collapsed back to their lounging positions, mute with frustration.

Not a half mile in the distance, an airship banked over the Market, seeming to have recently lifted off. From this angle, Senlin could make out the gondola, which was shaped like a square-nosed barge, and the heavy rigging that tethered the ship to the balloon. The voluminous envelope of gas was as round and red as a child's ball. Senlin felt a pang of envy. Oh, to fly! To be a balloon, to be a kite!

Edith stared dumbly at the byzantine sprawl of the Market and said, "You've heard what they do when they kick you out to make sure you can never come back? Tom," she said in such a familiar way, he felt disarmed, "they're going to brand me."

Chapter Fourteen

If you ever discover that you are bored in the Parlor,
wake up. You are asleep and having a tedious dream.
—*Everyman's Guide to the Tower of Babel*, III. LI

Ever since childhood, he had been fond of kites. He liked their
serenity. A kite might tug, and dive, and lunge about, but it
never panicked, not even if an unexpected gust snapped the
line. The person flying the kite might panic, but the kite never did.

He'd built box kites, shield kites, and sled kites of all shapes and
sizes. Every month, he'd order a new sheaf of colored rice paper from
Ms. Berks, and every month, she would puzzle aloud over his chosen
pastime. While other men in the village spent their idle hours repairing garden walls and framing rowboats, the headmaster was off in a
field with a kite. "How will you ever find a wife spending all your
time on toys?" Ms. Berks wanted to know. He didn't care. For many
years, he just didn't care. He flew kites. Ms. Berks rolled her eyes.

It was a more romantic gesture than Ms. Berks would've guessed
when, late in their secret courtship, Senlin built Marya a kite and
arranged an afternoon picnic. He constructed a simple diamond-
shaped kite from red paper because it was her favorite color. He chose
a secluded, dramatic spot for their picnic: Woolgatherer Bluff. The
bluff rose above the pebble cove where Isaugh's fleet of fishing boats
nodded on gentle waves. It was an uncommonly warm spring day. A

steady wind blew inland. The only obstacle in the expansive field of clover was an old, fruitless apple tree.

After launching the kite, he stood behind her with his arms around her waist, holding her wrists as she gripped the spool of string. He said, "The clouds give us a hint of what the wind is doing. See? We can see them stretch out and speed along and pile up together. But the kite shows the air in more detail. You can follow every jet and downdraft. It's like a flying weathercock."

She pulled at the kite string with a hooked finger and bumped against him, saying, "I was thinking the same thing. It's like a flying weathercock." He knew her teasing was good for him. It kept him from being so terribly earnest all the time.

And still, he blushed and backed away a step. He took refuge in the lesson, explaining how to make the kite dive and swoop and rise. She listened and practiced and yelled at the kite as if it were a poorly trained dog. Senlin gave her more room and tried to keep from kibitzing.

It wasn't long before the kite became snagged in the apple tree's branches. The collision occurred when Marya panicked at seeing the kite turn down from its towering perch and course straight down, directly at the solitary tree. Too excited to listen to Senlin's directions, she yanked hard on the line, which only sped the red missile on its way.

The crash didn't upset him. He had destroyed whole flocks of kites over the years. Marya was more sentimental. She insisted that the token be rescued. Senlin suggested, quite reasonably he thought, that they could wait for a gust to free the kite. It might be a little torn, but it would be easy enough to repair.

Marya insisted that she would save it, and while he protested, she stripped off her shoes and socks, knotted her skirt up above her knees, and began scaling the tree.

Though he could hardly admit it, he was stirred by the sight of her bare legs wrapped about the branch. Despite the town's later suspicions, their courtship had been quite chaste.

The limb swayed as she shinnied out toward the kite. Senlin made a conscious effort to not bite his nails. A moment more, and she had untangled the kite, shinnied back, and climbed down with it. Welts from the rough bark stood out on her arms and knees. She hardly noticed. She was giddy from her adventure and only laughed when she tripped over a root buried in the thick clover.

She was beautiful in the most unguarded, unaffected way.

He drummed up the courage to say what he'd arranged the whole occasion for.

He set his knee in the clover. He took up her hand, her arm like the string of a kite, her face floating above him with the sun lighting her auburn hair. She was suddenly so serene.

The kite never panics. This time neither did he.

He couldn't believe it would happen—not here. They would never brand a woman. This was the Tower, for pity's sake! If anything, the ordeal had made him doubt the morality and sanity of his fellow tourists. How different might the Tower be if the tourists would stop dragging their afflictions and flaws in with them! There were natives to the Tower, Senlin knew, who had never set foot on the ground. Their minds were naturally elevated by an environment that invented and ascended. Their influence would win out. Reason would prevail!

He refused to console Edith because he refused to believe she was in any real danger. An answer would come soon, and they would be freed. He gave her arm a pat-pat. It was the sort of cool reassurance he offered nervous students on a first day of class. His patting seemed to say, *There, there! It's not as bad as all that.*

Edith was too stunned by Ceph's news to notice Senlin's feeble consolation.

Despite his confidence that the registrar would offer a speedy response to their protest, night came without an answer.

The cage, which had seemed so exposed before, now seemed strangely private. The stars appeared like frost on a window. The moon rose, thin as a strap. They ate the hard rolls and shared the flask of water, their quiet seeming to amplify the clamor of the Market below. The sounds of flutes and fiddles and drums swelled from around numerous campfires. The songs overlapped like the field music of crickets.

The evening chill made them huddle together for warmth. Edith folded the excess of her skirts over their laps. The realization that she might be branded had stifled her previous talkativeness. As the hour grew later, Senlin felt his wellspring of optimism, of denial, begin to fail. His mind churned over the details of what Ceph had said. He couldn't make sense of it, and it grated at him. He wondered what was behind all of the Parlor's arbitrary rules.

"This obsession with fires, doesn't it seem strange to you?" he said, finally breaking the silence. "They don't insist that we wash the dishes or sweep the floors. We only have to stoke the fires. There must be some practical reason. Perhaps it mobilizes the air or warms the plumbing..."

"It's always been part of the script," Edith said, shifting her shoulder against his. "No matter what the play is about, the fires have to be kept up. I always remembered before."

"You had other things on your mind," Senlin said.

"You didn't forget the fires."

"Only out of habit. Whenever my wife lost track of me at a pub or a party, all she had to do was follow the chimney. I gravitate to fires. People leave you alone if you're stirring a fire."

"When you get out of here, you should find a chimney to stand near." Her tone suggested it was a joke, but feeling Senlin wince beside her, she said, "I'm sure she's fine."

"Coming here was my idea," he said. "I wanted to see the Tower. I brought us here. Why was I so determined to bring her here?"

"What's that old saying? Like water to a drain, we are drawn to the Tower," she said in a laughably formal voice. "Not what you expected, huh?"

"I liked it better in books. Have you ever been farther up, in the Baths or—what comes after that? New Babel?"

"This is as far as I've gone." She picked at the tattered tulle of her skirts. "As far as I'll go."

"Come on," he said, patting her hand. Even to him it seemed a condescending gesture. He stopped patting and squeezed her hand gently instead. "We're not staying here. You've got to go back home and lose your husband, and I've got to go on ahead and find my wife."

Marya ran her hand over the keys and along the lip of the music rack, up to the freshly polished top board of the upright piano. She turned to Senlin with an expression of amazement.

"How did you..."

Senlin pulled out the piano bench for her and bumped into his hat rack. The rack shivered but didn't fall. The piano was tightly wedged inside the little living room of his cottage. "I had it shipped in from Bromburry last week. It's a little old, I'm afraid. I bought it from your old conservatory. They were making room for new pianos."

"A piano, Tom. You're giving me a piano!" She sat down and tested the keys, still in a daze.

"I know most men bring a ring when they propose." He shrugged. "But I thought if you were ever to live here and be happy, you would need a piano more."

She glanced about the room, realizing that it had changed. "But where is your sofa?"

"You're sitting on it." He hooked his leg around the bench and sat down beside her. It swayed a little beneath them, and they both grabbed hold of the keyboard in case the old bench collapsed.

When it didn't, they laughed, and she said, "It's a very comfortable sofa."

Senlin cleared his throat and furrowed his brow. "Marya, I... I have a difficult time expressing certain...genuinely held feelings. I..." He swallowed and shook his head. This was not how he wanted the speech to go. She waited patiently, and he gathered his thoughts. "You've made it impossible for me to read a book in peace. When you're not here, I just gaze at the words until they tumble off the page into a puddle in my lap. Instead of reading, I sit there and review the hours of the day I spent in your company, and I am more charmed by that story than anything the author has scribbled down. I have never been lonely in my life, but you have made me lonely. When you are gone, I am a moping ruin. I thought I understood the world fairly well. But you have made it all mysterious again. And it's unnerving and frightening and wonderful, and I want it to continue. I want all your mysteries. And if I could, I would give you a hundred pianos. I would..."

She stopped him with a gentle hand on his shoulder. She rose, her hand moving to his cheek. He tried to stand and fell back onto the keyboard with a discordant bang of notes. She kissed him, shifting the bench with the side of her leg. He attempted to lift himself from the keyboard, but again she pushed him back with the force of a kiss, and again he banged upon the keys.

The villagers who walked past the headmaster's cottage that evening wondered where he had gotten a piano and why he insisted on playing it so poorly and so loudly for so long.

Chapter Fifteen

Most life in the ocean lives in the shallows. And so it is with those living on the land.

—*Everyman's Guide to the Tower of Babel*, I. III

He woke to a frigid gust of wind. The coop rattled softly; the wire links rang like a tambourine. The sky was a deep indigo, and the starlight painted the Tower the color of a glacier. The night was as brutally cold as the day had been hot. Morning was still hours away.

His arm had gone to sleep, and when he tried to shift it, he realized that Edith and he were in a tangled embrace. Her cheek pressed against his chest; his arms were around her. Her black, heavy hair blew about his chin and neck. Guiltily, he began to draw back.

Either she hadn't been asleep or was jolted awake by his movement because she quickly said, "Please, don't. I'm freezing." Her voice was muffled. Her breath warmed his chest.

He stopped, and she closed the gap he had opened. He could feel the full length of her body shivering against him. He rearranged the broadest part of his coat over her shoulders as best he could. "It'll be morning in a couple of hours. Try to get back to sleep."

For him, sleep did not return. He lay in the purple dark, thinking. He couldn't reconcile his idea of the Tower with his experience, and it gnawed at him. He had misled his students when he'd praised the

103

Tower so effusively; that much was certain. He would have to complicate his lesson come the fall and the new school year. He would still teach the Tower's technological advances and its vague historical accounts, but he would no longer exaggerate its character.

Something changed in people when they stood in the Tower's shadow. It sapped their humanity. It heightened their ambition. He couldn't imagine why anyone would return to the Parlor after being expelled. Why return for further torment? He didn't understand it. Was life really so grim in the Market? Was everyone so terribly dissatisfied with themselves that they could think of nothing better to do with their lives than to spend it in pretend? He thought of Pining, the poor affable sap. He'd been so effusive about the wonders of the Parlor. In the moments before he was killed, he seemed so confident and satisfied and happy. But why pretend love to a woman? Why woo an actor? It didn't make any sense.

"I imagine people would pay hundreds of shekels for a room with a balcony like this," Edith said, interrupting his brooding. "Do you think we could fit a sofa in here?" He smiled at the idea.

"I have a question, which you certainly aren't obligated to answer, but it's something that has been bothering me, so I feel compelled to ask—"

"Don't make a speech, Tom. Just ask your question," she cut him off, though not harshly.

He drew a breath. "Why did you come back to the Parlor so many times?"

She laughed and turned her face away from his chest. "I've been asking myself the same thing. I haven't a good excuse. There's just something nice, something comforting about being in the middle of somebody else's story. It's really clarifying, in a weird way, and it feels important." She heard Senlin sniff at this, a stunted little laugh, and she poked him in the ribs. "Don't laugh. I know it sounds stupid, but I look at my own life and all I see is ambivalence and confusion. Nothing dramatic happens, at least not suddenly. In real life, nothing happens quickly. Everything just erodes. And it's confusing and frustrating and dull. God, can it be dull. But then you have the Parlor, and everything has a point. Yes, it's simple. Yes, it's stupid. But there is a plot. A week ago, I would've given anything for a life with a plot. Now, I say, bring on the dullness. Give me chores and almanacs and nine hours of dreamless, exhausted sleep. Bring on the dullness!"

Senlin considered all of this. "I suppose it makes sense. But I prefer the story you told me about your past to the trite play we escaped. I think your life sounds interesting."

"Then I must have exaggerated." They paused to harden themselves against another snapping wind. He gritted his teeth and clinched his eyes shut until it passed. After it calmed again, Edith spoke, her voice abruptly lower. "I know you're in the middle of your own mess." She turned into his chest. "I hope you find your wife. I really do. I think you will. If you can survive this, everything else has to be easy," she said, and had to stop to clear her throat, and he realized that she was trying to keep from crying. "But I have a favor to ask. I know I don't have any right to ask, and you don't have any responsibility to say yes..."

"Don't make a speech," he said, trying to calm her and keep her from breaking down. "Just ask the question."

"Don't leave me till it's over. I can get through it. I just need a little moral support."

Hearing the dread in her voice, he said he would, of course he would. But, he was quick to add, it wouldn't come to that. The registrar would relent.

When Ceph's insufferable smile reappeared in the hatch portal the next morning, he repeated the previous verdict. Edith would be expelled. She could never come back. Ceph, having studiously avoided any mention of branding or bodily harm, referred now to the "ostracization process" that Edith would undergo. He made it sound like the most congenial thing in the world, and he assured them there was nothing more that could be done. The alternatives and appeals had been exhausted.

Senlin, having stewed on the subject all night, had prepared a fuming rebuttal. "Have you been entirely stripped of your conscience?"

he asked. "Don't hide behind duty and institution. Act like a human being! Don't behave as if this brutality is defensible just because an arbitrary policy and a bullying bureaucrat stand behind it. You do not need an appeal to confirm what you know. It is wrong to maim a person for failing to stoke a fire. You have a conscience, native to yourself, which is screaming through the bars of your very ribs: Let her go." There was an unfamiliar heat to his voice, and he found at the end that he was trembling with rage.

Ceph flagged his handkerchief over his face as if to swat away a gnat. "Hear, hear. A fine speech."

Senlin was taken aback by this strange response. The clerk had sounded genuine, if not a little bored. "Thank you."

"But in the final analysis, it's not a matter of conscience, really; it's a matter of constancy," Ceph said at last with a sad, resolute smile.

He swallowed a second argument. As much as he loathed giving in to this injustice, he could not argue with her request. He had promised to be a moral support. The obligation had already begun.

"Really, the ostracization process is quite humane," Ceph said with a tone that suggested much was being made of little. "For some, it's even revelatory."

Senlin had to clinch his jaw to keep from blurting a rebuke.

The verdict accepted, they were allowed into the hall again. Their backs ached, and their legs quaked beneath them. They stretched and shook the blood back into their legs. He felt like a man who had crawled ashore from a stormy sea. For the second time in the past day, he felt the disbelieving gratitude of a survivor.

Ceph led them to the hospital ward they'd passed through the day before. A dozen white-suited attendants patrolled the tile. The attendants weaved slowly, vigilantly through the grid of curtained stalls. Pistols hung at their hips under the hems of their coats. It occurred to him that if the two of them tried to run, they would not get far.

The empty beds they passed took on a more sinister light. Sobs and moans, which the tiled room amplified and duplicated mercilessly, sounded everywhere about them. And then Senlin abruptly understood. This wasn't a hospital at all. This was not where one came to be healed. This was where the unfortunate exiles were branded or had their eyes plucked out. This was where ensnared tourists were "ostracized." It was a white-tiled torture chamber.

Through a gap in the curtains of one cell, Senlin briefly caught sight of a scene that was so intense it stunted the passage of time. He saw a man being held upright in bed by two attendants. Concealing the man's whole head was one of the valved copper cylinders he had seen on their first pass through the ward. The valve stood in the center of the man's unseen face like an absurd nose. A nurse leaned over him, turning the valve in short, strained jerks. Spasms wracked the man's arms and legs, testing the strength of the two attendants holding him down. Despite his obvious agony, not a single sound escaped the sealed helmet. The man writhed in silence. They were torturing him. The nurse seemed to have no qualms about it.

Senlin supposed that the barbaric device was what they used to remove a person's eye. The thought filled him with disgust.

A cotton gown lay on the empty, tightly made bed where Ceph halted. A long curtain hung on a rod encircling the bed. Ceph directed Edith to ready herself for the nurse who would be around shortly. He called Senlin onward, babbling again about the beautiful peacocks that roosted all about the Baths. But Senlin remained planted beside the curtain after Edith closed it. He could see her shadow shift behind the drape.

"I'm going to wait with her," Senlin said.

"There really is no need. She will be—"

"I'm going to wait," he repeated more firmly.

Ceph looked genuinely puzzled. He seemed about to argue, then thought better of it. He gave a belabored shrug and removed himself some paces to scribble on a steno pad.

A short matronly woman in a cardinal-red apron and nurse's cap approached, pushing a white enameled cart ahead of her. A lidded iron crock rattled atop the cart. The long handle of a brand protruded from a notch in the lid.

Ignoring Senlin, the nurse peeked behind the curtain before casting it open. Edith lay under the sheet in the simple white gown that had been provided. Her tattered and stained costume lay folded at the foot of the bed. A moment before, Senlin's blood had been boiling, but the sight of her swaddled in white sheets was unexpectedly calming. Surely, none of this was real.

The nurse nattered happily about how pretty Edith was and how nice her outfit looked, even while she set about arranging Edith's right arm, straightening it, palm up, on the bed. Edith stretched her free arm toward Senlin. He knelt by the head of the bed, taking her hand. The nurse offered her a rolled cloth to bite down on, suggesting that it helped to diffuse the pain, but Edith jerked her chin away without response.

The nurse opened the iron crock with a thick leather mitt. Among the red coals, the circular brand glowed, large as a man's pocket watch. The sight made Senlin's stomach pitch.

When he looked back to Edith, she was staring at him intently. Her dark hair lay fanned over the pillow; her tanned and freckled collarbone glowed with sweat. "Don't hang around too long. You've got somewhere to be," she said, and shifted her grip from his hand to his forearm.

Sliding on a blacksmith's leather glove, which reached to her elbow, the nurse said, "I have to hold the iron flush for the count of three. It's very important that you don't move, dear. If it doesn't look right, we have to do it again." Edith didn't look away from Senlin to acknowledge the nurse. Her mouth was thin and bloodless.

"To the count of three," the nurse repeated. When the brand touched her skin, Edith's veins leapt in her neck and her eyes gaped and her fingernails bore into Senlin's arm and her cheeks darkened and the terrible but familiar scent of burning flesh filled the air and the nurse in a bell-clear voice said, "One."

When he last saw her, Edith was lying unconscious while the nurse wrapped her arm with gauze. Her blacking out had been a small mercy. She never cried out, and he sensed in her silence her defiance. The matron had resumed her unwanted pleasantries, despite Edith's unresponsiveness. Senlin had argued that he would stay until she had awakened, but Ceph insisted that if he lingered any longer he would have to reopen the review of Senlin's case.

"And you're becoming morbid, Mr. Senlin. You're losing sight of the prize! Galas and spas and peacocks await you," Ceph said with maddening insensitivity.

Senlin had no notion of what more he could've said to Edith, in any case. Perhaps it was just as well they avoid a final, awkward farewell. She was bound for home, and he still had more of the Tower to climb. He hoped she would be on her farm soon enough, hoped she could again become the Generaless, and hoped that he would become just a minor actor in a horror story she'd strive to forget. How could he say all of that in a goodbye? Better to leave them both with some dignity. So much had already been taken from them.

Rattled and spent from the ordeal, Senlin was silent as he was led out of the torture ward, back into the vast, officious halls. An attendant appeared with his clothes and satchel, and he was allowed to change out of his rumpled, sweat-soured butler's costume. He discovered that his money had not been stolen, but in that numb moment of depression, he found he didn't care. As he buttoned his shirt, he resolved three times to return to Edith's bedside. Let them throw him in jail and put a bucket on his head and unscrew his eyes. Let them try!

And three times, he convinced himself to go. Marya was waiting just up ahead. He hoped she was whole and unscarred. He wished she was there, right then, to comfort him. It was, he knew, a selfish wish.

Assistant Ceph seemed uncharacteristically subdued as he showed Senlin to a marble-walled stairwell. Chiseled in broad letters over the door were the words, THE BATHS.

Senlin had no intention of lingering on their parting, but the moment Senlin set his boot on the first step, Ceph reached forward and grasped his elbow. The young man offered an abrupt and earnest confession. "I know that was more than a little overwhelming for you. To be honest, I fear that I failed you with my own performance. You were so natural. I admire you. I had aspirations of playing the registrar myself. After this, I can't help but wonder whether I'm up to the part."

"Well, good luck," Senlin replied curtly, not grasping why the obnoxious assistant was suddenly fawning over him and divulging his professional aspirations.

"What I wanted to ask is, do you think I might be more suited to the role of a nurse? Do you think that character would be more appropriate to my talents? The role is traditionally played by a woman, but the potential for—"

Senlin butted in, "Role? What do you mean? You're an actor?"

Ceph could hardly contain his delight; he bit his knuckle and blushed. "Oh, Mr. Senlin, what a wonderful review. You have absolutely made my day!"

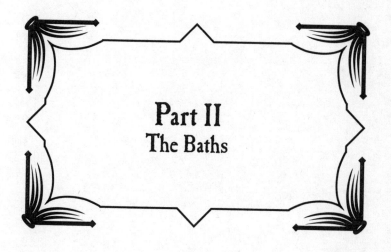

Part II
The Baths

Chapter One

The Fountain of the Baths can unwrinkle a crone's elbow, can mend sprained muscles and strained hearts alike, can dislodge the most stubborn tic. Whatever is worrisome will be forgot.

—Everyman's Guide to the Tower of Babel, IV. III

A troop of chattering young women in felt dresses and crocheted hats followed him up the switchbacking stairs. Their stairwell converged with another, then a third, until their upward path joined a great confluence: steps of pink marble, wide as a city block. The footfalls of ascending tourists chorused like falling rain, growing from a rhythmless patter into a thunderous beat. He was one of thousands making the climb.

The *Everyman's Guide* called the Baths "the nurse of humanity"—though Senlin's faith in the literature was not what it had been.

His time in the cage had stiffened his joints. His legs burned and shook. When he mounted the last step, he wanted to collapse, but there simply was no room. Without a moment to regain his breath, he was jostled forward into one of many queues inside the crowded customs station. The white porcelain brickwork gleamed in the gaslight of bronze chandeliers. Men in navy-blue uniforms patrolled and scanned the crowd. Billy clubs and rapiers hung from their belts. The black leather bills of their blue caps hid their eyes, but Senlin could feel the uniformed agents watching him, watching them all.

At the end of the great hall, some hundred yards ahead, a bank of caged customs booths stood, sturdy as molars. This was the only way through to the Baths, he knew. Either Marya had stood just here at some recent moment, or would stand here soon. After getting tangled in the mazes of the Parlor, he felt relieved to be standing again on the clear path.

A prominent banner above the customs booths advertised a 5 percent tax on all goods and currency. A second notice promised swift justice to anyone caught smuggling.

The tourist at his elbow wore a tall wig, powder white and boastful as a mainsail; his only luggage appeared to be an unlatched alligator-skin bag from which a toy poodle peered and yipped. As flamboyant as this man was, he was not remarkable. The crowd was flush with wealthy eccentrics. They carried frilled parasols and crepe bonnets, black thorn canes and gold watch chains. Though better dressed, the behavior of the mob wasn't much different than the mobs of the Market. The arriving masses were aggressive, single-minded, and aloof. If he failed to press against the person in line ahead of him, a swifter opportunist would wriggle into the gap. A woman carrying a large hooded birdcage knocked him on his heels jumping into his line. He felt hemmed in and panicky. He buried his hands in his coat pockets to keep from biting his nails: a nervous habit he had long suppressed.

His thoughts kept darting back to Edith, the agonized look on her face, the nurse's sadistic counting, and the repulsive yet familiar smell of searing flesh . . . He had left her. She'd wanted him to, but that didn't lessen his guilt. His conscience antagonized him: *You left her because you were afraid. You left her because she made you uncomfortable.* And he was. And she had.

But what could he have done? What would it have accomplished if he'd stayed and been branded and banned himself? And yet, if he discovered that another man in another ward had abandoned Marya the way he had abandoned Edith, he'd never forgive the scoundrel.

For the first time in his life, he had to confront a terrible fact about himself. Yes, he was shy, nervous, and a tad sanctimonious, but these were not his flaws. He was a coward. The Tower had proven that much. He was a coward, and Edith had paid the price.

After three hours of shuffling and self-recriminations, Senlin finally arrived at the front of his line. He only had to wait for the pushy woman with the birdcage to finish answering the agent's well-rehearsed catechism: "Have you any spoilable goods? Do you intend to earn a salary during your time in the Baths?" All went smoothly until the agent asked her to unsheathe the birdcage. She demurred. He insisted. She resolutely refused on the grounds that her bird was extraordinarily sensitive and she was a well-established lady with a husband who possessed nearly supernatural political powers. The mood of the agent soured visibly, the dark bill of his cap dipping over his eyes like a heavy, humorless brow.

At some discreet signal, another agent appeared, blocking the woman's passage. This agent did not hesitate in removing the birdcage cover, prettily printed with yellow flowers. He didn't seem at all surprised to discover that there was no bird. The cage was stuffed with banknotes. It must've contained hundreds of minas, a small fortune. Senlin couldn't help but gape.

The woman's bluster quickly turned to fawning: She batted her heavily charcoaled eyes and twisted her sharp hips flirtatiously. It was a grotesque display. Unmoved, the agent hooked her arm and escorted her away. As her voice receded, it rose into the higher octaves of panic. Senlin thought of the torment that awaited her, and his hair stood on end.

Then Senlin was shoved forward into the chute, and the agent asked what he had to declare. Without a second thought, he emptied the coins from his pockets and removed his boots so he could unpack the thin stack of large paper notes hidden there. He laid out his pitiful fortune: six minas and twenty shekels in all. He dutifully submitted 5 percent into the agent's open hand. When asked to present his bag for inspection, he quickly complied.

His copy of the *Everyman's Guide* slid about at the bottom of his otherwise empty satchel. "I was robbed," he explained. This information seemed to make no impression on the unsmiling agent. He directed Senlin through the doors at the end of the tunnel with a quick swing of his chin. Feeling as if he was stepping from a riot, Senlin staggered into the shattered sunlight of the Baths.

The light was simply dazzling. It took him a moment to discern how sunlight had been funneled into the cavern that held the city of the Baths. All about the top of the chamber, rectangular vents beamed in light. "The shafts must be hundreds of feet long," Senlin murmured. He could only imagine the contrivance of mirrors such a feat required. The light was further dispersed by scores of mirror balls, some as large as a carriage, which hung suspended from the blue-painted ceiling high above. The effect reminded him of how the sun lit the walls of a tidal cave by bouncing off the water. Everything here spangled and rippled. It was beautiful.

On either side of the cobbled pedestrian mall, three- and four-story buildings stood without so much as an alley between them. The pastel facades were finished with elaborate white cornices, making the buildings look like decorated cakes. There were playhouses, dance halls, restaurants, and hotels. The tourists were dressed in the diverse fashions of their native states, some in short riding jackets and breeches, some in elaborate kimonos, some in togas and leather thongs. Yet even among this chic flow, Senlin occasionally spied the bare backs and shaved heads of the hods, stooped and shuffling under heavy jute baskets. Customs agents half escorted, half drove these eyesores through the flocks of wealthy tourists, who scattered before the hods as if fearing infection. Senlin realized that he hadn't seen any hods in the Parlor. He wondered how they had progressed unseen to the third floor. He recalled Goll's remark that the Tower was not without back doors. Perhaps the hods traveled a less public road. He doubted it could be a very pleasant thoroughfare.

The wide avenue dead-ended into a reservoir that was perfectly round and blue as a sapphire. The size of the body of water was staggering, and Senlin wondered whether it had been drawn up from the deep aquifers beneath the Tower, or drawn down from the clouds that continuously masked the highest reaches of the Tower. Farther out from shore, reeds with white downy seeds grew. Flocks of pale flamingos preened and squawked amid the tall grass. At the center of the reservoir, a tower spiraled up to the ceiling, tapering like a conch shell as it rose. Hyacinth and ivy poured from portals and windows and clung to every surface. Steam wriggled through the greenery. Wrought-iron pedestrian bridges spoked out from the steaming tower, connecting it to the shoreline. Arched signs over the bridges advertised, ONE SHEKEL TO VISIT THE FAMOUS FOUNTAIN SPAS.

The reservoir, obviously the main attraction, was encircled by bathhouses. The cobbled, artificial shore teemed with bathers, young and old. At intervals in the deepening water, mechanical hippopotamuses opened and closed their maws, shooting jets of water from their throats, to the great amusement of many children.

This was the wondrous Tower Senlin had expected to see, a place befitting a honeymoon! He had underestimated the squalor and danger of the lower ringdoms, but equally, he'd underestimated the beauty of the Baths. It was glorious! He only wished that he could share this moment of revelation with Marya. It would've made her so glad to see it.

Senlin moved along the water's edge, winding a path through picnickers, lounge chairs, and cabanas. The air smelled strongly of a dozen different soaps. The fragrances itched his nose. Out of habit, his eyes darted toward any swath of red. It was absurd to think that she would always wear it. And perhaps the hat had been stolen. He liked to think that she was presently situated in a hotel suite, comfortably arranged and waiting, perhaps even at that moment standing on a balcony looking out over the tideless coast, thinking of him. Perhaps she'd found a piano and was entertaining the other guests with her fierce playing and thrilling voice...

"That is the face of a man who needs a welcome!" The mirthful baritone startled Senlin. He looked down and realized that he was standing very near a slatted lounge chair holding a large and barrel-chested bather. "Welcome to the Baths!" The man was bronze skinned and shirtless, wearing nothing but red bathing trunks and darkly smoked glasses. A two-pointed black beard accentuated his iron gray mane of hair. He seemed hale and athletic for a man his age. Senlin was a little intimidated by the width of his chest and shoulders, though his smile seemed amiable enough. "And that is the dazed look of a man fresh from the monkey pen." He gave an exaggerated shudder. "The Parlor is an awful place."

Despite his heightened suspicion of all the Tower's visitors, Senlin couldn't help but to feel an immediate camaraderie with this grinning giant. He asked the question that had been gnawing at him since he'd left Ceph at the bottom of the Parlor stairs. "Are they all actors?"

"I don't know. Perhaps they are just prigs. In the end, does it matter? They are terrible, and you are rid of them. Well, you are physically rid of them; it may take a bottle of wine to purge yourself spiritually, or, if you're very traumatized, a fortnight in the steam baths."

Senlin pointed his bony chin at the fountain spire. "It's an incredible sight, but I don't think I'll be staying as long as a fortnight."

"Ah. No, me neither. I leave tomorrow. Homeward bound!" The giant briefly described his background in mining, mostly in the Cyan Mountains to the north, though Senlin did not imagine, based on the man's appearance, that he had spent much time in the bowels of the earth scrounging after glimmers in the dark. He seemed more the type to count the gold than to dig after it. "And you, I take it, are"—the giant gave Senlin a long, appraising look—"a mortician?"

Senlin laughed. "A headmaster."

"Of course! All in black because you are mourning the loss of youthful innocence!" His deep bellow was half-reverent and half-joking; Senlin would soon discover it was a tone he used often: an ironic bark. "A man of letters. Good! I haven't had a reasonable conversation in months. Everyone here is too stuffy or witty to let an honest word slip out. I'm rabid for some intelligent discourse. Let's meet this evening at Café Risso for tea or drinks or dinner or whatever it is you scholars indulge in." The café, the man indicated, was located on the waterfront just behind them. "Risso's service is slow, but the snails are delicious."

Though Senlin was hesitant to set any engagements in case he was reunited with Marya in the next few hours, the happy titan wouldn't accept his excuses and promised that the engagement would be educative at worst and enjoyable at best. Eventually, Senlin accepted the invitation, and before they parted, the two introduced themselves formally.

Senlin shook the hand of John Tarrou, who laughed robustly when Senlin asked for a hotel recommendation. "They are all the same, Headmaster. They're overrun with luxurious moths that never tire of eating your money. Send a letter to your bank before you ask for a room with a view!"

Encouraged by his encounter with the friendly Tarrou, Senlin went in search of Marya. He quickly decided to focus his attention on the numerous hotels and the customs gate. If she was already here, she would have hired a room, and if she was still mired in the bowels of the Tower, the only escape was by the customs gate. He would catch her coming or going.

He wished again that he'd had the foresight to negotiate a hotel reservation. As things stood, he'd have to scour the panoply of hotels. There were nearly sixty in all. Adding to the difficulty, he would have to hunt for Marya discreetly. He couldn't just ramble about confessing that he'd lost his wife. He hadn't forgotten Finn Goll's advice to look without appearing to look. He didn't want to attract the attention of thieves or hucksters. Even Tarrou, amiable as he seemed, would have to earn his trust.

So, he devised a surreptitious means of discovering whether Marya was presently staying in a hotel. He approached the concierge as if he meant to check in and needed only to confirm that his wife, returned early from a matinee, had not already done so. When the concierge returned with the news that no guests under his name were currently on their rolls, Senlin would feign puzzlement and say, "This is the Montgrove Hotel?" knowing full well it wasn't because he had just come from the Montgrove next door. His mistake would be corrected, and he'd be sent on his way, just another absentminded tourist who had misplaced his hotel but not his wife.

Soon, Senlin had inquired in two dozen hotels. Though he'd still found no sign of Marya, he felt comforted by the fair start he had made. It would be a process; he had to be patient.

He was on the street between hotels when a carillon chimed a pretty musical phrase and then rang the hour of five. Recalling his engagement with John Tarrou, he made his way back to the Café Risso with a rapidly growing appetite. It had been days since he'd had a proper meal, and the prospect was quite appealing. Besides, he hoped he might learn something useful from a man who seemed in every way at home in the Baths.

He found Tarrou sitting at a wrought-iron table on the patio outside Café Risso, a wineglass and a bottle in front of him. Enclosed by a low fence, the patio contained an archipelago of wrought-iron tables and chairs. A few solitary diners sat engrossed by the reservoir, which was turning orange and purple in the refractions of the setting sun. An artist stood at an easel nearby, blending paint on his palette. It seemed an ideal hour for meditation.

Senlin greeted his new friend, who had added a canary-yellow shirt to his red swimming trunks. His flamboyant style amused Senlin, but it seemed to be the local mode: Everyone dressed like actors in a traveling theater troupe.

Tarrou looked at Senlin distantly as if he were a stranger who'd wandered into view. Senlin felt a flush of embarrassment. He had misinterpreted the man's politeness for a sincere offer of friendship. Goll had warned him: A man had no friends in the Tower. He was a fool to hope otherwise.

Senlin was about to dart back out into the street when Tarrou abruptly emerged from his trance. "Headmaster! No, don't go! You only surprised me. I was walking down a road a thousand miles away." He rubbed his face vigorously. "Muddit, this ghostly light makes the mind wander!"

Tarrou coaxed and flattered Senlin into the chair across from him, smiling over the prongs of his black beard. A young woman in a red apron appeared with a second glass. Tarrou made a show of ordering their dinner, bantering flirtatiously with the server as he did. He ordered the snails and lamb, potatoes, and stewed dates besides, and then turned the empty bottle upside down over his head and said, "My brains are going dry," at which the server giggled. She quickly returned with a full, uncorked bottle.

Soon, the siphoned sunlight dimmed and was replaced by a silvery cast of much paler moonlight. Senlin's face felt warm with wine, and his stomach was round with excellent food. Their plates were cleared, a bottle of port was brought, and they turned their chairs to face the dark water that flashed like cracked onyx. The painter closed up his easel. Gas lamps along the streets and pedestrian bridges were lit. Music from the dance halls mingled in the distance. A woman's laughter reverberated from a hotel terrace behind them. Senlin wished again to have Marya with him, though if she were there, she would almost certainly pull him from his chair and chase him to the nearest dance hall.

Though their conversation during dinner had been eclipsed by their appetite, the two men now began speaking with the ease of old friends.

"And there are no peacocks?" Senlin asked.

"There are two flamingos for every man and thousands of finches and parrots and swallows and doves, and I've heard of an eccentric who walks a dodo on a leash. But I've never seen a peacock."

Senlin laughed. "I met someone who was certain there were peacocks."

"I'm suspicious of people who are certain. I've known men who say that, without a shadow of a doubt, the Tower contains forty-six ringdoms. They'd start fistfights over this undeniable fact." Tarrou sucked his teeth. "And I have also met seemingly sincere airmen who swore the Tower had only thirty-two ringdoms." Tarrou tapped his nose. "I know the truth. The Tower is only as tall as the man that climbs it."

"To uncertainty!" Senlin offered by way of toast, and Tarrou raised his glass. "If there are no peacocks, there must be lamb at least. That was one of the sweetest chops I've ever tasted."

"There's no room in the Baths for lambs, unless you count the herds of courtesans flouncing around in those horrible wool wigs. You've seen them! Every one of them, I promise you, is hopping with lice."

Tarrou went on to explain that most perishable delicacies were carried up on airships, which was also the most popular passage for tourists. "It's only the adventurous and the frugal who climb the Tower by foot," Tarrou said, causing Senlin to feel self-conscious about his livelihood. He imagined that to Tarrou—who he'd learned owned three mines, one of which produced emeralds—teaching children to read, write, and multiply must seem a rather lowly living. "Don't scowl, Headmaster. So the lamb flies while you climb! You are no lamb. You have mettle and wits. Everyone else here is softer, dumber, and poorer than they pretend to be! They're all pig farmers and grocers in royal drag." Tarrou wrapped his napkin about his head like a turban. It made Senlin laugh.

"I'm sorry that you're leaving, Tarrou. It's refreshing to have good company."

"Ah! It can't be helped. To tell the truth, I've delayed my homecoming too long. My wife will have sold off all of my possessions."

"You're married?" Senlin was surprised.

"Twenty-eight—no, twenty-nine years. Though, between us, it feels not a day more than thirty. She is a patient woman, but I have made her wait too long."

Finding that Tarrou was married only endeared him to Senlin more, though he wondered why a man in the prime of his middle age would come to the Baths without his wife. Such a separation seemed to make a question of love and marriage. Why marry if you were going to walk the wonders of the world alone?

Though, Senlin had to admit, that was exactly what he had done.

Chapter Two

The only real danger is of growing so relaxed that one falls asleep while soaking in a bath. To prevent accidental drowning, go with a companion or seek out a new friend.

—*Everyman's Guide to the Tower of Babel*, IV. IV

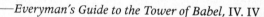

Days passed.

A regular schedule emerged, which was a comfort to Senlin. Mornings were spent discreetly searching hotel registries for signs of Marya. When Senlin felt panic creeping in, he reminded himself that Marya was resourceful, he was patient, and the Tower was finite. He read the *Guide*, his only book. He searched its many platitudes for practical advice and found little. He wished he had brought more books. When these consolations failed, he fortified himself with a glass of wine.

Days passed.

It wasn't long before he found his way behind the cake-decorated hotels and galleries to the narrower alleys where the porters, maids, and vendors lived. Those cloistered avenues were not slums exactly, but they were generally humble and often run-down. Shutters hung unevenly from glassless windows, and laundry lines sutured the alleyways. The air was muggy with human scents. The reflected sunlight was dimmer here, too, which allowed lichen to bloom on the plaster walls and cobblestones, turning them slick and spongy and gray-green.

Among the tenement apartments were boarding houses, which could be hired short term and on short notice. An effective search of the boarding houses was difficult because they were disorganized, overcrowded, and often run by suspicious, unhelpful proprietors. Senlin felt conspicuous and unwelcome in the back alleys of the Baths, and it wasn't long before he found excuses to avoid searching them. After all, he doubted very much that Marya would have to resort to such drab and unsafe accommodations.

Days passed, and the trauma of the Parlor dwindled in his memory. He had all but convinced himself that Edith had recovered and found her way home. The fall harvest wasn't too far off. The Generaless, he liked to think, had overcome her allergy and reclaimed her command. She would always carry the scar, the Parlor's brand, but she would enjoy a full and long life far from the shadow of the Tower.

He took his lunch outside the customs gate, where it was relatively easy to pass unnoticed amid the wash of tourists. Ever since his first exposure to the customs agents, he had been careful to avoid attracting their attention. It wasn't easy; the navy-coated agents were everywhere. They marched under the orders of someone called the commissioner, who was often discussed yet seldom seen in public. Otherwise, the rule of law was a mystery to him. Truthfully, he hoped it would remain one. The *Everyman's Guide* said nothing substantive about the laws of the Baths, but he wanted to believe the Baths was a more civil ringdom than the Basement or the Parlor. He wasn't looking for evidence to the contrary.

But the evidence, he'd soon discover, was inescapable.

In the evenings, he dined with John Tarrou. Tarrou had failed to follow through on his promise to leave in the morning, and Senlin soon understood that it was a kind of daily homage he paid his wife: Tarrou was always preparing to depart for home.

Senlin continued to keep his situation to himself, though it increasingly seemed ridiculous. And still, he could never quite bring himself to confess to Tarrou that he in fact had a wife and that he had lost her. Perhaps his discretion had turned to paranoia. Perhaps he treasured Tarrou's ignorance. So long as he didn't speak of Marya, they could laugh, bicker, philosophize, and drink. If not for these distractions, Senlin would have to face the dread that was ballooning inside of him. The dread was already as stubborn as a wine stain and as pervasive as a chill. Suppose Marya never came? Suppose she had found a way home without their train tickets? Suppose she was injured, or captured, or worse...

But the dread abated in Café Risso where Tarrou's ironic bark reigned supreme.

When Tarrou was not at the café, he could often be found lounging in his usual rented chair by the water, not far from where a clockwork hippopotamus spit its elegant jet.

"Today is no good for travel, Headmaster. The winds are coming in from the north. If I tried to fly home, I'd end up at the South Pole," Tarrou said from behind his dark glasses. The exquisite glare of the afternoon sun seemed magnified rather than reflected by the mirror balls twisting overhead. Senlin had been roaming the Baths for more than two weeks and still hadn't grown accustomed to the shattered light, or how it sometimes dimmed when clouds passed, unseen, over the sun outside. "Are you all done with your mysterious errands or ablutions or whatever it is you fritter your days on?"

"Only taking a break." Senlin waved a hand before his face, shooing the question away. In truth, he doubted Tarrou really cared to know; the giant just enjoyed teasing him.

Senlin paid an attendant a half shekel to rent the slat-backed chair beside his friend. In his long, dark coat, Senlin stood out among the tourists in bathing suits, though there was one other awkwardly dressed gentleman fidgeting not far from them. Tarrou nodded discreetly toward the nervous man.

"I have been watching this performance all morning. I think you've arrived just in time to see the end of this little tragedy," Tarrou said. The man in question was pudgy, middle-aged, and wore the farcical regalia of an admiral: gold-threaded epaulets, a purple sash, and a three-cornered hat. The well-fed and well-groomed man paced at the water's edge more like a cornered mouse than a military commander.

"He is flat broke—they always are—and terribly in debt," Tarrou said from the corner of his mouth. "And still he has carefully preserved his most ostentatious costume. Here is your peacock, Headmaster. But watch…"

A few moments later, a detail of six customs agents appeared. Clubs and rapiers wagged from their wide polished belts. The last agent dragged a basket heaped with coal. The agents surrounded the merchant, who immediately began dithering about the misapplication of justice, his powerful connections, and his reversing fortunes. He hopped from foot to foot, his arms raised as if he were trying to waltz through the circled agents. Unmoved, the agents grabbed him and began roughly stripping him of his clothes. Horrified, Senlin moved to interject, but Tarrou was quick to grab his arm and anchor him to his chair. Tarrou put his finger to his lips and gave Senlin a severe look of caution.

Now cowering in his stretched and stained long underwear, the man wept while two agents shaved his head first with rusty shears and then a notched straightedge. While they worked, another agent aired the man's name, described the exact nature and size of his debts, and announced how long he would have to work as a hod to level his accounts: twelve years. Twelve years! A whole era of a man's life lost. For what? An overdrawn account. It seemed out of proportion. The disgraced man sobbed through the judgment as nicks in his scalp welled with blood. At the conclusion of his sentence, the commissioner's authority was invoked, and a heavy cuff was locked around his neck. A six-inch iron tube dangled from the collar like a pendant. The agent rolled up the man's sentence and stuffed it into the tube, screwing the cap closed behind it. The freshly initiated hod was forced to pick up the load of coal, then escorted away.

"Where does he go?" Senlin asked.

"There is a passage that is only swept by the feet of hods…It's called the Old Vein, and it coils through the walls of the Tower, an unlit and unaired crag. It is more dangerous, I'm told, than any mine a man ever dug. Pray you never see it." Tarrou spoke in a low, dour tone. "That plucked peacock will not survive twelve years. He may not even survive the night. It is a lesson, Headmaster Tom," Tarrou said. "Be mindful of your debts."

Senlin put a fingernail between his teeth. "But surely, this isn't a common occurrence?"

"As common as the hods themselves."

Despite the vivid reminder that neither his time nor funds were infinite, Senlin began to detect an ebb in the urgency of his search. Something about the beauty and ease of the environment anesthetized his dread and made the episode with the hod seem outrageous.

A few days later, he completed his tenth circuit of the Baths' hotels. Most of the concierges had long ago seen through his ruse or had given up pretending to be fooled. When they saw him coming, they gave a quick shake of their head, and off he went to the next stop on his regular route. Sometimes he would dally under the window of a concert hall, listening to the merry refrains of a brass band. Sometimes he watched the children romp about the shoreline and thought of the coming school year. The school and his duties seemed somehow unreal and unimportant.

He lost the will to read. He'd still hold the *Guide* between his tightly pinched bony fingers and would set his eyes firmly upon the page. But then his mind would just slide off into fantasy. He'd envision the moment of their reunion. He dreamt up many versions of the scene while he loitered on the curbs outside customs, waiting for her to walk by with her arms swinging, or with a book to her face, or singing a pub song. In some versions of these fantasies, the two of them crashed together like cymbals, and right there, in front of everyone, he held her neck and kissed her.

Meanwhile, Tarrou played the merry friend. Tarrou's indulgence was contagious, though in all fairness to him, Tarrou wouldn't call it indulgence. He would call it reason. "You're in the Baths, and yet you have never been to the Fountain? That's like climbing a mountain and refusing to look at the view, Headmaster. Be reasonable!"

When Senlin finally acquiesced, paid the shekel, and went to the

Fountain, he discovered that after a few moments spent soaking in a tub, there was not a thought in his head. His feelings of dread just steamed away.

The Fountain, that garden spire that rose from the heart of the reservoir, was a true marvel of plumbing. The tiled interior was filled with aromatic steam, thick as ocean fog. Pipes and troughs moved water between hundreds of white marble tubs, installed one over the other like the scales of a pinecone. The higher a tub was inside the spire, the more challenging it was for a bather to reach it. One had to climb by ladder and ledge and narrow step. Spillage from one tub cascaded onto the lower tiers like a champagne fountain. The rain of condensation and displaced water was constant yet pleasant. Where the water was drawn from or how it was heated was a mystery that Senlin puzzled over once or twice. No one else seemed to give the question much thought. Soon, neither did he.

Knowing that the Fountain was the one spot everyone visited (it was, after all, the only place to take a hot bath), Senlin glanced about for Marya, though discreetly and sleepily. Later, when they were out of the Fountain spire and the fog had cleared from his mind, he wondered if his search was any better than the lip service Tarrou paid his wife. Was Marya really likely to be frittering time in a tub while lost in a strange land? Was she even in the Baths? For all he knew, she might still be stuck in the Mayfair nightmare, dutifully playing another man's wife. Perhaps she was lying in the beer slurry of a Basement gutter, or maybe she was camping at the site of their parting in the ever-changing Market. He wished he could be certain. He should be more certain. He should know his own wife better.

Senlin's lodgings did not include a window or a sink or a writing desk, but even so the room was a drain on his resources. His meals with Tarrou weren't without expense either, and then there were his occasional soaks to pay for...

After a month, he calculated he could only afford to stay ten days more, two weeks if he gave up drinking wine in the evening with Tarrou, which suddenly seemed a great inconvenience. This budding sense of entitlement horrified him. But such was the Tower's effect. First, it turned luxury into necessity, and then the Tower conspired to revoke all claims to happiness, dignity, and liberty.

This perverse metamorphosis, from tourist, to royalty, to hod, plagued Senlin's imagination. His dread returned with greater force. He could not sleep for days, and then finally when he collapsed into an exhaustion, he dreamt horrible dreams. Before his sleeping gaze, the peacock man was again stripped of his admiral's costume. Hunched under a great basket of coal, the wretch joined a river of wretches climbing the jagged Old Vein. In this dream, Senlin scoured the hobbling and gaunt procession of hods for Marya, willing, at once, for her face to emerge, and at the same time, fearing that it would.

As his sheets began to thicken with sweat, he followed the line of bald backs and knuckled spines up the infinite Tower for weeks, for years. When the plucked peacock finally collapsed, his exhausted heart bulging like a tumor from his rib cage, Senlin, forgetting that he was not one of them, forgetting his search for his wife and his old yearning for home, bent down and took up the load.

Chapter Three

Even beauty diminishes with study. It is better to glance than gawk.

—*Everyman's Guide to the Tower of Babel*, IV. V

The bell above the door jingled. The post office was as small as a closet but as high as a silo. The postal clerk, who sat behind a caged window in a seamless marble wall, looked like a swept-up pile of dust. His collar, though buttoned to the last, rattled emptily about his skeletal neck. He sat scribbling, the *scratch-scritch-scratch* of his pen nib constant and grating. Other than a wooden writing podium, the post office was bare.

Senlin asked the clerk for a sheet of stationery and a nib to write with. The request interrupted the clerk's scribbling, and Senlin could see through the bars that the clerk was systematically blacking out the words in a chapbook, starting from the back and working to the front. As soon as the clerk had taken Senlin's coin and given him his sheet of stationery, he returned to his methodical, obnoxious scratching.

Feeling a little disquieted, Senlin went to the podium and began to compose his letter. He did not deliberate. He'd written and revised the letter a dozen times over in his mind while lying amid his knotted sheets that morning.

Dear Ms. Olivet Berks,

I know you will be relieved to hear that all is well and we are enjoying our honeymoon in the Baths. The snails here are quite delicious, and they remind me fondly of the periwinkles back home.

We are enjoying ourselves so thoroughly, in fact, that we have decided to extend our holiday a few weeks more. As my kin, I am writing to request your assistance in preparing for the eventuality of my delayed return. The school year will commence in four weeks, and so I humbly ask that you use your considerable influence to lead the town in selecting a fitting substitute in my absence.

This is not a resignation, but merely a request for an extension of Isaugh's goodwill. I shall return with Marya before the end of harvest.

Your Loving Cousin,
Thomas Senlin

P.S. I am aware that you warned Marya against accepting my proposal, and I hold no grudge in the matter. She is a treasure. I strive every day to be deserving of your confidence, and so remain ever your faithful friend and servant, T. S.

He folded, addressed, and sealed the letter with the post office's wax and signet. He paid the dust-pile clerk a shekel more to post the letter. Again, the clerk only halted his scrawling long enough to take Senlin's money and to shove the letter into a slit in the wall behind him before he resumed his work on the vanishing chapbook.

Watching the mail slot gulp his letter, it occurred to Senlin that the chute might empty into a fire pit and he'd never know it. This realization of his helplessness filled him with a sudden fit of pique, and he said, "I'll buy that book you're ruining for another shekel," before he knew why he'd said it.

The clerk shrugged and slid the half-blacked-out chapbook under the bars without ever having uttered a word.

Returning to the street, Senlin resumed his usual route, reading the chapbook as he walked. He continued in this way, dazedly walking and reading, until the work so absorbed him that he had to remove himself from the impatient pedestrian traffic and perch upon a shoreline bench. There, he finished what he hoped was a work of maudlin fiction. It certainly couldn't be true.

The Confidences of a Wifemonger by Anon.

A wifemonger, simply put, is a man who identifies, isolates, primps, and delivers women who are fit for wifedom to willing and wealthy gentlemen. A competent wifemonger will have no fewer than three and no more than six women in his charge. Fewer than three prospects and gentlemen will feel starved for option, and more than six will make would-be husbands suspect they have blundered upon a harem.

Identifying the Would-Be Wife

The Tower of Babel is lousy with waifs, but princesses are in scarce supply. A wifemonger will spend most of his time spotting wifely talents among the feminine masses. Mongers anticipate three essential virtues of their wives-in-waiting.

Virtue One: *Healthy*. Wives must be fertile and free of disease, lice, and deformity. Ugliness is naturally considered a deformity. Personal experience suggests that 70 percent of the female population fails to embody the first virtue. The gentle reader will be unsurprised to learn that 95 percent of would-be husbands might graciously be described as *unhealthy*.

Virtue Two: *Wholesome*. Wholesomeness is less a positive force than the resistance of a negative quality. Or, in the parlance of my profession, "floozies make bad wivezies." While husbands would, of course, prefer to be joined with an *unblemished* woman, a wife need not be a virgin so long as she maintains some vestige of innocence, modesty, or, at the very least, coyness. Mothers, of course, are excluded out of hand. Of the remaining Babella stock, one out of two women will be suitably *whole*. Husbands-to-be, of course, remain whole regardless of how many partners they've broken in half, quarters, or eighths.

Virtue Three: *Charming*. Charm is perhaps the most elusive of virtues, and many a wifemonger has been ruined by his inability to judge a woman's charm. Novice mongers often confuse the bosom for charm. Charm, in my experience, is necessarily mysterious. Charming women will leave their masculine audience with questions. If the woman installs no curiosity or confusion in the man, then no charm exists in the woman. Men with the least amount of personal charm are most devoted to this quality in their spouses.

Isolating the Would-Be Wife

Once a wifemonger has identified bona fide bridal material, he must separate her from the influences of kin, friends, compatriots, colleagues, peers, and all familiar influence. This process, referred to as "stabling," is generally successful when the subject is in some distress. Experienced mongers don't try to separate a wife-in-potentia from a spouse or a father. Instead, they prey upon the wandering souls, the lost, the destitute, and the desperate.

When a woman has already confronted the inevitability of her ruin, she is much easier to separate from any lingering feelings of hope. If the woman is sufficiently terrorized, it may not even be necessary to lie to her.

It will probably be necessary to lie to her. Common lies include, "This man is a ship captain whose trade route will carry him near your home," and "This fine gentleman is a baron/registrar/port authority and will hold you as his sister until your family can be found," and "This man has been hired by your loved ones to whisk you back to your old bedroom, still exactly preserved, with your wildflowers pressed in your encyclopedias and your slippers under the bedside..." etc., etc. Under the guise of charity, a desperate woman can be convinced to accompany even the most buffoonish, malformed, and tiresome mate back to his princely hovel.

Primping the Would-Be Wife

Avoid the color red when buying dresses for your stabled wives. It is a lurid color and suggests a sexual aggressiveness that may intimidate the pseudo-functional male. Avoid white frocks as well, as these infer a prudishness that does not appeal to the libido of men who are incapable of attracting a mate naturally. Avoid black, too; it suggests severity and independence. Blues, pinks, and yellows are generally appealing to the stunted tastes of the hunchbacked gnomes who slink down from their filth-crusted birdcages and ignoble bloodlines to prey upon unguarded innocents.

If your would-be wife is roughly mannered, or shy at conversing, or afflicted with an unusual laugh, do your best to gently train her away from these habits. It is vital that you earn her trust and learn as much about her as possible. The wifemonger must cast lingering glances and lingering praises. Make your evenings long with her. Make elaborate promises. Expound on their elaborateness until you are swearing on your own head and by your own grave. Avoid, at all costs, falling in love with a woman in your stable. Do not forget you are a wretched man, a monster worse than the lecherous princes that slide down the Tower of Babella like dung down a camel's leg. Avoid, at all costs, falling in love. The door to ruin is heart-shaped and ringed with stone roses...

The remainder of the book was blacked out.

It was a fiction, surely, a crude romance written by a cynical man who'd been rejected by his lover. There was no conspiracy to trap defenseless women in unhappy marriages. This was the Tower of

Babel! And though he knew it was not an untroubled paradise, it was still, at its core and in its highest bowers, a civil place. No, the book was either a fiction or the ravings of a dim mind. Perhaps the postal clerk had had the right idea.

Senlin pocketed the wifemonger's chapbook with a dismissive snort.

It had been a productive morning. He had not relished lying to Ms. Olivet Berks—and certainly didn't like having the lie recorded on paper for all posterity—but he knew that raising the general alarm in Isaugh would do no good. If the townsfolk learned that Marya was missing, they might send a search party. Berks would certainly come. And then they would be plunged into the same chaotic mess that he and Marya had blundered into. God knows how many of them would be robbed or detoured or separated or otherwise ruined in the turmoil of the Market. No, it made no sense to add to the rolls of the Lost. His only recourse was to find Marya on his own and to return before their train tickets expired.

He was returning to the Le Gris Hotel to renew his inquiry when his attention was drawn to an amiable-looking crowd gathering about a waterside gazebo. An undecorated black banner hung from one white rail like a long, forked tongue. Believing that a troupe of actors was preparing a play, Senlin followed his curiosity to the edge of the gathering crowd.

Two men occupied the gazebo stage. The foremost was a young man, perhaps sixteen years old, dressed in the khaki apron common among hotel staff. Except for his anguished expression, he was quite a handsome youth with thick, oil-black hair. Behind him, an unassuming, relatively diminutive man fiddled with his white linen shirt, distracted by what seemed a red spot near his cuff. His round gut and slight limbs gave him a frog-like appearance, and his wide mouth only added to this impression. A broad straw hat hid the rest of his face. Something in his smile disturbed Senlin. It was too fixed and straight, like the carved grimace of a gargoyle.

"Has the show begun?" Senlin asked an old woman nearby, who was peeking and craning to improve her view. Her starched bonnet identified her as a laundry woman.

She looked in his direction only long enough to toss her chin in disgust. "Have some respect."

"I'm sorry. Are they celebrities?"

"What are you, fresh off the barges?" She gave him a second, more thorough look. "That's the Pall Bearer, the Grim Thresher himself. That's the Red Hand."

Senlin smiled at the woman's dramatic introduction of the actor. "His face is grim enough. Who's the boy, then?"

She continued in a crusty whisper, eyes darting to their corners, hunting for eavesdroppers. "A sinless nit. Works at the Mont Cappella Hotel. Least, he did. Poor Freddy."

A customs agent emerged from the crowd and climbed the first two steps of the gazebo. He began reading from a stiff sheet of stationery. "Mr. Frederick Haggard, you have been found guilty of theft, embezzlement, defamation, forgery, destruction of property..." The sentence went on and on for some moments. The counts against the young porter seemed impossibly, absurdly numerous. Senlin wondered what the meaning behind the farce might be. "...Conspiracy against the Customs Bureau, assault, lewd conduct, trespassing, and rape."

"Lies!" hissed the laundry woman at his side. "Freddy caught the eye of a rich old dame, and she tried to start a dally with him. Freddy fended her off, and she called the commissioner in to sort him out. There's the sorting."

"Does the condemned wish to repent?" The agent, coward that he was, faced resolutely away from the handsome youth. It dawned on Senlin that this was not a play. He had stumbled upon an execution.

In a voice hardly loud enough for Senlin to hear, the youth said, "I want to see my mother." It was a pitiful and honest utterance. Even without knowing the first detail of the boy's life, Senlin felt certain he was witnessing a terrible injustice.

Senlin wanted to cry out, to rush the gazebo and pull down the black banner... but he had learned to be afraid of the customs agents. And now he was learning to be afraid of someone new. That man—what had she called him?—the Red Hand. Something about him made Senlin tremble.

Transfixed, he watched as the Red Hand rolled up one loose white sleeve, revealing a bronze band about his forearm. Fitted to the metal cuff were six vials, like the barrels of hypodermic needles, each filled with some sort of sloshing serum that glowed like lit-up rubies. Hat drooping over his face, the Red Hand turned a series of pegs on the brass cuff like a musician tuning his instrument. The glowing serum drained from the cylinders and pushed into the Red Hand's veins.

A gargling cry, like something from a slaughterhouse, escaped the Red Hand's mouth, and for a moment, Senlin wondered if the man hadn't wounded himself. Then he raised his right hand above his head, and the crowd gasped at the luminous red tracery of veins glowing beneath the skin of his palm and arm, shooting out from the bronze brace like roots. The radiant lines speared up his shoulder, showing through his clothes like a wound seeping through a bandage. Soon the right half of his torso glowed red.

The Red Hand's posture became apish. Every rope and thread of muscle pressed to the surface. He circled the boy, now chattering with fear, pleading still to see his mother. Before anyone was prepared for it, the Red Hand leapt at the youth from behind. With the astonishing dexterity of an acrobat, he scaled the boy's back and dug one foot into either shoulder. The boy, staggering a little under the unexpected and awkward weight of the Red Hand, hardly had time to cry out before the executioner bent, placed his hands under the boy's jaw, and wrenched himself straight, carrying the boy's beautiful head from his neck.

Blood leapt into the air. The unnatural two-man tower collapsed. Senlin turned away too late, his stomach convulsing, and was sick at the cleaning woman's feet.

A short distance behind the gazebo, swimmers floated on their backs in the spangling waters of the reservoir.

Chapter Four

Conversations are a tedious symptom of an empty dance card.

—*Everyman's Guide to the Tower of Babel*, IV. VII

S enlin wandered the shimmering streets, hypnotized by the horror he'd witnessed. Though he hardly realized it, his steps were not without motive. He was searching for some sign of redemption, some hint that the human animal was not only horrible and violent. He needed some encouraging polemic, some cultural accomplishment or artistic ideal. His search drew him to the open shutters of a music hall, and he stood for some minutes listening to the lively play of a string quintet. But what might've sounded like a tuneful refrain an hour ago, now sounded like frivolous sawing. Uncured, he meandered toward a romantic fresco of three maids enlaced with ribbons and primroses. Their expressions were both ecstatic and innocent. Their arms and legs were plump and yet apparently weightless. The virgins floated and smiled, exuding an erotic sap that made him feel wretched and alone.

A group of young children played on the sidewalk. Hoping to hear some naive expression that would fill him with wistfulness for his students back home, Senlin slowed as he passed them. The children were playing hopscotch on a freshly chalked board. Balancing on first one foot, then the other, a young girl recited a nursery rhyme as she hopped. He had never heard the rhyme before, and as is sometimes the case with such minor discoveries, this new-to-him, old-to-the-world verse seemed to have been written especially for him.

> *The Tower grows up. The Tower grows down.*
> *The Tower holds up the hollow ground.*
> *The hod falls up. The hod falls down.*
> *The hod fills up the hollow ground.*

The simple verse was sung out happily again and again to the rhythmic stamp of the child's leather slippers. Senlin pressed one finger to his ear, as if to keep the song and its morbid vision from lodging there. He hurried his step.

He went in search of Tarrou and the consolation of wine. Finding his friend at Café Risso, Senlin imposed himself. He gulped from Tarrou's glass when his own was too slow to arrive and heatedly recounted the execution he'd witnessed. The words poured from him like a lecture that threatened to become a rage. "How can we tolerate such savagery? I thought the Tower was a moral pillar, but what has it shown me? Torture, sham justice, and public murder. Monstrous men with glowing, bloody hands. Madmen and actors without conscience. This isn't the sink of humanity; it's the sewer! Oh, don't look at me like I'm snoring through another lesson, Tarrou. You know I am right!" Unconsciously, Senlin had begun biting his fingernails, his teeth clicking together in sharp little snaps.

"Quit biting your nails," Tarrou said.

"I'm not biting my nails! I'm trimming them with my teeth because I've lost my nail clippers, along with everything else," Senlin said, swatting uselessly at the coins of reflected light that flared across his face. He almost revealed the extent of what he had lost, but stopped himself. "And better my nails than your head."

Tarrou reared back in mock fright, raising his hands to shield his face. "Heaven protect me from the spring cleaning of a man's conscience! Don't seethe at me, Headmaster. I'm glad your self-righteousness has given you some exercise, but you forget: We are not such a tidy, reasonable, and humane race. Our thoughts don't stand in grammatical rows, our hearts don't draw equations, our consciences don't have the benefit of historians whispering the answers to us. Oh, stuff your outrage!" Anyone happening past their corner of the patio would never have imagined the two were friends. "You overlook the beautiful and exaggerate the evil."

"You didn't see what the commissioner's circus did to that boy! His head..."

Speaking through a clamped jaw, Tarrou's voice lowered. "The Red Hand is a ghoul, I give you that. And no, I can't tell you the first thing about why he glows or how he gets his strength. It doesn't matter. He's just a bugbear for your nightmares." Tarrou, quick as a spark, reached across the table and clapped his broad hand over Senlin's wrist, nearly upsetting Senlin's newly delivered glass of wine. His voice was hoarse but forceful. "But you would do well to speak more quietly about the commissioner's sins. His ears are everywhere. There are men who would welcome a revolution, but we are few."

"Then why don't you just leave?" Senlin said with disarming honesty, peeling Tarrou's hand from his arm.

Tarrou looked as if he'd been pricked. "Of course, I am. In the morning."

"I need another glass before I dive after that little fable," Senlin said.

Despite the gruesome execution, despite his hopeless, floundering search for Marya, despite the hods and the vindictive commissioner, Senlin felt a glimmer of peace. Their argument and the wine had given him what he had numbly pursued in the streets: a sense of control and order. The feeling reminded him of the many summer mornings he spent crawling across his schoolhouse floor, hammering in nails that had been squeezed up by the wood's swelling. Alone and shuffling along on bare knees, trousers rolled up in thick, snug cuffs, he raised the hammer over the heads of old nails. Each blow echoed among the rafters like the report of a gun. It filled him with a small but warming sense of accomplishment.

Though every summer, the same nails sprouted anew.

Tarrou caught the attention of their server, who soon arrived with another bottle of tart plonk: cheap, acrid stuff that worked mercilessly on Senlin's stomach the following morning. They respected a truce while the wine was poured, but before Senlin could resume the subject of Tarrou's endless bon-voyaging, Tarrou diverted their attention to the painter working on the sidewalk beside their table.

Tarrou made a habit of heckling the middle-aged, hunchbacked artist. The artist, who hardly ever spoke, had paint in his hair and eyes that seemed always in motion. Other than painting, the only other activity he seemed to enjoy was smoking, which he often did, the sour yellow smoke rising straight as a flagpole in the breezeless atmosphere. Rows of his paintings leaned on the rail of the patio and around the spindly legs of his easel, but his work attracted little attention from passersby. Tarrou enjoyed teasing the painter for his style, which was distinguished by thick daubs of unblended paint. The effect wasn't bad taken from a distance, but on close inspection, his canvases reminded Senlin of a cutting board where a fish had been scaled.

"Painter, are you seeing spots? Have you suffered a blow to the head? Or perhaps you have only yet to connect your dots?" Tarrou laughed, obviously trying to move Senlin toward a merrier topic. He continued in a stage whisper to Senlin: "Notice how the artist reeks of old woman's perfume? Who do you think funds all these splatters? Widows and spinsters. Homely as a dog's hinder, but rich as the Tower. They model for him, I've heard, in the buff, and that's why he's half-blind and all his brushes have cataracts!" Tarrou leaned over the partition rail, sloshing wine onto the walk. "Look, Painter, I have a talent, too," he said, pointing at his spill.

The crooked painter patiently ignored Tarrou, though Senlin could tell he was affected. His already shortened neck seemed to shrink even further into his hump. Senlin felt a little scolded by the painter's persistence, his resoluteness. Tarrou, on the other hand, had gotten drunk and had raised his voice and had felt content, and there was no time for any of that. What was he doing with himself?

A woman in a fur stole stopped to consider some of the artist's work. Tarrou gestured grandly at the paintings leaning nearest them. "We're having a breakage sale! These, madam, are half off. And they come with a pot of paint so that you may repair them, if you like." The woman crossed the fur at her neck and hurried away. Senlin raised his finger to intervene, but was interrupted by the painter whipping about.

His large eyes were raw and red and dry with hate. Senlin half expected the painter to shoot Tarrou dead. "You tease away my livelihood, Tarrou." His voice sounded thin as a clay flute in comparison to Tarrou's theatrical baritone, but still it made Senlin recoil a little.

Tarrou looked only more entertained, but before he could reply, Senlin clapped his hands to dispel the joke. "Leave the man to his work. We haven't finished with our conversation."

"Did you just clap at me?" Tarrou rubbed his face, blunting one point of his beard and turning the other in a crazed direction. When he opened his eyes again, they were unfocused. The drink seemed to be steering the ship now. "No more conversations, Headmaster! The world is rotten. Leave it there. Why be upset?"

"I am upset because we have pooled our human genius into the building of an elaborate Tower and have filled it up with the same tyrants that have plagued our race since we crawled from the sea. Why does our innovation never extend to our conscience?"

"My conscience compels me to not throttle you or tackle the painter. That's progress!"

"That's not progress, it's fear of the law! And the law is corrupt! The innocent are still brutalized and murdered. I saw proof again of that today. The commissioner..."

"I do not endorse the man!" Tarrou said too loudly, and the painter's head swiveled around at him, his expression now one of incredulity, as if Tarrou were an idiot in addition to being a drunken wag. The look tempered Tarrou, and he continued in a more contained, though hardly more sober, tone. "He is a sneezy, wheezing little piggy. He is allergic to air. He sickens more easily than an infant. Every fortnight he hosts a buffoon's ball at his mansion where he poses as a human and a patron of the arts. A human! A patron! Bah! He employs a harem of art appraisers who tell him what a painting is worth. He is a conny... a conny..." Tarrou spit to one side to clear his dry mouth. "A connoisseur of accounting. If we want to see his collection, we have to be invited; we have to dress like a virgin sheikh; we have to look at the art through inch-thick panes of glass because the vapors disturb his sinuses." Tarrou thumbed his nose mockingly.

"Here I was concerned about murder. I had no idea the commissioner was also a bore," Senlin said acerbically, trying to sober himself now to compensate for his friend.

Tarrou only laughed. "Always so sour, Headmaster! What can we do to cheer you up?"

"I need smaller tyrants, Tarrou. Give me a stingy baker or a mayor who nods off during the spring recital. It is time I went home. The school year starts in a few weeks, and I must prepare." And, Senlin neglected to say, he was increasingly worried that home was where he would find Marya, long since returned by some easy means he'd failed to imagine. She was probably enduring all sorts of gossip and speculation. What had she told their neighbors? That her new husband had abandoned her? That she was perhaps a widow? What choice did he have but to go home? He was running out of money, and his ticket wouldn't be honored forever. If only he could afford to fly, he could bypass the whole slog back down the Tower!

"I am going home," Tarrou said, chin on his chest.

"I'm serious."

"So am I."

"How long have you been here, Tarrou? Six months? A year? You seem more a fixture than a visitor."

The large man's jaw worked, sawed nearly, until the words hissed out. "Sixteen years."

"Years!" Senlin's voice cracked with surprise. "Why?"

"I don't have to explain." The bottle seemed to chortle as he refilled his glass. "Suffice it to say, I lost track of time. And then, after a while, going home was impossible. What would I say to my wife? She took over the business years ago. The gold came out of the ground as easily under her watch as mine. We are not as essential as we'd like to think! She sends me a monthly allowance, has for years. I write her letters I don't send... pitiful, pitiful letters." At the mention of the letters, he winced as if suppressing a shudder. Senlin imagined what the letters must contain: a litany of promises. Tarrou sagged in his seat with a tragic sigh that rattled like a snore.

It was late. They were drunk. The imported light of the moon swam like silver minnows on their skin and the iron lattice of the tabletop. It was a slinking glow fit for melancholy. He ached to think that he would have to remember it alone. He would never want to describe it to Marya. It would only recall their spoiled honeymoon.

The chimes rang the ten o'clock hour, wrenching open the lengthening silence between them. The artist began packing up his easel and paints.

"I must gather my effects and buy a ticket," Tarrou said firmly, though his voice was still thick with wine. "Meet me at the south skyport in the morning, Senlin. I want a proper send-off. I will bring a bottle for you to dash on the stern. Or on my head. You are an all-weather friend. Good night." Tarrou jarred the table standing up, upsetting the empty bottle, which Senlin narrowly caught with the tip of his boot. Tarrou blundered then against the rail, and this started him laughing. He passed around the gate onto the walk, and whether out of intention or inebriation, he staggered into the artist, knocking his sling of paintings and box of paints from his hands. The artist careened forward and fell, splayed out under a lamppost.

Tarrou turned and bowed at the fallen man unsteadily. "Long dies the revolution! We have wasted our lives, Painter. But I, at least, have not burdened the world with proof of it." He began a leaning gallop away down the flagstone sidewalk and onto the cobbled street, his feet clapping flatly into the polka-dotted dark.

His conscience pricked, Senlin rushed to the artist, now sitting in dismay with his long fingers pressing the lines on his forehead into waves. Senlin apologized profusely for Tarrou, who was, he admitted, too often a bully to the poor painter. And while the painter stayed posed as a stone, Senlin began gathering the tubes and jars that spilled from the cornucopia of the painter's box.

Mercifully, the wet canvas he'd been laboring over had landed faceup. The paintings that had been on display were not so fortunately delivered. Many lay sprawled glory-side down in the street. Senlin inspected each piece in the lamplight for signs of damage, continuing his string of apologies while gently wiping scuffs of dirt from edges and blunted stretcher corners. His words quickly tapered, however, when he grasped the last of the toppled paintings.

The painted scene was of a bench. Behind it, the reservoir scintillated with morning sun, and the conch-like silhouette of the Fountain spiraled upward, jets of steam whistling out in white spokes. It was an evocative scene, if not an unusual style. But it was not the style or backdrop that struck him now. Sitting on the bench in the near foreground was a woman. Her form had been captured in just a few strokes, yet Senlin couldn't mistake her figure or the crimson-colored helmet.

The humiliated painter had finally risen and was brushing the street dust from his knees when Senlin hooked his arm tightly, holding the canvas before him.

"Where did you paint this? When did you paint this? Where is this woman?" he asked desperately, and pointed to the captured image of Marya.

Chapter Five

There are endless currencies beyond the bills and coins in your pocket. Sometimes a ticket may be bought with a smile; a glass of wine may be payment enough for an entertaining tale.

—*Everyman's Guide to the Tower of Babel*, IV. XI

Senlin stood on the rooftop terrace of a two-story perfumery. It was the artist's apartment. An intense but muddled scent suffused everything: the rough stucco walls and the rounded stairs they had climbed, the tapestry draped over the entranceway, and the bouquets of paintbrushes blooming from terra-cotta pots. The air was so cloyed with perfume it smelled almost like rot. Senlin would've found the air intolerable if he hadn't been so distracted by the elation and doubt that warred within him. What if it wasn't Marya in the painting? The style of the painting was so vague! Even if it was her, what if she had emerged only briefly from the anonymous crowd, only to disappear into it again, this time for good? And if she'd been so nearby, how had he missed her? Though he was filled with turmoil, he maintained his customary outward poise.

The majority of the terrace was devoted to the painter's work space. A sturdy four-posted easel dominated the floor. Stacks of canvases leaned against the parapet that encircled the roof, and other than a modest cot and a frayed chaise lounge, draped in colorful fineries, the only furniture was a flimsy card table and two cane chairs.

"I don't understand why people pay for a second roof when we already have one over our heads. Custom, I suppose," the artist said, retrieving a stubbed-out cigarette from a full ashtray and lighting it. The painter had yet to respond to Senlin's initial outburst over the familiar figure in his painting. Senlin felt the artist was circling the subject, and it made him uneasy.

The painter formally introduced himself as Philip Ogier. He had a nervous habit of tucking his thin, jaw-length blond hair behind his ears, which were round and prominent. His facial features were noble enough, his bright darting eyes and active brow serving to offset his long, aquiline nose. The hump on his back seemed to swell a little more to the right, which made him appear always slightly crooked when he stood still or sat. His voice and expressions were almost feminine, but Senlin detected a powerful ego beneath his mild facade.

Ogier invited Senlin to sit, and he did, though he stayed vigilantly on the edge of the seat, partly to keep his besotted mind from wandering. "I know you are new to the Baths, but I can't say I like the company you've chosen to keep," Ogier said.

"Tarrou is too often drunk and too much brokenhearted."

"Drink and self-inflicted sorrows hardly excuse it." Ogier smiled humorlessly. Senlin thought he understood Ogier's subtext: He was unlikely to be sympathetic or generous to a man who cavorted with his enemy. Senlin could only hope the artist was susceptible to bribery. Though he had little enough to bribe him with.

Ogier retrieved a bottle and two etched flutes from a blue-painted cabinet. Before taking his seat again, Ogier set a large skeleton key on the table just before him. It was a black, menacing thing with a ringed grip large enough for two fingers to pass through. Senlin didn't recall there having been any locks on the doors they had come through.

"You seem to prefer wine, but would you take a little sherry? It's viciously dry, I'm afraid, but good," Ogier said, and Senlin, feeling he could not refuse, accepted the pour. Ogier toasted Senlin's health, and Senlin graciously returned the gesture even as dread and wine made his stomach churn. This was exactly the situation Finn Goll had warned him against; exposing his desperation to Ogier had made him vulnerable. He was entirely at the man's mercy. But since the day he'd lost sight of Marya, this was the first glimpse of her he'd had. The thought that she might still be, or at least had been, in the Baths gave him hope enough to endure Ogier's agenda.

"How do you know this woman?" Ogier asked, gesturing toward the painting that had gripped Senlin's attention. The painted board now leaned on the sturdy easel facing them.

"She's an acquaintance, if it is her. It's difficult to tell."

"An acquaintance? If that's the extent of your connection, I hardly feel comfortable sharing her particulars," Ogier said, picking up and fidgeting with the substantial iron key.

"I misspoke. We are family, of course."

"Ah, yes. An absentminded cousin, perhaps?" Ogier lit a second cigarette and then pointedly muddied the air between them. The addition of the smoke to the fragrant air made Senlin's eyes tear. "You know, your initial reaction seemed genuine, and so I thought that you might really be in need of some assistance. But now you are so cool. I wonder if you aren't perhaps some vile opportunist. Some deviant with a gross agenda."

Senlin's calm cracked a little; a pleading light weakened his gaze. "She is my wife, though I have no proof of it. I promise that she will confirm it."

Ogier smiled at having coerced this revelation. His smugness made Senlin want to leap across the table at him. The urge surprised him. "And she is lost?" Ogier coaxed Senlin on with the draping smoke of his cigarette.

Senlin could think of no advantage now to concocting a story for their separation. He had gone as far as looking could take him. He was nearly out of funds. He could go no further without some assistance. Ogier seemed reasonable enough. A trifle hurt by years of scorn from Tarrou, perhaps, and a little smug, and perhaps conniving...but he did not seem to be a criminal. Besides, what choice did he have? He decided to tell Ogier the entire truth, though it pained him.

Senlin dryly and succinctly described their arrival on the train, the tumult of the Market, his error in letting her go, and the moment of their unexpected parting. He summarized his search, leaving out (he scarcely knew why) Edith, their perplexing imprisonment, her torture, and his abandonment of her. He didn't wish to complicate the narrative of his devotion to Marya, and so he hurried on to describe his inefficient scouring of the Baths.

Having never been very good at emoting, Senlin worried that Ogier might mistake his reserve for indifference. He could only hope that the frankness of his confession would be enough to elicit some mercy from the artist.

"So, she has been lost for . . . nearly five weeks?" Ogier asked, and Senlin confirmed it.

The artist sat considering the pots of orchids that enlivened the terrace wall, and even in meditation, his eyes never ceased darting about. The artist seemed to weigh the merit of Senlin's tale. After a moment, he shrugged himself from his reverie and refilled their glasses. "You wonder whether it's really her, the woman in the picture. It's so difficult to say, really, from a few strokes of paint," Ogier said without a trace of sympathy.

"It is."

"And also, I imagine, you wonder if I know where she is now, or if she was just sitting there by chance one day while I worked."

"You have a wonderful imagination, Mr. Ogier." Senlin could hardly keep the sourness from his voice. Though he risked everything if the painter took offense, he was embarrassed that his honest confession had been met with such austerity. "I'm sure you're proud."

"Pride is a funny thing." Ogier drained his little flute and smirked. "It's enjoyed most by those who deserve it least. Take our friend Tarrou. He is proud, but he has lost his purpose. Some time ago, there were those who loved him. There were those who thought him a great man, but now . . . Well, you know how available his evenings are. He has many acquaintances but few friends, Mr. Senlin."

"You certainly are more gregarious when he's not around to defend himself. Or do you want me to report your opinions to him?" Though

Senlin couldn't disagree with any of Ogier's assessment, he still felt it necessary to defend his troubled friend. "To be frank, I played no part in that history. I have treated you only with respect."

Ogier retucked his hair, the tips of which were tinted blue and green by the transference of paint from his stained fingers. "I only tell you this to warn you. If you are waiting for him to help you, he will ruin your patience, or worse, he will break your heart. I, on the other hand..." He rose and walked, stiff as a man pacing out a map, to one of the many piles of canvases leaning against the parapet. He flipped through the boards until he found the one he was looking for. It was a small work, no larger than a schoolboy's slate. He returned to present it to Senlin. "Let me turn up the lamp for you." As he raised the light, Marya's face emerged from the gloom, captured in Ogier's strange but affecting pointillism. Her hair was loose, and she was not wearing her red pith helmet. She was posed with one shoulder forward, her head turned so that the slope of her nose seemed to echo the waves of her auburn hair. Behind her, ivory, tangerine, and canary orchids flowered, making the setting immediately recognizable as the same terrace he occupied now. Her expression was one Senlin had never seen before. It reminded him of the rapturous yet glazed expression of old icons. But, of course, what Senlin absorbed most was that she was undressed to the waist.

Senlin understood that violence was probably the expected response. He should be outraged to find his wife naked, her beauty exploited. But his emotions were too disorganized. He felt flashes of sorrow and shock, anger and desire. It was like two great horned rams were butting their heads violently together in the very center of him. Confronted so forcefully by this likeness of her, he could no longer console himself with reason. His prudishness could not repair the world; his search would not turn back time. His old comfortable sense of himself and his wife and their life together was lost. His shoulders began to shake. He could not keep from weeping.

When Senlin looked up, he found the artist reared back in embarrassment. Ogier seemed startled by this sudden collapse of composure.

Strangely, the artist was pointing the heavy key at Senlin, though as Senlin regained himself, Ogier turned the key away. "I'm sorry," Ogier said, his active eyes finally meeting Senlin's. They were luminous, intelligent eyes. "I forget that not everyone is as ruthless as the Tower. All right, let us discuss this as gentlemen. I'm laying down my arms." He gingerly set the key again on the table. "Will you do the same?"

"I'm not armed," Senlin said, looking at the key in confusion. "What is that?"

"It's a very discreet and ingenious pistol. Are you really not carrying any protection at all?"

"Why would I?"

Ogier shifted his hump against the back of his chair, crossing his arms with an expression of pleasant surprise. "You really are as naive as you seem. Spectacular. I can hardly hold you responsible for befriending Tarrou. I bet you would befriend a badger." He indulged a brief, light laugh. "All right, I will tell you about your wife. But I doubt you will like it," Ogier said, nodding at the nude of Marya, which Senlin still held slackly on the table.

A month ago, Ogier had been painting by the shore of the reservoir, at a spot not far from his usual haunt outside Café Risso. It was late morning when a woman in a red pith helmet came and sat down on the bench before him. Typically, Ogier did not include occasional pedestrians in his work, not unless they were in the distance and could be captured in a few strokes. But this woman had sat in the very center of his view, had sat there as if transfixed. She hardly stirred, only stared over the artist's head for hours. So, Ogier had included her in his scene. Then, when the afternoon glare was beginning to diminish, Ogier packed his paints and collapsed his easel. As he was leaving, he interrupted her reverie briefly to thank her for being such a willing subject.

And that, as far as Ogier was concerned, was to be the end of it.

Only, the woman began to follow him.

He didn't notice until she caught him going up the stairs to his scent-soaked terrace apartment. She, seeming a little embarrassed but nevertheless brave, asked if he ever paid anyone to model for him. He said that he generally did not, with the occasional exception of the nude models he sometimes hired, most often a poor maid or au pair.

The red-hatted woman went away, apparently upset—though, Ogier assured Senlin, he'd made no overtures of any kind. He hardly expected a tourist to be interested in posing for him, nude or otherwise. He put it out of his mind, in fact. Chalked it up to a momentary fancy by a tourist caught up in the exoticism of the Baths.

But she returned the next day, determined to model for him and to be paid for her work.

"I hope that you take me at my word when I say that nothing inappropriate occurred." Ogier emphasized the oath by laying his hand over his heart. "She sat for me. I produced the painting you hold before you. I thanked her. I paid her, and she left. Again, I expected that would be the end of it." The blue moonlight shimmered across the mirror balls far above, making them spangle like fishing lures. Ogier's cigarette flared its orange eye and then was crushed into the darkness. "But I did see her again. And every day for a week after. In that time, she told me many things. She spoke of tragedies and disappointments and her plan to rescue herself and, she hoped, her husband."

"I will give you everything I have—" Senlin began in the firmest voice he could muster.

"Thank you, but you don't have what I want," Ogier interrupted, his sympathetic simper hardening now. "You have lost something that you love very much. I have also lost something that I love. So I have a very simple, very fair proposal. I wish I could say that we could be friends and assist each other out of the valor of friendship. But there are no friends in the Tower. There are only partners in business. So. If you will help me recover what I have lost, I will help you."

"I'll agree to any terms," Senlin said quickly.

"A painting of mine was taken. Stolen, I should say. I realize one painting might seem inconsequential. I have many, and I can always make more. But I am not a printing press. I am subject to fits of inspiration and ability. I can count on one hand the works that I'd consider to be my true successes. It was the greatest of these successes, my one true masterpiece, that was stolen. I cannot remake it. I have spent years trying."

Ogier leaned forward, his eyes no longer darting about. He seemed to have finally arrived at his point. "Two years ago the commissioner fabricated an excuse to seize my masterpiece. Mr. Senlin, I want you to steal it back for me."

Chapter Six

Tourists who talk too often and too fondly of their homes can expect a lukewarm reception. Locals call such nostalgic tourists "dirt-headed" or "mud-minded." One can hardly blame them. "Home" is an exaggeration made true by distance.

—*Everyman's Guide to the Tower of Babel*, IV. XII

Since the day he'd let her slip from his sight, this was the first genuine hope of finding Marya he'd had. The thought that she might still be, or at least had recently been, in the Baths gave Senlin hope enough to endure the perils that lay before him. He was prepared, if necessary, to knock the Tower down for her.

Senlin spent the night conspiring with the artist. He learned much about the commissioner: his palatial home, his opulent galas, his allergies and galleries. Whenever possible, Senlin tried to curve the subject back to Marya to learn more of her time with the painter, her current situation, her condition. But each time Senlin approached the subject, Ogier locked his lips. Senlin pleaded with him to accept some other payment, going so far as to empty his boots on the table, but Ogier was unmoved. He would accept only his masterwork. It was love in exchange for love; nothing else would sway him. Senlin had no choice but to listen and to learn about the eccentric tyrant and the Baths' societies, which included, in part, Tarrou's troubled history and the painter's own fallen star. The headmaster felt like a freshman studying for his exams; he was overstuffed with facts.

Every new piece of information he learned only made the task seem more impossible. The commissioner's mansion was under heavy guard. Every hour of the day, there were two armed agents posted at each entrance and window. Many of the guards were armed with flintlock pistols, and the rest carried clubs or sabers. Worse yet, the house was also patrolled by a unique breed of dog that had a singular talent for ratting—for catching a scent and chasing it down.

Ogier's painting hung in the ballroom under an inch of glass. It was displayed near a balcony entrance, which seemed a stroke of luck until Senlin learned that the balcony was considered the keep of the mansion, and so was fortified with two thirty-pound demi-cannons and six men with long guns. As if that wasn't enough, there was also the Red Hand to worry about, who regularly prowled the grounds. He was rumored to walk the mansion at will, or perhaps he slept at the foot of the commissioner's bed, or perhaps he lived in the walls, or perhaps he merely appeared when his name was spoken too loudly.

"What a desperate mess!" Senlin moaned.

"Precisely. And so it calls for a desperate man," Ogier replied.

As the embers of morning appeared on the streets, Senlin left the painter with a promise he had no hope to keep: He would return with his masterpiece.

Senlin walked the nearly deserted thoroughfares of the Baths. The distant burble of the fountains sounded like the ocean caught in a shell. He felt a vague annoyance at the Baths' nauseous impression of the seashore. It was a shore without a sea; it was a shallow, stupid place. But what of it? His mind was roving away from the matter at hand, turning to the comfort of criticism to distract himself from the looming reality.

Even if he'd had the courage to run at the commissioner directly, it would take an army to make it past the door. No, it simply couldn't be done by force. Senlin tried to imagine himself sneaking through the mansion at night, a black scarf wrapped over his face like a common burglar, a gangly, graceless, and loping burglar. No, stealth was out of the question, which left only deceit. The commissioner would have to be tricked into giving him the painting or moving it out into the open where it was vulnerable, if such a place existed in the Baths. The commissioner was a deeply suspicious and conservative man. Fooling him would not be easy. Senlin was not used to conniving.

The music halls stood silent; the brasseries were empty. It was beyond late; it was early morning now. It occurred to him that a bath might focus and inspire him, but he quickly dismissed the idea as a cowardly indulgence. He must face the challenge. He must transform himself into a criminal mastermind. The thought made him laugh. If his students could see him now, stripped of all confidence and authority, a fish out of water. A sturgeon, indeed.

He wondered how all his old virtues had become failings. His calm, his patience, his love of deliberation, his rationalism and fair-mindedness—all were now flaws. He needed to be cocksure and shrewd. But even then how could a cocky bookworm compete with a powerful commissioner? Senlin couldn't challenge him on any point, unless it be a contest of flaws.

A contest of flaws. The thought made him laugh and, soon after, made him plot.

Morning vendors began to walk the streets behind carts heaped with fresh pastries and fruit. Then came the early bathers and the elders who spoke incessantly about vitamins and their constitutions. A pair of plump children under the watchful eye of a governess broke the glass of the reservoir, splashing the flamingos awake. The coral-colored birds began breakfasting on the abundant algae pooled about their stalks. A customs agent flirted with a young woman selling bathing salts and scented soaps from a tray hung about her neck. The clockwork hippo resumed its impressive gout. Senlin passed through it all so lost in thought that he hardly realized where he was going until he arrived.

He stood before Tarrou, snoring under a towel in his usual lounge chair near the tidy shoreline. Senlin pulled the towel from Tarrou's face and slapped him with it until he awoke with a snort.

"Muddit, man! Let me be." Tarrou's grimace hardly softened when he realized it was Senlin who had disturbed him. "I know, Headmaster! I've missed my ship. Don't whip at me. My head is ringing!"

"Get up. I'll buy you a coffee."

"I haven't even had my morning steam yet. Why are you pestering me so early?"

"Because there is much to do, my friend. Tonight, you are escorting me to a gala."

Over coffee at Café Risso, Senlin explained his plan between Tarrou's bursts of ironic laughter. The giant, despite his hangover, was entertained by Senlin's audacious scheme. He thought it a lark, an articulate jest. Who would be mad enough to steal from the commissioner, from the man who held the leash of that psychotic dog, the Red Hand? Besides the absurdity of the proposal, Tarrou was mystified by Senlin's sudden desire to help the painter.

"What do you care about him? Let him fetch his own masterscrawl. I wouldn't take two steps to pick it up off the street," Tarrou said, his head tracking the passage of a fresh-faced young woman in high-waisted shorts. When Tarrou turned back to Senlin, he found the headmaster was studying him closely. "What?"

"A few facts came to light last night while I was owling with the painter. Sixteen years ago you did not, as you say, lose track of time, Tarrou. You came to the Tower with your wife, and you lost her." Senlin's words bleached the mirth from his friend's face. "You waited for her, certain she would find her way back to you. But she didn't." The young tourist with scissoring, bare legs passed by again, apparently lost, but this time Tarrou did not inspect her. "You could've gone home, but what if she was not there? And what would you tell her father, her mother? No, don't fidget and slouch down in your chair, Tarrou. I am not chiding you; I am reminding you how it was that you became lodged here, became a lump that could neither move up nor down. You searched for her; you waited, sick with despair and humiliation. The flights of hope were no less painful. Your funds dwindled. Then, just when hope was all but eclipsed, a miracle occurred: A letter from your wife arrived at your hotel. Somehow, over the weeks after your separation, she'd beaten a path home. She feared you were lost or dead but sent money anyway, just in case. And you..."

"Please, no more," Tarrou said pitifully.

"You," Senlin pressed on, "took the money. You repaid some debts, dallied off the rest, but wrote nothing in response... because what was the need? You'd go home and explain everything in the flesh. But shame kept you from going home. The next month, another letter and another sum arrived. She was tithing the universe. Seeding some of your fortune just in case you were alive to enjoy it. And you had new debts to pay and not quite enough left over to pay for a flight home. You spent weeks swinging between shame and indulgence, boasts and self-reproach. Gradually, you fell in with the local socialites. You became a staple of soirees; you could fill a room. Ogier tells me that many, many parties were born on your toe and died at your heel. Still, you didn't write your wife because it was better for her to think you were dead."

"I will whip that painter with his own tongue!" Tarrou said, but looked as if he were going to strangle Senlin, if for no other reason than he was nearest at hand. His dark gray eyes burned under his flushed forehead, and he fairly trembled with rage. "He hasn't told you half the story. Don't pretend to stare through me!"

Senlin shook his head with the stiff severity of a patriarch. "He showed me a portrait he painted of you in the days of your friendship. There was a little less gray in your beard then, but there was no mistaking it was you. He told me all about your falling out after you drunkenly confessed everything to him. After that, you couldn't bear his company."

"Oh, is that his story of our souring!" Tarrou snorted and rapped his fist on the table. "Let me tell you the other half, and we'll see who looks gallant then!"

"I don't care. I am not scolding you!" Senlin grabbed his friend's hand. "We are the same man. I have recited my own story in telling yours. Listen! I have lost my wife in this terrible place. I have searched and floundered and proven myself a coward. I've gone half-mad with hope and guilt. I've drunk myself stupid. I've hidden from my life. I am ruined, Tarrou. I can never go home. Not alone."

For the second time in recent hours, Senlin found himself recounting the saga of how he'd lost Marya. His tragedy revealed, he then shared what he'd learned from the painter, sparing no detail, despite the discomfort it caused him. It was so galling to think that she had been so close at hand. They may have passed each other a dozen times on the street and only looked the wrong way each time.

Ogier had said Tarrou was unreliable, a false friend, and Senlin could only hope that his present abject honesty would be enough to prove him wrong.

At the conclusion of Senlin's startling confession, Tarrou sighed and rounded his shoulders. His eyes glowed wetly as he gazed out at the evanescent traffic that passed under the churning mosaic of sunlight. "I'm sorry about your wife, Tom. I'd not wish this demoralization on anyone. It is the most hollow feeling . . ."

Senlin couldn't afford to let Tarrou slip into self-pity, though perhaps a better friend would've offered some consolation. It was too late now for pity. "I haven't much time. I may seem reckless, but I have a chance, a small chance, to find her. My wife is not safe at home, Tarrou. She is here, somewhere, and lost. I have proof of it." Senlin heard the echo of Ogier's warning under the words that were rising now in his throat, felt the old dread return. Perhaps the painter was right to say that the Tower made friendship impossible. But what other hope did he have? "Please, my friend, for my sake, for my wife's sake, help me steal this painting."

"You are running at the wrong end of the rabid dog, Headmaster. Why risk your life when we could more easily confront the painter and compel him to talk?" Tarrou said. "He's stubborn, to be sure, but we could work the truth from him." Tarrou raised and squeezed his fists.

"Returning a painting that was wrongfully stolen is one thing. Torturing a man is quite another," Senlin said, and whether it was affected outrage or genuine conviction, Tarrou saw that Senlin was firm on this point. "I won't let the Tower turn me into a tyrant."

"You have no idea what the Tower will turn you into!" Tarrou laughed and swatted the air, trying to dispel Senlin's sudden piety. When Senlin didn't flinch, Tarrou's laughter turned to an uncomfortable haw. "Oh, it is too late. You are already insane. Do you have any idea what the commissioner will do to a man caught stealing from him? Do you think your wife prefers a martyred husband to one that is gone but living?" Tarrou searched Senlin's face for some healthy symptom of fear. Instead, he saw the headmaster craning forward resolutely. "You mean to go through with it?"

"I do," Senlin said.

Tarrou pulled a little silver flask from his white robe and bobbed it to his lips. "Your plan is bad. You do know that? If your plan were a horse, it would have three legs, two heads, and no end to it." He sucked his lips and screwed the stopper back on his flask. Senlin sat without argument, though Tarrou seemed to be waiting for one. The giant flinched first. "Oh, all right!" Tarrou said. "We'll roll your horse to town, Headmaster, your rickety, unlikely horse."

Tarrou stood abruptly and patted his pockets for his purse. "I will need a new suit. Something peacockish and horrible."

From the outside, the commissioner's mansion resembled a lavish hotel. A colonnade led from the public street to the house. Each column was striped with a broad black ribbon. The white marble facade of the mansion beyond was festooned with green garlands hung above windows that glowed with electric light. Two files of immaculately presented customs agents stood by paneled doors that were as tall as the colonnade itself.

Senlin studied these features while he waited for his fellow conspirator to arrive. He was freshly scrubbed and pressed and brushed. He seemed nearly dapper, thanks almost entirely to the top hat that Tarrou had loaned him and insisted he wear, and still he might as well be wearing a fishmonger's smock for all the extravagance pouring past him. The fashion of the commissioner's guests was so intense and diverse it made Senlin wonder if he wasn't about to blunder into a masquerade. And there were hundreds of them. Men in white wigs or tricornered hats escorted women with spangling tiaras and hoop skirts or exotic robes and jeweled turbans. He still wore his plain black waistcoat and narrow black trousers, which he had pruned of loose threads for the occasion. He looked more like a shadow than a guest. He could only hope that Tarrou's opulence would be sufficient for them both.

And indeed it was. When Tarrou appeared, Senlin couldn't decide if he looked more like a king or a king's fool. His gold-embroidered pantaloons ballooned absurdly at his knees, his enormous hat looked like a cushion fit for a sheikh's throne, and his green felt shoes curled up at the toe. His beard and hair had been trimmed and waxed, and his skin still glowed from a recent soak. He bowed theatrically to Senlin. "Behold, the suicide of fashion! No, no, excuse me: the fashion of suicide!"

Senlin managed a wan smile. "I must warn you, I am appalling at parties. I'm accustomed to hiding behind my wife's sparkling personality." He straightened his narrow black tie.

"You'll make a better impression on our host dressed as an undertaker. He's not like his guests, all high as fireworks and dim as smoke. He doesn't like sparkling personalities; no offense to your wife," Tarrou said, clapping his friend on either shoulder. He pulled Senlin nearer and whispered through a showman's smile. "The commissioner is as good humored as a guillotine."

"That is not comforting," Senlin said, cringing down against his sharp collar. A numb, floating sensation filled his stomach. His courage fled and returned and fled again. "I feel a little ill."

"You must exhaust your wife," Tarrou said and laughed.

Chapter Seven

The politics of the Tower are like garden politics,
like neighbors bickering over the ownership of a
plum tree. You may detect undercurrents of rivalry
and feud, though none are very serious. Even so, it
is best to have a supple opinion in matters of local
governance.

—*Everyman's Guide to the Tower of Babel*, I. XIV

They joined the line of guests flowing through the doors, which
were tall as oak trunks and stationed with butlers in white bibs
and black tails. Senlin found their livery all too familiar.

The vestibule seemed to stretch up about them like the walls of a
gorge. Guests flung cloaks and overcoats at butlers, who were disappearing under the heaps. Brilliant electric chandeliers painted everyone with a halo, the light both beautiful and unnerving. He had read a
little about electricity, had even seen a few crude models of generators,
which spat out sparks, short as an eyelash, but he'd never seen and
hardly imagined electricity used in such abundance.

The high walls of the great lobby were shingled with artwork; the
gilded frames began at the wainscot and climbed to the ceiling. This
salon arrangement was crowded but showed the hand of a curator.
Indeed, the hall seemed more like the wing of an overstuffed museum
than the entrance of a residence. As museums went, it outshone the
most fabulous he'd ever seen.

Stationed intermittently along the wall, customs agents stood like lead soldiers, expressionless and severe, each holding the leash of a small, hairless dog. The crowd thinned here, as guests were careful to give the watchful dogs a wider berth. The breed most resembled a terrier in size and shape, though their naked pink skin piled and hung grotesquely at their jowls and haunches. The dogs, Ogier had explained the night before, were used to screen guests before they were allowed to enter the commissioner's atmosphere.

The commissioner's allergies were legendary. He was so sensitive, a single boutonniere in a shared room was enough to send him into a fit of sneezing and wheezing. If the dogs detected any trace of perfume, or tonic, or pollen, or any other pollutant, they would growl and nip at the offender, who would be unceremoniously frog-marched out the door and not invited to return. Such had been Ogier's fate. His skin and clothes were permanently suffused with scent from living over a perfumery. He wasn't allowed within a hundred feet of the commissioner.

Senlin and Tarrou had carefully scrubbed themselves and their clothes in preparation for the evening. Though, Ogier had assured him, being scentless did not guarantee safe passage. The commissioner had been known to feign an allergic attack when annoyed by someone in his company. He would say that some whiff, imperceptible to even the dogs, tickled his nose. The commissioner was quite proud of his sensitivity. It was this that first inspired Senlin's plot.

The slow pace of the procession, and the constant elbowing and shouldering that resulted, drove Senlin to seek the refuge of observational study. He scanned the works of art they shuffled past, all of which were sealed under glass to keep the paint from off-gassing into the commissioner's atmosphere. All styles and subjects were represented in the collection. Senlin recognized several of the artists from the rudimentary art lectures he gave his students.

Beyond the hall, a wide stair curled up to an immense ballroom. The glare from teardrop chandeliers made the pink marble columns and floors gleam like a carousel. Black silk banners, emblazoned with a gold astrolabe, hung on the walls. Senlin had never seen the flag before, and he didn't know what country it belonged to.

A string quintet played an exuberant waltz while couples bowed, spun, and fairly smashed together on a dance floor that was overrun on all sides by spectators. He'd never seen anything like it. This was not like the crowds that piled around the dozy shore in the morning. There was no chance of blending in here. Everywhere he looked glances were being thrown, stares leveled, winks delivered; it was a great ogling madness. Through it all, butlers ferried silver trays of champagne flutes and hors d'oeuvres with the imperviousness of sleepwalkers.

Bouts of high laughter challenged the music's dominance in the room. A yellow-haired woman climbed onto a grand piano, sitting unplayed under a white sheet near Senlin's corner of the room. She hiked up the thick membranes of her petticoats, showing her white bloomers in a display of such vulgar gaiety, it made Senlin wince. His out-of-place expression made him stand out, and she locked her gaze on him, and with an expression between coy and aggressive, cupped her bust and pressed until her cleavage overflowed like a loaf in a bread pan. He tried to conceal his revulsion with a tight smile. The woman bit her thumb at him. Tarrou hissed at him to stop grimacing at everyone like a ghoul. He would've fled had it not been for Tarrou gripping his arm and forging a path onward, inward, deeper into the convulsing heart of the gala.

Tarrou moved through the party as if it were his own. He slapped men on the back, rallied pouting couples with bawdy jokes, and pestered every passing servant for a drink. He was, it seemed to Senlin, born for bedlam. Senlin worried that Tarrou would forget the plan and fall entirely into the arms of his old society. But amid his flirtations, Tarrou continued to tug the headmaster through collapsing gaps in the crowd, moving them ever nearer their goal.

As agreed, Tarrou escorted Senlin to the spot where Ogier's masterpiece hung, lonely, between the balcony doors. The enormous balcony seemed to attract young dandies and adventurous women. They flew in and out like swallows from a barn. But there was a small gap in the migration where the painting hung, and it was here that Tarrou finally deposited Senlin.

"I might be gone a little while. I have a lot of hands to wrench and bygones to rehearse. I haven't shown my face at one of these comedies in months. Be patient. Take a drink. Take three." And with that, Tarrou disappeared into the mass of skirts and coattails.

He felt as if he'd found the party's fireplace, and the thought reminded him unexpectedly of Edith. He flinched at the memory. Behind him, dancers careened with unsteady elegance. He turned his attention to Ogier's painting. He stared into it as if it were a fire.

The painting was, as he'd been told it would be, small: fourteen inches tall and eight inches wide. The thick gilded frame, which doubled the painting's size, almost enveloped it. The style was immediately recognizable as Ogier's. A young girl in braids and a white swimming dress faced the blue reservoir. The water stood just at her ankles. Other bathers stood farther out, but she seemed removed and alone. The girl was the subject and the center of it all. Her back was turned at the viewer. Even without seeing her face, Senlin could sense her hesitation. She seemed to be deciding whether to go farther out or stay near the shore. A bright, white paper boat dangled loosely from one hand. Though the mirrored light was dazzling, the girl's dark shadow spread under her like a hole. She seemed to hover over deep water. It was odd and beautiful...

He was startled from his reverie by Tarrou's broad hand on his shoulder. He turned to face a small, slight man in a closely tailored gray suit. The cuffs of his pants were set so high that his socks showed. A lock of sterling hair, delicate and stiff as a fishing hook, curled on his formidable forehead. His eyes were the color of wet mortar, and his pale, wax-white skin made him look like a black-and-white print of a man. "Mr. Senlin," the man began in a high, sing-song voice, "I hear I have you to thank for Tarrou's reappearance. You've done what a dozen invitations could not." He stamped his boot and gave Senlin a little ironic bow.

"May I present his eminence, the Commissioner Emmanuel Pound," Tarrou said with a grander, more swelling bow, though it seemed to Senlin every bit as ironic as the commissioner's.

Senlin had been warned against trying to shake the hypersensitive commissioner's hand, and so he bowed, too, but as sincerely as he could. Coming up again, he said, "You have a most fantastic collection, Commissioner. I congratulate you."

"Yes. This Ogier is a favorite." He pronounced Ogier's name differently than the artist, hardening the *g* and making the whole sound like it was being gagged upon. "Appraised at three hundred minas." The amount was staggering. Senlin could've built a second and third schoolhouse for the amount. "A bargain, I know. It'll double in value, I promise you, before I'm done with it." The commissioner tapped his lower lip as if it was a secret and he was taking Senlin into his confidence. Senlin doubted that the commissioner wanted any estimate of his fortune kept secret, but he tapped his own lip just the same. He wanted to win the man's confidence, so he would play the parrot. "Tarrou tells me you are an art scholar?" the commissioner said, leaning backward as if to study Senlin from a new angle.

"I have penned a few essays." Senlin then went on to expound, peppering his speech with little proofs of his expertise. He knew enough to affect an accomplished art scholar, though really most of what hung on the walls was new to him. When the commissioner mentioned a particular artistic movement Senlin wasn't familiar with, he vehemently dismissed the entire thing as hackwork. It was a tactic his poorer students used; they mocked the subjects they'd failed to study.

The commissioner quickly agreed. "I don't trust critics who like everything. If everything is good, nothing has any value. Without garbage, there is no gold, is it not so?"

"Absolutely true," Senlin lied. "But this piece"—he turned again toward Ogier's painting—"*Girl with a Paper Boat*, this is something remarkable. The character of your local light seems to have inspired a novel style. It's primitive, perhaps, but evocative and precise in its way."

"I agree. I have impeccable taste," the commissioner said, and signaled Senlin to continue with a slight roll of his wrist.

"I would love to write an essay on its novel palette. Here, for example..." Senlin leaned nearer the thick pane that sealed Ogier's painting, and as the commissioner leaned in to follow his point, Senlin affected a series of abrupt, spasmodic sneezes.

Horrified, the commissioner flew backward into Tarrou with his arms thrown over his face. Gray eyes bulging from his smooth doll's head, he shrieked for his guard. The barks of his dogs rang over the noise of the room.

Gasps and stifled cries rippled through the waltzers. The band stumbled, faltered, and sawed to a halt. Blue-breasted agents appeared from several directions. Very quickly, Senlin found that he was surrounded. One of the agents presented the commissioner with a pewter tray that carried a black rubber gas mask. Two gold foil filters protruded from the cheeks of the mask like blunt tusks. With the deftness of a reflex, Commissioner Pound fitted the mask over his head and cinched it tightly against his face. Dark lenses, large as the lids of jam jars, hid his eyes. The commissioner had gone from obvious to impenetrable in the span of a few seconds. How could Senlin pander to a man who had no visible expression? There was no time to fret over it.

Senlin hurried to explain: "I'm not ill, Commissioner, I assure you. I'm only sensitive to scent." He produced a handkerchief and blew his nose delicately, almost noiselessly. "This may sound absurd, but I think someone has gotten perfume on your painting." Senlin dabbed at his eyes, sneaking a glance at the commissioner as he performed. He saw nothing behind the blackened lenses. The mask distorted the commissioner's breathing, even as he threatened to hyperventilate. The room seemed to be listening and leaning in.

The commissioner's breathing gradually returned to an even swell and whoosh. After a moment more, he uncurled and raised a single finger, signaling the ensemble to resume their play. The music broke the tension in the room: A laugh escaped, the woman atop the piano gave a tentative kick, and the party recommenced. Everyone, it seemed to Senlin, was quite accustomed to the commissioner's fits and had learned to handle them efficiently.

Still in his gas mask, the commissioner exited onto the large balcony, the agents sweeping Tarrou and Senlin along behind him. Since his fate wasn't clear, Senlin tried to appear as if this were all part of a tour. The young men and women canoodling along the parapet saw the agents and the masked commissioner and quickly drained back into the ballroom.

When the commissioner finally removed his mask, Senlin found that the diminutive and allergic tyrant was scrutinizing him. He held the expression of a man squinting into a heavy wind. "It seems we share more in common than just our appreciation of the arts," the commissioner said at last. Senlin fought to remain straight-faced, though a chill ran up from his stomach to the top of his scalp. Of course he hadn't smelled even a trace of perfume on the painting, but he gambled that the commissioner would go along with the charade rather than risk his standing as the Baths' most sensitive nose. Hoping the man's vanity extended even to his failings, he had made a contest of a flaw.

"As ingenious as Ogier's work is, it is all tainted by perfume, the result of his studio's proximity to a lady's boutique. All his work is soaked to the atom in scent. I'd hoped the glass would contain it. A pity. I will have to return it to the vault." Pound straightened his collar and waved the agents away with another roll of his wrist.

"Commissioner Pound," Senlin hurriedly interjected. "The work may be salvageable."

"I'm sorry, Professor Senlin, but I don't take risks when it comes to my sinuses."

"Then allow me. Let me suggest a simple deodorizing process. A technique I've had to learn." Senlin dabbed his handkerchief at the corner of one eye. "If I fail to rid the paint of every trace of perfume, you will have lost nothing. If I succeed, your masterpiece can retain its prominent place on your wall. It seems a pity to shelve such a jewel unnecessarily."

The commissioner returned the stiff silver lock on his forehead to its former glory, the rubber gasket of his terrible gas mask having upset its shape. "I am suspicious of Good Samaritans, Mr. Senlin."

"I have ulterior motives, of course. While the painting is being defumed, I'd like to study it and, with your endorsement, write an essay on it." Senlin tried to sound as if he were making a minor confession.

"I don't feel comfortable releasing my property to strangers."

"I would not ask you to, Commissioner. In fact, the process I have in mind requires only sunlight. Direct exposure to sun, I've learned, neutralizes almost any pollutant, though with paintings the exposure must be managed to avoid bleaching and craquelure." Craquelure was one of the more obscure painting terms he had gleaned from his studies. He used it now to establish his credentials, and it seemed to have the desired effect: The commissioner smiled. "Perhaps, you could rope off a little corner at one of your skyports, and I—"

The smile vanished, replaced by a scowl, straight as a mail slot. "The port? Out of the question. It's impossible to secure. Beside the professional sinners, the pirates, and smugglers, there is a whole host of amateur cretins: imbeciles, drunks, henchmen, lapdogs, whores, spoon-snatchers..." The commissioner did not so much conclude his list as douse it with the tipping back of a champagne flute he snatched from a tray. This paranoid litany reminded Senlin of the charges he'd heard read before the boy was wrenched in two by the Red Hand.

Despair welled within Senlin. His whole plan depended on this point; he had to separate the commissioner from Ogier's painting, had to get it out in the open and away from the agents and their cannons and vigilant dogs. Failing this, the rest of his plot was a useless ravel.

Tarrou gave Senlin a discreet smirk, which he took to say, *See how the plot collapses, Headmaster! Look at your three-legged, two-headed horse try to run!*

"Commissioner, if I may." Tarrou swept his hat, which resembled a poisonous mushroom cap, from his head and genuflected. "There are many ways to cook an egg. As I recall, you own a little portion of the sun. Your solarium! Good for entertaining, yes, but also very secure. You once told me it was accessible only through the Bureau building. Don't your men have barracks there? What could be more secure? The professor can take his notes and watch the sun do its work." Tarrou seemed very pleased with the suggestion, though Senlin hardly shared his enthusiasm. He wasn't familiar with the Bureau building, but he didn't like the sound of it.

"It's not an idiotic suggestion," the commissioner said, but Tarrou continued to charm him: The professor could act as their canary in the gold mine; when he no longer felt the tickle of perfume, the painting would be declared fit for the commissioner's air.

The commissioner was soon persuaded. He invited Senlin to his solarium in the morning. "I'll tell my men to expect you. I will desire a copy of your book, once it's published," the commissioner said in parting, sliding now toward other guests inside his mansion. "I trust I'll get a mention in the credits."

"I will dedicate it to your generosity," Senlin said, smiling as he bowed.

Chapter Eight

Often the simplest way to unlock a door is to knock
upon it.

—*Everyman's Guide to the Tower of Babel*, IV. I

O vernight, the champagne bubbles turned to sand, and Senlin
woke to a heavy head.

He rolled from the rut in the hotel mattress and turned
up the gaslight by his bedside. The light pinched his eyes, and he grimaced. His coat, trousers, shirt, socks, and boots lay in a trail across
the floor.

Foggily, he recalled celebrating with Tarrou after leaving the commissioner's gala. His friend had begun the revelry by kicking his
ridiculous hat into the reservoir and hiking a jeroboam of champagne
onto his thick shoulder. Senlin had no idea where he'd gotten the huge
bottle. Tarrou insisted that they go carousing. Before Senlin could protest, Tarrou tipped the jeroboam toward him, dousing Senlin's face,
compelling him to gulp defensively. Oh, he wished he could pretend
he had been coerced! But when Tarrou said, "Go to bed if you must,
Tom. I am a fly who lives for a day! I must buzz until I die," Senlin had
gone off buzzing willingly.

He poured water into the chipped ceramic basin atop the hotel vanity and splashed his face. He shaved slowly in the mirror without looking himself in the eye. He couldn't fathom why the evening deserved

celebrating. His plan, ill conceived as it had been from the beginning, was spoiled. What was there to celebrate?

His plan had been to get the painting out in the open where there were more escape routes and fewer agents. A bustling skyport had seemed the most opportune place; it was as chaotic as the customs gate but not as heavily patrolled. Shiploads of wealthy tourists arrived almost hourly at the port. Distractions would be plentiful. Senlin would wait until a tourist, some socialite with a birdcage stuffed full of banknotes, caught the agents' attention. Amid the furor, he would swap the original of *Girl with a Paper Boat* for one of Ogier's inferior copies. The artist said he had many, and hopefully one would be serviceable. Senlin doubted the agents would notice the difference (they weren't art critics, after all), and he hoped it would be days or weeks before the commissioner studied the painting closely enough to realize that he had been robbed. By then, Senlin would be halfway home with Marya on his arm.

Such a pretty delusion!

Tarrou had been right to call his plan a three-legged, two-headed horse. Tarrou doubted Senlin was capable of the sleight of hand a swap required, doubted that Senlin would be able to remove the painting from its frame in the span of a few moments. And how did he propose to sneak the copy in or the original out? Did he intend to stuff it down his shirtfront?

It hardly mattered anymore. He had failed to convince the commissioner to move the painting to the port. Now he would have to brave the headquarters of the Bureau, which Tarrou had described as a hive of offices, barracks, armories, and oubliettes. Perhaps his chances of stealing the painting had been better while it still hung in the commissioner's mansion. There was nothing to do now but carry on and hope for an opportunity.

As soon as he had reassembled himself, Senlin went to the concierge of his hotel and requested a blank sheet of stationery. The concierge, who weeks ago had marked Senlin as a poor guest who tipped accordingly, offered him a thin, musty, slightly crumpled sheet. Too queasy to respond to the slight, Senlin took the paper and penned a note to the artist.

Dear O,

    I need a good copy of the *Girl*. Bring it to the café this evening.

Yours,

S

    He hoped the artist would interpret it correctly. It seemed prudent to be discreet. He addressed the folded note to Ogier's perfumery apartment and gave it to the concierge to deliver. The concierge was surprised then to receive a shekel, a reasonable tip. This wasn't the time to be frugal; Senlin needed to know the note would be delivered. The concierge snapped a young porter over, then graced Senlin with a prim bow.

    Senlin might have been more gratified by the rare expression of respect if it hadn't reduced him to his last six shekels. He was almost broke. The next time he saw Tarrou, he would have to compound his debt of gratitude by asking for a loan.

    In the narrow back alleys of the Baths, under the flags of drying hotel sheets, an aged peddler sat behind a ratty collection of books, splayed across a threadbare rug. If Senlin hoped to impersonate an art critic, he'd need something to write upon.

    He asked for a journal and was offered a book bound in rawhide. It was roughly cut but sturdy. The first ten pages were filled with some poor sot's attempt at romantic verse. Senlin scanned a few lines: "The gleeking hippopotami sprays our paddleboat. Your flaxy hair swamps the prow, as I row your petticoats."

    He cringed. After paying the seller two pence for the diary, he ripped the poems out.

    The Customs Bureau building clung to the chamber wall like an immense mollusk. Its rearmost cornerstones, each twice the height of a man, melded with the limestone superstructure of the Tower. The Bureau, set too far from the dazzling mirror balls, sat in permanent twilight. Tongues of condensation and swarthy lichen darkened its granite masonry. The building reminded him of a mossy castle keep. Arrow loops, crudely paned over with foggy glass, slitted the walls, while high above, men patrolled the ramparts. Agents flowed in and out of the entrance, black shellacked batons gleaming at their hips. The raised portcullis inside the archway reminded him of a wolf's open mouth.

He reset his satchel's strap on his shoulder and allowed himself a deep and settling breath. He must do this for Marya. He must pretend to be brave.

True to his word, the commissioner had made preparations for Senlin's visit. The agent stationed at a rosewood podium beneath a now-familiar black banner recognized Senlin's name immediately and called over a cadet who had been pushing a broom about the lobby. The acned youth, dressed in a pale blue version of the customs uniform, was told to escort Senlin to the solarium. The cadet clicked his heels and saluted with a curt chop of his arm. The young man's glassy-eyed obedience struck Senlin as tragic; he had seen how much esteem the Customs Bureau had for youth. He had watched, and watched again in his nightmares, a boy's head pulled from his body like a cork from a bottle.

The interior of the Bureau was whitewashed and lit with electric bulbs that burned bright as crucibles. Racks of rifles and sabers were around every corner. Iron doors rasped open and clanged shut. Boot heels rang against the flagstone floor like hailstones. Senlin couldn't tell if the distant human sounds he heard were those of men howling with laughter or wailing in pain. He was still waiting to feel brave. He felt as brittle and small as a piece of chalk.

They passed a map room that was glassed in like a terrarium. Inside, models of the Tower stood on pedestals. Like countries on a map, each ringdom was painted a different color. It was incredible to consider how much of the Tower still lay unexplored above him. A few officers stood about a tea cart parked outside the map room, their double-breasted jackets open and showing a red lining. They watched Senlin like cats, their postures relaxed, their eyes active. The cadet hustled on, unfazed. Senlin was glad to have the excuse to hurry past the officers. He was then led through a barracks that was large enough to be measured in acres. A team of laundry women stripped the bedclothes from the rows of bunks. It was obvious the commissioner had an army of men at his disposal.

Senlin matched the cadet's brisk pace for a quarter hour before it occurred to him that the facade of the Customs Bureau had been much too shallow to accommodate such a long walk. But then it only made sense: The entire building had been carved out of the Tower wall like a rabbit warren in a hillside. Every step forward brought him nearer to sunlight.

They came at last to a spiraling stair that ended at a large, iron-bound door. The cadet stopped and swiveled on Senlin, his young, ruddy face straining with the effort of making eye contact with his taller charge. "I beg your pardon, but may I ask a question, sir?"

Senlin nodded, stiff with surprise.

"What is spring like?" the cadet asked. He was obviously uncomfortable with addressing Senlin, and so he hurried on. "I've read that the ground breaks open and all the flowers leap out at once. Does it make a sound? Does the earth shake? What does it smell like?"

Senlin's concentrated frown lifted at the corners. He recognized it was a genuine question, so he rallied to respond with a sincere answer. "Spring is gray and miserable and rainy for three or four weeks while the snow melts. The ditches turn into creeks, and everything you own is clammy as a frog belly. Then one morning, you walk outside and the sun is out and the clover has grown over the ditches and the trees are pointed with leaves, like ten thousand green arrowheads, and the air smells like"—and here he had to fumble for a phrase—"like a roomful of stately ladies and one wet dog."

The cadet considered this with smirking wonder, then his face blanked and his back went ramrod straight again. "Thank you, sir," he said, clicked his heels once, and retreated. Senlin watched him go and marveled at the idea: to have lived and never seen springtime. The boy may never have even set foot on the ground. Surely that would be the case with more and more people, the farther up one climbed.

He refocused himself on the door and turned the thick knob.

Blinded and teary-eyed, Senlin stood blinking in the doorway of the solarium. He felt an unanticipated swelling sense of relief at seeing the sun again. He felt like a drowning man who had come again, at least briefly, to the surface.

The solarium protruded from the Tower's facade like a blister. A half dome of framed glass peaked twenty feet overhead. Light streaked across a meticulously waxed parquet floor, which stood empty except for an easel and a chair. A lone agent with a grandfatherly paunch and a gray drooping mustache presented himself with a similarly droopy salute, his head dipping to meet his raised hand in a half-hearted effort. Despite his languidness, Senlin did not overlook the long flint-lock pistol jutting from his belt.

"I am Kristof," he said. "You are the critic with mud on his boots." Kristof regarded him with what seemed paternal suspicion, and Senlin felt like a boy caught rifling through his father's pockets. "Please present your bag for inspection." Kristof took Senlin's satchel, feeling along its seams, first squeezing and then probing its pockets. He glanced over Senlin's guidebook, wrapped lunch, and empty notebook. While Kristof riffled through his pitiful belongings, Senlin's eyes adjusted enough to see past the dazzling light and into the landscape. "Pull up your sleeves for me, sir," the agent asked with a little impatient wave, as if this were obviously routine. Senlin showed Kristof the thin reeds of his forearms, the pale onion bulbs of his elbows.

In the far distance at the edge of the arid basin, mountains cut upon a cloudless sky, the same mountains their honeymoon train had climbed weeks earlier, the same mountains where they had made use of the privacy of their sleeper car even as it yawed back with the train's ascent, and their ears popped, and their hearts flew against their ribs like caged birds.

Though, it was not this tender memory that held his attention now, because here in the immediate foreground the balloons of an airship rippled grandly in the wind. Not one balloon, but three, each separately larger than any single gas envelope he'd ever seen.

Senlin had once been to a fair where a hobbyist with a hot air balloon gave tethered rides for a shekel. He'd been too shy of heights to buy a ticket but had watched the gondola float up and slide down for hours. That balloon had seemed large as the moon at the time, though it only had to lift a small jute basket and a couple of brave souls two hundred feet into the air. The trio of balloons he gaped at now seemed like planets in comparison. Senlin took two steps to see past the horizon of the handrail that encircled the solarium, so that he could see what sort of magnificent vessel required three Jupiters to hold it aloft.

The vessel dangled from a jungle of cords. It hardly looked like a sea-going ship, as airships often did. Rather, it looked like a coliseum that had been yanked from the earth. He counted three levels of hatches and saw at the base of it an open drawbridge. The ship was moored to the immense cantilever of the skyport. From one of the ship's rails, the same black-and-gold flag that hung in the commissioner's mansion twisted in the wind.

"She carries seventy-eight guns." Kristof surprised Senlin by speaking just over his shoulder, his breath stinking like a barman's rag. Senlin stiffened but did not turn. "Thirty-two-pound demi-cannons that could put a dimple in a mountain. Her hull is one hundred and sixteen feet across, one hundred and eighty-three around. I walked the watch on her for eighteen years, until finally"—he backed away and slapped his gut, which bounced against his hand like a drum—"I'd had my fill."

"What's she called?" Senlin asked.

Kristof's neck piled under his chin and spilled over his cornstarched collar. He seemed to be sizing Senlin up. "You really do have mud on your shoes. Thick mud. Everyone knows that ship. That is the commissioner's flying fortress, the *Ararat*."

Senlin shrugged at his ignorance. "She looks fierce."

"Good, because it hangs like a millstone and pitches around like a bat. Once the guns start firing, it's a victory if you hold on to your breakfast." Kristof belched and then waved Senlin toward the chair that faced the easel and the center of the room. "Look at the painting. Make your jots. Our talk has made me nostalgic."

Kristof began pacing the perimeter of the solarium with a laborious and shuffling step, his blue cap drawn low over his eyes. Sometimes, when he passed behind Senlin's line of sight, Senlin would hear the gurgle of a tipped bottle.

Senlin pretended to study Ogier's painting. With the glass removed and the sun, the real sun, adding to the dazzling spectacle of the little painted scene, it seemed more wonderful than it had on the commissioner's wall. Even so, Senlin only pretended to observe it. He made little nonsensical notes and uttered thoughtful exclamations of discovery. Whenever he could, he glanced at Kristof in his slow orbit. He was trying to deduce the man's intelligence. Kristof seemed a little exhausted by life, a little drunk, but Senlin did not think he was as lackadaisical as he appeared. This was an easy assignment. It was the type of soft work that was given as a reward to a good soldier, a vigilant and perhaps wily one.

Senlin invited Kristof to share his lunch. He hoped to stir a little more casual conversation between them. They sat, Kristof on the floor, Senlin in the only chair, eating the cold chicken kebabs Senlin had brought. Once they finished, Kristof produced a second lunch from his coat pocket and ate it without offering Senlin any. He expressed no interest in any of the olive branches of small talk Senlin offered, responding only with long, bovine looks. Kristof chewed, a little cow-mouthed, apparently untroubled by thought, his eyes red at the corners. Senlin wondered if he hadn't given Kristof too much credit; perhaps he was a simple man who could recite a few technical details. He could be some captain's daft uncle or the childhood friend of a far-removed duke, for all he knew.

After another two hours, the sun fell dead even with the little room and began baking rather than lighting the air. Dabbing the back of his neck with a handkerchief, Senlin proclaimed his work done for the day, though he promised to return the following morning. He directed Kristof to remove the painting to a shadier room in the internal halls, instructions Kristof received with a poorly stifled yawn. Kristof again examined Senlin's satchel, saying in parting, "I may ask you a question tomorrow, Mr. Mud."

Senlin drew little attention as he passed unescorted through the halls of the Customs Bureau. He felt optimistic. His gait was almost jaunty. Perhaps his plan wasn't so awful after all. Perhaps it would work. He wondered what sort of question Kristof had in mind to ask, and whether it had anything to do with springtime.

Chapter Nine

The longer you linger in the halls of Babel, the more strongly you will feel the pull of allegiances, of clans, kings, and guilds. A man who stands alone is generally thought a lost tourist or a rogue. Many have found the one is a natural sibling of the other.

—*Everyman's Guide to the Tower of Babel*, IV. XX

His high spirits quickly steamed away when he returned to Café Risso.

He'd expected to find Tarrou huddled about a bottle amid a smattering of afternoon regulars. Instead, he found the patio deserted, save for one table where two buttoned-up customs agents sat. A pair of full wineglasses sat untouched before them. Senlin had seen many sotted agents in the past weeks, had seen them half peeled out of their blue coats, teetering and singing among the bathhouses, groping after the girls who sold cigarettes and oranges. Agents were far from moderate in their relaxations. These men did not look like they had come to unwind. They looked like a couple of owls, heads turning above rigid torsos, their eyes wide and scanning.

Senlin veered away from the patio gate. He tried to appear as if he had been casually diverted rather than chased off, but he sensed them watching his about-face. He felt as if his whole plot was written out on his back. The hair on his arms stood on end.

Ogier worked at his customary corner outside the café rail, but when Senlin began to approach him, the painter caught his eye, flared his own in warning, and then darted his glance toward the seated agents. Understanding his meaning, Senlin curved his path a second time, moving away and toward the shoreline of the reservoir.

Prickling with paranoia, Senlin stalked along the water's edge. He wound his way around to Tarrou's usual spot by the water, but his favorite lounging chair was empty. Senlin asked the attendant who rented the chairs if he'd seen Tarrou today, and the young man shook his head.

For a horrid moment, Senlin wondered if his friend was not avoiding him. Perhaps Tarrou had finally decided that the boorish headmaster brought more trouble than entertainment. Senlin could hardly remember a time when he'd felt more alone.

To keep from lurking about and drawing attention to himself, he found a bench with its back to the water where he could sit and keep an eye out for Tarrou or Ogier. A meandering peddler carrying a crate full of clanging bottles cried, "Four pence for a grip of grappa! Four pence for a grip of grappa," over and over like a determined whip-poor-will. The peddler stopped by Senlin's bench, repeating his call until Senlin could stand it no longer. He told the peddler he would buy a bottle if the man agreed to take his song elsewhere. Senlin counted out four small copper coins and then briefly considered the remaining palm-full of change. It was all that was left of the small fortune he'd spent years saving. Years! And for what? To hang himself and lose his wife? He wanted nothing more than to uncork the bottle and drain it.

It wasn't self-control that kept him from doing it, either. It was fear. He was afraid that when he climbed out of the bottle again, it would be as a hod.

Where was Tarrou? Probably scared off by the agents squatting on his patio, or sleeping off the previous evening's celebrations. If Tarrou was off snoring somewhere, he'd picked a terrible time for it. Senlin needed his friend. He needed, of course, to ask him, plead with him if necessary, for a loan, but he also needed a foil for his thoughts. He still had to figure out how to smuggle in Ogier's imitation and sneak out the original.

A half hour later, Ogier appeared through the stand of bathhouses that divided the mall from the shore. He toted his easel, paint box, and a sling of canvases. The burden made his hump seem more distinct and inconvenient. Red-faced, Ogier sat down on the opposite end of the bench without glancing at Senlin.

"What did you do?" Ogier said, wheezing softly. He lit a cigarette from a match he struck with his thumbnail. "Those agents were sitting there all day. Were they after you?"

"I hope not. Perhaps it's just a coincidence," Senlin said, though he doubted it. At least the painter was finally sharing in his dread. It only seemed fair. "Have you seen Tarrou?"

"No." Ogier tapped his cigarette rapidly until the ember became an angry, orange cone. "I hope you aren't counting on him. I told you, he is unreliable." He rehung his stained hair behind the platters of his ears. "How are you making out?"

Senlin briefly explained his plan and the setback of the solarium, concluding with the hours spent under Kristof's eye. "He went through my bag like a hound." Senlin thought of how Kristof had checked his sleeves, and how he'd snuck up behind him like a cat, and of his familiarity with the armaments of the *Ararat*. "He could be a drunk, or he could be an admiral, for all I know."

Ogier didn't seem overly pleased with any of it. "How will you sneak the copy in?"

"Is it off the stretcher?" Senlin asked, and Ogier nodded. "Perhaps if I folded it ..."

"It's a painting, not a newspaper!" Ogier said, his voice cracking with alarm. He quickly regained his tone. "No. The creases will show. They'll spot the copy in a moment. Besides, I don't want the original returned in squares. You can roll it, but under no circumstances should you fold it. I'd rather not have it at all."

"Well, it hardly matters. And I still have to figure some way to get Kristof out of the room." Senlin squeezed the long bat of the grappa bottle. The bland label that wrapped it appeared to have been drawn by hand, though not by a very talented one. The solution to both problems came to him abruptly. "Do you have the copy with you?"

"Of course," Ogier said, and pulled a small, rolled-up canvas from his sling of supplies. "It's the best I have. I only had a few sketches and my memory to work from. I don't know how much scrutiny it will stand up to."

"Pound knows what his collection is worth, but I don't think he really knows the pieces half as well as you think. Your copy may hang on the wall for years before anyone notices, if anyone ever does."

"You think this is a permanent solution?" Ogier asked.

Senlin shrugged. "Even if Pound does suspect the copy for what it is, what would he have to compare it to? Of course, if he does get suspicious, you'll be the first person he visits."

"That has occurred to me. It's a risk I'm willing to take," Ogier said.

"Good," Senlin said with a tight smile. Inside, he was boiling again. Ogier was willing to risk everything, including his life, including Marya's life, for a single painting. To Ogier, Senlin was nothing but an errand boy. If Ogier decided to go back on his word and not divulge what he knew of Marya's circumstances, Senlin would have no recourse but violence. Perhaps Tarrou had been right. Perhaps he was running at the wrong end of the rabid dog. If Senlin and Tarrou surprised the painter at his rooftop apartment, they could make him confess...

Unbidden, an image of a red-hot brand flashed to mind. He again saw the nurse, or rather the awful woman pretending to be a nurse, press the seething iron against Edith's smooth skin. The nauseating smell of burning flesh was so fresh in his mind it was almost palpable.

Senlin suppressed the memory with a shudder. He was ashamed to have even considered such a thing. When he looked at the artist again, his anger toward the man had fled, and what he felt most of all was pity. Here was another man who had been made desperate by his love. He took a deep breath and said, "It must be done tomorrow. Would you lend me a couple of matches and a bit of wax?"

"I have a stub of a candle. Will that work?" Ogier asked, and Senlin nodded. As the painter handed over matches and the stub, his expression clouded. "This is where I first saw your wife, on this very bench." The confession seemed to trouble him. Had his conscience finally been pricked? Had it dawned on him that he was essentially holding a woman hostage?

"I am risking my life for your painting," Senlin said. "Before I go to face capture and execution, tell me, is Marya alive and safe?"

Ogier scowled down at the cobblestones looking every bit as wretched as Senlin felt. "Yes," he said finally. "Meet me here at five tomorrow. Have my painting. Not a crease, now."

The next morning, Senlin presented himself again to the registrar of the Customs Bureau. No escort was offered him, and he was left to retrace his path from memory, which had been sharpened by fear. The halls felt a little more pinched and the agent's expressions a little less glancing today. He felt like the cheating student tormented by the scrap of paper tucked in his sock. Only his stubborn poise kept him from breaking into a trot.

He was relieved when he found the solarium and almost glad to see Kristof, leaning on the rail and eating a croissant. He held the long bars of his mustache up with one hand as he shoveled his breakfast in with the other. Senlin presented his bag for inspection, and Kristof nosed through it sleepily, still chewing, his jaw sawing slowly like a cow. When Kristof saw the full bottle of grappa rolling at the bottom of the satchel, he pulled it out and examined the hand-drawn label.

"Grappa. Very good." He patted the bottle affectionately and placed it back in Senlin's bag. "Take off your boots and pull up your pant cuffs," Kristof said wearily, as if this were the same routine of their previous encounter. Senlin did as he was directed, hopping awkwardly on one foot as he stripped his boots. Kristof peered into the boot barrels and then waved Senlin to his seat before the easel.

The morning proceeded much as it had the day before: The sun prickled his neck; Kristof circled the room, listless as a vulture; the girl in the painting hesitated near the shore.

At noon, Senlin unpacked a lunch of potato dumplings and cured dates. Kristof seated himself cross-legged on the floor, presuming that

Senlin would again be willing to share, which he was. Kristof was delighted to see the tall grappa bottle liberated from Senlin's satchel. Kristof drank from the bottle as if he were dousing a fire. Senlin took a much shorter draw while Kristof sucked on his brandy-dewed mustache.

They ate in silence. Senlin repeatedly took a small drink from the bottle before passing it to Kristof, who always drank more deeply. Kristof finished Senlin's lunch and again produced his own, which he devoured with mechanical swiftness. Senlin sipped the unrefined brandy and gazed at the world outside. Distance transformed the Market below into one of Ogier's paintings, a scene of daubs and colors devoid of hard edge. It felt as if he had climbed onto another Earth.

Kristof climbed unsteadily to his feet, his ears red as tomatoes under the unruly gray fringe of hair. His mustache hung crookedly to accommodate a smirk. He gave Senlin a stuttering heel-stamp salute, marched unsteadily to the door, and leaned his back against it. Slowly, he slid to the floor, lowering his cap as he went. He laced his pudgy fingers over the shelf of his gut and soon began to snore.

Fearing that the agent was staging a ruse, Senlin crept across the lustrous parquet floor, wobbling on tiptoe. If Kristof woke, he decided, he would ask to be shown the restroom. The barrel of the guard's pistol had been turned upward by the man's collapse, and the oiled iron barrel seemed to wink at his approach. After a few skittish advances and retreats, Senlin reached down and swatted the tip of the man's spit-polished boot. Kristof gave no sign of waking.

Satisfied that the rotgut had done its work, Senlin returned to the painting. Popping Ogier's canvas free of the gilded frame took little effort, but removing the canvas from its rigid wood stretcher where it was held by dozens of staples proved to be a challenge. He undid his belt, pulled it from his pant loops, and used the prong of the buckle to pry loose the wire horseshoes around the edge of the painting. He kept one eye on the snoring Kristof as he labored.

He'd smuggled Ogier's copy in by rolling it around the long grappa bottle, the back of the canvas facing out. For all intents and purposes, it looked like an oversized label. He had affixed the canvas to the bottle with a nearly imperceptible seal of wax, and then redrawn the crude label in pencil. The result was reasonably convincing: It looked like the swill anyone might buy on the street.

Now, Senlin unfurled the copy and fitted it to the newly empty stretcher. Replacing the staples proved more difficult than he'd expected. His fingers quickly began to throb from pressing staples back into place. If one became stuck, Senlin was forced to go through the nerve-racking process of tapping the staple with the butt of the wine bottle. The chore took a quarter hour to finish, and erasing the label took another few minutes. But in the end, the painting appeared straight, flush, and centered when viewed from the front.

The back of the painting was another matter entirely. If it were ever removed from its frame, his hackwork would be immediately apparent. There was nothing to do about it now. He could only hope the painting would hang with its back to the wall for decades to come.

He scrolled the original around the dark bottle with the painting facing in. He softened the nub of wax he'd brought with Ogier's match, and rubbed it on the seam to seal the new, blank wrapper in place. He didn't have time to redraw the label's heraldry, and he doubted that Ogier would forgive him for defacing even the reverse of his masterpiece. Senlin could only pack the bottle back in his satchel and hope that Kristof didn't peer too closely when he conducted his exit inspection. With any luck, the man would be too drunk to uncross his eyes.

The swap complete, Senlin sat again with the easel before him, his notebook casually open on his lap, the sunlight lapping warmly at his nape and the tips of his ears. Having stared so long at the original, Senlin immediately recognized the copy for what it was: an inferior vision. The copy was by no means artless, and had he never seen the original, it might have even seemed a work of modest accomplishment. But he had seen the original. In the imitation, the girl's proportions seemed a little inelegant and dwarfish. The water, though heavily highlighted, appeared flat. The once magnificent, tantalizing shadow beneath her seemed now an inconsequential gloom. The composition, palette, and style were all similar to the original, but Senlin could understand, almost, how Ogier had become obsessed with the one and indifferent to the other.

It was a half hour more before Kristof snorted himself awake. He roughly cleared his throat and rubbed his mouth. His eyes winked and slowly returned to a concerted blinking. Rising in the same leaning fashion that he had descended, he straightened his cap and pulled on the hem of his coat. He resumed his circuit around the room as if he had never paused.

When he came up behind Senlin seated before the forgery, the agent stopped. Senlin felt the man's presence swell behind him. Perhaps it had dawned on Kristof that Senlin had been too generous with the brandy, suspiciously generous, in fact. Kristof might, even at that moment, be moving his hand to the grip of his flintlock, was even now sighting the back of Senlin's head, ready to earn the commendation that awaited him. Senlin squeezed his eyes shut.

And he stayed like that until Kristof's voice forced him to steal a glance over his shoulder. He found Kristof leaning on the rail, staring indolently down at the Market, his head rolling dreamily from side to side. "I would've liked to have been a merchant. The travel, the exotic, sunburnt women, the fresh beef, the rain, and the puddles," Kristof said, breaking his long silence. "I have never tasted a fish that wasn't salted or drowned in oil."

"You were born in the Tower?" Senlin said, relieved that Kristof seemed oblivious of the forgery.

"Of course. In the House of Pell, long may it stand." The agent pointed up with his thumb and then flicked the tip of his nose with it. "My mother had hoped I would climb a little higher over the course of my career. Become a chancellor or a duke or a lord of port. But it turned out that I wasn't very good at bowing and scraping, and that was two-thirds of high society, though I liked the other third," he said with a wink and a drinking gesture. "And now, Mr. Mud-Boots, I'm ready to ask my question."

A little charmed by Kristof's confiding tone, Senlin replied, "All right."

"I was a lookout on the *Ararat*. I kept her from running into trouble: wind shear and pirates. I had the eyes for it and a head for understanding the signs: bird swoops and cloud breaks and the little funnels that devil the sands. Personally, I don't care one way or another if you want to steal the commissioner's painting, Mr. Mud-Boots. But I am curious, are you toadying for the House of Algez, or are you a lone wolf?"

Senlin nearly leapt up but managed to only stiffen his back a little. He kept all trace of surprise from his voice. "I don't know what you mean."

Kristof turned to face Senlin, who still craned awkwardly around in his chair. His mustache seemed now a theatrical frown. "Look, I'm tired of making life easy for Commandant Snot. He has made life so tedious for me." Senlin recognized a seditious bitterness in Kristof's expression, and it gave him a glimmer of hope. "Every post I draw is twice as dull as the last. If I turned you in, I don't doubt Pound would reward me by shifting my patrol to the Fountain toilets."

Kristof sounded almost sober now, though he still sawed a little on his feet. "I know you aren't an Ostrich because your arms aren't branded. If you came up from the dirt, you must be fairly clever, probably quick with a bribe or handy with a sidearm." The fact that Kristof's estimation flew so far above Senlin's accomplishment came as a surprise. But this surprise was quickly trumped when Kristof drew his pistol, though without much haste. "Your boots were stitched in Algez. I saw the *A* stamped on your insole. Which may mean nothing; Algez boots are sold here and there, I hear. It may be a coincidence. Or it may mean that your credentials were forged and you're a spy of the House of Algez."

The accusation baffled Senlin. He had never read or heard a word about Algez. The angle of Kristof's gun made it difficult to think. He doubted that a denial would convince the agent, and he was too flustered to think of a convincing lie. So he blurted, "I am the headmaster of the only school in a fishing village called Isaugh. I came here on my honeymoon with my wife, but I have lost her. The original artist, who is withholding information about my lost wife, coerced me into stealing this painting for him. I am only doing this for my wife."

Using the barrel of his pistol, Kristof knocked his cap back on his head and scratched his brow with the bead of the gun. "You're a good liar."

The same attentiveness and suspicion that made Kristof a successful lookout also apparently blinded him to honesty. Which was probably just as well. Senlin could think of nothing to say except "Thank you."

"I wish you were half as good at painting. This is a terrible forgery. The commissioner will spot it, or one of his beetle-brained curators will. How much money do you have?"

"I have two and a half shekels to my name."

"A very poor pirate. Imagine that! For two and a half shek, I can give you an hour's head start." Kristof holstered his pistol and asked, "Do I smell of drink?"

"Strongly," Senlin said, straightening his arm as he dug into the pockets of his trousers and coat. He placed the last of his coins in Kristof's palm.

"Then I will give you two hours." Kristof shooed Senlin from his chair with an exhausted sweep of his arm and sat down with a grunt. "If you ever decide that you do work for the House of Algez, tell them that I'll entertain offers. I'd make an excellent rat."

Senlin refused to run at the door, though his heart beat at him to do just that. Instead, he walked with determined and loping steps, like a king at his coronation. He would not run. He would not.

Kristof called after him when he'd reached the door, and Senlin turned to find him pointing at the painting with a smile that was yellow as old ivory. "Why does the dwarf walk on the water?" he said, a hiccup turning into a belch.

Chapter Ten

The Baths are like a chrysalis. Exhausted men and women wrap the Baths about them and, in a fortnight, are transformed. One may come in a worm and go out a butterfly.

—*Everyman's Guide to the Tower of Babel*, V. III

The Customs Bureau building was crowded now with the changing of the shifts. A cacophony of boots, exaggerated by the odd acoustics of the corridors, drummed everywhere like an unbalanced engine. The air was thick with the musk of leather and sweat. No doubt the atmosphere would've been toxic to (what had Kristof called him?) *Commandant Snot.*

Senlin couldn't help but imagine that the agents leered at him more knowingly now. He came around a blind corner and collided with a man who stood a head shorter than him. It was a minor bump, but Senlin felt like a train had struck him.

The man, dressed in white, craned his neck back and peered at Senlin from under the frayed brim of a straw hat. His unwrinkled, poreless complexion reminded Senlin of a boiled egg, and his large round teeth seemed to have been worn down by habitual gnawing, as if he made a point of worrying the bones left on his dinner plate. The Red Hand's pale blue eyes were distant, almost sleepy. "Isn't he tall! Yes, quite the specimen; prominent brow, thin lips," the Red Hand said in a low, meditative grumble. "Sharp chin and cheeks—such a tragic

Josiah Bancroft

visage! Must be from the land of cod and ballads and lighthouses. Like something straight out of a textbook: Eastern Ur Male."

The Red Hand's deduction was startling in its accuracy. Even amid his shock, Senlin couldn't help but be impressed by the man's intelligence. But before Senlin could formulate a coherent reply, the Red Hand swept past him, his hands balled in his pockets, the soles of his leather sandals clucking against his heels. Senlin gulped at the lump in his throat and hurried on.

He could only hope that Kristof was as good as his word. Though, really, what were two hours worth? He'd planned on it being weeks before the forgery was discovered, had planned to borrow a little money from Tarrou and collect Marya and be halfway down the Tower before the commissioner could loose his hounds. He'd planned to vanish into the human maze, Marya clutched to his side—not just clutched, but also tied, like the old spinster sisters had been lashed together in the Market. But so much had gone wrong.

A chorus of bells rang three o'clock as he exited again onto the gloomy street. His satchel seemed to pull at his neck like a millstone, the bottle biting into his hip like a riding crop. Many blocks stood between him and the bench by the glittering reservoir where he was to meet Ogier. He had no choice but to run.

If the painter turned out to be a liar or a villain, if it turned out that he was behind Marya's present difficulties, and all of this had been a ruse to trick Senlin into doing his dirty work, Senlin wasn't sure what he would do. He might strangle Ogier in the streets, right in front of everyone. He wondered if a single soul would try to stop him, or if the tourists and drudges would part and pretend to look away. The thought horrified him.

For the moment, he was still anonymous. No one paid his hurry much attention. He dashed like a rabbit between the curbs of the street, bounding over the gutters full of sudsy gray water and dodging the crones and wenches toting laundry baskets. He apologized until it became a string of indiscriminate pardons. By the time his feet struck the clean flagstones of the mall that ringed the reservoir, he was shining with sweat.

190

The promenade was overflowing with vendors. The gaps between booths, which were buried under produce, tonics, and soaps, were clogged with wagons at almost every end. He could hardly squeeze through. He veered toward the shoreline where the crowd appeared, for the moment, more fluid, and regretted the decision as soon as he saw what had parted the crowd. Customs agents encircled a man, freshly shaved and stripped to the waist. A basket of coal sat at his feet. Senlin had stumbled upon the making of a hod.

When he saw who was reading the declaration of the man's crimes, he stopped dead. It was Commissioner Pound, dressed just as he had for the ball, in a black suit that seemed to have shrunk a few sizes. He wore his nightmarish gas mask. The lenses over his eyes were as black as the bottom of a well. They seemed to stare straight at Senlin, and the illusion made his skin crawl.

It was unfair. As hard and as far as he had searched, he could not find Marya, and yet he could not stop running headlong into his enemies.

Senlin tried to dissolve back into the crowd but found himself hemmed in between a wagon that was filled with fragrant melons and a perimeter of children in striped bathing suits, all gawking at the poor, ruined man. His crime was apparently entirely one of debt: The commissioner read a list of the man's unpaid bills to restaurants, clothiers, dance halls, theaters, hotels, and every other trap of pleasure the Baths had to offer. Senlin didn't doubt that the charges were exaggerated like those recited at the boy's execution. Regardless, this wasn't his tragedy, and he hadn't time to share in the man's misery. He'd be joining him soon enough if he didn't hurry.

Senlin dug his forearm into the crowd, trying to open a gap. His efforts were rewarded by one of the children slamming her heel down on his toe. He let out a pained yelp, and the commissioner's litany halted. The cans of the gas mask whipped about and pointed at him. Pound called, "Mr. Senlin! Mr. Senlin. I'm so glad I caught you." The words froze his blood, and the children recoiled from him. He felt as if he'd been shoved onto a stage. "I've heard that you have been very active in your notes. Good. I like a thorough scholar. A man who makes up his own mind can be trusted. Is it done fuming?"

Senlin nodded, relieved that he had not yet been discovered. "The sun is doing its work. Your Ogier is nearly cured." He rubbed at his nose and sniffed daintily several times. "It has been exhausting for me, but I have drafted some excellent impressions."

"Excellent impressions!" Pound echoed, and slapped the decree he'd been reading against the chest of an unprepared agent. The agent fumbled to catch the papers before they spilled. "It occurred to me that perhaps an interview would make a nice frame for your article. Bald facts are so dull. We should sit down and discuss my thoughts on the art world."

"Yes, indeed. Of course," Senlin said eagerly. The minutes were slipping by. What if Marya wasn't conveniently placed? What if she was locked in a room across the Baths or sitting in a tub in the Fountain? It might take him hours to find her even if Ogier knew exactly where she was staying. He'd have to sneak about town like a thief. As a thief, in fact.

To Senlin's relief, the commissioner was already losing interest. The headmaster was preparing a bow when the bare-chested, swarthy wretch, the newly made hod, leapt through the agents and grabbed Senlin by the coat. He pulled Senlin into a fierce embrace and dug his fingers into his back. Senlin's revulsion was automatic: He turned his head and fought to bring his arms up between them, but the hod only gripped him more tightly.

"My friend, it is me!"

Senlin turned back to reexamine the man's wide face, threaded with sweat and blood from where the unforgiving razor had scored his scalp and cheeks.

Without his imperial beard or his iron mane, Tarrou seemed now like a ghost cut from its shell. Only his slate eyes and warm baritone were recognizable.

Senlin quickly turned back to the commissioner. "Commissioner Pound, there must be some mistake. This is Tarrou! He was in your home two nights ago."

"I am just as surprised as you, Mr. Senlin. There is no mistake;

ledgers do not lie. He has not paid his bills in more than a month and yet has gone on living like a sheikh."

Senlin thought of all those dinners and bottles his friend had bought for the two of them. He had been stubbornly generous. "So, he is a little tardy; I'm sure he will pay his debts now." Senlin gripped his friend's hard shoulders. "This is no time to be shy with your wallet. Out with it!"

"I cannot," Tarrou said. All his humor, his acid wit, was gone. Senlin looked into Tarrou's eyes and saw a man who had passed beyond humiliation, passed through despair and fear. Some primitive kernel had burst open inside him. Tarrou was now livid with rage.

Abruptly, Tarrou roared over Senlin's head at the goggling crowd: "I betrayed myself and my friends. I grew fat and tired." Tarrou gripped the sides of his gut, a softened swell of abandoned muscle. "I drank and danced and soaked myself silly, but I was never free. I was only distracted! I now appear to be what I have been for years: a slave." The crowd blanched when Tarrou, in a gesture of pique, smeared the blood from his scalp down over his eyes. "We have society, but we are alone. We have light, but we have no sun. The Tower sucks our lives and gives us only a little diversion and a little death. Do not accept a little death! Demand a great, booming demise!"

As each phrase burst with more hatred and bile than the last, the men and women who had come to stare, to watch with voyeuristic pleasure, found themselves becoming the focus of attention. The commissioner and his agents watched the audience for any wince of sympathy or revolt. The onlookers stood motionless as startled rabbits. They blinked in the shadow of a hawk.

Amid this horrible tension, Senlin vaguely registered Tarrou's hand passing into his coat pocket. Then Tarrou shoved him so violently he was sent reeling backward against the cowering mob. "And here you only care about your paintings and your book. Academic! Anemic! You are as cowardly as a clam! Your death will go off like a fart!"

Senlin was pained by his friend's abrupt betrayal, and his shock registered baldly on his face. But, in the very next moment, he understood

Tarrou's motive. It wasn't to hurt him; it was to protect him. He was making it apparent that they were not really friends and certainly not coconspirators. Nevertheless, Senlin was shocked by Tarrou's seditious outburst. He had always shied away from political statements, had seemed always afraid that they might be overheard. It was only now, when there was nothing left for him to lose, that Tarrou was free to speak his mind, and it had been, Senlin thought, a fine speech.

The commissioner flicked his hand, and his agents leapt on Tarrou. They swung their black lacquered clubs at his legs, and his knees buckled. A second rain of blows to his back and shoulders made him collapse entirely. Tarrou refused to cry out, even as he was driven into a ball on the ground. Senlin wanted to leap into the frenzy of batons and scrabble down to his friend and split the abuse. But that would make an end of everything. Tarrou's sacrifice would be worthless, and Marya would be lost forever. He would have to be the coward once again, and once again leave a friend behind.

The commissioner casually resumed their conversation. "Come by my home this evening at eight, Mr. Senlin." Pound's voice sounded like a wasp in a can. "Bring a sharp pencil or two. I will add some flamboyance to your facts." He turned from Senlin, concluding the exchange, and pointed at Tarrou where he lay panting raggedly, his eyes already swelling shut. Without a hint of inflection, he said, "Put that in the wall."

In the distance, bells rang the half hour.

Senlin pushed outward with his shoulder. No one tried to stomp on his toes now. They parted before him like water about a stone. Nor did they gawk at him, but only looked down as if they were afraid. And why shouldn't they be afraid? Ruin was contagious. If Tarrou, who was so well liked, could be ruined so summarily, undefended by anyone, what hope did anyone have?

Marya. What hope was there for her?

Senlin found the artist sitting on the bench by the shore, as promised, the sleeves of his paint-spattered smock tied up around his elbows. Ogier sat with his hands in his lap, a serene, unfocused expression on his face. He would seem, to the casual observers, a lamentable sort: a poor hunchbacked outcast. But Senlin knew better. There was nothing about Ogier that deserved pity. Ogier was clever and commanding. He had marched Senlin around easily enough.

When Ogier saw Senlin, he did not stir much but only nodded at the opposite arm of the bench. Senlin sat down and without looking at the artist spoke to the air and the uninterested migrations of bathers. "They have Tarrou. They've turned him into a hod." Turning his head finally toward the painter, Senlin felt his face flush with anger. "I hope the painting is worth it to you. It was not worth it to me." He felt his composure slipping. He wanted very badly to blame the artist, to hold him accountable, and to punish him. "I have only an hour before the alarm is raised because of your incompetent copy."

Senlin watched the plot unravel on the stage of Ogier's face. The painter's expression bloomed and wilted and bloomed again as disbelief and despair ran through him. It was frightening to watch Ogier's confidence collapse, and fascinating to watch him struggle to rebuild it, first with the smoothing of his brow and then the untangling of his mouth. His composure regained, the painter dispensed with his earlier discretion and turned to face Senlin. "Then we haven't time for this. The painting is still around the bottle?"

"Yes," Senlin said, sliding his satchel down the length of the bench. Ogier snatched it quickly, a little alarmed by Senlin's cavalier shuttling of his precious cargo.

"Wait here," Ogier said, and left Senlin on the bench. The artist took the satchel to one of the green-painted bathhouses, hardly larger than an outhouse, paid a dozy attendant two pence for the key, and then disappeared inside.

Several minutes later, Senlin was on the verge of rising and beating the flimsy door of the changing stall in when the artist emerged. Ogier gestured Senlin to his feet. "We must hurry."

"Tell me about Marya," he said with planted feet.

"As we go. There's little time before they will close the ports to trap you here. That will be the commissioner's first move, to tighten the noose." Ogier opened a small paper accordion and consulted the printed grid. He scanned the port schedule for a moment before announcing, "A ferry leaves at the top of the hour from North Port. We'll be pressed to get there in time."

"I haven't any money."

"I will get you aboard."

"Is Marya there, at North Port? Tell me where she is, or I promise you, I will..." His voice quavered, and he gulped. He found he was clinching his fists and bringing them up. Heat ran up his spine like a fuse.

The artist gave Senlin a disarmingly fragile smile. His expression was sympathetic, genuine, and devoid of the arrogance that had seemed permanently chiseled there. It was as if Ogier had, all in a moment, pulled off a hood he'd worn since the first time Senlin had set eyes on him. "I am sorry I had to treat you with such suspicion, but I had to be sure." Bewildered, Senlin dropped his hands, and Ogier pressed on, "This place is full of spies and traitors. I had to be sure you were Marya's husband. You have given me all the proof I need. You would risk anything for her. I will tell you all I know, but we have to leave for North Port this instant. We must hurry without seeming to."

Chapter Eleven

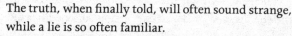

The truth, when finally told, will often sound strange,
while a lie is so often familiar.
—*Everyman's Guide to the Tower of Babel*, V. IV

With their heads drawn so close that they looked like conjoined twins, Ogier and Senlin plowed a way toward North Port. They skirted the agents who prowled among the bathers scrabbling about the perfectly curved shoreline. They didn't dare run. Brass music brayed from an unseen bandstand, the piccolo rising shrilly over the joyless band. The afternoon sun no longer dazzled but seemed rather like a scaly disease that scabbed the tourists and blighted the pastel hotels. The Fountain vented steam like a factory stack. A girl selling oranges from her apron, still years from womanhood, was trying to evade a cotton-headed, lecherous gentleman who tried to pinch her hips and stroke her hair. The girl dropped the corners of her apron, letting the oranges fall and bounce and roll underfoot as she made a nimble escape. Senlin thought of his own students for the first time in weeks. The memory seemed like a fable: an ancient and unsophisticated ideal. He used to occasionally dream of bringing his class to the Tower of Babel on a grand field trip. Now he couldn't imagine anything more specious.

Through it all, Ogier spoke as if he was reciting a well-rehearsed tale, as if Marya's story had occupied his heart and mind for weeks.

And so it had been.

Marya had surprised Ogier with her interest in his work: how he mixed his paints and organized his palette, how he'd developed his novel, blobby style. She listened keenly to his explanations.

At the conclusion of their first session, Ogier counted out her payment while she dressed. A dazed expression softened her face. One of the many landscapes that leaned against the parapet caught her attention. She approached it and retreated from it as if trying to bring it into focus.

"It's like the mottling of a bird, isn't it?" she said. "It seems one hue from a distance, but up close, there are many colors." Buttoning the cuffs of her yellowing blouse, she turned her attention to the canvas on Ogier's easel. She recognized herself immediately: Her reddish hair was, here and there, flecked with shades of green; her red lips were daubed with blue; and the skin of her bare stomach and breasts was a pastiche of pinks, browns, and purples. She had never seen herself outside of a mirror, and she found this view quite different. "It's not like seeing yourself in a glass at all. Is that what I look like?" she asked with more wonder than doubt.

"To my eye," Ogier said. "Often the most difficult part of painting someone is convincing them that they look like their portrait." It was an unusual conversation. Ogier didn't usually burden his models with his philosophy. The young women who sat for him had neither the interest nor the capacity to make it worth his effort; they came to him for pocket money and nothing more. But this woman radiated an intelligence he rarely saw in the anesthetized crowds of the Baths, so he went on. "Flattery in portraiture guarantees a long but miserable career."

Marya saw the logic in this and nodded as she buttoned the waist of her skirt. "But if you paint us as we wish to appear, we would be unrecognizable. What good is a portrait that doesn't match the subject?"

"Exactly right," Ogier said. "One has to tell lies that don't hide the truth."

By the time she left, Ogier was a little charmed by her curiosity and wit. Again, he found himself wondering why such a woman would spend an afternoon modeling to make a modest sum. He could only imagine that she was in some trouble.

He wondered if she even realized how much trouble she was in.

When she returned the next morning, he wasn't entirely surprised.

She was less sheepish in her offer to model for him, suggesting that she could be engaged for several days in a row, if he liked. For anyone else, Ogier would've demurred and felt insulted at the suggestion that his inspiration worked on a model's schedule. But the prospect of a longer study, a more complete work, with this astute and exotic woman was enticing. So he agreed. He asked her to pose much as she had the day before, though he fussed more with getting the sheet to drape just so across the back of the chaise lounge. He wanted the work to be larger, to capture her entire figure, but he was hesitant to broach the subject of further disrobing.

A moment later, as if she had read his mind, she emerged from behind the curtain fully undressed, settling on the sofa with the natural grace of a falling leaf. His white and yellow orchids seemed to fan the air about her hair, shoulder, and bosom. He was enthralled.

As he worked, they began a natural dialogue, not like the rapid lisping of gossips, or the conversational tug-of-war between young wits, but rather they talked like two old men playing draughts: with ponderous silences, unspoken consensus, and shrugged replies.

Over the course of the session, Ogier listened as she slowly unspooled her history. He learned of her recent marriage and how her honeymoon had been quickly derailed. She described her first hours alone in the Market, the realization that she was without a ticket or a means of acquiring one, and her quick reasoning that she should ascend to the third level of the Tower, to the Baths, where, after all, she and her husband had planned to spend the majority of their days. She had passed through the beer-slushed streets and waterworks of the Basement. She scavenged a moth-eaten cloak from the gate of a rubbish wagon and wrapped herself in it. Her red sun helmet was entirely too conspicuous, so she kept it tucked under her arm. She spoke to no one in the Basement, and whenever she was approached, she would cough as violently as one dying of consumption. Even notorious-looking men would squint at her and give her a wide berth.

Ogier found her resourcefulness quite entertaining.

She had passed through the Parlor's quagmire in less than a day by affecting the most boring, charmless version of Mrs. Mayfair she could muster. She pretended to fall asleep at the height of their stilted professions of love, and then snorted when she pretended to come awake. She laughed during their arguments and acted as if she had choked on a biscuit when Mr. Mayfair swore, for the second time, his undying love. Her performance was uniformly panned by the other players who, in exasperation, quit the play.

Two days after she'd lost her husband in the Market crowd, she entered the Baths, fearful that she had kept him waiting. (She had no way of knowing that at that moment Senlin was just entering the Basement, blundering through the crowds, his progress slowed first by denial, then by shock.) Very quickly it became apparent that finding her husband among the touring masses and the scores of hotels was a nearly impossible task.

Her initial inquiries were met with either derision or extortion. One hotel purveyor went so far as to propose a corporeal form of payment that Marya might offer in exchange for his assistance. Having spent many hours in pubs among men who'd drown their discretion, Marya knew exactly how to reply to such a proposal and paid the man on both shins with one boot.

As the sun set on her first day in the Baths, realizing that she had to be frugal with the money she had left, Marya asked a young woman selling soaps where she lived. She was directed to a women's boarding house that was run by a mouse-faced old woman named Ms. Curd. The crone's eyes were dark and sharp as pencil lead. Marya installed herself in a closet of a room in the attic of Ms. Curd's house, stowed her money under the mildewed mattress of her coffin-sized bed, and slept in her clothes, too exhausted to dream.

The next day, she took a little pocket money and her red pith helmet and went in search of some professional assistance. She was certain that there had to exist somewhere in the Baths an institution that helped the wayward and the lost. Ms. Curd informed her that there was nothing so organized as a mission, but she suggested that Marya might ask one Mr. Horace Fossor, a retired customs agent known for his social connections, for help. Ms. Curd offered to arrange a brunch meeting at the Crepe House. Marya thanked her profusely, and the beady-eyed woman responded with an arthritic curtsy.

Mr. Fossor, it turned out, was an exceedingly well-mannered man who was free of vice, except for snuff, which he took only with apologies, excusing himself after each inevitable sneeze. He had been handsome once, probably. He was still relatively thin, with the slicked, inky hair of a young man, but his heavy jowls and receded chin betrayed his age.

Marya was hesitant to confide in him, having learned caution from her previous encounters in the Baths, but Mr. Fossor had an uncanny ability of deducing from the vaguest of cues the exact nature of her troubles. It was as if her whole story was written out in her clothes, her subtle shifts, and the timbre of her voice. He guessed her history, and she only had to confirm his suppositions, which she did with some amazement.

Was it some sort of trick, she wanted to know, this ability to guess her history?

"No trick, my dear, just a special attunement," Mr. Fossor said demurely.

He insisted that he be allowed to use his contacts to help locate her husband. He was willing to do this for the very modest retainer of a shekel a day, all of which he would return if he failed to produce her husband in a fortnight. Then he paid for their lunch and departed on his mission even before Marya was entirely committed to it.

But then, what else could she do but accept?

She returned to Ms. Curd's boarding house to budget her remaining funds with this new expense in mind only to find that her cache of money had vanished. She flipped her dank mattress three times before she could believe it. She had been robbed.

Confronting Ms. Curd proved fruitless. Curd proclaimed that all the girls in the house were the worst sort of immoral trollops: Thievery was the least of their sordid habits! Curd assumed Marya would have had more sense than to leave her valuables in a room without locks. "I run a boarding house, not a bank, missy," she said. "Rent's due in the morning."

In a daze, Marya wandered out into the daily furor of the Baths and the mob of shoppers and peddlers that stood as thick as clover. Oh, what she would've given for a patch of grass or tree shade amid the infinitely circling sidewalk! She found a bench by the shore, posed herself politely, and then retreated into thoughts that seethed with self-reproach. How could she have been so stupid? She had ascended the Tower with such clever nimbleness—and now everything turned on a single mistake.

Her only hope was to be quickly reunited with her husband, but the only way to do that was to pay Mr. Fossor his daily allowance to plumb his contacts.

It was at that moment that an artist with paint in his hair thanked her for being such a willing subject for his work. Which brought them, Marya concluded, to their present arrangement: She sat, and Ogier paid her just enough to keep Mr. Fossor on call and her head on a cot.

"I don't suppose you've heard of Mr. Fossor?" Marya asked. "Perhaps overheard his name at a party or a pub?"

"Madam, I am persona non grata in the Baths. I hardly know anyone anymore."

"Being unknown has its advantages." Marya shrugged her shoulder an inch, which seemed an exaggerated gesture under the microscope of the painter's eye.

"Never say that to a painter," Ogier quipped.

At the end of their second session, Marya announced that Mr. Fossor was arranging interviews for later that week.

Ogier was a little disturbed to find that Marya didn't know who she was meeting. All she could tell him was what Mr. Fossor had told her: They were a secret society of altruists, as yet untainted by Babel's immoral influence, who were willing to help the deserving. These were men of principle. They believed in two economies: one material and one eternal, whose currency was goodwill and self-sacrifice. They called themselves the Coterie of Talents, and they had, according to Mr. Fossor, "galleons of gold" at their disposal.

"I've been thrown a lifeline," Marya said, and the relief she felt deepened the corners of her mouth into the dimples of a smile. "Do you know how I prepared for the possibility of our separation? I dyed my hat red! If I'm ever going to find Tom, I'm going to need help. I can't just strut around the cafés, hoping to be spotted. I need help."

Unwilling to cast a shadow on her optimism, Ogier smiled and kept his reservations to himself. For the first time in years, he wished he had a wider society of friends and resources.

The Coterie of Talents: He didn't like the sound of that.

The next day, she arrived in a new dress: a pale blue, strapless gown that flattered her figure and accentuated her slender neck. The dress was free of the usual foofaraw, the frosts of sequins and explosions of feathers that seemed popular of late. It was a classic and stately dress, free of any ornament except for the staging of her décolletage. It was a dangerous dress.

Trying his best to appear undisturbed by her transformation, Ogier asked how the search for her husband was progressing. Marya confided that Mr. Fossor's methods were a little circuitous.

The previous evening, after their session, she'd again met Mr. Fossor at the Crepe House, and he had insisted that they postpone dinner until she'd had a chance to change into her proper evening attire.

"My dear, I have been busy sowing the seeds of your virtue with my friends," Mr. Fossor said, taking a pinch of snuff and turning his head to delicately expel it on the sidewalk. He apologized, and then repeated the process twice more. When he finally regained himself, his eyes were red from sneezing. "I have written dozens of letters on your behest and already there are some in the Coterie, I believe, who have developed an interest in you." He leaned over their table, his jowls pinched in around his earnestly puckered mouth. "One or two of them may be prepared to throw all of their resources behind the search for your husband. Believe me, these are the most principled of men, but they are also practical. They won't endorse someone who appears"—he glanced mournfully at her tattered blouse—"destitute. They have learned that poverty naturally makes a person dishonest. So, they are suspicious. You must appear hopeless but not helpless, if that makes sense. In short, we must polish you."

Marya confessed that all of her luggage had been stolen in the Market and that she was, at present, short on resources. Paying Ms. Curd for room and board and retaining Fossor's services was the limit of her finances.

Fossor immediately, almost eagerly, proposed that he buy her a dress. "I'm sure that your husband will be able to compensate me for any out-of-pocket expenses, and I know a brilliant seamstress who owes me a favor." When Marya argued that she would be uncomfortable being too greatly in his debt, he insisted. "Think of it this way: You must at least give me a chance to succeed. I have already invested so much in this effort. If I fail to find your husband, you may keep or return the dress, as you like." He smiled, his jowls rising a little wolfishly.

Though unhappy with the arrangement, she could not argue with his logic. If she appeared as a pauper, she likely would be treated as one. So, she spent the remainder of the evening being fitted for a new dress, as directed by Fossor, at a rather posh boutique.

While he painted, Ogier listened to her account with increasing alarm. Though he couldn't be sure what Fossor's true motives were, he doubted very much the existence of a coterie of wealthy philanthropists. No matter how these nobles preferred to dress their charity or what currency they preferred to deal in, there was only one economy in the Tower, and it was not the eternal sort.

"Tonight, I am to be introduced to some of Mr. Fossor's friends," Marya said, redressing at the conclusion of the session. Ogier frowned as he squeezed the paint from his brushes and stirred them in baths of turpentine. His scowling made Marya worry that he was unhappy with the work or with her modeling.

Ogier reassured her. "No, it's coming along fine," he said, gesturing at the canvas and the emerging, almost spectral figure. He was pleased with the proportions and the tone of the work, though he was still dissatisfied with her expression, which seemed conflicted: Her mouth smiled with a natural grace while her eyes appeared to glare intensely. "It will be a great work, I'm sure, I hope. No, I am worried about you. Are you sure this Mr. Fossor has your interests at heart?"

"Most likely he does not," Marya admitted. "He seems greedy and vain and a little shallow minded. I'm sure he'll squeeze every last cent from Tom, but it is only money."

"The rich say the same thing, but they never mean it," Ogier said, and paid her for her day's work.

Chapter Twelve

One shouldn't feel compelled to attend every ball, or accept every proposal, or finish every glass that is raised. The sun is sometimes brighter when watched from the shadows. Sometimes to enjoy a scene fully, we must first retreat a little way.

—*Everyman's Guide to the Tower of Babel*, V. XIV

Senlin's heart felt like the air bubble of a level: It slid up and down his throat, searching for a center that had apparently vanished.

It was Ogier's description of the pastel blue of her dress that did it, that made him recall the queer, half-blacked-out book he had saved from destruction weeks ago. *The Wifemonger's Confession*, or whatever it had been called, had recounted a theory of color that had, at the time, seemed impossibly esoteric. Now, he was not so sure.

The marble faces of hotels seethed with the embers of afternoon light. Senlin clung to Ogier's arm, and they barreled on under the shadows of marquees of dance halls and dinner clubs, the shadows appearing moth-chewed under the mirror lamps turning above like disembodied eyes.

The next few days continued in much the same way. Marya arrived in the morning and departed midafternoon. During their occasional breaks, Ogier made tea and set out pastries that she would eat while he smoked cigarettes. They looked out from their rooftop fort, guarded by orchids, timeworn tapestries, and exquisite fumes, and felt serene.

Marya was a natural model: She was aware of her figure but not enamored of it; she was at ease without being limp. The resulting pose was more beautiful than anything the younger maids had ever achieved.

And always, while he sat mixing his paint and laboring over her obscure expression, dropping in and wiping off a dozen failed strokes, she regaled him with reports of her evenings.

Every evening she would accompany Mr. Fossor to a different private party. Fossor selected their ports of call and, when she inquired, refused to explain how he chose them. These soirees, as he called them, were mostly held in lavish rented drawing rooms and parlors, which were invariably wallpapered with silk and gold leaf or silver foil.

The soirees were more staid than a gala but less formal than a dinner. A few dozen well-groomed men and primly arrayed women, apparently all strangers, would be in attendance. There was always a gregarious, tireless host, who did not so much mingle as stir the room. And there was little for her to do but sit around and nod and smile and glance wistfully at the piano. There was always a piano, and without fail, it was abused by a parade of unshy amateurs and tone-deaf flirts. It was torture. If any one of them sat down at the upright piano in the Blue Tattoo public house, they would've been booed into a weeping pulp.

Before each evening began, Mr. Fossor ritualistically repeated thorough directions of how she must conduct herself. She had to wait to be approached by the other guests. She wasn't to mention her grave circumstance or make any reference to her tragedy unless asked directly. Fossor would broach the subject of her need when appropriate; Marya only had to be charming and to appear deserving of attention and assistance. "They are, my dear, very discreet people. The Talents are extremely generous, but they think charity crass. They prefer patronage." He emphasized the word with a wag of his jowls.

Marya was a little offended by Fossor's lack of faith in her social polish, but being generally ignorant of this society, she imagined there were probably a few points of etiquette with which she was unacquainted. "And, please, please, my dear, do not converse with any of the other young ladies. Their families are very protective and will be nervous at how an...exotically grown young woman like yourself might influence their sisters and daughters. I know it is ridiculous, but it will save me from having to smooth many feathers if you will just keep to yourself."

Exotically grown. He made her sound like a white stoat, or a nugget of amber, or a desert lemon tree. Marya couldn't imagine a more dreary and counterproductive way to conduct herself at a party. But she dutifully kept his council. At least, she did for several nights.

The first few evenings, she'd felt a little confused by the gatherings. She smiled and nodded herself dizzy and was generally ignored by everyone. She spent most of the evening eating finger sandwiches and sipping sherry or champagne. She entertained herself by privately inventing stories for the coiffed men dressed in all manner of suits, some courtly, some military, and some comically roguish. She'd never seen so many frilled collars. Every now and then, Mr. Fossor would appear with a captain or courtesan in tow, and Marya, understanding that these were members of the Coterie of Talents, would grace them with what she believed was sparkling banter. Yet, each time, her new acquaintances quickly found a reason to excuse themselves, leaving her alone with Fossor, whose jowls stood on either side of his frown like grim bookends.

It was hard not to be offended; she could only conclude she was doing something wrong, though she couldn't imagine what.

After several evenings of feeling like the appendix of the party, she asked the exasperated Mr. Horace Fossor what she should do differently. In the corner of a conservatory, while a piano was haltingly plunked at by a young man who possessed more humor than talent, Fossor replied in a whisper, "I'm having trouble getting any interest in your circumstance, my dear. It can't be helped, I suppose. You just naturally blend in."

"What did you expect? You won't even let me strike up a conversation.

It is hardly my fault your parties are so dreadful. If I smile any more, my cheeks will shatter," Marya said in a whisper that ran hoarse.

"Is that really the limit of your charm? I thought you were more ingenious than that," Fossor replied sourly, taking a pinch of snuff. He did not excuse himself when he sneezed. She began to worry that he would soon tire of trifling with her predicament and move on to other affairs, other charities. She doubted she could afford a better retainer and did not doubt she would have to return the dress, which seemed her passport to these affairs.

"Let me make a direct appeal, Mr. Fossor. Perhaps a forthright request will be met with more—"

"Out of the question. If I'm caught with a begging woman on my elbow, I'll be ruined for a hundred years. You don't know who these men are. Believe me, they aren't interested in pitiable creatures, in panhandlers and lepers. They are interested in souls that may yet be redeemed. No, obviously I've made a mistake..." A round of tepid applause interrupted them as the amateur's playing faltered to a full stop. "I will make an excuse for us, and we will leave," he said stoically. He didn't give her time to argue before turning away.

Marya described to Ogier in some detail the sudden gall she felt. She knew she had just been summarily dismissed by her champion, ignoble as he surely was, and would be soon left begging. Her decorum had its limits, and in truth, her pride had been pricked at the suggestion that she was too drab a personality to catch anyone's attention. She decided that if she were to be cast from the aristocratic bosom, she would at least make a scene of her exit.

No one in the room took any notice of her smoothing her skirts under her as she lowered herself onto the piano bench, or her momentary petrification at the prospect of playing publicly after weeks of not practicing and with no sheet music to guide her. The only song that came to mind was an old sailor's ballad, a romantic lament that was popular at the Blue Tattoo. It was, she was sure, horribly suited to the refined tastes of her audience, but with little choice and a new impish indifference, she dove into her performance with such force and volume that a gentleman who had been leaning on the piano leapt into his drink as if he'd been burned.

Her voice rang over her fierce playing like a bell in a storm. She abandoned her emotions entirely to the tragic lyrics that described the drowning of a young fisherman and his despondent widow's suicide. She played through the gasps and the smattering of boos; she closed her eyes and sang herself to the brink, sang herself home to the cottage she shared with Tom, dear Tom, sang until his sincere, unsmiling face appeared before her and her heart broke.

Exhausted, she concluded with a drum of bass notes that fell upon a silenced crowd.

When she opened her eyes, a man with a close-cropped blond beard sat on the bench beside her, studying her profile closely. "You play like a deer runs: with terrified grace."

Before she could reply, Fossor was at her elbow, though he seemed more aware of the man at her side than her. "An unusual performance, madam," he said.

"Oh? I was trying so hard to blend in," she replied, enjoying Fossor's uncomfortable squirming. Fossor was about to offer a rejoinder when she turned her back to him and began a closer inspection of the man at her hip. He was richly dressed in a gray wool suit, and his face was handsome though his cheeks still carried a little of their youthful fullness. The beard seemed a means of compensation. "And you, sir, did you find my playing unusual?"

"You meant it to be unusual. You are proud of your strangeness," he said with an intelligent smile, though he seemed a little overly impressed with himself.

"It is better to be pleased by one's own distastefulness than to please another man's tastes," she said, eliciting an unguarded laugh from her new acquaintance.

"Marvelous! Mr. Fossor, you must introduce me to this charming hedonist."

She spent the remainder of the evening conversing with the bearded young aristocrat, under the watchful eye of Mr. Fossor. She was careful to not directly mention her bad fortune or her lost husband, but still dropped discreet hints that she was not without care or need. For his part, he seemed sympathetic to her cause, vague though it was, saying that he was always willing to help a friend.

After they had taken their leave from the party, Fossor expressed his enthusiasm for the man who had occupied himself with her. "He is enormously important, a veritable prince. And he seems very keen on you. I think he is willing to help."

Marya took this as some comfort, though she was still bothered by what seemed a byzantine process. Why were they all behaving like coquets? The man had been evasive about his own background, keeping even his name a secret. Surely local customs couldn't require the omission of one's own name! "What is his name?"

"Be patient, my dear. He is famous and famously private, though I'm sure he will be more open with you in the very near future."

All this Marya confided in Ogier the next morning while she sat for him.

And the morning after that, which would prove to be the last time Ogier ever saw her, she returned again with more stories about the mysterious aristocrat who she called the Count. "I call him that because it bothers him. And I don't see why I should be easy on such a smug young man." She had attended another party, a more exclusive one, and the Count had renewed his fascination with her, devoting most of his time to trading quips with her, with teasing her, with elaborating on the virtues of one sherry vintage over another. The remainder of the attendees seemed annoyed by her monopoly. The Count, oblivious to the scowls of the other young ladies, insisted that she play another song for them, insisted that she take a turn on the veranda with him, and finally insisted that she confide in him her greatest wish.

Overcome with relief to have at last arrived at the point of all their flirtations, Marya said, "I have lost my husband, and I need your help if I'm ever going to find him."

The Count clasped her hands in his own finely gloved hands and immediately agreed. "I will find your husband."

"Oh, that is wonderful! Wonderful! I was beginning to think..."

She trailed off to stop herself from gushing. Their hands, his held over hers like oyster shells about a pearl, leapt joyfully.

To Marya's great delight, the Count promised to produce her husband the following evening.

"Mr. Ogier," Marya said that final day in his company, "I will be reunited with Tom this evening, if the Count has half the influence he pretends to." She, again dressed in her pretty powder-blue dress, came around Ogier's easel to observe the fruit of a week's labor. Ogier pronounced it finished, though he still felt he needed to tinker with the orchid leaves that periscoped over her pale shoulder. She examined herself only briefly before bursting into pealing laughter.

Understandably distraught, Ogier cringed before her as if he had been slapped.

"No, no, it is beautiful. A masterpiece! I was only thinking what Tom will say when I show him how I've spent the interim of our honeymoon. And I will show him. I must!" She laughed again. "Please, let me bring him by tomorrow."

Ogier looked nervous; the eventuality of showing a married man his undressed wife hadn't occurred to him. "I hope he has your sense of humor."

"Absolutely not, but he is the most reasonable man alive. He will accept it as a fact, a strange and complex fact, but a fact nonetheless. He will understand it was this exercise that helped me survive until we were rejoined."

"Then I'll look forward to the introduction," Ogier said, rallying his confidence.

Marya pulled the painter from his chair and embraced him with sisterly vigor. A contented smile pinked her cheeks. "You have saved me. I will never forget it. And it is a wonderful painting. I wish I could see all the world so. You have such a romantic eye."

When she did not return the next morning, Ogier took it as a good sign: Perhaps she had been reunited with her recently betrothed, and in the natural course of the morning, had thought better about exposing her husband (and herself) to the exact means of her survival. He could hardly blame her. Still, Ogier couldn't help feeling a little disappointed. She had been such a liberating, encouraging presence. She had been good for him. Though as he examined his painting of her figure, he had to admit the effort was flawed. His infatuation with her character had colored his re-creation of her: He had captured the ideal but not the woman. This struck him as poetic. She had sat without pretense, and he, without meaning to, had made her appear vain.

Ogier was deliberating whether he should undertake a revision from memory, a risky prospect to say the least, when a young, bearded man interrupted his meditation by bursting onto the rooftop.

He was dressed in an unusual riding outfit, complete with stiff collar and puckered breeches. A red leather belt held the long holster of a pistol with a gold-plated grip. He was closely followed by two others, less richly dressed, each with squared shoulders and sabers swinging at their hips. By Marya's descriptions of him, Ogier recognized the young man as her mysterious Count. They barged into his terrace apartment as if invited. Ogier did not think he should tell them they were not.

"You are Ogier," the Count said without a note of question in his voice. "I have come for the painting you recently completed. Ah, here it is," he said, and positioned himself before the portrait Ogier had been recently critiquing. The paint still gleamed. "I'll be honest, I expected much worse. This is absolutely an adequate likeness, Mr. Ogier. Congratulations. I will pay you ten minas for it; twice what it's worth, surely."

Baffled by the Count's appearance in his home, Ogier didn't immediately grasp the implication of his presence. "Why are you here?"

"Well, when Marya told me how you'd taken advantage of her destitution, my first instinct was to have you killed." His hand dropped to the gold butt of his gun, and for an electrified moment, Ogier believed he would be shot where he stood. "Preying on young women to satisfy some carnal urge is really quite loathsome, Mr. Ogier." The Count moved his hand from his pistol to open his collar a little. He leaned into the painting, his back to the painter, whose eyes darted toward the two men blocking his escape. "But then, a man loathes most what he reviles in himself." Now he turned toward Ogier with a lecherous sneer, and everything became clear to him. "It's no use fighting who we are."

"You haven't found her husband at all," Ogier said.

"I have found him," the Count replied, taking a step back and bowing for cute effect. "I am he, all but sworn." Then, returning to the painting, the Count looked to the bottom corner where Ogier's signature stood in bright black letters. The Count pressed his gloved thumb over the letters, smudging them beyond reading. "I will let you live today because I am trying to be discreet. But if I ever see you again, or hear that you have spoken one word of me or my bride-to-be, I will do to you bodily what I have done to your signature. I will place my thumb upon you and press down. I hope I've been clear." He removed the stained glove, showing the most pristine set of fingers, white as piano keys. "Take the painting," he said to one of his men. The conscript saluted, grasped the painting as if it were a howling infant, and carried it out with arms stretched before him. The Count dropped a felt purse on the painter's table. "You haven't any sketches of her, have you? No other studies?"

Ogier shook his head vigorously.

"If I hear that you do . . ." The Count slapped Ogier violently across the face with his stained glove. While Ogier still stood with a round expression of shock, the Count dropped the glove at his feet, turned on his heel, and marched from the terrace.

Chapter Thirteen

The trade winds climb the Tower along a spiraling, tangled course. Ships do not rise up and down the Tower like plumbs on a line, but rather twist their way up like ivy climbing a tree. *Up* is not at all a straightforward direction.

—*Everyman's Guide to the Tower of Babel*, I. XIII

He had not liked her. He did try to, much as any fair-minded educator worth his salt would try, but she seemed determined to be unlikable and to repel his weary patience like the mountain peak repels the exhausted mountaineer. He finally gave in to her incline and let himself roll down the hill of her unlikableness.

He inherited her from the retiring headmaster, who looked like the very picture of the Old Year, departing with a white beard that was as long as a windsock. Senlin, for his part, looked as much like the New Year personified as he ever would: cheeks still pink and a little plump, eyes polished almost to tears with optimism for the young minds of tomorrow. Mr. Regimond DeSeay, wizened headmaster of fifty-three years and some eleven hundred students, bequeathed Senlin the keys to the schoolhouse one sultry summer morning, the inauguration attended only by a pair of clover-fat rabbits hiding by the hedge.

His thoughts already flying to the grand improvements he would make to this hopelessly antiquated shrine of learning, Senlin expected some final piece of sapient advice from the gray headmaster, who seemed to be still chewing through the residue of his breakfast, though perhaps he was only warming the machinery of his jaw. DeSeay drew a shuddering breath. Senlin leaned in. DeSeay said, "That Marya Berks is a quizzical little turd. Good luck."

Precocious was perhaps a more accurate (and certainly more generous) way of characterizing the young Miss Berks's behavior in class. With chin cupped in her hand and elbow propped upon her desk, she seemed every inch the philosopher, an impression that was only compounded by her limpid eyes and crookedly pursed mouth. But if she was a philosopher, it was only a philosophy of the contrary.

She challenged everything he said, his logic, evidence, and authority, with such torturing persistence that Senlin was driven to punishing her on a near daily basis. First he took away her blotter and inkpot, a privilege of upperclassmen, giving her instead the slate and chalk that were the utensils of the novice. Then he assigned her the zinc pail and towel, which must, every night, skate across the blackboard, squelching all evidence of the day's diagrams. And still she pounded him with insubordinate curiosity: Mightn't the sun be made out of coal? Is zero really a number or is it more like an abstract letter? If we don't know who built the Tower of Babel, could it have been built by some other species of animal that has since gone extinct—a species of ingenious beetle, perhaps?

He moved her desk to the front of the class so that the edge of it touched the front edge of his own, but she was not intimidated by the doubling of his attention and instead took it as an opportunity to criticize the leggy nature of his chalkboard cursive. He turned her desk toward the wall, but she only raised her voice to interject, which made her echo as if she had the tonsils of a giant. None of it seemed to faze her in the slightest. The only thing that changed from day to day was the color of the ribbon lassoed about her hair, which was as ruddy as a maple in autumn.

Having not yet developed the wiles or elephant skin of a seasoned teacher, Senlin's confidence was sorely tested by her schoolgirl interrogations. As that first year passed, he came to loathe the quizzical redhead because he wondered if she wasn't right to question him. Perhaps he was a fraud, an incompetent dolt, and a polluter of future wits.

But then that first summer came—and a little distance with it. With time to build his kites and walk the cliffs and peruse old letters from his beloved professors, he realized the situation was not as insufferable as it seemed. He decided that what Marya Berks lacked was responsibility and difficulty. She was bored. So, he decided to find some entertainment for her.

When the new school year began, but before she had an opportunity to derail his lesson with some ponderous question that was ultimately unanswerable (at least to her satisfaction), Senlin announced that she, Miss Berks, would be his teaching assistant for the fall, and that in particular, she would be in charge of the lessons for the children in the lower levels in the subjects of history and writing. She would conduct her lessons in a back corner of the schoolhouse while Senlin taught the upper levels in the front. Of course, Miss Berks would be responsible for keeping up with her own studies, and there were a half dozen other caveats besides, but Marya was not perturbed in the least. She leapt at the opportunity.

There were false starts and missteps, but soon these were overcome, and Marya was conducting well-organized and well-received lessons on the basics of grammar and the elementary epochs of Ur.

Her inquisitions did not immediately or entirely cease, but the more she taught, the more patience she developed with Senlin's lessons. She was more likely to stay after class to pose her questions privately, and her questions were more likely to be deliberate than contrary. He still found her a little egotistical and pestering, but she was, for the first time, tolerable.

Three years later, Senlin was an established headmaster who no longer suffered the howling insecurity of the amateur, and Marya's youthful thorns had been ground down, allowing humor and grace to bloom. Their relationship became cordial, almost collegial. He would be sorry, he had to admit, to see her go.

Whenever students departed Isaugh for a higher institution of learning, it was tradition that the headmaster see them off. Disliking goodbyes, especially public ones, this was not a favorite duty, so Senlin was prone to forget it. On one or two occasions, he had arrived at the train station just in time to watch the great bouquets of steam erupt from the departing train, much to his small guilt and great relief.

The day of Marya's departure, Senlin was making an effort to forget the train schedule, and was, even a half hour before her embarking, standing atop a ladder plucking clods of grass from the gutter of his cottage, sweating in the mid-July swelter with a handkerchief tied about his head. A spasm of some unfamiliar emotion pulled him off the ladder. He had to see her off. He hadn't time to wash his hands, comb his hair, or change out of his summer breeches and work sleeves. So, he looked like a stable boy running down the great green bank toward the town and the station that lay clear across the valley of the inlet. The villagers he tore past could hardly believe it was their headmaster blurring by. He ran like a startled ostrich, and they were convinced, though not surprised, that he had gone mad.

In all honesty, Senlin was a little surprised himself: He could not say why he was running or grinning as he ran.

His boot soles skidded when they landed on the weathered boards of the train platform. Recalling the handkerchief tied about his head, he hardly had time to whip it off before he spotted Miss Berks, standing beside a steamer trunk, which the local porter was busily weighing and labeling. No ribbon was in her hair today, and her hair stood turned up in a practical bun that made her seem more mature. Her dress was high collared and long sleeved, and the skirts hung nearly to the toes of her boots, which were as bright and black as a collie's nose. Since he spotted her first, he got to see her honest state. And she seemed, he thought, sad.

When she saw him, shuffling now with handkerchief clutched in hand, her look changed entirely. She smiled warmly and said, "You are late, Headmaster."

"Impossible. Headmasters cannot be late," he said. "The sun must be running fast."

This delighted her, and he felt strangely pleased to see it. Soon, they both realized that they had been standing there entirely too long, grinning and swaying and saying nothing else. She rescued them both by saying, "Have you picked a new assistant for the fall?"

"I was thinking I might give Mr. Barret a turn."

She sucked in a breath and grimaced. "Mr. Barret is a bit of a gander."

"Oh, no, he's just unaccustomed to speaking publicly."

"An ideal teacher, then. He can pantomime his lessons," she said, and gave a brief performance with her arms. Senlin was baffled by the laughter, the giggling, that poured from him.

The porter heaved her luggage up the steps of the train car, ignoring both her and Senlin's overtures of assistance, though accepting the two pence she offered him next. The engine began to hiss as the steam built, and the engineer rang the bell, tolling the last passengers aboard.

This, then, would be the awkward part that Senlin so entirely detested. He was in the process of deciding how to offer her his hand, when she settled her own on his shoulder, hiked herself onto the tips of her collie-nosed boots, and kissed him on the mouth.

And then she whisked herself aboard, and he was waving dazedly at the impassive valves of the train and the invisible stain she had left in front of him, standing entirely too near the drive wheel that bathed him in cumulus clouds of steam.

The engine slipped forward on the tracks. The wail of the train harmonized with the hills, and she was gone.

You are late, Headmaster. His mind felt as shriveled and parched as his tongue, which stuck to the roof of his mouth as he shuffled through the gloom of the bore to North Port. A medallion of sunlight swung back and forth hypnotically ahead of him, and then the coin became a saucer, and the saucer grew into a platter. He could smell the salts of the desert air. *You are late, Headmaster,* her voice lisped from behind his eardrum, driving him onward through the husk of the Tower, arm in arm with her confessor. *You are late, Headmaster; you are late.*

North Port had been scalloped from the Tower's facade. The stepped archway reminded him of the band shell of an amphitheater. Broad dock boards fanned out from the opening, leading first to the customs booth before splitting like a trident into three separate piers.

The piers were supported by a great matrix of girding. There was only one airship in the port, and it bore the scars and patches of an old working vessel; it seemed the sort of thing a man might wager in a late night game of cards. It looked like a gray mollusk hanging from a bluish jellyfish.

Judging by the slack posture of the agents who leaned against the blue customs booth, the alarm either had not yet been raised or hadn't spread as far as the ports. A pair of longshoremen unloaded crates from the lone airship, knocking softly against the jute-wrapped pylons. Crowding near the gangplank, which warped violently when men crossed it, was a line of women, apparently waiting for the unloading to finish so they could board. The women, though young, seemed sallow and frail in the firm sunlight.

Ogier handed Senlin a little scrap of paper and then filled his palm with ten shekels. "Give the shekels to the guards and the note to the skipper. He owes me a favor. He won't talk to you, though, so don't bother trying to strike up a conversation. In fact, that's good advice: Say as little as you possibly can. People up there don't like wits, Tom."

Senlin was trying very hard to focus on what Ogier was saying, but he was in such a state of confusion. Questions flew through his mind. He could hardly consider one before the next occurred: Who was the Count? How could he marry a married woman? Was he dangerous? Was he violent? Where did he live?

"New Babel is the nearest port," Ogier said. "That's as far as my favor can carry you."

One question stood out. Really, it was the only question that mattered. "How do I find her?"

"The glove the Count dropped was monogramed with the letters *WHP*. I'm almost certain the *P* stands for Pell. The Pells are more than a family; they are a wealthy and powerful centuries-old dynasty, and unfortunately, there are dozens of minor royals running about, happily abusing the moniker. The Baths are essentially a Pell colony, though the nobles treat it more like a fraternity house. The commissioner is their local enforcer: He flies their crest, the gold astrolabe, collects customs under their authority, and trollies heaps of gold up to their ringdom. If this Count was indeed a Pell, and he certainly was arrogant enough to be, he will take Marya there, to Pella."

A cabin boy on the waiting ferry rang a bell three times, and the women began to file across the treacherous, jouncing gangplank. "Thomas, I am sorry that I couldn't trust you from the beginning. I thought that the Count had sent you. I was sure you were a spy trying to catch me out. I know I tested you viciously. I'm sorry."

An unexpectedly crisp breeze whipped down at them as some jet of higher air shot down the length of the Tower, and for a moment they could not speak over the rush. Senlin set his hand on Ogier's drooped shoulder, thorny with misgrown bones. The wind cleared his mind of questions and incriminations for the moment, and when it had passed, Senlin said, "Thank you for helping Marya. You were wrong, I think, to say the Tower forbids friendship."

Ogier's expression brightened with gratitude. "Yes, friends just in time to never meet again." He turned Senlin by the shoulders and began gently running him down the dock toward the customs booth. "I put a parting gift in your bag." He spoke just behind Senlin's ear. "New Babel is full of villains. Be mindful of my key. It fires a measly pellet and the trigger is not exact, but it may be enough to save you someday. I am afraid you will need it."

"What about you? What if Pound suspects—" Senlin began, but Ogier quickly broke in.

"As much as he might like to, the commissioner won't touch me. There are greater forces at work, and fortunately for me, greater forces need me alive."

"I don't understand," Senlin said.

"And there isn't time to explain. Bon voyage, my friend."

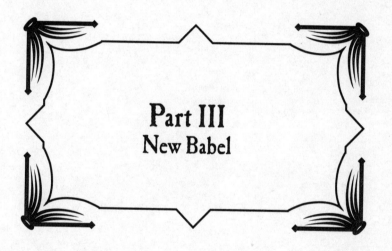

Part III
New Babel

Chapter One

Volume II in the *Everyman* series describes the many marvels of New Babel: the Lightning Nest, the Chrom chapels, its population of exotic moths and bats, and how it earned the titillating nickname the Boudoir. Request a copy from your local bookman today!

—*Everyman's Guide to the Tower of Babel*, V. XXII

The galleon swayed beneath him. Clouds migrated over the distant mountains, dreamily as unherded sheep. Perhaps the ship stood still, and the world swayed. It was hard to tell. He felt their ascent in the building pressure behind his eardrums, but otherwise, flying was not at all the harrowing experience he'd expected. It was quite serene. He recollected reading that serenity was often a symptom of shock. It occurred to him that he was taking the news that Marya had been abducted by a foreign nobleman quite well. Too well. Perhaps he didn't believe it yet, or perhaps he had anticipated a much worse fate for her. She was alive, at least. However it was, for the moment, he didn't care where the feeling of peace came from or how long it would last. The world swam about him like a nursery about a cradle.

The ship was built from materials chosen for their lightness: pine, cord, and wicker. The rail at his elbow and the bench beneath him were both made of bamboo. Everything creaked like old hinges and chirped like crickets. The wind ran through everything. He sat among twenty or so young women in the aft of the ship. His size and relatively fresh clothes made him stick out like a heron among seagulls. Their frocks and sarongs were stained and torn. Their hair was wildly frayed and made worse by the wind that grabbed hold of it and beat it upon their faces. Each had an exhausted expression, the glassy eyes of a deer that had been chased until it collapsed. Bruises and sores and smirches of dirt colored their faces. One woman with wild yellow hair squinted at him amid his observations. She seemed vaguely familiar to him but not in a significant way. She probably had a common face and was only curious what a man was doing on a ferry that was apparently reserved for women. Wrinkling her nose to show she was not impressed by him, she abruptly looked away.

He wondered how these women had been so utterly robbed of their dignity and spark. Had they been lured away from their families? Had they been, like Edith, independent and adventurous once? Had they come to the Tower, or been born to it? He wondered if their present fate was better or worse than Marya's.

The Count, or W. H. Pell, or whoever he was, had gone to some trouble to entice Marya into going with him willingly. Which meant he probably wouldn't hurt her. He might be short on scruples and spoiled by his station and wealth, but the Count didn't seem psychotic. He hadn't killed Ogier, though he easily could have. When Senlin found him—and he would find him—he'd attempt to reason with him first. It might be more difficult for the Count to claim another man's wife if the husband stood present before him.

And if reason didn't work, then what? Senlin attempted to picture himself challenging the Count to a duel, or something similarly brutish and hopeless. He couldn't see it, couldn't even drum up a boast of what it might look like. For a man choked full of esoteric wisdom, he had very little idea what he was capable of. He knew himself but poorly.

So why was it that he kept wriggling through the traps of the Tower, while those about him—Edith, Tarrou—were caught and punished?

They were stronger than him, more resilient, more deserving of a second chance. It hardly seemed fair. Senlin hoped that Ogier would be overlooked, though it seemed unlikely. Pound would be suspicious. He would send his agents to dismantle Ogier's apartment. When they found the stolen painting, the ponderous Red Hand would be engaged; a crowd would gather; a head would come loose.

No. Ogier would escape. He was shrewd and careful; he was not eager to die.

Senlin recalled the gift the painter had mentioned, and indeed, his leather satchel felt heavier than it had any right to be. Senlin undid the brass clasps and peered in. At the bottom, Ogier's key-shaped pistol gleamed with fresh oil. Ogier had called it a jailor's key and had described its original double duty as a prison cell key and a defense against rowdy prisoners. With no lock to fit it to now, it had been reduced to the single purpose of a firearm. Senlin had never loaded or fired a gun in his life. He wondered if it wasn't time to learn.

Carefully replacing the key, Senlin saw an unfamiliar wooden edge. He pulled the paper-backed frame halfway from his bag and recognized the work at once. It was Ogier's nude study of Marya, the contraband he'd kept from the Count. It was the greatest gift he had ever received. The unexpected sight of her face, her iconic smile, made his breath catch. He sat hunched over the painting like it was a flickering candle about to go out. Longing passed through him like a shiver, and a hundred vivid memories of her surged to the forefront of his mind. He stopped the welling emotions with a formal clearing of his throat and slid the frame back into the weathered folds of his attaché.

His only other possessions were the *Guide*, its pages swollen from repeated thumbing, a few humble sundries, and the journal he'd lately bought and begun to fill. If Tarrou had been present for this inventory, he would've remarked that the artist had been cruel to take the bottle of grappa. Senlin winced at the memory of his friend stripped and shaved. Tarrou had looked as pitiful as a bear who'd lost its fur to mange.

He remembered that Tarrou had slipped something into his pocket during the commotion. After a brief rummage, he drew out a piece of stationery that was folded into a small, wrinkled square. He opened it and recognized Tarrou's stately cursive, which grew larger and more rushed toward the letter's end. It read:

My Dear Tom,

Forgive me for being dramatic, but I am done for. The commissioner's Blue Bells are coming for me, and I am sure they mean to take my beard. My debts, both economic and cosmic, have caught up with me. You might say they have caught me by the toe. It is a sad story.

I did try, my friend, to go home. It is a longer tale than I have told. I think you, great grim scowler that you are, will understand how difficult it is to be forthright about sad stories and caught toes.

Ogier is a reliable man. He is insufferable, but reliable. Trust him. I think he never strayed from the course of his conscience. I retired from that path some years ago, and I had lived happily after. Happily, that is, until one mad-as-mud tourist embarrassed me into action. (I hereby confess to all the incidental readers of this letter: I am the mastermind of the plot against the commissioner. Tom is quite innocent; he is far too unimaginative to invent such a conspiracy.)

Tom, as a superior student of the Tower, keep after your wife. It is easier to accept who you've become than to recollect who you were. Go after her.

Drearily Yours,
J. Tarrou

The signature ran off the edge of the page.

He read the letter twice and then released it to the wind. The sheet darted between the bowed heads of the defeated beauties and then vanished through the harp strings of the rigging. The note was better off lost. Senlin didn't understand Tarrou's allusions to the course of conscience or cosmic debt, and he was surprised that he had endorsed Ogier with this, his last gasp of freedom. The final sentiment, however, was not confused. Senlin understood him exactly.

The Tower had seemed as thin as a crack in a mirror from their train car weeks ago. Now, it seemed as broad as the horizon. The edge of the Tower was like the curving limb of a moon. He felt as if they were in orbit about it, felt its immensity and gravity. They flew so near the blond sandstone that Senlin began to wonder what happened when a gas envelope scraped the Tower. Did it pop? Did it burst into flames? Did it just snag open and bleed slowly until the whole kit dropped from the sky? Looking up at the balloon above, he marveled at the fragility of the venture. They dangled from something that looked about as flimsy as a silk camisole.

No one else looked concerned, so Senlin supposed it was all very normal, and so he settled back again into the peace and the respite from terror. The immense blocks of the Tower's edifice were each as large as a room. They were carved with decorative sinuous knots and spattered with ancient flecks of paint. This surface reminded Senlin of an antique rug: a well-made, well-worn artifact. All this splendor was wasted on his fellow passengers, who seemed to find it as dull as an unlit train tunnel.

The ship whooshed along, fast as a frigate, on a coiling course around and up the Tower. They rose like a ribbon around a maypole. It was exhilarating. It was like riding a kite.

The port appeared in the distance, rolling up over the Tower's limb, and the lookout who clung to the jungle of ropes dangling from the gas envelope cried down to the captain: "Port ahead!"

It was coming up fast. In the short time the port was visible before the ship's balloon eclipsed it, Senlin saw that their approach was too low. They would fly far under the platform. He wondered if the captain meant to circle all the way around the Tower again. He wondered how long that would take.

Just as Senlin began to entertain serious doubts about the man at the wheel, the unhurried captain adjusted the furnace, and they shot upward. It felt as if they had stepped out of a raging river. The jet stream became a breeze that puffed them gently away from the Tower. The port reappeared under the horizon of the balloon, and Senlin saw that the breeze had pushed them too far out. They would miss even the tip of the jutting skyport altogether! It was such a dodgy business, this flying of airships.

They were nearly level with the platform when a large kite leapt up from the arms of several dockworkers. It resembled a ship's sail, it was so large, and it carried along a drooping tail of jute rope. The port was sending out a towline.

It was a fascinating process to watch. The kite swooped toward them while the ship's lookout reached for it with a boat hook. After a few failed attempts, the lookout managed to snag the towline. He drew it in and cut the little leash that connected the jute tether to the kite's silk line, and the kite leapt away from the ship.

Looping the towline about the rigging to keep from being snatched overboard by its awkward, swinging weight, the lookout slid down to the deck. He wrapped the line about a cleat while the captain unspooled a red flag on a short stick and waved it at the port. The dockworkers began to work a winch, drawing the ship out of the thermal vent and into a slip.

The platform sat on a triangle of rusting trestlework and was perhaps a hundred yards long and a quarter as wide. Yardarms stood like naked trees on a mall. Dockworkers unloaded sacks from the only other ship that was currently docked. The entrance to the Tower, unlike the band shell of the Baths' port, was a humble, undecorated arch.

Two mooring arms stretched under the slip they were being reeled into, and dockhands slid out onto these prongs, legs dangling over the naked abyss. They caught and secured the ship's anchors. The crew of the ferry threw lines to waiting stevedores, who coiled them about iron bollards, each one substantial as a forty-two-pound cannonball.

The women stood and filed off. Their silence was almost funereal. All were under the trance of a private despair. Not knowing what else to do, Senlin fell into line with them. A stevedore in leather overalls waved at them to follow him, and they began to wind through a maze of pallets and crates toward the Tower and the entrance of New Babel, which, admittedly, held all the charm of a cave.

The impression of this skyport was much different than the commissioner's ports, which were clean, regimented, and lovely in their way. Here, open crates of produce attracted pillars of flies, coal dust crunched underfoot, and the lanes were cluttered with empty pallets, cracked kegs, and the legs of drowsing, lazy men. The customs gate was a crooked post with a board nailed atop it. An oafish man leaned on the cobbled pulpit, a menacing sneer hooking his lip. Senlin saw no tourists, no gentry, only a mass of hard-worn men. He wondered who could possibly be in charge of such a shambles.

The oaf was dressed mostly in old leather and heavy denim. His gray-brown beard blended into his collar of rabbit fur. He looked like a trapper from some remote mountainside. It might've seemed comical in another setting, but here in the open air, in the beating sun, in this friendless place, the man was every inch a terror.

The oaf processed the line of women as if they were livestock in a market. He felt their necks for plague lumps, checked their arms for the telltale brand of the Parlor, and rubbed his grimy finger along their teeth. The women had to confess their names and sign his registry. They were then swatted unkindly on the posterior, and the oaf moved on to manhandle the next in line.

Once cleared, the women were loaded onto the open bed of an unusual wagon. Where one would expect to see horses or mules or oxen, there was instead an engine, shaped and sized roughly like a buggy, which burped steam and jittered on its two axles. Its rear wheels were broad and treaded with steel chevrons, while the front wheels were small and apparently made of rubber. It was a liberated train. A rail-less car. An autowagon! Despite everything, Senlin wanted to run over and inspect its ticking gauges and valves, its blustering pistons...

"You're an ugly woman," the oaf said. Senlin looked around with a start, surprised to find himself at the head of the line.

Before Senlin's brain had a chance to censor it, his mouth ejected the reply, "Whatever you say, sister."

The only person more surprised by this blurt than Senlin was the oaf, who gave a startled snort. "Just what the Boudoir needs. Another comedian!" The oaf snatched Senlin's bag from him before he could react. He stirred the satchel with his hairy arm and pulled out the *Everyman's Guide*. Snorting again, he held up the book to show a taller, grimmer sentry who stood behind him with arms folded. Senlin looked again at the second guard, or agent, or gate-keeper, or whatever, who he'd at first mistaken for a man. She was, in fact, a square-shouldered amazon, who was every bit as broad as Tarrou and half a hand taller. Much older than the women who'd lately filed off the barge, she had the smooth eyelids and wide fore-head common among the natives of the grim arctic ring. Her short hair appeared to have been cut by a blind man wielding a sickle and was the color of ashes. She wore a thick chain wrapped about her waist three times as if it were a perfectly acceptable belt. Senlin couldn't look away.

"Look, Iren! I found his jokebook," the oaf said. The amazon's wide brow showed no wrinkling hint of amusement. The oaf cocked his arm and threw the *Guide* over Senlin's head in one deft gesture. The book fluttered open like a bird and dropped over the port edge into the blue.

Though surprised, Senlin was not particularly sad to see the *Guide* go. He had clung to it once, and desperately, for all the good it had done him. "Old jokes," he said.

The oaf showed no interest in Senlin's leather-bound book of notes or the jailor's key, which he mercifully mistook for its apparent func-tion, but he homed in on Ogier's painting. Turning the frame toward the light, he whistled horribly. As Senlin watched, he ran his thumb over the image. "You filthy beggar! Smuggling in a nudie." The oaf moved to drop the painting into a barrel that overflowed with pocket watches, lockets, ivory combs, and other valuables. It was a trove of mementos.

A tiny explosion went off in Senlin's head, like a popping kernel of corn.

He grabbed the oaf's wrist with one hand and the painting with the other. The oaf clutched Senlin's throat, the skin of his hand rough as coral. His smirk was gone. There was nothing so hot as murder in the oaf's eyes. His gaze was indifferent. He might just as well be untying a difficult knot as strangling a man.

Though starved for breath, Senlin refused to slacken his grip on the painting. He feared the frame might wishbone apart in their hands, but he would sooner be thrown by the neck over the precipice than let go of her image. This came as something of a surprise to him; he had reached the limit of his cowardice. So, they stood like two warring crabs, claws locked.

The oaf, surprised by Senlin's determination, slowly let his yellow dam of teeth show. "I can respect a man who loves his nudies more than his life." He released Senlin's throat and dropped the painting back into his satchel. Then, even while Senlin gasped the color back into his cheeks, the oaf asked, "Name?"

"Mud," Senlin said hoarsely.

"Mud it is," the guard said, and turned his ledger toward Senlin. A spike of a pencil lead lay in the margin. "Make your mark, Mud." The ledger was filled with scrawled X's and hieroglyphic jots. There wasn't an honest signature in the book. Senlin wetted the tip of the nubbin of lead on his tongue and drew out the most glamorous, flourished signature he could muster: Thomas Senlin Mudd, Doctor of Letters. He dropped the pencil back in the book with a daring wink. He felt a little mad.

The guard wrinkled his lip at Senlin's efforts. "Oh, a gentleman's come up on the whore barge. Make way for Doctor Thomas Senlin Mudd!" he hollered through a cupped hand.

Senlin was feeling bold and a little pleased with himself right up until the moment that the amazon's head swiveled toward him like a stone gargoyle that had sprung to life, her formerly unfocused eyes now clear as a hawk's. She said in a clear and chilling baritone, "You are Tom Senlin." It wasn't a question.

Something told him that he should recover his old cowardice and run.

Chapter Two

The simplest way to make the world mysterious and
terrifying to a man is to chase him through it.
—*Every Man's Tower, One Man's Travails*
by T. Senlin

The tunnel was so rough and uneven that it appeared to have
been chewed out by a monstrous worm. There were no brass
rails, or arabesque carpets, or white wainscoting here. The passage was as unglamorous as a mineshaft. Engine steam clung to the
stone like fog upon glass, so every step forward ended in a reckless,
unsteady skid. A chain of electric bulbs, yellow as egg yolks and
hardly more illuminating, hung from the ceiling. Through the gloom,
Senlin saw no alcoves to hide in and no intersections to dart down.
The only way to escape the amazon at his heels, her chains jangling
like a tambourine, was to outrun her.

A dark, rocking mass blocked and scattered the light ahead. It was
the autowagon. As it passed under a bulb, the elaborate shadows of a
dozen women animated the walls. Plodding at a wounded pace, the
autowagon was as good as a dead end. Any attempt at going around it
would almost certainly end in Senlin being crushed against the rock
wall. He had no choice but to go over it. He leapt onto the wagon's
bumper, crying, "Coming through! Aside! Aside!" as he threw his leg
over the gate.

Already packed to the bed rails like refugees on an ocean raft, the women's frustration suddenly erupted. Those who could find room to raise their arms swung at him, catching him under the ear, in the ribs, between his shoulder blades; others cursed shrilly into his ear. He wedged between their hips, offering a string of apologies. Their anger had one positive effect, at least: The frenzy made it impossible for the amazon to mount the cart. She was being rebuffed by a slew of kicks and stomps. She seemed hesitant to throw these women aside, though Senlin had no doubt that she could part them as easily as a lion parts the grass.

Senlin took that instant of confusion to scramble up the back of the driver's box. He set his toe on the transom, gripped the seat irons, and hoisted himself up. The driver, whose white fringe of hair whiffled in the steam of the engine, was startled by Senlin's appearance on the seat beside him. He gave a phlegmy caw and cowered to the corner of the bench like a kicked dog. Senlin apologized again, though the clamor of the pistons swallowed up his words. The engine was awkwardly placed in a yammering stack before them, obscuring much of the tunnel floor and the string of lights with great mushrooms of steam.

Realizing the only escape lay over the engine, Senlin hunted about for a foothold among the spearing rods and racing belts. He put his boot forward tentatively and had it knocked away by the arm of a piston. His cuff snagged upon something at his hip. Craning about, he saw what his cuff was hung upon. A powerful hand reached over the heads of the incensed passengers. The amazon bolted him with a pitiless stare, tightened her grip, and seemed about to yank him down, when one of the women dug her teeth into the crook of the amazon's arm.

Her grip flinched just long enough for Senlin to hike himself free. There was no time to hesitate now. He drew his legs up beneath him and laid a hand on the lime-scaled dome of the boiler. A tremendous shock ran up his arm as the boiler scorched his skin, but he did not recoil. He threw himself forward, vaulting the front block of the dynamo like a boy leaping a fence.

It was a miracle he didn't snap both ankles when he landed or fall under the wheels of the plodding autowagon. Somehow, he kept his feet under him. He bunched his seared hand into a fist, as if he might squeeze the throbbing pain smaller, and ran on.

Soon, the passage opened upon a chamber, large as a city block, into which a chaotic station yard had been stuffed. Dozens of porters swarmed to unload carts and sleds. Drivers struggled to get wagons turned around in the graveled yard, while other men sat atop ziggurats of crates, drinking from bottles and heckling their friends. What Senlin initially mistook for the start of a riot turned out to be a raucous game of cards being played atop a pickle barrel. An austere two-story building, the only structure in the chamber, stood like a deaf grandfather amid the furor, its white plaster gables and square exposed beams looking every bit as old as the chisel marks in the chamber walls. For a moment he was amused to think that this charmless cave had been flattered with the namesake of "New Babel." But quickly, he recognized the space for what it was: a minor cavity in the Tower's immense superstructure. He had not yet come upon the ringdom of New Babel. This was a weigh station. He plunged ahead, satchel gripped to his chest.

It was not unlike picking one's way across a cow pasture: He had to pay particular attention to where he set his feet. He stepped over a little avalanche of rotting apples, danced between spatters of wet tar, and shuffled through a spill of iron filings, which seemed ideal for transmitting a fatal infection. While he negotiated the pitfalls of the station yard, he began to wonder why the amazon was chasing him. She had responded to his name as if she were waiting to hear it. Senlin reviewed his meager list of enemies. It seemed unlikely that she worked for the commissioner. Even if his influence stretched as far as New Babel, word of Senlin's burglary could not have traveled faster than he had.

Perhaps the amazon answered to the mysterious Count. The Count knew of his marriage rival and might have reasonably concluded that it would be easier to have Senlin killed than to risk an eventual confrontation. But then, the Count had no way of knowing which course Senlin would take. There were dozens of ports and gates, hundreds, perhaps. How could he possibly cover them all? And, more to the point, why would he bother? In the grand scheme, the Count had little to fear from a penniless, powerless cuckold of a lowly fish town.

By the time Senlin had arrived at the continuation of the tunnel on the far end of the cavern, he was certain the Count was not behind this present spree of panic. But if not the Count, if not the commissioner, then who and why?

He took these questions into the mouth of the dim tunnel where a breadcrumb trail of lights lit the dark road to New Babel.

Indigo tendrils of light flashed over the city.

Senlin's fear shriveled before the spectacle. He searched for some analog from past experience, some theory to make sense of it, but history stood empty. What he was seeing was beyond the imagination or study of a poor headmaster. He stood just outside the mouth of the port tunnel, gaping at a distant, domed monolith that was haloed with blue lightning.

It was difficult to look directly at the ragged thorns of electricity that leapt against the bars of the dome. The cupola towered over the city's bleak, windowless buildings that, except for an occasional door, seemed as impenetrable as bricks. Bats gyred about the nest of lightning, knifing through clouds of moths that fizzed about the dome. Every second, scores of moths fluttered into the arcs of electricity and were consumed like scraps of flash paper. Even observed from this distance, the lightning cracked and roared with all the volume of a waterfall. Senlin had to turn away before he gawked himself senseless.

And then all at once, the storm of indigo sparks quit, and the dark that replaced it seemed so awful and total that Senlin wondered momentarily if he had died.

But it was only the false dark that surrounds a campfire. After a moment his eyes adjusted, and Senlin saw scores of dim, electric streetlights standing vigil over a grid of paved streets. Horseless carriages and all manner of strange steam engines ran in traffic patterns so intricate they verged on entropy. The running lights of vehicles bounced and ran like ghosts in a swamp of steam.

A tambourine jangled behind him, and his instinctive impulse to run reasserted itself so violently that he leapt from the corner into the street without so much as a precautionary glance.

Senlin knew almost immediately that the reflex was fatal.

At the same moment that he was careening forward, a tall steam-coach was running at breakneck speed about the street corner. Its smokestack pushed out steam as thick as wet dough. The goggled man in the driver's box spotted Senlin and stiffened with alarm, but the angle of his turn and the dense traffic left him with nowhere to swerve. Senlin hardly had time to cringe before the inevitable.

A flash of silver snaked through the spokes of the carriage's rear wheel. The fluid metal turned abruptly rigid, as the grappling chain was pulled taut. The effect on the wagon was like a leg breaking on a galloping horse. The hook stripped out a half dozen spokes, and the wagon careening at him buckled on the broken wheel. The other end of the chain, looped about the corner lamppost, uprooted the pole. The coach lurched violently into the curb, throwing the goggled driver from his high seat. The lamppost crashed onto the yawing carriage, batting the engine to a stop just at Senlin's feet. A volcano of steam erupted to one side of him, as a piston snapped loose of its arm and hammered at the ground with dumb fury. He had just enough time to close his eyes and picture Marya before the boiler exploded. The brass dome flew out like it had been launched from a cannon. It skipped upon the street once, twice, three times, gouging the road like it was nothing but wet sand as it went, before finally cratering the corner of a building a full block away.

When Senlin turned about, his limbs petrified by the cramps of terror, he found the amazon staring at him from behind the wreckage. She tugged her chain free of the devastation. How she had managed to hook a running carriage to a lamppost was almost as mystifying as why she had done it. She had saved him, which could only mean one thing: She was trying to catch him alive. Someone had plans for him. He couldn't imagine what those plans were, but he had a strong suspicion that he didn't want to find out.

Recovering his wits, Senlin scrambled through the traffic that had begun to snarl about the wreck. He scanned the surrounding blocks for some refuge. All he saw were rows of buildings that were set as close as tombstones in a potter's field. He couldn't tell which were offices, or factories, or shops, or homes, because all were a uniform, windowless cement box.

Except one.

Through the fog, at the end of the street a few blocks away, a round disc of colorful light glowed like a beacon. Running toward it, he soon realized it was a rose window set high in the gable of a building that was slathered in pretty white stucco. Its broad doors were open and welcoming. Perhaps it was a mission. In a fit of optimism, Senlin wondered if he might be offered sanctuary. By the time he reached the doors, breathless and cramping, he was drunk with hope. The block letters painted over the broad lintel read, HOUSE OF WHITE CHROM. It even sounded like a mission.

He looked over his shoulder at the street, full of clangorous engines. There was no sign of the amazon among the pedestrians, who were dressed in the dark clothes of factory workers. He shivered in the cold damp and peered through the doors. A breath of warm air stroked his face. The air inside seemed to swim with chalk dust, as if someone had been beating out erasers. He couldn't imagine a more welcoming sight. He ducked his head and went inside.

By the time he realized he had walked into a drug den, it was too late.

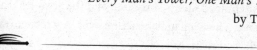

Chapter Three

There is a narcotic, unique to the Tower and in particular New Babel, called White Chrom or Crumb, among other things. The porters call it Crumb because it makes the real world seem like the sort of thing a mouse could eat in one bite and still be hungry.

—*Every Man's Tower, One Man's Travails*
by T. Senlin

At first, he didn't notice what it was because it looked so familiar. It looked like a friendly pub stuffed inside a meetinghouse. There was no bar, but the ceiling was high and the edges of the tables were round with age and lustrous with hand oil. He wasn't alone; other men sat at the tables, calmly, serenely, with their heads bowed under little white blankets. Which was odd. The light was odd, too. It poured from the streetlamp outside and through the rose window, which cut it into all sorts of magnificent colors and shapes. It was like peering into a kaleidoscope. Everything was shattered and beautiful.

Except for the woman who greeted him. She was an age-blanched matron. Her white hair was done up in a snowball of a bun. Her immaculate pinafore was starched to crispness and, he was sure, studiously protected from stains. She was the spitting image of a proper tea lady.

The matron escorted him to an empty table, and he let himself go with her because he had begun to confuse the pub-that-was-not-a-pub with a tearoom he had frequented during his time at university. She sat him on the end of a long bench, and he looked down at the men who were pretending to be little white mountains. There was something in the air, a dust that wafted about overhead, thin as the glow of the moon.

In front of each man sat a basin, and they all had their faces buried in these basins like men with head colds. A white linen napkin was draped over the back of their heads, shrouding their profiles.

Senlin turned to see a white bowl sitting before him. The water was so clear and immaculate, he wouldn't have been able to see it if the woman hadn't tapped the rim with a white envelope, no larger than a teabag. She tore it, tipped it, and white sand rolled out. When it struck the water, a vapor climbed up his shirtfront and the great length of his nose. He felt it come. The woman helped him over. A white curtain fell around the world. And then...

It was a spectacular dawn, and he was standing in a basket high above the arid hardpan of the Valley of Babel.

Above him, long sections of a balloon glistened like a freshly peeled orange. His fingers ached with cold from the thin frost on the wicker rail. The floor of the gondola dimpled gently beneath him when he turned away from the sanguine sunrise, toward the mountainous column of the Tower. He could just make out the shadow of the balloon sliding across the edifice like a tick across the face of a boulder.

Stooping a little, he glimpsed thick clouds swaddling the higher rings of the Tower. He was overcome by a sudden urge to break through those clouds, to see what was being hidden from the ground dwellers and the poorer tourists. It must be splendid and sacred, the throne of philosophers and engineers.

He feverishly hoisted the sandbags at his feet, heaving them overboard, then wrestled with the knots of the ballast sacks that bumped against the outside, until every last ready ounce of weight had been shed. The skirts of the envelope luffed as the balloon rose into a new current. He had no idea how fast he was rising until the clouds collapsed about him, milky and dense as cataracts, and the Tower vanished from view.

The clouds swelled and flowed about him like a mob of ghosts. He floated endlessly, lost in the quilted mist, lost among bulbous, spectral bodies. Faces formed in the corners of his vision and then deformed and fled when he tried to focus on them. He began to feel as if the basket he rode in was nothing but a shell, a skin from which he was coming loose. He was not flying; he was ascending from the earth. He was turning into a ghost.

Feeling madness swell in him like a deathbed panic, he prepared to scramble up the ropes. There was nothing else to do. He would sabotage the balloon. He cast about for something sharp to hack at the silken envelope with, sure now that he would rather plummet to his death than rise any farther into the cloudy abyss.

The gondola broke through the cap of the clouds, and he quit thrashing about. The sun was there, and a vast bowl of azure sky, and the Tower was there beside him, too, but it was not the Tower he knew.

It looked like an immense burnt match: blacked, still smoldering, and curling into a fragile, unstable shard at the distant pinnacle. It was a total ruin. Inside its shattered walls, he could see the jagged debris of collapsed buildings, the parapets and buttresses of devastated ports, the torn tissues of flags and airships, the black statuary of burnt corpses, splayed beneath funnels of vultures that numbered in the thousands. Rubble spilled down from the upper echelons like sand in an hourglass as the Tower continued to fall and sag.

He realized with a start that he was being blown toward the ruin.

Instinctively, he took a step backward and found himself bumping against something taller and more solid than himself. He turned to find Marya, dear, sweet Marya, bending over him, her cheeks red as apples. At first it seemed entirely natural that it was her, but then he doubted that it could be because she had almost doubled in size. Or perhaps he had shrunk.

He tried to embrace her, but his arms were as useless as empty sleeves. He swatted them about haplessly as his eyes began to flood with tears. Hoarse from all the smoke that billowed from the devastated Tower, he could only accept her when she reached down, hooked him in her arms, and hoisted him up like a child. His head rolled against her chest. She smelled like a forge, but he found the smell oddly comforting.

He bounced in her arms for a while, and then she dipped again and stood him up on his feet. Behind her, his balloon drifted away; he did not remember climbing from it. Looking down, he found he stood atop a charred outcrop of stone. Above, the black peak of the Tower, frozen midcollapse, seemed to lean in. Marya placed her unnaturally large hands on either side of his head. He said in a thick, croaking voice, "I love you."

She withdrew one hand, keeping the other cupped about his cheek, her expression as bland as a sphinx, and then slapped stars into his head.

The sky, and the balloon, and the burnt match of the Tower all winked out, and Senlin found himself standing under the sulfurous beacon of the streetlamp outside the white chapel. Where Marya had stood a moment before, the amazon now loomed. She gripped him by the side of the neck and held her other hand raised at such an extreme distance he mistook the action for a yawn. Working his newly loosened jaw, he prepared to speak, to say something in his own defense, when the hand came down again, broad as an oar, and spun him around by the face.

He saw his gaping reflection in a carriage window that stood conspicuously near. Even amid his disorientation at the receded hallucinations and the amazon's blows, he still suffered a dull throb of shock at seeing himself. He looked like a fish, like a white koi peering up through the surface of a pond, all goggling eyes and colorless grimace. He looked deranged.

The coach was opulently arrayed in panels of black lacquer and gold molding. Like the other wagons of New Babel, this vehicle was horseless and trembled even as it sat motionless. His sleeves tightened sharply under his arms, alerting him to the fact that he had been gripped by the scruff of his coat from behind. The door of the carriage opened, and his own reflection was replaced by a not entirely unfamil-iar face.

It was a moment more before Senlin identified the swarthy cherub grinning down at him from the red velvet carriage bench.

"There you are, Tom," Finn Goll said. "You didn't die after all. What a treat."

Chapter Four

Goll's Port is not an original feature of the Tower. It was dug out eons after the Tower's erection, and the fact shows in its shoddy form. It has been renamed throughout the centuries by a parade of ambitious men, and yet appears to have stubbornly remained little better, little nobler, than a smuggler's cove.

—*Every Man's Tower, One Man's Travails*
by T. Senlin

In stark contrast to the coal and sulfurous smell of the city, the carriage was scented with camphor and orange oil. It was an opulent little cabin. Between the high-piled red velvet couches, a teardrop lamp swung like a hypnotist's charm. Crystal decanters chattered in a cubby, inlaid with fine cork bumpers. The drawn shades over the windows swam with minute paisleys. The carriage swayed as gently as a hammock, and Senlin was reminded of his most recent train ride: that sense of encasement and casual speed, that sense of luxury laid over brute mechanical force. Except in this case, he didn't know where the engine was going or when it would stop.

How fondly Senlin had once recalled Finn Goll's advice! The ensuing weeks after their meeting in the Basement were so fraught with treachery and suspicion that Senlin had begun to cling to their brief acquaintance as an example of the Tower's better nature. If Finn Goll lived here, he'd reasoned on several occasions, then other good souls must live here, too. In a land of few friends, Goll was a man without conspiracy or ulterior motive.

Senlin could hardly have been more wrong.

Goll's prior humble appearance, his camel-train merchant garb, was entirely transformed. His tweed coat and wool trousers were immaculately presented. His thick hair was styled in a black wave that seemed to be forever cresting but never crashing toward one side of his head. Goll sat across from Senlin, pinching his bottom lip, his thick, dark brows animated by some private amusement. The more Senlin's head cleared, the more disturbed he was by Goll's appearance. It seemed anachronistic, a cosmic mistake. What was he doing here?

Senlin might have thought it all a continuation of his hallucination had it not been for the amazon. She sat beside him on the rocking carriage bench. While Senlin studiously maintained eye contact with Finn Goll, she sat glaring at him without subtlety. She leaned into him so intimately, Senlin could feel the breath puffing from her nostrils.

"You make quite an entrance, Tom. Getting choked in the port, terrorizing the poor tarts on the cart, hurling yourself into traffic, and then getting stoned in a Crumb house. Bravo! I am impressed." Goll rolled his palms on his knees. "My favorite part was when you told Iren that you loved her." He barked a laugh in the direction of the immense woman, who absorbed the joke with a single, languid blink. "Between you and me, I don't think she's the marrying sort." He laughed again. "I bet you didn't learn those tricks from your guidebook!"

Senlin refused to cringe at any of this, despite a sudden sense of humiliation. He turned and frowned in a shrugging way, and said, "I'm not going to defend that pap. I find it incredible that a guidebook could be so misguided and still see a fourteenth edition."

"It's not so surprising if you know that most of the writers who worked on it never actually set foot in the Tower."

"Surely not," Senlin scoffed.

"But it explains a lot, doesn't it?" Goll said, his voice lilting up merrily. "Let me tell you the most useful fact that every one of those bog rolls leaves out: The Tower is a tar pit. Once you put a toe in her, you're caught forever. No one leaves. No one goes home."

"Of course people go home," Senlin said, suppressing a rueful snort. He was finding it increasingly impossible to be convivial. Who was Goll to patronize and intimidate him like this? "I wouldn't have taken you for a conspiratorial sort, Mr. Goll." Senlin pulled himself up. He attempted to tidy his cuffs, though both were soiled with grease, the result of his recent flight. Goll watched his preening with amusement. "People go home," Senlin insisted. "I and my wife will go home."

"Aha!" Finn Goll pointed at the amazon, Iren, and said, "I told you I liked him for the job from the moment I laid eyes on him. He is just so earnest." Iren gave a little grunt of acknowledgment, and Goll turned his stubby finger toward Senlin. "It was a long interview, Tom, slogging your way up through the plumbing of the Tower. I really didn't know if you'd survive the Parlor. The fact that you escaped the Baths without getting turned into a hod is a minor miracle. I hoped you'd make it, though."

"I don't know what you're talking about. I came up of my own free will and not for any job."

"Yes, yes. Of course you did." Goll rolled his eyes. "Don't act like this is somehow obscene. This is a negotiation, Tom; it is business. My port hasn't had a port master in six months, not since the last one... retired abruptly, and I can't find a living soul who is willing and fit to do the work. I need a new port master, and you need a job. You didn't even know it at the time, but you needed a job the minute you stepped off that train in the Market. Everyone in the Tower finds work sooner or later. It's just a question of whether you get paid for it or not."

"I admit this has not exactly been the vacation I'd hoped for, but I do not need a job. I have a job waiting for me back home," Senlin said, even as he doubted the truth of it. He felt a pang of grief at the thought: They would've had to replace him by now. His students would've received no warning, no explanation. The school year had begun, and they had found a stranger waiting for them. Whoever it was, they wouldn't be a stranger for long. The bond between teacher and student was quick to form and quick to set. Senlin choked off the expanding sense of loss, letting his anger redirect him. "And don't act like you were somehow essential to my survival. There was no inter-view; this is not my destination. I do not care about you or your job. And as soon as you decide to stop this carriage and open that door, I will be on my way."

Goll continued in his own vein, unperturbed by Senlin's protest. "But why, I'm sure you're wondering, why not just recruit a new port master from the comfort of my own port? Why go all the way down to the Basement to scrabble about for talent? All I have to do is sit on my back stoop and quiz the incoming masses. I could just ask every knuckle-dragging mouth-breather through the gate, 'Are you any good with numbers? Are you loyal? Are you honest? Are you reason-able?'" Goll ticked the virtues off on splayed, thick fingers. "That's exactly what I did, too, and I ended up with a string of incompetent, unreliable liars who almost robbed me blind. Because, see, by the time they get this deep into the Tower, most have had the character beaten out of them. They are willing to say anything to get what they want. You can't reason with them or trust them. To know a person, to under-stand their character, you must know who they were before the Tower shook them to their roots. If you do not know how they changed, you do not know who they became. The very fact that you are resistant to me now is a sign that you are the man for the job."

"Do you give them all the same bad advice you gave me?"

"What bad advice? To be suspicious? To rely on one's own eyes? How is that bad?"

"You told me not to trust anyone," Senlin said, and he wanted to intimidate the man with some emphatic gesture, but he was nervous about making sudden movements while the amazon glowered at him. He tried to stuff his words full of the passion he felt. "But the only way I escaped the Parlor and the Baths was by trusting my friends."

"Really? Is that really what happened?" Goll scrubbed playfully, almost compulsively, at his beard. This seemed high humor to him. "Are you sure that you didn't just develop a rapport with strangers, and then use them? Where are these friends of yours now? Did they make out as well as you?" He opened his hands, waiting. "I take your sullen silence to mean they did not. Knowing what they know now, do you think they would trust you again? Would they still call you a friend?"

"Yet, you expected me to trust you."

"No. Muddit, no! The powerful never trust. They respect and are respected. Trust is a weak bond, and it is for the weak."

"I have other, stronger bonds in mind," Senlin said, his expression turning oblique.

"Ah..." Goll rocked back against the buttoned lobes of the red upholstery, an expression of understanding dawning on his face. "You're talking about your wife." He reached over and opened the window shade. Outside, the buildings of New Babel, plain as mileposts, closed as caskets, slid by in the ashen gloom. The world smelled like the underside of a paving stone. Moths fizzed about the streetlamps. As Goll's hand lingered on the shade ring, Senlin noted, for the first time, the gold wedding band on his finger.

When Goll spoke again, his voice had lost some of its blustering lilt. "You are acting as if you haven't lost her. You're like a dog keening at its master's grave. But she is gone, Tom." Finn Goll gave Senlin a candid, almost melancholy smile. "People think that the difference between the rich and the poor, the powerful and the hod, is the absence of failure. But that's not it." And now Goll's tone began to bounce and leap again. "Powerful men fail just as much, if not more often, than the failures. The exceptional thing is that they admit it; they take and hold up their failures. They claim their disappointments; they move on!" Goll sat roiling his fists in the air as if he had gripped some invisible scoundrel by the collar. "Don't be a hod. The hod is in denial, Tom! He cannot admit he is beaten, and so he can never escape the beating. Your wife is gone!" His voice leapt to a hoarse, strained note.

Senlin had begun to stare at his open hands halfway through Finn Goll's diatribe. They were filthy. A blister the size of a sand dollar filled his palm, his reward for laying it on a steam-filled boiler. Senlin flexed it experimentally, watching the angry skin as it swelled and stretched. "My wife is not lost," he said. "She has been kidnapped by a wealthy rogue named W. H. Pell, but she is not lost. I know where she is. I am going to fetch her, and not you, nor anyone else, is going to stop me."

The passionate mask on Goll's face deadened so abruptly he appeared to have suffered a stroke. He glanced at the amazon, the woman he called Iren, and she, interpreting the cue, grabbed Senlin by the neck and shook him about the cabin as if she were punishing an irritating rooster. Pops and sparks of pain ran up and down Senlin's spine as the cabin jerked violently around him. He was helpless in her grip.

Outside, the lightning in the dome guttered back to life, the drone of its power whooping higher and louder as purple bolts boiled against the cage and lit up the city. The interior of the carriage became a stark tableau. Senlin realized he was no longer being shaken, and he gasped after an elusive lungful of breath.

Then the lightning was pinched off as the carriage passed into a tunnel. The chug of the carriage's engine and the grinding of the wheels reverberated more noticeably.

Senlin felt as if his thoughts were the echo of some long gone utterance. And yet, empty-headed as he felt, he propped himself back up, cleared his bruised throat with a muddy cough, and said with unperturbed surety, "My wife is not lost."

Goll leaned forward, his heavy brows drawn so low they looked like a blindfold. "You aren't the only mope coming up, Tom. I set a dozen other candidates in motion that day I talked to you. Dozens more in the days before." He snapped his fingers at Iren. "Recite!"

Immediately, the amazon began to drone names from memory. "Haden Peal, Farooq Jiwa, Geert Van Dijk, William Mercer, Edgar Cole, Jean Flaubert, Chin Mawei, Thomas Senlin, Colin Hannah..."

Having made his point, Goll impatiently waved her to silence. "You think you're the only one who can write and read and pile up numbers? You lettered men are as rare as bedbugs!" he shouted and then calmed himself with abrupt, almost manic grace. He sat back. "Don't take the job, Tom, and good luck to you. But I warn you, the one commodity that is never in short supply in the Tower is desperate men."

"Desperation isn't such a bad thing," Senlin said.

"It is when it's got no money behind it," Goll quipped.

Much as Senlin hated to admit it, Goll was right on one account: He needed money. Finding Marya and traversing the Tower would require fares and bribes and who knew what else. He couldn't carry on any longer as a tourist. He couldn't keep depending on the sacrifice of his friends and acquaintances. He had to formulate a plan, gather his forces, and make a concerted effort. And all that required time, and time required money.

Goll, watching him narrowly, seemed to recognize the machinations Senlin was going through. Senlin pursed his lips to punctuate his meditation. "I don't like being strong-armed, Mr. Goll. If you want to propose business, I'll entertain it, but if you're going to browbeat me and behave as if I owe you some debt of gratitude for being taken advantage of, then I'd rather join the hods."

"I want to make this perfectly clear: I have employees. I don't keep hods. You'll be paid for the work you do."

"What is the work, exactly?" Senlin asked, and listened as Finn Goll outlined the duties of the port master, which included organizing the dockworkers and inspecting, pricing, buying, and selling the imported goods. He would schedule the shifts of porters, balance the ledgers, pay the men, and, most importantly, prepare the daily eight o'clock report for Goll.

"The work isn't easy or simple. You've seen the port, the station, and the men. It's all a bit..."

"...of a shoddy, disorganized, and riotous mess," Senlin finished.

Finn Goll opened his hands, accepting the characterization. "So, you will have to earn your money. Your salary will be one mina a month, after room and board."

It was less than his old school salary, but Senlin doubted that he was in any position to haggle for a better wage. He gave a considered nod and stuck out his hand. They shook once, glaring at one another, the gesture devoid of trust or confidence. This was, as far as Senlin was concerned, not unlike the Parlor. He would act the part for as long as was required, but he was no more an honest employee than Goll was an honest employer. The handshake merely signaled their agreement to share an illusion for as long as was mutually convenient.

The next moment, the carriage arrived at the same weigh station Senlin had recently charged through. The carriage door opened, and Senlin clambered down. He expected for Goll or Iren to follow, but neither made any move to disembark.

Goll seemed to enjoy watching Senlin through the now closed carriage door, gawking back, trying not to look like a boy on his first day of school. Senlin was elbowed into a yardarm by a laborer dragging a poorly packed sled of jangling crates. A bottle inside one of the crates burst, and a plume of suds sprayed through the slats. Senlin leapt out of the way and then had to fight his way back to the carriage's side.

"Where do I begin?" Senlin called up to Goll, who cupped a hand behind his ear, shook his overlarge head, and pretended not to hear. Senlin felt his hackles rising. Already, he regretted this decision.

Goll made a little twirling motion with his finger, and the carriage lurched forward.

Senlin turned, gaping after the lustrous carriage rumbling back toward the shaft to New Babel, and for a moment he considered chasing after it. He felt as lonely and desolate as a castaway. He was unprepared to find the tan, young man standing so close behind him, and he gave a surprised little leap in a manner that immediately embarrassed him. The young man, muscular but shorter than Senlin, didn't seem to notice. He wore a brown leather eye patch and stared up at Senlin with his remaining eye, bright as a gold coin. It was Adam Boreas.

Here stood his mugger, the young man who had sped along Senlin's doom.

Senlin had often conjured up the image of Adam when he'd felt the need to scold someone for his misfortune. In those bitter daydreams, he had condemned Adam to all sorts of absurd punishments. He exiled him to a leper colony on a volcanic atoll; he forced him to scrub the Tower, from top to bottom; he made him memorize and recite the dictionary while jumping rope.

These cruel fantasies, once so amusing, sprang to mind again as he stood there like a statue, and he felt ashamed. Adam looked as if he had suffered much in the ensuing weeks. His broad shoulders were slumped, his dark, splendid hair was matted, and his copper skin had an almost greenish cast to it. From under his eye patch, an old bruise radiated; a scabbed-over crack bridged his nose. Though still young, he had the gaze of a yeoman who had spent the better half of a century scratching at a miserable, stony field. He looked beaten, and he seemed to be steeling himself for another attack.

The tension struck Senlin as absurd. This aged boy was not his enemy. And furthermore, he was determined to prove Finn Goll wrong. Desperation did not make friendship impossible, and the bonds of trust were not weak.

Senlin made a stoic show of adopting a smile and offered Adam his singed and blistered hand. "It looks like we'll be living under the same thumb, Mr. Boreas."

Relief, like a break in a cloud, showed on the young man's face. "Call me Adam," he said, shaking Senlin's tender hand.

"Adam, call me Tom. It's nice to see a friendly face."

Adam's expression clouded again, and his grip weakened. "You have no friends."

Senlin laughed, startling Adam. "That's what all my friends say."

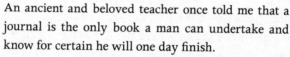

Chapter Five

An ancient and beloved teacher once told me that a journal is the only book a man can undertake and know for certain he will one day finish.

—*Every Man's Tower, One Man's Travails*
by T. Senlin

September 7th

I am the one in charge of making things run.

The list of "things that must run" includes the skyport, where negligence is only eclipsed by incompetence; the weigh station, with its ancient hoist and rusted weigh plates of dubious calibration; and the station yard, where perishable imports bloom maggots and crates of port wine mysteriously vanish with regularity. Everything must be haggled after and sold at a profit, and the records of purchases, stocks, wages, and losses must be rigorously kept and copied for the "Almighty Eight O'Clock Report," which goes daily to Goll, care of Iren the amazon, along with most of the money and copies of the manifests. The men are uniformly surly and indifferent to my direction, and they are so seldom sober, I have yet to distinguish the unfit from the lethargic, the imbecilic from the inebriate. I am master of the port in name only. I hardly know where to begin.

It's not like the Baths or the Parlor here. There is no head clerk or commissioner or lord of the Boudoir. New Babel is ruled by the port authorities, the whoremongers, and the factory bosses. The men in power are always scrambling after more. And there isn't a single reputable, empathetic soul among them.

The station yard sits midtunnel like an undigested bulge in a snake. The station house is two stories of rambling timber and stone and boasts a humble barracks of rotting hammocks for the men, a mess hall that's not fit for cleaning fish, and a kitchen that is fairly lacquered in mold and tallow. The second floor holds my office and two apartments; one is mine, the other, Adam's. My office is whimsically fitted with a desk that appears to have once been the prow of a ship. It might seem more whimsical if it weren't buried under piles of inscrutable ledgers and unmet schedules. Everything is covered in pencil shavings, dust, and dead moths. I can hardly sit in my office without screaming. I will clean it as soon as I can find a rag that isn't filthier.

My apartment smells like a cave where generations of cheese makers cultured their wheels. It is furnished with sticks and splinters that hold the rough shape of a table, two chairs, a bureau, and a bed. A loose floorboard by my bedside is as sensitive as a wolf trap. I have already stepped on it wrong twice, plunging my foot into a jagged maw. The cavity beneath is large enough to hold this journal, and since it seems prudent to keep my private ruminations private, I have decided to stow this account there along with Ogier's jailor's key. At least something useful came of my shaved shins.

I have placed Ogier's painting of Marya on my nightstand. I have turned it toward the wall and then back again about once a quarter hour for the past two hours. Both sides of the frame are equally painful to look at.

I hardly know where to begin!

September 12th

I began by choosing an example.

I asked Adam who he thought was most responsible for the

disappearance of the crates of alcohol. He quickly returned with the name of Tommo Carric, chief stevedore, third in command after Adam and myself, and the very same man who had welcomed me to the port by choking me and fondling my wife's portrait. (I realize "portrait" is an inaccurate term, but I shudder to call it "my wife's nude," even privately.) Iren is often about on one errand or another, and so I conscripted her in the effort. She expressed no qualms with my plan, though in all fairness, she is generally as expressionless as a spade. I do not pretend to be comfortable around her; my hand is still bandaged and my head still sore from our recent introduction. But she is under orders from Goll to assist in all reasonable efforts to redeem the port and not to kill me unless absolutely necessary. I know this because she told me.

And still, Iren is exactly the sort of presence one wants when firing an oaf. Tommo Carric made the exact spectacle I'd hoped for. Adam, Iren, and I confronted him by his open-air pulpit on the port. When I informed him that his services were no longer required, he pulled the pulpit from its anchor and prepared to beat me with it. He would've succeeded, if Iren had not grabbed him by the waist and shaken the spittle from him.

Carric shouted a string of the most elaborate obscenities as Iren carried him like a bawling child, held stiffly at arm's length, through the tunnels, station yard, and finally into the fog of New Babel. Though it was not done out of petty revenge, I won't pretend that I did not savor the sight of the brute splayed upon the pavement. He stood and lunged again at me, but Iren dealt him a slap so fierce it knocked his nose from joint.

Shortly thereafter, I gathered the men and announced that the wine thief had been identified and dismissed. The men listened and seemed to understand that now, at least, they could claim innocence, and we could begin afresh. Hopefully, this will open the door for reformation. I do suspect that there might be a riot if I tried the trick again. But if I can keep the men's confidence, I can win Goll's confidence. And if I have that, I can lull him into believing that I have given up on her. And then, I will escape.

I found a clean rag and something like soap. I have scrubbed my office and room into little islands of sanity. Tomorrow, I tackle the station yard. If this account ends here, future readers should assume that I was lynched midinventory by my men.

September 16th

With Carric gone, I have the added duty of reviewing outgoing manifests and collecting signatures from departing captains. The gap between what is declared on the manifest and what is present belowdecks is sometimes marked. Crews are eager to circumvent Goll's tax on exports and have grown quite wily in their smuggling methods. (I think back to the days when I carried my money in my boots and laugh. I was such an amateur, and concealment is a fine art in the Tower.) To combat this loss of revenue, spot inspections are required, and I have witnessed some tense exchanges between my stevedores and the mates of ships.

The major occupation of New Babel concerns the production of hydrogen, a gas that is as ephemeral as it is volatile. The four other skyports of New Babel, all legitimate and well greased, supply the local factories with iron filings and sulfuric acid for the creation of hydrogen. Steel is imported for the construction of specialized kegs, which are loaded with the gas once it's been compressed. These drums are fuel to the airships, and are the major export of the ringdom.

The ubiquitous, squat, windowless buildings of New Babel resemble bunkers for a reason. They were designed both to contain the gas and prevent the escalation of chance explosions, as well as protect non-factories from such accidents. Escaped hydrogen is a perennial fear, especially considering the regularity with which a spark is applied to the atmosphere. Incredibly enough, catastrophes are rare.

But this noble effort does not describe the Port of Goll's industry. No, we are not so noble. We are importers of vice.

September 19th

Visiting captains and crew call New Babel the Boudoir for a depressingly obvious reason. The ringdom is fairly stuffed with bordellos and cantinas shrouded under bleak concrete shells. Inside these colorless crypts... well, if the broadsides and flyers that litter the streets are anything to go by, the entertainment is anything but drab.

Nothing depresses me more than the shiploads of women that arrive weekly. Their faces seem like panes of leaded glass; they are toughened but transparent. They are all lost. Finn Goll seems to think of them as being no different than a crate of oranges or a keg of Basement beer. They are added to the registry, shifted to whatever account is deficient, and are carted off to work on stages and in bedrooms. Goll has his own seedy venue, the Steam Pipe, to which he diverts the most well-presented women. The Steam Pipe is managed by a whoremonger named Rodion, who I hope to never meet but am certain I one day will. From what I've heard, he is dangerous and ambitious.

The dockworkers, of course, save their wages for just such entertainment. I am not naive. This is the old business of the world. But it seems a sad business. When I think on it, I turn the painting of M away. But when the thought persists, as it sometimes does, I turn her image back again.

September 24th

I have succeeded finally in compiling an accurate roll of all the stevedores, wharfies, drivers, sentries, and peons employed by Mr. Goll in his port. After firing some fourteen loafers, there are fifty-two fit men in all; eighteen are moonlighters who also work in one of the more legitimate New Babel ports, such as Ginside or Erstmeer. Of the thirty-four full-time workers, not a single one is literate or capable of anything more than rudimentary counting done upon the fingers. If the number of something is greater than ten, two men are required to count it.

Adam, of course, is the exception. He is well read, a reliable calculator, and absolutely gifted with mechanical repairs. I routinely forget his relative youth, and so often find myself confiding in him about one practical dilemma or other. (No one ever speaks of his miserable past or anything else of personal importance.) We have transcended the mistakes of our first meeting, though he was suspicious of an easy reconciliation. He first wanted all of our cards to be laid on the table before we decided to be friends. So, he explained why he'd robbed me only hours after meeting me.

The scheme had been Finn Goll's entirely, of course. Goll insisted on importing talent from the ground because he believed such men to be smart, naive, and unaffiliated with his enemies. In short, such men could be trusted. (Ironically, Goll trusts no one well enough to let them recruit for any position better than a porter.) Adam's role in the plot was to identify isolated, vulnerable, and educated tourists. He'd earn their trust, lead them toward an unsuspected rendezvous with Goll, and, as soon as the opportunity presented itself, rob them blind. Adam then delivered the tourist's personal effects to Goll, who would all too conveniently stumble upon the ruined tourists.

After that, it was just a matter of manipulating the tourist into believing that Goll was also a victim of the same thief, which, as I can attest, creates an instant and surprisingly strong bond. Goll's philosophy of sowing many prospects to reap a single resilient hire meant that Adam had robbed many, many men. Knowing Goll, knowing his persuasive and brutal extremes, I can hardly blame Adam for the part he played. He was only doing what was required of him. How can I hold a grudge?

Besides, Adam is the only man in the yard not rooting for my involvement in a fatal accident. I am unpopular with the men. They think my schedules and routines are arbitrary and excessive. It has never occurred to them that overstocks of rotting meat and produce are the result of poor management, or that bottlenecks in traffic can be avoided, or that money is being lost to faulty indexes. For them, the rotting bushels of figs, and the dented wheel fenders, and the evaporation of alcohol are just natural phenomena that may be bemoaned but not corrected.

Adam is teaching me the rudiments of steam engines. Since our tractors break down religiously, we are left to repair them or carry in the imports by hand, so it is prudent to learn. In honesty, I enjoy those claustrophobic sessions under the carriages of engines because it at least liberates me from my desk where I feel increasingly chained. Also, this work with engines has sparked a theory about the Tower that I would like to pursue...if I ever have energy for academic thoughts again.

September 29th

Ah, the nightly airing! Every evening I stand upon the base of the weigh crane in the yard, adopt my headmaster's bawl, and make announcements about productivity and assignments. These sessions, much loathed by the men, have only been recently redeemed. One evening a week ago, our cook, Louis Mawk, asked me to read a scrap of paper. It was an IOU of which he was suspicious, but being illiterate, he could not satisfy his curiosity. I read it, and with no trouble of course, though it entertained the men greatly. The next night, another man approached with another document he wished to have deciphered. And ever since, I am beset each night by a half dozen men with limericks, letters, and flyers.

While I would expect these men to wish to keep their affairs private, no one else seems troubled by the publicity. It is just the opposite: The men stay in assembly to hear what news of the world will be read. In general, the news is quite banal and sometimes profane. But I treat it all as literature, and so manage not to squirm even as I am forced to read the bawdy advertisement of a brothel or the charmless love notes the men sometimes receive.

I almost laughed this evening to see the young Adam Boreas blush at just such a recital. Old Louis Mawk came forth with a particularly lurid broadside for the Steam Pipe, Goll's own den of iniquity, which, beside a menu of vulgarities, included an etching of a beautiful young woman with a writhing abundance of curly black hair. She sat perched on a trapeze bar in an acrobat's leotard. The copy said, and I read, "Come see, come see the Flying Girl! The Amazing Voleta! Slim of bust but broad of back, will she go flying into the sack?"

It was crude enough, but I was surprised to see the usually implacable Adam turn a furious shade of red and then disappear for the remainder of the evening.

September 30th

I am an insensitive fool. The name of the girl on the flyer was only vaguely familiar, and even so, I should have remembered. Voleta was who Adam addressed his note to, the one he'd posted to the Lost and Found in the grim shadow of the Tower. Voleta, starlet of the Steam Pipe, is his sister.

Why did he lie about her being lost? Shame? Denial? Superstition? Oh, the question answers itself. Honesty is so often full of defeat. We do not talk about our past. To do so would invite despair. We talk of the port, the men, the state of the tea mildewing in crates in the yard. We are friends, but I have yet to ask how he came here, or why, or how he lost his eye, or how it was that his sister became Finn Goll's showgirl. What horrible questions to ask. What horrible answers to conceal.

October 5th

Every day, Iren comes to my office to collect the "Almighty Eight O'Clock Report" for Goll. I have not seen Goll myself since my hire, and have no sense of where he lies ensconced inside New Babel. For all I know, he lives on a ship in a cloud.

Every morning, without fail, Iren startles me half out of my wits by erupting into my office with all the civility of a famished bear. She is ingenious at catching me off guard, arriving on a different minute of a different hour, and always without making any noise in her approach.

The door merely flies on its hinges and bangs upon the bookshelf, and the famished bear rushes in.

This morning, I leapt in such fright that I knocked over my ink-pot, throwing a black lake across an open ledger. While I mopped at the mess with my now-ruined handkerchief, I told Iren to collect the envelope containing the eight o'clock report herself. It lay on the edge of my desk among several others, clearly marked, "Port of Goll Figures of Commerce for the Fourth of October."

She was instantly irate (a fierce prospect), and demanded that I hand it to her. I sat there with my hands blackened to the second knuckle, and in my distress, refused her request.

It was only later that I realized she could not read the envelope to distinguish it from the others. It shouldn't have come as any surprise, and if I had not been so discombobulated by the early hour and the tide of ink creeping across my desk, I would never have made the mistake. What did surprise me was how ashamed and angry this revelation made her. The men in the yard express no embarrassment at having another man read their mail. But Iren was...upset. And she quickly reminded me why I should make it a point to not upset her.

She rapped me once on the top of my skull, like she was knocking on a door, and repeated her request. I was sufficiently inspired to fulfill it.

I wonder if Goll was curious as to why his regular post was decorated with blackened fingerprints this morning.

October 8th

A ship, small and dreadful, hardly better than a dingy tied to a goat-skin gasbag, arrived with a load of White Chrom today. The shipment agitated the men, who alternately leered at it distrustfully and were drawn out by it like worms in a cloudburst. The men call it Crumb. It is too dangerous to leave it in the yard. It would vanish or spark a riot; more likely, it would do both. So it is sitting in my room. Ten pounds of White Chrom squats on my dresser in a pine cube crate.

That first day in New Babel when I was chased into what I mistook for a mission, I fell under the trance of Crumb. It showed me a vision of a burnt-match Tower, but it also showed me something better than a painter's impression, better than a memory, or a fitful dream. It brought Marya back in such a tangible way that it felt as if we had never parted. Strange as it was to see her, gigantic and in the basket of a balloon, I believed with all my heart that it was her. She was really there.

I have seen the dockworkers who've crawled one time too many into the Crumb's convincing dream. They have the soft smiles of a sleepy child. It is a pitiful, unaware expression. And sometimes I envy it. Marya is in that crate on my dresser. Not in flesh and blood, but in the conviction of memory and mind. She is in there, and I could go in after her.

I must find Adam and see if he is interested in playing a game of cards.

October 15th

It has been ninety-three days since I last saw Marya vanish into the underwear bazaar, and forty days since I shook hands with Goll. The burn on my hand has healed, though it looks like a splotch of candle wax dried upon my palm. It is strange to look at, strange to think that I will always have this mark with me now. When I consider the scars my friends have accrued—Edith's malicious branding, Tarrou's carved scalp, and Adam's undone eye—I feel fortunate.

Now, the port and weigh station tick along like two clocks. The station house is tidy as a library, and the autowagons run as regularly as the tides. I have Goll fairly convinced that I am Port Master Tom Senlin, a reliable man who is satisfied with his salary and his lot. He believes that I have forgotten my old crusade.

A ship arrived today with a miraculous cargo. The captain himself escorted to the station the four waterlogged crates. He opened one and showed me layers of straw packed about a crust of ice—ice!—which he had harvested himself, from the horn of a mountain, before flying to a port, not a skyport, but an honest oceanic port, where he took on his precious cargo: five hundred oysters. He pulled one of the horned shells from the ice pack to prove the oysters were still tightly closed and redolent of the sea. He deftly cracked it open with a pick and offered me the shimmering morsel to sample. What had always seemed peasant's food to me before now was a capsule of a lost home and an old life...I have never tasted anything so wonderful.

That captain walked away from the port with a king's purse, which the port coffers quickly recouped and doubled after selling the treasures to a private cantina. But more importantly, that unpolished, unremarkable captain left me with the clear revelation that a man with a ship is capable of all sorts of miracles. If five hundred oysters, those most perishable of creatures, can be plucked from the sea and carried to the heart of a continent, unspoiled, is anything impossible with the advantage of a ship?

What good is money? It can be skimmed and extorted, taxed and burgled! Tickets will strand you. Customs will rob you. I do not need money to buy passage upon a ship. I need a ship entire and my own. Let Goll think I have lost my resolve! I am determined. I will find her.

I am going to take a ship.

Chapter Six

Presuming that I can obtain a ship, I wonder how I would crew it. Of course, I cannot afford to hire airmen, nor can I tolerate the pirate option of violent salaries. No, each one of my crew must come on their own, for their own reasons.

—*Every Man's Tower, One Man's Travails*
by T. Senlin

It was midday in late October when Adam slunk cross-armed into the port master's office under the burden of a terrible secret.

Senlin was too distracted to notice his friend's brooding because he had just that morning made an absorbing discovery. While cleaning the corner cobwebs from the underside of his ship's-prow desk, he'd found stowed on a receded ledge a strange and dusty artifact. It was a steel rod, a straight yard in length and about as thick as a broom handle. It was quite heavy but in a satisfying way. At first, he had mistaken it for a bit of plumbing, but it was not hollow like a pipe, and its surface was scored with regular rings. After polishing away a thick film of soot and grime, Senlin discovered names had been engraved minutely between these rings. No, not names: destinations. Between the heel of the rod and the first line were the words, "The Genesis." Then, above the next line, "Algez's Parlor," and above the next, "The Baths."

It was a model of the Tower—a three-dimensional map!

It took him a half hour to clean it fully and a half hour more to oil it and file down several obnoxious burrs. There were thirty-five segments in all, and though many of the segments were blank or had been purposefully scratched out, nineteen of the sections were clearly marked. Senlin saw evidence of at least three different hands in the shaping of the letters. It was marvelous!

In the fifth segment, Senlin found the inscription he was looking for: "The Ringdom of Pelphia, Seat of the Pells." He worried those pristine serifs with his thumb, repeating the words to himself until the utterance became almost a mantra. The Ringdom of Pelphia, Seat of the Pells.

The state was eponymous with the man: W. H. Pell, the Count who had deceived and abducted Marya. For the first time, Senlin knew, knew with thrilling certainty, where Marya was.

Now, wearing an expression that verged on giddiness, Senlin held up the steel staff, polished to a gleam, and asked, "Have you seen this before?"

Adam closed the heavy door to Senlin's office, which swung unevenly on hinges that had been loosened daily by the amazon's visits. He dropped into the chair before Senlin's desk, which was bookended by great leaning shelves of ledgers and manuscripts, so much paper that Senlin sometimes felt like he was in the spine of an immense book that was slowly coming shut. The old red leather of the chair crackled under Adam's self-conscious shifting. "It's called an aeronaut's rod, or an aerorod," Adam said with hardly a second glance, as if the totems were common enough. "Captains carry them for navigation."

"An aerorod!" Senlin said approvingly. "It's unfinished, though, and what is written upon it seems to have been added by several hands. I imagine additions were made as new lands were discovered. It must be decades old!" Hardly taking his eyes off of the staff, and still oblivious to Adam's apparent misery, Senlin went on: "Again, this is evidence of the importance of literacy. Uneducated men could not have made this record. I've been thinking," Senlin said, turning the heavy staff in the air, "I'm going to teach Iren to read."

Despite his poor mood, this pronouncement goaded Adam into brief laughter. "I can't think of a worse idea," he said.

"Why? I've seen many brutes reformed by the ability to read. Iren knows there are open secrets written all around her that are invisible to her because she cannot read. She knows how easily she could be taken advantage of, knows her ignorance makes her vulnerable, and so she compensates with force. But she can't hope to go on being a bodyguard into her dotage. One day she'll have to retire, and then what will she do?"

"It's a noble thought, Tom, but..."

Senlin looked up, and his eyes narrowed with abrupt concern. "Why are you making such a miserable face? Are you sick?"

Adam's mouth hung open, his eyes on the floor. He gathered up a breath and said, "The organ at the Steam Pipe is broken again, and Rodion has called me in to repair it this evening before tonight's show."

"Well, that's—"

Adam interrupted. "He wants you to come, too. He wants to meet the new port master."

"Ah." Senlin quickly divined the root of Adam's discomfort. It was not the repairs to the pipe organ or the repulsive whoremonger, Rodion, who had upset him. The Steam Pipe was where Voleta performed and lived, and Adam was embarrassed to think that Senlin might see "the flying girl," his sister, amid her humiliation.

The subject of Voleta had remained unaddressed in the weeks following the awkward reading of the Steam Pipe's advertisement, and Senlin had respected Adam's silence on the matter. But now, it seemed, something had to be said, or rather, Adam wished to say something. "I'd like to tell you, Tom, about where I came from."

The young man cleared his throat and lifted his gaze to Senlin's, who was in the process of quietly setting aside the aerorod. The once-headmaster folded his hands on his desk and gave Adam the time he needed to gather his words and courage. The pages of the office seemed to close a little more about them, while the dangling light bulb, like a luminary at a fall festival, softened the darkness. Then Adam began his tale.

*   *   *

Adam Boreas was born in the grasslands of Khayyam in the west of Ur, where the land was golden with perennial drought and the sky was a blue desert. His father worked in the Depot of Sumer, where many vital railroads intersected, swapped cargo, and snaked again into the expansive fields of tall buffel grass like black millipedes.

In the far distance, a hazy form rose from the earth like a single hair from an ancient head: the Tower of Babel. It was the dream catcher of his boyhood.

The city of Sumer had been built on stilts above the depot's matrix of rails and switch tracks. The buildings were all thin and flimsy as playing cards. No matter where one stood or sat or slept, the rumble of trains was immediately underfoot. Steam jetted and seeped up through every crack and knothole, as if a volcanic spring churned just beneath the baked-gray boardwalks. There were no streets between buildings, only empty canals where trains ran submerged just beneath the surface of the city.

Voleta, born just ten months after Adam, was near enough to be his twin, and he was fiercely devoted to her. She was a happy, adventurous child who possessed a natural physical grace that was only honed by the environment. The city of a hundred footbridges and a thousand guy-wires was the stage of her very own balancing act. Rigid cables flew over canals that, with little notice, would fill with blunt tons of rushing iron. Gouts from smokestacks shot up in waves that could cook a man at a pass. Only the brave and the witless used the guy-wires rather than the bridges to traverse the city, and Voleta crossed them all as confidently as a squirrel. She leapt between gutters and chutes, and danced along the wires as if unaware of the twenty-foot drop that followed her everywhere like a shadow.

Adam lived in mortal fear that she would one day miss a toehold and fall onto the iron arms of a track. But Voleta was more nimble than his imagination.

If only their father had been so.

Accidents were commonplace on the floor of the Depot of Sumer.

The lighting was poor, the atmosphere bleak with steam and smoke, and the rails were so densely laid that one could hardly help but to stand on one line or another. The droves of porters and switchmen were in constant peril, and still it came as a surprise when the foreman rapped on the door of their house, making the whole facade shiver, and informed their mother that her husband had slipped on the toe of another man's polished boot and had fallen under a crawling car wheel up to his thigh.

His death, she was told, had not been merciful.

Their mother, an entirely practical person, did not ask for elaboration. Details were only good for resolving denial, and she was not the sort to disbelieve the brutal facts of life. She thanked the foreman, closed the door, pulled her black dress from the cedar chest, and began ironing it. Adam hoped that he had inherited her pragmatism. It was a very practical wish.

Sturdy-minded as she was, their mother had suffered a severe fever in her youth that had returned later in her life, first intermittently and then more frequently, making her incapable now of supporting Adam and Voleta during their final years of school.

Adam had been a dutiful student all through his youth, had made high marks, and had even hoped to attend a university. But that was impossible now. He had to find work, and high marks would not help him. In the Depot of Sumer, there was only one kind of work for young men born to unremarkable parents: the gory, deadly sort. He was sure his father's old foreman could find some place for him in the yards, and though he would have to begin with a pittance of a salary, he would be gainfully employed, at least. Even the thought of it was enough to chill him. After his father's death, the underbelly of the city on stilts had become as awful as a bottomless pit. Even looking down into the gloom from a footbridge filled him with dread.

Then, while the catastrophe was still fresh and unsettled, his mother was driven to bed by the return of her childhood pyrexia. Even while the fever cooked her, she resisted the delirium, which a less practical person might've succumbed to. She lay rigid for two days, staring clear-eyed at the ceiling of her bedroom before calling Adam in and announcing in her matter-of-fact way that it was time he struck out on his own. "If you have to worry about taking care of me, you're going to drown; and if I have to worry about taking care of you, I'm going to sink. That's how it is, Adamos. But if we go our own ways and save ourselves, we'll be saving each other, too." Adam could think of no reason, no practical reason, to disagree.

His mother would move in with her sister, whose husband was an assistant to the scheduler. He stood in line to become, one day, the scheduler himself. Adam's aunt and uncle were riding on the cusp of what passed for wealth in Sumer. He knew his mother would never go hungry while under their roof.

She would take Voleta, too, who would be useful in her uncle's kitchen; there were six cousins who needed looking after as well, which was also partly why there was no room for him. Partly why. His uncle already had two sons of his own to educate, dote upon, and insinuate into the local industry. He couldn't manage a third son. Meanwhile, Adam's whole inheritance, his father's entire wealth in death, was only enough to buy a single train ticket.

Adam was strangely relieved by all of this. It was as if he had been put to pasture just as the rest of the herd was being gathered up for the slaughter. He knew instantly where he would go: the Tower of Babel, the sink of humanity, the promised land of young men. He packed his meager bindle of possessions, kissed his feverish mother, and left with Voleta as if it was a matter of course that she would go with him. He could not leave her.

It wasn't until he was on the train with Voleta, sipping the weak, cold tea that was served to the third-class passengers, that it occurred to him this had not been a practical choice. His sister was guaranteed a home in Khayyam in their uncle's house, and he was stealing her from that certainty. It would have been the life of an unwanted cousin and a wanted scullery maid, but it would have been a stable life. He felt the sting of this new responsibility. Outside the car window, the buffel grass luffed in the wind. He watched it and fretted about the future.

As is so often the case with older brothers, Adam had presumed to have more responsibility than he did, and presumed his sister was acting only out of devotion to him. He couldn't imagine that she had her own reasons for leaving. Of course, Voleta would not have let him go alone. He was her dear, near-twin brother. But that was not the reason she had decided to follow him to the Tower. She would not tell him the truth for some weeks, but she would eventually confess that she had left with him because the fear had gone out of her daily leaps. Her hours were filled with confident, minor feats and toothless dangers. She would not call it such, but Adam would later name it for her: It was boredom that had driven her from her mother's side and a secure home.

Her father's death mystified her. It seemed such a silly accident. How could a man slip on another man's boot? Was he tripped? Had some unspoken grudge made the other man throw a foot under him? It seemed impossible. Even if she halved the agility of her legs, and then aged those legs twenty years, she still could not believe that her father had stumbled on such sturdy and able legs. It was too stupid.

The moment she heard the morbid news, she was sure that he had thrown himself under the train. And why not? He had worked in a coal swamp beneath a pine-board sky for twenty-nine years. Iron-nosed, devil-hot boilers flew past him on knives every minute of every hour, all twelve hours of the day. He had never been struck before. He had leapt nimbly among them all, in the dark and the low, rotten clouds.

He was an acrobat who had, in a moment of despair, let himself be killed. It was not suicide, though. It was worse. It was boredom. So she had to leave and go someplace where she did not know every chasm and every foothold and leap. She had to rediscover fear and, tucked somewhere inside that fear, life.

Wisely enough, the younger near-twin did not put it this way to Adam for some time. She merely mentioned one of their cousins, an eighteen-year-old maid named Delphie, who was homely and desperate to get married, saying, "Delphie told me she would pay two minas for my hair, and that will buy my train ticket."

So, she sawed off all her hair, her roundly curled, jet-black, pride-of-her-mother hair, and bought her own passage to the Tower.

They were gone forever before their mother's fever broke.

When their train pulled into the station under the Tower of Babel, it was a man who disembarked.

The boy had evaporated over the course of their two-day journey like ore from a smelted ingot of gold. Climbing down, hardly touching the stairs, Adam did not step into the umbra of the greatest monument to human industry, ingenuity, and daring; he stepped into manhood, into his potential, which the spiraling Tower, at that moment, seemed hardly able to contain.

He swelled to his full height on the station platform, which quaked under the feet of a thousand immigrants, while Voleta's hand wrenched his own. He could feel the fear in her grip. But she was smiling, beaming up at the trunk of the Tower, the white marble blending into limestone, limestone into sandstone, sandstone into clouds. The beetle bores of high portals winked minutely as figures and machines moved inside them. Airships nosed and fled from the Tower like gnats about the leg of a great bull. And he was not afraid.

It would only be much later that the memory would become a sort of sad fable to him, and he would see the boy proudly descending to his ruin like a mad king being led to the executioner's block.

They walked into the maddening Market, hands locked together. Two days later, he had found work as a clerk in the Parlor.

Chapter Seven

Even with a crew and a ship, escaping the port requires the right wind. A single airstream feeds the entire Port of Goll; all ships come in from the low south and depart to the high north. When there is only one road out of town, runaways are easy to catch.

—*Every Man's Tower, One Man's Travails*
by T. Senlin

W ait," Senlin interrupted Adam. "You worked in the Parlor. You *worked* in the Parlor."

"Well, I thought I did." Adam shrugged. "When we got to the landing with the four Parlor doors, an usher tried to give me a role. I stopped him and said I hadn't come for the play. I wanted a job."

"Incredible."

"Not to me. It seemed pretty straightforward. I was interviewed by one of the—what were they called—assistants to the registrar. He offered me a six-month contract as a clerk, and I signed without hesitation. He asked for a deposit on room and board, which I paid. I was naive enough to think this was all a matter of course. A few minutes later, I was being measured for a new uniform. I hadn't a shekel left to my name, but it didn't matter. I had a job."

"What about Voleta? Did she get a job, too?"

Adam shook his head. "No. She was fifteen years old, and they didn't have any work for her. Honestly, I meant to take care of her, so I wasn't bothered by it. We had our own cabin. It wasn't much, and I know she went a little stir crazy, but I'd brought some of my old school primers. All she had to do was stay out of trouble and study while I worked."

"What did you do?"

Adam's snort seemed part chagrin and part disdain. "For one hundred and eighty days, I sat on a stool in a dim hallway, looking through a peephole and taking notes."

"I saw you," Senlin murmured, and then when Adam looked understandably confused, Senlin corrected himself. "No, not you. I saw the clerks in the backstage corridors, looking through little brass loupes."

"That was me. I was so nervous I could hardly eat my lunch that first day. I was afraid I'd miss something. I didn't really know what I was looking for. So I noted every sneeze and awkward phrase and drunken giggle. I was shocked by how pitiful my subjects were; I couldn't imagine why anyone would want to spy on such a thing. But I had been told to observe and report, so I filled my steno pad, and at the end of the day, proudly presented it to the head clerk. The only things that interested him were the fires and the exits. He wanted to know who had added fuel and who had used which doors. It was all quite... dumb. I never understood their obsession with the fireplaces."

Senlin nodded sympathetically. "I have a theory about that..." He waved the thought away, as if it were a bothersome odor. "But, never mind—you were just an actor reporting on other actors, correct?"

Adam made stuttering, qualifying noises that finally resolved in a full-chested sigh. "The strangest thing about the Parlor is that you can't tell the difference between people who are in character and people who don't know they are acting. There must be some legitimate management there, but I don't think I ever met anyone who was part of it. Then again, who can say?" he said, and his revitalized frustration raised a deep blush on his neck. "At the end of my six-month contract, I went to the head clerk and asked for my wage and a promotion. I wanted to become an assistant to the registrar. They had full apartments, not just cabins with a bed and a chaise lounge—I was so tired of sleeping on a lumpy sofa! Spying on people through a fish-eye lens was not my idea of a career, and I was beginning to worry about Voleta. She had become jumpy and moody and strange. And it was my fault.

"Asking for money really confused the head clerk. He said that if I was interested in becoming an assistant to the registrar, I just needed to finish paying out my contract and sign a new one. The whole thing fell apart pretty quickly. I had misread the contract; really, I hadn't read it. I saw a figure, sixteen minas, and I presumed that would be my salary. It seemed plum enough. So, I went six months believing I was a responsible working adult, but I was a tourist the whole time, just like all the fools I'd spent twelve hours a day studying through a bunghole in the wall. One hundred and eighty days in the Parlor is not cheap. I owed sixteen minas."

As he had spoken, Adam's posture seemed to melt like a candle into the slouch of an old man. He looked at Senlin with his one eye that was the color of dead grass and said, "My arm was branded. I was taken into the wall to where the hods are. Tom, there are places in the dark of the Tower, places I hope you never see, where men and women are put in pens like cattle. The bones are pounded to dust and become part of the road." He did not describe it further, seemed incapable of describing what he had seen, but Adam's haunted look was enough. Senlin could not hold his morose gaze. He looked down at his blotter, picked up the stock of a pen, and fiddled with the nib.

"Voleta saved me, in the end," Adam said, with a swell of pride. "She is so fearless. She went with me into the dark, though she had to fight me and the ushers to do it. While I was being fitted with an iron dog collar in an airless slave market, she...found a man who would make a deal with her."

"Finn Goll," Senlin said grimly.

"He paid my debt and took her life as bond, and I have been here trying to work our way out of it ever since. More than two years now."

"How much longer until the debt is paid?"

"Three years," Adam said, and looked at the rut of the callus in the palm of his hand. "She will be twenty-one years old when she is free again."

"Three years!" Senlin echoed it, his voice filled with the pains of empathy. "Why so long? Even two years of your salary would cover sixteen minas and then some."

"Because my sister attracts a lot of...attention." Adam gulped as a sudden welling of emotion caught in his throat. He shook his head clear and said, "I have to bribe Rodion to keep her on the stage and out of the boudoirs; I have to bribe him to keep her from being sold to some rich noble. Most of what I earn goes straight back to Rodion, and I'm sure Finn Goll takes a cut. I work to pay the man who works me. I hate that she has to parade around in front of all those muddy oglers, but it's better to be on the stage than behind it."

"But why not escape, take your chances? Three years!" Senlin stifled his horror, realizing that he was just rubbing salt in the wound. "How can you wait?"

Adam gave him a soft smile of defeat that seemed years beyond his age. "I felt the same way," he said. He had been edging forward on his seat for many minutes, but now he settled back into the crackling leather. "And then I lost my eye."

The words hung heavily in the air. Sympathy and the desire to fix this tangled mess, to somehow advise a retroactive solution, had already exhausted Senlin. He wished that he could put off the remainder of Adam's miserable confession. But, as is often the case with men, once the silence has been broken, it can't be recovered until everything has been said.

Adam, sensing Senlin's discomfort, tried to lighten his narration. "Not long after I ruined your day, I robbed a bunch of tourists, fresh off a train in Babel Central Station. I wasn't supposed to; it wasn't part of the job. Goll gives a shopping list, a schedule, a budget, a timetable, and a postcard so you never forget to write. But I saw them standing there, just like I had stood months before, happy and confident and dumb as they come. I thought, 'Here it is! Here is your chance to shorten your sentence and save your sister.' I told them I was a porter from the train company, come to take their luggage to the ferry. And they couldn't wait; they were so excited. They gave me everything they owned. I had to hire a wagon to carry it all." Boreas scratched the edge of his brown leather eye patch and gave an unconvincing laugh. Senlin could sense the guilt that loitered beneath the surface, but Adam rushed on. "I sold it all as quick as I could, dresses and bassinets and hats and shaving kits and jewelry. I walked away with nearly twenty minas. If Finn Goll had found out, he would've sent Iren over to pound it out of me. So, I decided to sneak my way back to New Babel, come in through Ginside Port on the other end of town, bribe Rodion with everything I had, and be gone with Voleta before Goll could cock an eyebrow."

"What happened?"

"Pirates," Adam said with a dry scoff. "Me and five other worthless souls bought passage on a ship that looked legitimate; really, it looked like a classic courier ship: a tall barque with three envelopes and two boilers. Built for load and durability, but a pretty ship. But I should've paid more attention to the crew. Instead, I was hanging over the gunwale like a kid, picturing Voleta's face when I told her we were leaving.

"Then, the barque got up in the high air, and the captain wanted to renegotiate the terms of our voyage. His proposal was this: We would give him everything that we had, and he would not push us off a plank. One man argued. They threw him over. The rest of us emptied our pockets. Afterward, we were dumped at the most convenient port, which happened to be the Parlor. I didn't think I could argue, though I knew I was stepping into deep mud. I'd been careful for two years to avoid that awful place. I wanted to forget. But..." Adam pointed at the circular brand on his arm. "They remembered me. And they made sure I would remember them." Adam flipped up the egg-shaped patch of soft leather, showing a purple, drooping gash in the center of an empty eye socket. The scar seemed sacrilegious on the young, handsome face, but Senlin did not grimace or look away. "Tom, don't tell me I can't wait. I can only wait. We have to be patient. We have to work our way free." Adam flinched with the final words, reset the eye patch, and looked down at his empty hands.

Senlin wanted to argue. He wanted to rouse the young man from his despair and inspire him with some grand plan. He tightened his jaw to keep back the flood of advice. This wasn't the time for motivational speeches or proposals; Adam had emptied his heart, and his confession needed no critique. Adam sat like an understuffed doll, and Senlin knew the only thing to do was to break the pall of misery that had fallen over the room. He stood and began shoving his arms into the sleeves of his black overcoat. "I have never seen the inside of a pipe organ," he said, and took up the aerorod, holding it now as if it were a cane. "You know what the old organist at my college used to call his instrument? The plumbing that sings. He joked that every time he pulled out a stop, somewhere on campus, a toilet flushed."

With this and a half dozen other silly anecdotes, Senlin endeavored to revive Adam's spirits. Adam hardly resisted as they departed the station house, requisitioned a steam carriage, and began the trip into New Babel. Whatever was to come, Senlin was not about to let his friend face it alone.

Adam steered the shambling autowagon through the streets of New Babel. Steam clung to the road and curb like a piecrust. Seated on the high driver's box alongside him, Senlin watched as traffic careened in and out of the gloom, mad as jacks. Ashy white buildings rose about them like grim teeth. Bats swooped through the fog, which glowed a molten gold in the electric light of streetlamps. The air was heavy with a damp chill. He hated the stygian city and had avoided it for months.

Had it been left up to him, Senlin would never have found the notorious Steam Pipe. From the outside it looked like every other building on this and every other block; it looked like an undecorated crypt. But Adam was well versed in the subtle variations of the New Babel grid and had no trouble finding it. He parked the autowagon on the street and led Senlin to a metal service door at the end of a narrow alley.

They were met and let in by an older cleaning woman, whom Adam obviously knew. The two of them chatted amiably about her sore foot, and the inconsiderate young women she had to clean up after, and other banalities Senlin could not contribute to. He was distracted by the room anyway. The broad ceiling stepped closer to the rough plank floor the farther they went in. Senlin supposed that they were under the risers of some great room, probably the tiered seats of a theater. Crammed inside the shrinking room were the brass intestines of a leviathan: pipes snaked out from a central tank, running to every corner of the room. Black needles danced across the white faces of gauges. The room was pleasantly warm, a rarity in the Boudoir. Senlin took the opportunity to open his coat and loosen his collar.

"Wet steam comes up into that boiler and is superheated," Adam said, materializing at Senlin's side. Senlin glanced about and realized the cleaning woman was gone. "Most of the pipes go to heat the theater and the bedrooms upstairs, but these," Adam said, and pointed at a trio of thick pipes, "power the turbine, which inflates the bellows of the organ."

Adam continued his technical explanation, and Senlin could sense the young man's passion for the intricacies of the machine, even as the details flew over his head. He tried to force himself to follow Adam's explanation, but he was distracted by their stooped passage behind the boiler and its medusa of pipes that sweated and hissed about them, through a tunnel that thrummed with the drone of an engine, and up a narrow, unlit stair.

They stood before a model city of spires. Some of the towers were made of wood, others of copper, or tin and lead. They stretched up between a black-painted wall full of scaffolding and rigging and an immense red curtain. Such a strange, unexpected spectacle! The towers of this model city, he quickly realized, were in fact the pipes of a mighty organ. There were hundreds of them. Adam explained that they had passed under the main stage of the Steam Pipe and were now backstage.

"There are pipes on stage that look like diapasons, but they're just dummies. They blow air, but don't produce sound. They're just for show," Adam said, concluding some lengthy mechanical note that Senlin had missed the start of.

"If they're dummies, why do they blow air?" Senlin asked gamely, but before Adam could answer, they were interrupted by a man entering from the backstage wings of the theater. Over a tuxedo, he wore a cape that was silver-lined and crimson-backed. Senlin couldn't decide whether it made him look theatrical or insane.

The man was in his prime, at least. He wore his dark hair oiled and in a queue, and the skin of his face was tightened to the bone, unlined when relaxed and, Senlin suspected, heavily rouged. This could only be Rodion, the whoremonger.

"There's something wrong with the Ottava Diapason, Adam. It has no oomph. A crack in the pipe, or perhaps the rats have been at the seals again," Rodion said lightly enough, as he swept to a stop before them. He eyed Senlin like a dominant rooster. The metallic threads in his cape glittered ridiculously even in the dim backstage light. Perhaps if he had met Rodion at a dance social last spring, Senlin would've been intimidated by the man's ostentation, but as it was, the whoremonger reminded him of a watered-down commissioner: a weak man in strong costume. Senlin was afraid the commissioner might pursue him to the ends of the earth, but Senlin doubted Rodion was capable of such persistence. He looked like a dramatist, a man with more props than power. Far from being impressed, Senlin wanted nothing more than to put his thumb in the man's eye.

Rodion continued. "Voleta goes on in twenty minutes. If the organ isn't fixed, I'll have to find some other work for her this evening."

The implication was clear enough. Senlin could feel Adam's tension, which came on as reflexively as a salute. Adam seemed to calculate how long the repairs would take, frowned at the worrisome conclusion, and curtly excused himself to work on the problem.

Rodion turned back to Senlin. "Port Master Thomas Senlin, finally we meet," Rodion said without a hint of warmth to his voice.

"I came to assist Mr. Boreas," Senlin said.

"Liar. It doesn't take two men to stuff a rag in a mouse hole. You came to see some knickers." Rodion leaned in to the port master.

"All right. I came to see, um . . . the show," Senlin said.

"Of course you did. I'll find you a seat," he said, with a sizing glance. He seemed to be gauging Senlin's level of interest in his sordid business. Obviously, the whoremonger was accustomed to capitalizing upon other men's lust, so he was testing the port master, tempting him in the hopes that Senlin would expose some exploitable weakness. Senlin saw a clear advantage in allowing Rodion to believe that he held something over him. Let the man think what he wanted. The whore-monger's mislaid confidence would make him vulnerable to flattery and manipulation later. All Senlin had to do to coddle the man's ego was sit through a burlesque performance that starred Adam's sister.

Senlin suppressed a shudder, quickly replacing his grimace with a smirk that reflected Rodion's own knowing smile. "You really must see what all the fuss is about," Rodion said.

Chapter Eight

Today's candidate: the *Fat Alistair*. She's a merchant ship, forty-six feet, stem to stern, with two twenty-pound guns and bunks for twelve. A good candidate on the surface of it; unfortunately, she flies the colors of Pelphia. Stealing from the Pells, who I must one day infiltrate, seems beyond stupid. The search continues.

—*Every Man's Tower, One Man's Travails*
by T. Senlin

S enlin sat rigidly in the plush theater seat he had been ushered to, his aerorod laid across his knees. He was sure the boiler room was beneath him; he could feel the slight pulsation of machinery through the floor. The contrast between that gloomy underworld and the golden theater that soared about him was almost surreal. Senlin was surrounded by hundreds of men decked in what passed for formal attire in a city of laborers; moth-chewed coats, threadbare hats, and collars the color of cigar smoke were in evidence everywhere. The men were agitated and eager. Ornate theater boxes, arrayed with plaster friezes of reclining nudes, hid wealthy spectators from the prying eyes of the rabble below.

Midstage, Rodion sat at an organ keyboard that was shaped like a crescent moon. He played with stiff-armed vigor. The organ sounded like an aviary. Each note was loud enough to prickle the skin. Rodion pulled at the banks of ivory stops as expertly as a cherry picker, changing and layering the tones to suit the passage he played. The man's talent was undeniable.

Behind the organist's console, a bank of pipes rose in tiers from the floor halfway up the presidium archway, filling the stage. The lush red curtain, which Senlin had recently seen the back of, fluttered from the wind that burst from those dummy pipes. Most of the gleaming copper resonators seemed large enough to swallow a man. Above him, the high, domed ceiling had been painted the color of a clear sky.

But it wasn't the vast and polished pipes, or the flamboyant organist, or the thunderous chords that enthralled the men who filled the theater. It was the women who came on stage and climbed the face of the brass mountain with flirtatious immodesty. They climbed up and pranced along the tops of the pipes, agile as mountain goats, graceful as ballerinas. They were uniformly young and made up, their eyes exaggerated with charcoal and paint, their mouths lurid as smashed cherries. All were ribbed with tightened corsets; frilly skirts flowered at their hips. Blasts of air erupted from the pipes beneath the climbing and bounding dancers, blowing their skirts above their waists. The dancers covered their mouths in a parody of modesty. The audience leaned and rocked and applauded in their seats. The black stockings. The white garters. The flashes of bare thigh. It was as if the erupting music was peeling them bare.

The thought that Marya might somewhere have been reduced to the same fate was enough to make him want to shoot out the lights and strangle the organist and plunge the whole horrible scene into silence. But he was in the obvious minority. The rest of the audience didn't see sisters and daughters, lost souls and adventuresome hearts. They saw beams of limelight swinging across banks of kicking legs. They saw greased teeth and jouncing bosoms. When their locks were blown straight above their heads, the women appeared to be hanging by their hair like fruit from a tree.

Senlin wondered which one was Voleta.

Rodion concluded his song with a volcanic flourish and turned on his bench to face the crowd. The ladies grabbed their skirts and curt-sied above him. The applause slowly died as he held up a white-gloved hand for calm. "Good evening, gentlemen, and welcome to the Steam Pipe." He paused for the wave of sincere cheers. "Please see the door-men if you're interested in a more private performance. My staff is as clean as my pipes!" Laughter pealed. "Not all women are created equal." He continued, and Senlin recognized the words as scripted. "Some are beautiful; some are daring. Some have a talent, athletic or exotic." An obscene call from the crowd elicited a new bout of laugh-ter. "But I have only ever known one woman capable of flight! And so without further ado, the girl you all paid to see, Voleta the Flying Girl."

A hatch opened at the apex of the blue dome, and a woman seated on a trapeze was lowered through. The voluminous black hair that hung in wild kinks about her shoulders made her head appear large and her body slight. She wore a purple leotard that covered her mus-cular bust and broad hips, and bared her lithe, olive-skinned legs.

Even from a distance, Senlin could've identified her as Adam's sis-ter. She had the same broad mouth and the sharp nose, but her eyes were all her own: large, violet, and painted round with green. Blue sequins glinted at her temples. She smiled, not seductively but like an artisan taking delight in her work. She pumped the trapeze until she swept up the incline of the audience, then back up the cliff face of the pipes. Such fluidity and nonchalance! Rodion played a haunting, theatrical tune that seemed full of danger. Senlin was mesmerized. In one deft motion, Voleta flipped over the bar, and for a moment, he was sure the trapeze would leave her behind. But she twisted in the air like a wisp of smoke and caught the bar again. Dangling by her arms, her slippers brushed the outstretched fingers of the more brazen men who reached after her from their seats. Then, at the limit of her swing, she released the bar and corkscrewed like a maple seed, catching the bar as it began its return. When she somersaulted, her unruly, beautiful hair accentuated her body like the tail of a kite.

Senlin's heart rose into his throat, enlarged by fear and awe. She was spectacular.

After a few further acrobatic feats, she slowed the swing of the trapeze, waved with childish abandon at the crowd, and was hoisted back through the hatch in the dome. This time Senlin found himself contributing to the manic applause.

There was a brief but touching reunion backstage among the rigging, fire buckets, and the sparkling dandruff of a thousand costumes. Adam's usual haggard expression fell away as he swung Voleta about in a glad embrace. Senlin felt privileged to be present for the happy moment. The grounded Voleta seemed somehow smaller than the Flying Girl. She was unreserved, almost silly in her expressions, and seemed in many ways the opposite of her brother. Adam introduced Voleta to Senlin, and she shook his hand with the soft, shy grip of a child. But she was not a child, and there was a quick intelligence behind her gaze. Even so, she had her tics; she often guffawed after anyone spoke with any seriousness, as if she found earnestness itself funny. The guffaw was short, not at all feminine, and sounded more like a baritone's "huh-huh" than an eighteen-year-old girl's laugh. It was an oddly endearing quirk.

Voleta talked rapidly about her routine and her frustration with being kept always inside and her jealousy that Adam got to see the sun anytime he wanted. She concluded this single streaming sentence with an effusive description of a box of four bonbons she had been given as a gift, three of which were heavenly, and the fourth, disgusting. Adam said little, but his smile was eloquent enough. Senlin suspected these occasions were rare for them, and he wondered whether lost loved ones were perhaps sometimes preferable to imprisoned ones.

Then, all too soon, Rodion appeared, followed closely by a retinue of young women, ushers, makeup artists, and a slew of other stagehands. He preceded them like a king, still wearing his foil and crimson cape, but now with a new addition: The silver butt of a pistol protruded from a holster at his hip.

Rodion insinuated himself into their happy little trio, driving the smile instantly from Adam's face. He pointed at Voleta. "The next show is in a half hour. You need to eat and get back to wardrobe. Go on," the whoremonger said in a tone that parodied parental concern. Voleta gave him a sour smirk, though one that was free of any real rebellion, and turned to peck her brother on the cheek.

"Don't eat the bonbons, Voleta. They aren't gifts. They're installments from men who are trying to buy you," Adam said.

Voleta let out one of her honest huh-huh's. "If somebody wants to buy me with chocolate, they're not going to like what they get," she said, ballooning her cheeks and hooping her arms around an imaginary large belly. This time Adam didn't laugh; he looked pale and bereft. Voleta turned her violet eyes on Senlin. "You're his boss. Order him to be happy, and then hit him with a stick until he is. Just follow him around with a broom handle and give him a whap when he sighs," she said, clapping her hands. Before Senlin could answer, she rose to the points of her toes and kissed him on the cheek just as she had with her brother.

Voleta was absorbed again into the procession of dancers and stagehands, the group fizzing away into the bowels of the theater where changing rooms turned into bedrooms, and some spectators paid handsomely to become leading men for a while.

As the group was turning the corner, one straggling yellow-haired dancer glared back at them...no, not them, but at Senlin. Her glare had a sinister edge to it, and he realized he'd seen her before. Yes, he'd seen her on the barge on which he'd escaped the Baths. Hadn't she glowered at him then, too?

Before Senlin could pursue the bothersome thread of thought, Rodion grabbed the reins and whipped the conversation toward his own destination. "Such priceless genius," he said, nodding after the receding chatter of the group. His chest puffed with undeserved paternal pride. "Priceless! I would never dream of letting that sort of talent languish in obscurity. The whole world deserves to see her act."

Senlin could tell that Adam knew the whoremonger was baiting him. The young man did not rise to the bait. Senlin was proud of him, though the victory was short-lived.

"An Algezian baron caught her act the other night and was impressed. He wanted a private performance, but, per our agreement, I told him that such exceptional beauty and skill was not for rent." Rodion's tight, anemic skin piled about his mouth like an old man's knuckle; it was a ghastly smile. "I'm a whoremonger. I prefer dealing in whores. There's no courting, little turnover, no complex negotiations or proof of maidenhead or questions of pedigree with whores. The life of a wifemonger is exhausting! But your sister does all the work for me. She goes on stage, and she courts them, and haggles with them, and proves herself a hundred times more convincingly than any doctor or genealogist ever could. She is making this old whoremonger into a peddler of wives. I said she was priceless, but she has been searching for her price. The Algezian baron suggested that it might be twenty-five minas. But what are your thoughts? What do you think your sister is worth?"

Adam strained forward, his ears red; the veins in his neck stood out roundly. Senlin knew what was coming. He had on many occasions in his time as headmaster seen the victims of bullies abruptly arrive at their breaking point. The fight that followed was invariably bloody. Rodion was pushing Adam to the edge of self-restraint. He was looking for an excuse to shoot the troublesome brother of his star performer. Senlin had to intervene.

Senlin swung the heavy aerorod low, striking Adam at the back of his knees. The young man, caught off guard, dropped like a stone. Sprawled on the backstage floor, Adam rolled awkwardly at Senlin's feet, staring up at him with an expression of shocked betrayal. Senlin hiked his head toward the backstage door and said in a flat, pitiless tone, "Boreas, start the wagon."

Adam rose and collected himself, never once taking his eyes off of Senlin, his initial surprise quickly hardening into anger as he headed with a slight limp for the door. Senlin could only hope the youth would forgive him.

Rodion was squinting at the port master as if he had sprouted horns. "Well, the bookworm has a spine after all," he murmured, and then squaring his shoulders, he asked, "Why did you come here? Why, really?"

"Finn asked me to poke around." The lie came out casually, as if Senlin was too bored by the deception to continue it. "He wonders if he's getting his full take of ticket sales, so he asked me to count heads. He can sit on his thumb for all I care, him and that elephantine woman," Senlin said. It was all bravado, of course, but Senlin's many years of observing playground sports had taught him that a little chest thumping was often the best way to discourage a bully. "Tell me your headcount, and I'll report it."

"One hundred thirty-six," Rodion said. "I don't believe in generosity or fraternity. So tell me why you're sparing me this trouble."

"The man's paranoid enough without confirming his suspicions. If he finds one leak in his purse, he'll look for more, and I don't want that." He rapped his aerorod once on the floor in punctuation, drawing a boom from the hollow stage. Senlin turned to leave and then, pretending to be inspired by a pestering thought, pivoted back to face the whoremonger. "And I would think the girl is worth thirty minas at least. Such a spectacular creature!"

It was a weak goad, but Senlin hoped it would be enough to stir the whoremonger's greed and buy them a little time to plan. If there had been any question in his mind before, there was none now: He would do all he could to help Voleta escape this black-hearted cad.

Adam wasn't fuming. He was deflated, which was infinitely worse. Senlin had hoped the youth would just repay the blow with one of his own. Instead, the young man sat slouched over the spindly wheel of the autowagon, his eye half focused, unconsciously kneading the back of his leg. Senlin apologized for hitting him, and Adam's only response was to stop massaging the sore spot.

"He would've shot you." Senlin had to nearly shout to be heard over the knocking of the pistons.

Adam mulled the point over, first nodding, then shaking, and finally rolling his head miserably. He seemed on the verge of breaking down. He said with choked pride, "He hasn't broken her. You saw her. She is indomitable." The lightning in the barred cupola over the city sparked with sudden ecstasy, pausing their conversation. The thorny light pierced the fog and immolated scores of moths and bats. When the bottled storm ended, Adam continued with renewed force. "I am responsible for making sure she stays unbroken. I am responsible. I must do something..."

Senlin wanted so badly to say something, to blow upon the spark of Adam's revelation, but he worried that doing so would only undermine Adam's confidence in it. So, instead of lecturing, Senlin decided to confess his own failure. "I tried patience in the Baths. I had a method and a schedule I kept for weeks. I expected a fair result, expected the Tower to reward my self-discipline with...a miraculous reunion." He made a throaty sound of disgust. "If I had kept to my timetables and nursed my entitlement any longer, I'd be a hod now. I have no doubt. And Marya would be lost to me forever."

"So what did you do?" Adam asked.

"I robbed the commissioner. No, first, I conspired, then I infiltrated, then I flattered, then I conned, and then I robbed the commissioner." A little satisfied smile lightened his face. "Oh, if Finn Goll knew how much of a mess I left behind...I'm sure there's a bounty on my head in the Baths; I'm probably worth a little fortune to the commissioner. I took something of his, and I'm sure he'd like it back." He heard the bragging tone that had crept into his voice and coughed to cover his chagrin. He needed to circle the conversation back to its purpose. "My point is, we must sometimes take calculated risks, Adam. We cannot expect the Tower to treat us fairly, or expect the powerful to respect us."

"Calculated risks..." Adam scowled and wrung the wheel until his knuckles were bloodless and white. "Do you have a plan?"

"The plan's still forming, but I know the pieces that we'll need."

"That's a place to start, I suppose. What will we need?"

Senlin counted the points out on his fingers. "A ship, a crew, and a wind."

Adam straightened in his seat as the enormity of the list sunk in.

"I was really hoping you'd say that we needed a bit of rope and a sausage," he said, scratching at the patchy shadow of a three-day beard. "A ship, a crew, and a wind, hmm? That's going to take a lot of calculating. And what about a captain? We'll need one of those, too."

Senlin laughed. "Let's not get ahead of ourselves."

Chapter Nine

Tucked among the old ledgers on my office shelves
are a dozen flawed dictionaries, several primers on
aeronautics (which I have thoroughly perused and
the best of which I've claimed as my own), and at
least thirty unique and useless guides to the Tower.
When I read them, I want to shout, *Draw me a map!
Show me the way!* But all the authors do is describe
their footprints and talk about their shoes, which are
always the best, the only true shoes.

—*Every Man's Tower, One Man's Travails*
by T. Senlin

Swift action was undermined by duty, which suddenly overwhelmed Senlin and Adam and every aspect of the port.
Barges and ferries filed into the docks in such quick succession that Senlin felt like he was drowning in crates of rum and haggling captains and pie-eyed women bound for the boudoirs. The port
workers, plunged into shifts that lasted twenty hours or more, might
have rioted if they'd had any energy left. Senlin had to abandon his
accounting to assist at the weigh station; the scales had to be loaded and
unloaded as rapidly as a catapult besieging a city. It was near madness,
and yet Senlin's systems somehow held: No ships were turned away;
no valuables were absconded with; and no perishables perished. The
autowagons overheated but did not explode, and after three days of
furious activity, the port was calm again.

Senlin canceled the evening assembly, and instead of standing on it like a soapbox, he sat on the lip of the weigh station, arms on his knees, watching the men move toward the tunnel to New Babel. A few stopped to ask him to read an address on a broadside, which he did automatically. A stevedore named Emrit asked Senlin to decipher a note from his sweetheart. Emrit was missing a prominent tooth, but when he smiled, the gap didn't seem like a flaw. It reminded Senlin of a dimple in a cheek; it was an attractive quirk. The note, written in the uncertain, tight cursive of a novice, asked Emrit for a meeting, asked him to bring chocolate, and made a rather clumsy reference to an intimate act, which Senlin recited with a physician's professionalism. Emrit thanked him for these revelations and joined the vein of men moving out.

Despite their exhaustion, they were all in the happy throes of anticipation: Some would go to the boudoirs, some to the Crumb houses, some to the pubs, and they would all slink home to the yard at some miserable hour, all the joy wrung from them, all the anger exhausted, and all the anxiety spent. Senlin was a little surprised to find that he wanted to go with them. He could do with a little distraction, a little oblivion. But no, there was work to do.

Later that evening, Adam tromped up to Senlin's apartment carrying a small wooden cube, a late delivery from the port. Adam found the port master seated at his uneven table with an open book and an open bottle. Senlin glanced up at the hardy little crate, recognized it, and hiked his chin toward an empty corner of the room. Adam set the shipment of White Chrom down and backed away from it quickly. Neither of them liked having to handle the stuff. Senlin had nervous visions of the crate being dropped and cracking open; he imagined the powder erupting into a fog, an overdose in a single breath, a cloud full of nightmares.

"The men are drunk," Adam said in a voice flattened by exhaustion. He settled into the rough wood chair across from Senlin, and though he was tired, he still tested the chair before giving it his whole weight.

"They've earned it," Senlin said, hardly looking up from the prone book as he scooted the bottle nearer his friend. "As have you." Adam accepted the offer and enjoyed a long, contemplative drink.

Outside the windows of Senlin's apartment, the revelry of the men reached a new, exalted pitch before settling again into a low slur of laughter and song. "I gave them a raise," Senlin said in a way that suggested Adam shouldn't be surprised, though the young man was.

"In the nearly three years I've been here, there has never been a pay raise. How did you talk Goll into it?"

"I didn't," Senlin said, not glancing up from his book and the complex schematics of a steam engine that lay there, obscure as ancient hieroglyphs. "The port is so efficient now that the increase won't affect the eight o'clock report."

"Are you serious?"

Senlin looked up. "Trust me, he won't notice. And if he does, I'll just explain that it was an overdue act of self-preservation. I staved off a revolt. You can't work a crew half to death and expect them to come lapping back for more punishment."

"Maybe so," Adam said with an edge of doubt. "But why now? If he does find out, he'll have Iren put your head on a spit. Why risk it?"

"Well, because I've been thinking. And I've come to the conclusion that our prospects are pretty grim."

Adam started to laugh, tried to catch himself, and then gave in to it. "Oh, but your list is so short: a ship, a crew, and a wind. Easy-peasy."

Senlin closed the book, but his expression did not open any further. He had the concentrated, pained look of a man playing a card game he could not afford to lose. For a moment, there was no movement in the room except for the shuttering shadow of a moth beating itself to death on the sallow electric light overhead. "Here are the problems as I see them. First, we need a ship. A tug or a barge won't do. If the ship isn't reasonably agile and minimally armed, we won't get a mile from port before we're boarded or shot down. But if the ship is large, we'll need an equally large crew to fly it. That's something we can't afford. Never mind that for the moment.

"Let's say we find a modest ship that can be operated and defended by a crew of five or six, a ship that had a cargo hold large enough for a few weeks' rations of food, powder, fuel, and water, a ship that is neither so ostentatious that it attracts unwanted attention, nor so pitiful that we're turned away from the nobler ports. The perfect balance would be like the dress code for the Steam Pipe: shabby formal. Even if such a ship exists, how would we take it? We haven't the numbers to overwhelm a crew.

"So..." Senlin paused with a finger raised to hold his place as he took a gulp from the bottle. He gasped a little and continued. "We will need to use someone else's strength and numbers to do our work for us. But they, whoever they are, will of course have no interest in throwing themselves into our battle to risk their lives for our reward. Which leaves us with a difficult question of how to empty the ship... presuming, of course, that we can gather a small, faithful crew to fly her once she's off the moorings.

"Added to this impossibility is your sister, Voleta. And it is the same problem. Rodion is sealed up in his very own fortress, and he has, by my count, at least thirty men. They play usher and stagehand, but they are, without a doubt, his armed guard. We don't have the strength to muscle our way into the Steam Pipe and extract her. We must use someone else's arm to beat in the door. So we need two proxy armies: one to clear the ship and one to save your sister. And presently, we have no armies."

"And no crew," Adam said.

"And no ship," Senlin added helpfully.

The moth that had been battering the light raised a fatal clank and fell to the floor. Adam shook his head and said, "But what does all this have to do with giving the men a raise?"

"I'm currying favor. We may need them to stand with us."

"In that case, however much it was, the raise wasn't large enough."

"You're probably right," Senlin said, deflating a little. "At the very least, they might hesitate to wring our necks, should it come to that."

"It sounds like your plan is really coming along, Tom. You even have a contingency for when the porters try to wring our necks. That's wonderful."

Sharing an impulse, both men reached out to grip the bottle standing between them. Neither released it. Senlin met Adam's eye amid the unexpected stalemate. Obviously the young man was working up to saying something more, to speaking his mind, and the bottle remained stranded between them while he did. "All right, out with it. What's on your mind, Adam?"

"Is this really the thing to do? Steal a ship? I mean, you're arguing against it yourself. It seemed a fine idea when we were both stirred up by the whoremonger, but now in the clear light of day..." He pulled at his collar until the second button popped open. Senlin sensed that the young man had been thinking about this for longer than he'd been sitting in the room. Perhaps it had been on his mind since their visit to the Steam Pipe. His phrases were a little too exact, a little too practiced to be spontaneous. "We'll make a hundred enemies: Rodion, Finn Goll, the port workers, the crew and captain we displace... Once we begin running, I don't think that we'll ever be able to stop. How will we live without steady work or homes or a patron? Who will we trust? Will we have to steal our fuel? Will we have to scavenge for food? What sort of life is that?"

"What sort of life is this?" Senlin said.

"You told me that you were worth a small fortune to the commissioner. You robbed him; why not ask for a ransom? Negotiate a deal. Give him what he wants, and he will pay you for it. I'm sure of it. Instead of running, we could buy our freedom."

"Adam," Senlin said, abruptly releasing the bottle and rocking back in his chair. He crossed his arms. "Powerful men don't bargain with men like us. They don't respect us or fear us, so there's nothing to keep them from backing out on a deal. There's no honor. Remember your pirates, the ones who are responsible for the loss of your eye!

How did that happen? You had a deal, didn't you? But you hadn't any power, and they knew it." Senlin's mouth was dry, and spit was beginning to foam against his teeth. "Even if—and I do mean if—the commissioner was willing to haggle over a ransom, he would only be interested in paying for two things. First, his precious painting, which I do not have. And second, my head. My sincerest hope is that he has forgotten all about me. That is the best-case scenario."

In response to all of Senlin's passionate reasoning, Adam only shrugged. "I'm not saying it isn't without risk, a calculated risk, but you're presuming an awful lot about how the commissioner will react to a proposition that saves him effort and time. I don't see how that is any more ridiculous than engineering an elaborate plot and stealing a ship." Adam radiated obstinate, youthful confidence, which struck an old nerve in Senlin: a headmaster's nerve. Adam concluded his argument smugly. "I'm only trying to be reasonable."

"And I am trying to save your sister!" Senlin shouted more violently than he'd intended.

Though thrown off balance by the outburst, Adam stubbornly pressed the point. "Even if you don't have the painting, you could sell him information about who does. With just a little money in our pocket—"

Senlin cut him off. "No, Adam! No, I am not going to bargain with the commissioner. That's the end of it!" Senlin pounded the table once, making his book jump. Adam looked as if he'd been slapped, which Senlin regretted, though it did not cool his response. "Look, you will never have enough money to pry Voleta loose of her contract because Rodion sees no advantage in letting her go. He will just take your money and sell her again to someone else. Why not? What will you do to stop him? If you want to see your sister freed, we will have to do it ourselves!"

Adam scowled but said nothing. A long burst of hoots from the porters outside gave the gulf between them time to grow. Senlin wiped his mouth and felt an unfamiliar tremor in his fingers. It wasn't the thought of Voleta that had driven him to the brink of manic rage. It was Marya. It was always Marya. A week earlier, he'd finally given up his obsessive turning of her portrait and had stowed it out of sight under the loose floorboard along with his journal and Ogier's key-mold pistol. He'd done it because she was becoming an abstraction, an image, an ideal. He felt it happening. The woman was disappearing. The memory of her thrilling voice, the taper of her agile fingers, and the subtle flirtations she used to console him in a crowded room... all of it was fading away, and in its place, growing larger and more real every day, was Ogier's painted icon. So, he had hidden her from himself in the hope that when he did glimpse her picture again, it would give him a little shock of memory, a little jolt of hope, and keep him a while longer from accepting the plodding, desolate life that stood in evidence all about him.

Without another word, Adam stood and walked from the room. Senlin did not try to stop him. He realized that he had made a mistake by confiding his fears and the flaws in his plan to the youthful Boreas. Adam was looking for direction, for a leader, for a captain, and having meant to or not, Senlin had taken on the role. And now he had to act accordingly. The crew doesn't want to hear that the captain has doubts or that the captain's plan is full of holes. It ruins their confidence, and then they begin to grasp at straws, just as Adam had done. It wasn't Adam's fault that Senlin had made no progress in finding a crew, or a ship, or a wind. Pretty soon, if that lack of progress continued, Adam would just find some other piper to follow.

Senlin woke in the middle of the night to a wooden bang.

The sound was like a door being slammed but lower to the ground. Blearily, he wondered if it was a trapdoor. But his room didn't have a trapdoor. Perhaps it was an echo from the station yard or a forgotten nightmare that had fooled his waking ear. In a daze, he opened his eyes, anticipating the dim golden gloom of the shuttered lamps outside.

A red glowing figure loomed at his bedside, twisting and struggling like a man amid a seizure. The revelation was immediate: It was the

Red Hand. Impossibly, incredibly, the commissioner's executioner had found him.

The assassin was pulling at his own knee. He had stepped on the faulty floorboard, and for the moment, his foot was caught in Senlin's secret cubby. Adrenaline flooded Senlin's extremities with sudden sensation; every nerve felt like a sparking fuse.

Senlin rolled out the far side of his bed, intent on making a break for the door. Instead, he tumbled to the floor, tangled in his sheets. He flailed like a fish caught in a net. Boards splintered behind him, and he turned in time to see the Red Hand lunging over the bed like some cosmic phenomenon, like a fireball blazing through the atmosphere. Then the meteor crashed down. The Red Hand bowled into Senlin, and they became a knot of bedsheets and limbs.

They crashed into the flimsy bureau, popping all three of the drawers out. Shirtsleeves roped about them. The assassin's brass cuff clipped Senlin in the jaw, making his eyes pool with tears. Senlin could see nothing but a red glow shrouded by white linen. It was like watching a forest fire through dense smoke. A sudden pressure on Senlin's arm kept him from swiping away the clean laundry.

"Where is the painting?" the Red Hand said, his enunciation so flat and calm he might've been asking Senlin for the time of day.

"I don't know!" Senlin said through gritted teeth.

The tracery of veins made the man appear as a frozen firework, a spew of volcanic light. With his free arm, Senlin pulled a shirt over the vivid skull and looped the sleeve about the assassin's neck. The Red Hand seemed to gasp, and Senlin felt a little flight of hope: Perhaps he could fight his way free. But it was not a gasp of surprise. It was a sigh. A weary, contemptuous sigh. Senlin was boring his assassin.

Before Senlin could tighten the makeshift noose, excruciating pain lanced up his shoulder. The Red Hand wrenched his arm with overwhelming, almost mechanical strength. He rolled with the pressure to keep his arm in its socket. Forced onto his stomach, he was left entirely helpless. He kicked like a child throwing a tantrum, but his heels hit nothing. The Red Hand yanked him up by the hair, and his spine bowed against the knee that dug into his tailbone. He felt like a stick of kindling preparing to snap. Then the floor flew at him. He had just enough time to look away before the side of his head bounced against it. Splinters bit his ear and cheek. For an instant, he was deaf. Then a ringing note, higher than hearing, slowly descended the scale like a falling bomb. His head was lifted and bounced a second time, and the wood now splashed beneath him. Motes appeared in his vision, yellow spiders crawling upon a red web. The red web opened its mouth, showing a little glowing furnace, a flame-like tongue.

Senlin could feel the man's warm breath when the Red Hand said, "You intellectuals are always so surprised to discover how fragile your body is. The mind is so robust, so remote. But muscles and bones are as simple as tied-up straw. They unravel and snap. And the more they break, the more the mind shrinks. In the moments before the cascade into death, the great intellect is reduced to a silent kernel. The mind is nothing more than a door into the dark." Senlin wanted to scream but couldn't. "That is where you're going, Thomas. The voracious, indifferent, eternal dark. Where is the painting?"

Made desperate by fear and dumb by the beating, Senlin cast about for something, anything, to defend himself with. His hand slapped along the floor, searching. The wood tingled under his hand. He was disoriented. Which way was the door? If he could only get ahold of his aerorod, he would at least be able to die while defending himself. But there was nothing, just laundry and splinters.

He realized he couldn't swallow before he understood that he couldn't breathe. The assassin now sat on his back, pulling his neck like a rider trying to stop a horse. A sudden, unexpected rush of euphoria filled Senlin. Dimly, he recognized the gladness for what it was: the coming of death. And he was oddly relieved. The Red Hand was wrong. There was light in that expanse; there was peace to think. He let his mind wander. He wondered about Ogier. He must've hid the painting well because it hadn't been found. Maybe Ogier had died before he confessed the hiding place of his beloved *Girl with a Paper Boat*. Senlin saw the girl now, standing in the full brilliance of the

Baths' kaleidoscopic light, standing over her shadow, dark as a hole in the world. And in his vision of the painting, Marya was standing with her, skirts bunched up in one hand, her other hand holding the girl's. He watched from the shore. Neither faced him. Neither needed to. They were happy; the world was bright.

Amid this fondness and calm, a fly began to buzz: a single, dark speck of thought. The fly refused to be caught and refused to go away. He batted at it. Whatever small revelation was trying to disturb his paradise, it wouldn't have much longer to live. How long did houseflies live? He would ignore it. It bumped against his face. He swatted again, and the fly seemed to slow, to let itself be caught. He felt it fizz in his closed hand. He pulled his fist up to his face and uncurled his fingers. In the middle of his palm lay a key.

Then the world began to shake, the subtle tremor quickly becoming a grinding, stampeding earthquake. The water leapt and boiled and splashed up the legs of Marya and the girl whose hand she held. Fine mortar began salting his upturned face in the utter darkness.

He realized he wasn't ready. He wasn't ready. Then the ground leapt out from under him, and he began to fall.

He landed in his body again on the floor of his room. He was lying on his back. The red glowing figure shook him roughly, and it didn't seem like the first time he had done that. Senlin felt warmth pooling in his mouth. He swallowed and coughed until he could breathe; the sensation was painful but full of relief. "I'm sorry it has taken me so long to find you. I don't like to be tardy. I visited Ogier months ago. I was right on time for that conversation. It didn't go well for him. Either your compatriot was fatally stubborn, or the truth was unfortunate. I asked him the same question I ask you now for the last time. Where is the painting you stole?"

Senlin felt a pang of sorrow for the painter, but he was equally amazed that Ogier had been willing to die to keep his painting from the commissioner. It all suddenly seemed so out of proportion. And the fact that the commissioner had continued hunting for Senlin in the ensuing months, had somehow found him, and had then loosed his dog on him . . . All for a painting!

Obviously, he wouldn't be able to convince the assassin of the absurdity of his mission. If Senlin wanted to survive, he had to tell him something. Then he recalled the key that had appeared in his hand in his deathly vision, and an idea, slim and unlikely, sprang to mind.

His voice came out as a croak. "It's in a locked drawer," he said. "I need to get the key."

Chapter Ten

The *Banyan o' Morrow* is a flat-bottomed scow that's as ugly as a pig's nose. One thirty-pound gun, heavily corroded, is its only defense. The motley crew of six would probably surrender without argument. A charmless but feasible candidate. (On second inspection, rot has turned the bulwarks soft as cake. It is a death trap.)

—*Every Man's Tower, One Man's Travails*
by T. Senlin

Senlin braced himself over the shattered gap in the floorboard. As he reached into the darkened cubby, a boot heel settled on the back of his neck, threatening as a thumbnail to a flea.

"If you come up with anything but a key, I will step on you," the Red Hand said.

Senlin hesitated. Sweat or blood trickled around the rind of his skull and down his jaw. The jailor's key lay under the painting of Marya. He had no choice but to pull her out first to get to the key.

"There's a painting here," Senlin said. "But it's not the one you're looking for. The key is under it."

"Let me see it."

As soon as the painting emerged, a glowing hand flashed down and snatched it from him. Senlin could not watch the assassin's scrutiny of the painting, but he saw the result. Hurled against the wall before him, the frame exploded about the painting. Senlin winced. He couldn't tell if his painting was ruined, but there was nothing he could do about it now. He reached again into the hollow with deliberate slowness.

The pressure softened on his neck when he came up with the key. The Red Hand removed his heel. Senlin stood, and his legs were as rickety as one of his chairs.

"What does the key open?" the Red Hand asked in his distracted, almost dreamy way.

Senlin cleared his muddy throat. He teetered on his feet and said without inflection, "You."

He pulled the small trigger inside the key's bow. The report was no louder than the crack of a wooden spoon. The pea-wide barrel gave a snort of smoke. It was, Senlin had to admit, a more pitiful result than he had hoped for.

Unruffled, the Red Hand glanced down at the stain forming on his shirtfront. The slow ooze of blood was garnet-bright.

"You know what's funny," the Red Hand said humorlessly. "You look at me and see a man, a head shorter and a hand wider than your-self, but a man nevertheless." The assassin reached forward and gath-ered the folds of Senlin's nightshirt into his deceptively small fists. He pulled Senlin closer to his bland, jack-o'-lantern face. "So you assume that I am like you, that I share your cognition, your burden of conscience, your intestinal parasites. But I am nothing like you." His breath smelled strongly of formaldehyde, and up close, Senlin saw that his skin had the rubbery appearance of a preserved frog. Senlin was raised to his toes and then lifted from his feet. "I am the riddle in the mouth of the Sphinx. I am the slaver that chews the living chain. I am the farmer of dead seeds, the filler of holes. Who am I?"

Senlin answered at a whisper: "Death."

"Yes," the Red Hand breathed.

An explosion arrested the tightening at Senlin's throat. The apart-ment window across from them blew out into the station yard. The blast came from the opposite side of the room, and they turned as one toward the origin.

Illuminated by the light of the hall, Adam stood in the doorway with his second pistol raised. A troop of dockworkers drummed up the stairs behind him. With unnatural speed, the assassin flung Senlin at the door, ruining any chance of Adam getting off a second shot. The Red Hand leapt through the jagged remains of the window into the murky light of the station yard and was gone.

Adam caught Senlin, the pistols in his hands making for an awkward embrace. Senlin, his voice momentarily crushed, gestured at the devastated window. Adam didn't wait for further direction; he yelled over his shoulder at the coming troop of porters, "After him! He's headed for the port!"

Adam propped Senlin on his heels and ran for the stairs, raising the alarm as he went.

Senlin's bedroom looked like it had entertained a bull. Rubbing his raw throat, Senlin made a half-hearted attempt at gathering up his sundries and his clothes. He dropped the tangled mass into one of the broken drawers and shuffled to the heap that had once been a picture frame. His knees trembled when he knelt to the painted board, which miraculously had landed faceup among the nest of wood and brown paper backing. The painting had survived. This simple fact was enough to chase the terror and the shock from his mind. He had also survived.

He was surprised by the texture on the reverse side of the painted board. It felt like fish scales. The papered-over back of the painting had been torn open. He turned the board over and let out an unexpected blat of laughter.

Taped to the reverse side of the board and staring back at him was a girl. She stood in ankle-deep water. A paper boat dangled from her hand.

A scrap of paper fell out. The few words on it had been written out hurriedly, but Senlin still recognized the hand. It was Ogier's. It said, "Don't let him have it. It is not what it seems. It is a key—it is a key to the Tower and happiness and death. Hide it, and keep it safe. For her sake."

A half hour later, Adam returned to find the port master sitting on his bed with all the lights on. The gunny curtains hung limply over the destroyed window. Senlin had had the presence of mind to hide Ogier's contraband painting. Whatever happened, he was determined to not add to Adam's burden any further. It wouldn't do the young man any good to wrestle with the mystery of a painting that Senlin had been compelled to steal by a man who did not keep it, even while insisting that it was a "key to the Tower and happiness and death," whatever that meant. Such mysteries were part of the burden of leadership. Besides, Ogier's painting might turn out to be a bargaining chip yet, and he didn't want anyone to know that he had it, at least for the moment.

"He got away," Adam said. "We chased him to the port. Don't ask me how a man who glows in the dark vanishes in the middle of the night." He tried to laugh, but the noise came out raw as a bray. Adam, badly shaken, sat heavily on a corner of Senlin's bed. "I've never seen anything like that. I don't know what that was."

"Thank you for coming to the rescue," Senlin said, recovering some of his usual ramrod posture.

"It was either that or lie awake listening to you break every piece of furniture in your room," Boreas said with a tenuous smile. He was quiet for a while, his brow knitted in reflection. After a moment, he asked, "Tom, who was that?"

Senlin wheezed, his swollen throat constricting his breath. It took him a few breaths to work up to saying, "That was the Red Hand, the commissioner's executioner. I think it's clear that we're past bargaining with that tyrant." He retrieved the broom that stood in a corner of his room and began sweeping up the shattered glass from under the window. "I'm afraid that my glowing assassin will be back...eventually. I'm glad you interrupted him when you did, but he doesn't seem the sort to be discouraged for long."

Adam stood and pursued the port master as he shuffled about the floor, dragging the broom in long pensive strokes. "Well, you say we're past bargaining, but you're also past hiding now. What are you going to do? If you have the painting, if you felt like you had to hide it from me, why hide it from him? Just give it to him. It's not worth dying for."

"I agree," Senlin said, presenting the broom to Adam. "And since you feel like pacing, I'll give you something to push."

Adam yanked the broom from Senlin's hand but did not cease pleading his case. "Then tell him where the painting is. Tell him who has it, and who you stole it for. Or tell me, and I'll talk to him on your behalf."

"No. It's a brave offer; you probably don't realize how brave, but no. You're right about one thing: There'll be no more hiding. But for the time being, I think the commissioner's uncertainty is what will keep me alive. The Red Hand could've just wrung me dead in my sleep, but no, he wanted to talk. I think, Adam, there is more to this painting than we know. I think the commissioner is desperate to have it back and just as afraid to lose it. Which I find interesting. And as long as I can keep him guessing . . ." Senlin trailed off when he saw Adam hanging upon the broom like an old crone holds her cane. He leaned on the broom, looking bereft of all hope. And why not? He had just seen a monster, full in the flesh. The peril was undeniable.

Senlin strode to the table and picked up the jailor's key that lay there. He wanted to give Adam something else to distract him, something useful, so he said, "All right, it's about time I learned how to reload a gun. Come and show me."

Adam gave him a long, disbelieving look, but the port master did not back away from the request, which had sounded remarkably like an order. After a moment Adam set aside the broom and began the instruction.

The next morning, driven by curiosity, Senlin went out on the pier and looked for how the assassin had escaped. A ship would've been noticed, even a small one, which meant the Red Hand had come by more discreet means. Scouting the perimeter of the dock turned up nothing suspicious, though he wasn't entirely sure what he expected to find. He repeated the circuit twice, moving more slowly each time. The porters, waiting idly for new freight, were amused to see their port master out of his office and away from the station yard. They were further delighted to watch him sprawl flat and hang half over the side of the dock like a man who'd had too much to drink. Senlin ignored their snickers.

It wasn't long before he found what he was looking for: a silk cord tied carefully to an eyelet screwed close to the edge on the underside of the pier. He couldn't see where the cord ended because it ran down and around the limb of the Tower, but he was sure it led to the Baths. The Red Hand had had a long and treacherous climb up, but a quick slide back down.

Senlin set a hook knife to the cord and snipped the line.

One thing was certain: Someone in the Port of Goll had tied the line and let it out. Someone in New Babel was conspiring with the commissioner.

Later that morning when Iren burst into his office, Senlin was prepared. He received her calmly, his hands steepled over the absurd prow of his desk. She stuck out her hand, large as a dinner plate, and waited for the envelope filled with bills and the summary of imports.

"You can't read," Senlin declared, "which means you can't write, which means you are more helpless than a woman of your stature should be."

The lines of her broad, smooth brow turned down, pointing toward a deep and frightening scowl. With practiced deliberation, she unlatched the chain about her waist. The links clanked as they straightened at her side. Senlin regarded all of this with a small, implacable smile. Iren adopted a fighting stance, the leather of her apron creaking about her trunk-like thighs, her feet nearly connecting the walls of the room. Senlin refused to flinch, even as she began to swing the chain over her head. The whoosh of the chain filled the narrow space. She let it out, link by link until the hook at the end whizzed within inches of his bookcases. The tree of rubber stamps on his desk trembled. The beads of his abacus chattered; his papers fluttered. It was as if a storm had been born inside his office.

Through it all, Senlin regarded her with level-eyed patience. He said, "I've gotten used to having my life threatened, Iren. I'm bored with it. Knock my head off or sit down."

Her face reddening, Iren turned the chain's propeller nearer the top of his head. Senlin felt his hair begin to part from the gust. He had to raise his voice to be heard over the wail of the chain. "You can't punch the sense out of a book. You can't torture a letter into talking. You can't strangle a sign into giving you directions. Everywhere you look there are secrets standing out in the open. You are vulnerable because of it. But I can help you if you'll let me."

Gradually, her anger dwindled and her chain slowed, until with a final jerk of her arm, she snapped the hook back to her hand. Breathing heavily, she wrapped the chain about her waist again. "What do you want from me?" she asked in her mournful baritone.

"See this?" Senlin turned up his chin to show the garish bruise collaring his throat. "I need you to teach me how to keep this from happening. I've written a letter to Goll, asking him to let you train me to defend myself. I think he'll want to keep his investment—that is, me—from getting strangled in his sleep. I'm sure you've heard about last night." Iren inspected the bruise with the vague interest of a connoisseur. She didn't seem overly impressed. "An hour a day," Senlin continued crisply. "We'll spend the first half hour sparring and the second reading. What do you say?"

"Mr. Goll won't like me wasting time on books."

"Then don't tell him," Senlin said, holding out the letter he'd prepared. "He's the least of our worries. I'm going to feel very weak, and you're going to feel very dumb. But that's how it always is in the beginning. Learning starts with failure."

Iren scrutinized the face of the clear-eyed stickman sitting before her, searching for signs of shrewdness or pity, any trace of which would have brought her down on him like a guillotine. Making up her mind, she nodded and said, "Okay." She grabbed the letter and pounded from the room. It was the longest conversation he'd ever held with her.

Chapter Eleven

The *Double Fond* is a pot-bellied galleon, with an
S-shaped hull, eight long guns, three fat envelopes,
a grappling cannon, a glorious deckhouse, a great
cabin complete with teardrop chandelier, and a crew
of sixty-two armed marauders. All dreaming aside, a
ship is only as good as her course. I must find a new
wind.

—Every Man's Tower, One Man's Travails
by T. Senlin

He had ulterior motives for tutoring Iren. Senlin knew she was
capable of doing the work of two men, and he wanted her on
his crew. But buying her loyalties would require more, much
more, than he could afford. Since he could not hope to buy her loyalty,
he meant to earn it.

So, her lessons began. Midafternoon, behind the closed door of his
office, stooped over the primer he'd written out for her, Senlin treated
her exactly as he had the illiterate bullies of his past school days: with
patient and firm encouragement. At first, she held the pen like a knife
and attacked the paper. She bent and snapped nib after nib, and shot
black spiders of ink across the page. It was days before she could even
close the loops of her letters, though every day she destroyed fewer
pages and pens. Every day she improved.

And he learned that she was not entirely illiterate. Her education
was sped along by her familiarity with a few essential words. She

could read the common labels of crates and the regular verbs that appeared on broadside advertisements. She proved to be a quick study and took her lessons in earnest. She practiced on her own, and within a week she could read rudimentary sentences. Senlin found her determination inspiring.

Iren's patience was not inexhaustible. She suffered fits of frustration. At the peak of her frustrations, she would accuse Senlin of making up rules, of contradicting himself, of mocking her attempts at sounding out words. More than once, she grabbed whatever was at hand, an inkpot or paperweight, and raised it menacingly over her tutor's head. But he carried on explaining the logic of the grammar in the same calm, lilting tone: "See, the *J* jumps back while the *L* lays the way. Try again. 'John likes to beat the drum. Liza likes to ring the bell.'" Eventually, Iren would lower her makeshift weapon, and her halting efforts would resume.

And she always got her revenge. At least, Senlin suspected that their sparring lessons in the station yard were colored by her irritation with her education. Her preferred method of teaching Senlin to defend himself was by attacking him relentlessly, until, inevitably, he ended up flat on his back, winded and bruised. Then, as she watched him struggle to his feet, she would explain with the fewest words possible what he had done wrong. When they sparred with staffs and she swept his legs from under him, she said, "Your feet are too close together." When they boxed and Senlin was left doubled-over from three quick jabs to the stomach, she said, "You wind up your punches." When they practiced with wooden swords and she clipped him on the ear, she said, "Don't attack my sword. Attack me."

It was a humiliating process made more so by the crowd their practice attracted. The men of the yard gathered about the sparring ring they'd cleared between crates of olives and kegs of vinegar. At first, the porters observed the lessons casually, afraid to gawk at their port master and Finn Goll's enforcer scrapping in the yard. But soon their observations grew more focused and vocal. There were exclamations, which became volleys, which became cheers of the sort one might hear around a professional ring. By the end of the first week of their afternoon bouts, wagers were being made. An enterprising stevedore found a cracked slate and began chalking up the odds.

Senlin tried to ignore the nature of the bets. They presumed he would be overwhelmed by Iren's size and ability. It was a given that he would end up on his back. The bets regarded how long he would stay on his feet and whether he would ever land a successful parry or punch. Even those odds were bad.

But he was learning. For the first time in his life, he felt like he was developing his reflexes. He began to sense the rhythms and patterns of her assaults. Strength, he discovered, was not as important as balance, and balance was not as important as anticipation. He began to predict some of her attacks by the slight shifts in her stance or the tightening of her shoulders. He could sometimes anticipate the trajectory of her foot or staff, even if he couldn't always get out of the way of the blow. Occasionally, he'd enjoy a little success, a dodge or parry, and immediately afterward would begin to analyze his success. He'd ponder how fighting had a grammar all its own, and war had its syntax. His mind wandered. These flights of fancy always resulted in him being laid out.

"Don't think about it so much," Iren said after one of Senlin's daydreams had been punctuated by her delivery of an unexpected uppercut. "Better not think at all."

So it was they developed camaraderie out of necessity.

The whole arrangement made Adam nervous. He tried to convince his friend that Iren was a monster playing the pet. "Don't believe for a moment that you are friends," Adam said one afternoon while washing out a large abrasion on Senlin's shoulder blade. The port master had earned it while attempting to strike his teacher with a graceless riposte. Instead of landing the blow with his wooden dowel, he'd thrown himself off balance and had slid painfully across the gravel yard. Though injured, Senlin felt pride in the attempt, which Iren deemed "gutsy."

"She can be swayed," Senlin told Adam, and believed it.

Air currents, Senlin had learned from his readings on the subject, were similar to sea currents. They were invisible but persistent conveyor belts of varying widths and strengths. They braided the sky in intricate systems of energy. Airships, at least those that came to the Port of Goll, had no means of self-propulsion and, much like a sail, were entirely reliant on the wind for speed and direction. Ships could be moved vertically by warming the trapped gas or releasing ballast, allowing them to leap from one current to another. Captains, at least capable ones, had some measure of control over their course.

The locations of the ports that jutted from the Tower had been chosen for their proximity to relatively calm, stable currents. Well-placed ports were reliably accessible, but the trade-off was that many could only be entered and exited along a single course. This posed no inconvenience to righteous traders, but it made hijacking docked ships a risky business. Running away was easy enough, but getting away would be hard.

If Senlin and his as-yet-imaginary crew on their as-yet-imaginary ship hoped to get very far, a novel escape route was essential.

So, to the amusement of the aeronauts and dockworkers, Senlin took up a new morning hobby. As the rising sun sparkled upon the frost-slicked port, Senlin paced behind the white, wax-paper kite that he had built. The pinch of the autumnal air had given way to the bite of winter. The sky was as cold and flat as a frozen sea. He flew his kite between the enormous balloons that tugged at moored ships. The kite dove like a sparrow along the curving face of the Tower, battering its corners against pink sandstone. It tangled about the yardarms of cranes, and he'd have to climb to free it. He lost his hold on many kites while stumbling over crates and bales of cargo, and could only watch helplessly as the plain diamonds fled into the distance. The men laughed. The bitter wind stung. And always, his kites flew eastward on the same persistent current of wind: the trade wind, the only wind.

After a couple of days of lost kites and stubbed toes, Senlin found what he was looking for. It happened one morning when the dock was unusually empty. Senlin had given the dockworkers the previous evening off after a two-day lull in traffic, and most of the men were sleeping off their drunken liberty. Above, a long, shallow depression in the facade of the Tower seemed to attract the kite. The dip in the Tower face would've seemed little more than a dimple from a distance, but locally, it was large enough to generate a little vacuum. The kite tugged intermittently at the spool in Senlin's hand, reminding him of how a fishing line would dip and jerk with the explorative bumps of a cautious fish.

Then, all at once, the kite took off, flying straight up the face of the Tower for fifty feet before pulling sharply west. His line exhausted, Senlin held the last foot of silk, watching the kite fight to follow the newly discovered current. Then he let it go.

Watching the kite escape on that untapped current charmed a smile to his face. It would be a little difficult to reach, and missing the edge of the current would probably result in the ship being dashed against the stone face, but he had found his course. Hazardous as it was, he had found his exit.

Adam did not receive the news of the miraculous discovery with the enthusiasm Senlin had hoped for.

Senlin found his friend in the gloomy damp of the station yard, under the skating bats and egg-yolk lights, trying to pry the lid from a stubbornly shut crate. When his crowbar slipped out and nearly caught him in the chin, Adam, in an unusual display of anger, began beating the crate furiously. "Why?" Adam asked, once he had exhausted himself. "Why seal up a box of pears like it was a coffin?"

Senlin laid a hand on his friend's heaving shoulder. "It's just fruit. What's got you so mad?"

The crowbar clanged out three notes as it bounced on the ground. "Rodion," he said with concerted calm. "He's squeezing the last pence out of me. In the past three weeks, he's come to me with three marriage contracts for Voleta. Each time, I give him a mina to delay the agreement, and he goes away to find a new husband-in-waiting with a fatter wallet. I'm out of money." He picked up the crowbar and reset its claw under the lip of the lid. "Voleta says she should break a leg or set her hair on fire. She thinks that no one would want to marry a gimpy, bald girl. But that's the trouble. The only thing keeping her out of the bedroom is the stage. But it's her act that attracts the lechers. I'm afraid that I'll just wake up one morning and she'll be gone for good." The lid finally came open with a squeal of nails. Adam shook the soreness out of his arms and plucked a blushing pear from the bed of straw. "So, I'm glad you found your wind, Tom, but I don't see how we're any closer to getting out of this place."

"I will talk to Rodion," Senlin said.

"And say what?"

Before Senlin could answer, their conversation was interrupted by the arrival of a familiar autowagon. The ebony panels of the coach were like black mirrors, fluted with gold leaf. The windows were lidded with blood-colored shades, and the brass and copper stack of the machine spilled wads of steam over the gaunt driver. Finn Goll's autowagon cleared a path through the porters in the yard as effortlessly as a shark through a school of sardines.

Senlin hadn't seen much of the port's namesake in the three months he'd worked as the man's port master. His unexpected appearance now might be nothing more than a surprise inspection, but Senlin was certain that Goll hadn't come to the port on a social call. Senlin cataloged the worst-case scenarios: Goll had learned about the raise Senlin had given the workers and had come to squeeze compensation out of the port master's hide; or Goll had deduced the interest behind the midnight attempt on Senlin's life and was preparing now to turn him over to the commissioner and collect the ransom; or the lord of port had somehow caught wind of Senlin and Adam's plot and was coming now to mete out the punishment that came to all deserters: the plank.

Iren preceded Goll out the door of the coach. Her shoulders, usually squared, were now slumped. It was a bad sign. Worse, she didn't meet Senlin's eye when he came to meet the carriage. Goll emerged onto the running board where he stayed, standing nearly at eye level with Senlin. The driver did not shut off the engine, making it clear their business would be brief.

"Iren has developed some new talents." Goll put his hand on Iren's head in the familiar way that a boy might handle his dog. "Imagine my surprise this morning when I find her writing this," he said, producing a page from his vest pocket. He unfolded it and began to read in the mocking tone of a simpleton: " 'John likes to beat the drum. Liza likes to ring the bell. John and Liza march and sing all around the wooded dell.' "

Senlin recognized the verse as having come from his primer, and he quickly deduced where this conversation was heading. Goll had correctly identified the lessons as a threat to his authority, and he had come out to reassert that authority.

"Tom, can you imagine how useful it was to have a secure, reliable, untroubled messenger? Who wants a dog that can read what it fetches? Now I find I am in the uncomfortable position of having to trust my courier." Goll pulled a second slip of paper from his pocket. This, with a flourish of the wrist, he gave to the amazon. "And since trust requires trials...Iren, dearie, please read the directions I've given you."

She studied the scrap of paper, her brow furrowing with the effort. The words came in fits and starts. "Make...a fist...with your hand and...put it to Tom's head...three...tims."

"That last word is *times*, dearie. Seems you didn't enact such a miracle after all, Tom." Goll drew a whistling breath. Iren stood in a stupor, staring down at the note in her hands. Senlin watched as she grappled with the decision, and he found himself silently willing her to strike him before it was too late. Goll was testing her loyalty. She had to strike before suspicion set in.

She recovered herself in an instant. Stepping forward, she took Senlin by the collar and without ceremony, struck him in the face again and again and again. The only mercy she paid him was to spread her blows evenly across his head, and still it felt like the kick of a mule.

"Ho, ho, hold there, Iren. That's good. That's five! I only asked for three!" Goll was greatly amused by the extra blows.

Senlin's face streaked with blood and tears. Iren dropped him, and he fell right through his knees to his tailbone. He bounced against the ground and spilled onto his back. The world was haloed in red, and at the center was Goll's round face.

"Tom, you would've done well to have taught her to count before you began the alphabet," Goll said. "At our age, education is a waste. You can't defend yourself, she can't count, and I can't learn to trust.

We are too deep in our ruts to turn onto fresh tracks. In the future, I'd appreciate it if you didn't meddle with the natural order of things." He disappeared back into the carriage, then through the window he concluded, "And another thing, Tom. I expect that men who make it this far up the Tower will come with a little baggage. But if what I've heard is true, and it was the Red Hand who came a'callin' last month, I want nothing to do with it. The commissioner and his thug aren't to be trifled with. Whatever it is, sort it out. I don't want to lose my book-keeper because of some grudge, but at the same time, I'm not sticking my neck out for you. If the commissioner decides to press the point, I'll hang you out to dry."

Goll's parting words resonated through Senlin's pain. If Goll didn't know why the Red Hand had come, he couldn't know about the paint-ing. Which meant he hadn't been the one to turn Senlin in. It made sense, of course. Goll had no reason to be subtle; if he had wanted to collect the bounty, he would've done it openly and immediately. Finn Goll might be a heartless boss, but he wasn't the one trying to get Sen-lin killed. But if not Goll, then who?

Goll rapped on the door twice, and the driver let out the throttle. As the coach pulled away, Iren grabbed the rear rail and pulled her-self into the jump seat. She glanced back at Senlin briefly. There was a subtle shift in her expression, which would've gone undetected by anyone who hadn't spent hours sitting across from her. To Senlin, that look spoke volumes; she was unhappy. Perhaps the beating had driven her nearer to his cause.

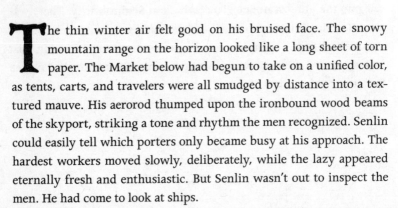

Chapter Twelve

Everything I've read on the subject suggests that five able bodies are required to make a skeletal crew. Counting myself, Adam, and Voleta, and presuming that I can recruit Iren, I'm still one short. I suppose I could advertise in the station yard: *Aeronaut wanted for crusade into certain peril and probable death. Low wages, moral reward; philanthropists preferred.*

—*Every Man's Tower, One Man's Travails*
by T. Senlin

The thin winter air felt good on his bruised face. The snowy mountain range on the horizon looked like a long sheet of torn paper. The Market below had begun to take on a unified color, as tents, carts, and travelers were all smudged by distance into a textured mauve. His aerorod thumped upon the ironbound wood beams of the skyport, striking a tone and rhythm the men recognized. Senlin could easily tell which porters only became busy at his approach. The hardest workers moved slowly, deliberately, while the lazy appeared eternally fresh and enthusiastic. But Senlin wasn't out to inspect the men. He had come to look at ships.

He was well aware of how strained the situation had become in recent days. He would lose Adam if they couldn't save Voleta from Rodion soon. And Iren might like him, but Finn Goll would be watching her closely now, and Senlin doubted she would abandon her life just to continue her reading lessons. Goll had made it clear that there was a limit to his patience. He might at any moment decide that Senlin was a greater liability than an asset. Senlin couldn't afford to be picky now. Today he would choose a ship; tomorrow he would steal it.

The port was full at least; all four slips were occupied. The *Cornelius* sat in the Tower-side south bay, a hulking, multitiered ship that reminded Senlin of a great flat-bottomed river boat. Its boiler room alone probably required three men to maintain. Though it hardly mattered; the ship was scheduled to cast off before nightfall. Across from it sat a gray wind-scalded ship called the *Stone Cloud*. It was not much larger than a twelve-man sloop and oddly shaped. Its hull was reminiscent of a nesting robin, with a bulbous fore and a flattened aft. It had one thirty-pound gun at the bowsprit, a filthy, clam-shaped balloon, and a full crew of gold-toothed pirates. The outer north bay held a miserable, unarmed ferry christened the *Sally Quick*, which looked as sturdy as a rat's nest and every bit as charming. Then there was the *Gold Finch*, a sleek merchant ship from the south of the continent that had come in loaded with olives, tea, pistachios, and incense. Freshly painted a brilliant yellow, the *Finch* had four big guns and a single, long envelope that was tapered like a cigar. It was a little large for a five-man crew, but manageable, he thought.

He stood atop a coffee crate considering the *Gold Finch*. This was the ship. His ship. Now he only had to figure some way to empty it. He tried to discreetly count the heads of the crew as they moved along the immaculately scrubbed deck. He had just lost count and had started again when he heard someone speak his name. It was a woman's voice, a familiar voice. He turned and found Edith standing behind him with a wondering expression on her face.

His second thought was that it was not Edith: This woman's dark hair was bobbed above the jawline; she wore the mismatched leathers and rough wool pants popular among unaffiliated aeronauts, which was just a polite way of saying "pirates." A piece of polished brass capped her right shoulder like a lone scrap of plate armor. This rustic privateer was nothing like the countrywoman in a peach gown who'd once huddled and shivered against him while locked inside a wire coop. It could not be her.

And yet it was.

Since she had spied him first, she had the unfair advantage of having composed herself; a lopsided smile bunched the freckles on one dusky cheek, and she held her head cocked in a mischievous manner as if she'd been trying to sneak up on him.

He recovered himself quickly, and since he was unsure how to react, he stayed poised atop the crate like a statue in a town square. "What are you doing here?" he asked.

"Well, hello to you, too, Tom," she said, feeling, or perhaps feigning, hurt.

Senlin softened his tone. "I beg your pardon. I only meant..." His mind drifted back to their days in the cage, a memory he had long suppressed. With no further prodding, the whole ordeal came rushing back, swamping him with unaddressed guilt and an uncomfortable ache. He had left her in her hour of need with a sadistic nurse and a fresh wound. While he'd escaped with scratches, she had been maimed. She had every right to hold a grudge. "You're supposed to be farming."

Her smirk stiffened at that. She didn't seem to enjoy the reference to her past life. When she replied, it came out as a jab. "And you're supposed to be teaching brats and making some of your own. How is your wife?"

It was his turn to be wounded now. His expression, he was sure, betrayed everything, but he felt compelled to confess it anyway: "I haven't found her. Not yet."

"Oh," Edith said, and flinched with a silent self-rebuke. Their unexpected reunion was going terribly. Senlin began to think of an excuse for a quick exit.

A dockworker, gesturing sheepishly at the crate under Senlin's feet, interrupted the clumsy moment. He asked, "Are you done with that one, Port Master? It's for the truck if you are."

Senlin climbed stiffly down, not letting the dockworker see his broken composure. "Yes, take it," he said. Standing level with her, he realized that she was not wearing a brass pauldron, as he'd first thought. The shoulder armor ran all the way down her arm and ended in an intricately jointed gauntlet. He glanced at the metal arm, then to her charcoal eyes, then back to it, attempting not to gawk and failing.

She gave an unguarded laugh. "Port master! Headmaster! Are you a master wherever you go?"

"Hardly." He snorted. "I was conscripted into it, but I'm not terrible at it. They haven't lynched me yet, anyway."

"That is a fine standard of excellence. I'm a first mate, myself," she said, swelling a little with pride.

Senlin no longer wanted to bolt, but he was having trouble not staring at her brass-sheathed arm. "Oh, really? That's an admirable title. Which ship are you mate of?"

"The *Stone Cloud*," she said, hiking her head toward the vessel bobbing in its crib behind her. Senlin followed the motion and gave the ship he had previously dismissed a second examination. It looked like something that had lain submerged in a bog for years. The wood that formed the hull appeared to still have its bark. Or perhaps it was just some sort of aggressive burl. He wasn't sure. "Why do people always make that face when I introduce them to my ship?" she said, interrupting his scrutiny. "It's not a bad ship, Tom. It's fast enough."

He cleared his throat. "I'm—I'm sure. And how's the crew?"

"I had to break them in. They weren't used to having a woman aboard, and it took a little while to convince them that I wasn't the ship's madam or anyone's mother . . . All right, we might as well address it since you're not going to stop gawking at it."

He had been caught looking for signs of skin between the metal joints of her armored arm. Now he tried to act as if it was purely an academic interest. "It's just such an unusual"—he swallowed noisily—"ornament. How does it attach to the arm?"

"It doesn't," she said with the aloofness of one who has entered a necessary but uncomfortable spiel. "I lost the arm to gangrene six months ago. It was removed just short of the shoulder." Edith studiously avoided Senlin's gaze, which embarrassed him more because he wanted to reach out through his stare and offer some solace. But her shying also saved her from having to watch his initial revulsion turn to anger and then to pity, all in the span of a few seconds. "Yes, the infection started with the branding, and no, I won't talk about it."

Sensing how uncomfortable she'd become, Senlin made a concerted effort to return his attention to the arm. It was truly a marvel: as sophisticated as a wind-up bird and as solid as a derrick. A beautiful arabesque pattern ran down the length of the arm like a tribal tattoo. When she flexed the arm for him, a valve at the shoulder gave a little puff of steam, fine as pollen shaken from a bloom. Clockworks hummed inside the brass shell as her digits unfurled one by one. She demonstrated the fluid and nearly human range of her fingers by reaching out and unbuttoning the top button of his coat. It was a forward thing to do, and it made Senlin briefly flinch and then, very soon after, laugh. He was relieved to find that the bold woman he'd met in the Parlor had not been eclipsed by her novel limb or humble ship.

"It's a demanding little engine," she said. "I have to put water in it. I have to oil it and fuel it. I've owned prize thoroughbreds that needed less attention. And it didn't come cheap, I'll tell you that. New arms aren't free, Tom. You have to make a deal." She bent and scooped up a pine slat from a broken pallet. She squared the wood board in her mechanical palm and with a slight jerk, crushed the board to splinters. "But the damnedest deals have the damnedest perks."

Realizing that she was trying to make him recoil, Senlin refused to indulge her. He ignored the menacing nature of her demonstration and instead complimented her on it: "It is incredible. It reminds me, oddly, of a music box with its thick, hearty drum and its delicate comb. It's part hammer and part tweezers, isn't it? But I am sorry, I'm so terribly sorry that it came at such an awful cost. Edith, it is..."

She dropped the arm abruptly and hiked her chin at him. "Ha. You remembered my name after all," she said.

"Of course I remember your name. You're the Generaless of the

Garden, Mrs. Mayfair with a fist. You're Ms. Edith Ex-Winters. I didn't forget."

She slouched a little, looking almost vulnerable, though the splintered board lay still fresh at her feet. "It seems like everyone I meet knows nothing about me but still wants something from me. It's so tiring, Tom, to always be on your guard. It's been an exhausting six months."

"It has," Senlin agreed, and stamped down the guilt that was already balling inside him. Could he pretend to be any different? Didn't he want something from her, too?

She looked around, appearing uncomfortable with the conversation, and said, "I have to go kick my crew softly in the pants. We have a half ton of eggs to unload, and if I don't glare at them while they do it, they'll break half of them and then blame your porters for it."

Senlin nodded, his hands wrenching his aerorod nervously. "When do you shove off?"

"Tomorrow. The crew has shore leave tonight."

"Oh. Well, then maybe we could have dinner together," Senlin said.

"I can't. First mate has to stay aboard so the captain can go carousing. Besides, I don't care for the local entertainment much."

"No, of course," Senlin said. "But could I call on you? I have a bottle of very average port that has been aging on a shelf for . . . for days now. It really needs to be drunk."

She laughed, but he could feel the hesitation in the sidelong way she looked at him. Perhaps she was thinking of his wife and wondering if this was some sort of romantic overture, or perhaps she already sensed that he, too, wanted something from her. The months had made her guarded. But she didn't waffle for long. "Bring your port, Port Master. If it needs to be drunk, we'll drink it. I'll be free after moonrise."

Senlin watched her stride off toward the *Stone Cloud* that squatted like a molting bird in its nest. The flawless *Gold Finch* swelled grandly behind him. He heaved a sigh. Yes, her ship was plain, short on guns, probably infested with termites, and aptly named, but the *Stone Cloud* had one very appealing quality, and she, unlike the rest of them, was familiar with airships. While he'd been mastering another man's ledgers, she'd learned how to fly.

So, it had to be the *Stone Cloud*. This was the ship.

Already feeling a little devious, though he had done nothing yet and was not exactly sure what he would do once given the chance, Senlin arrived back in his office to find that he had company. The yellow-haired woman sat in his desk chair with a book in hand. She appeared to be reading what he recognized as a particularly inept guide to the Tower. On closer inspection, he realized she was not reading the book. She was scouring it with the nib of a pen. She scratched at the pages with such determination that it seemed she was trying to dig through it. Then he recalled where he'd seen this odd behavior before: The postal clerk in the Baths had been likewise engaged with the book Senlin had rescued, *The Confidences of a Wifemonger*.

When the yellow-haired woman saw Senlin stalled in the doorway, she did not immediately cease her work. Instead, she laid the book out for him so that he could see the words she was carefully redacting, beginning from the last word on the last page and working her way toward the start.

He recognized her as one of Rodion's girls, but he didn't show it. Instead, he said, "Put down my book. Get out of my chair."

This she did, though with a sarcastic pout that made it clear she was only humoring him. She circled around one side of his desk as he came around the other. Plopping into the cracked red chair across from him, she said, "You have a lot of stupid things."

"Yes," he said coldly, picking up his scribbled-upon book with unfelt reverence. "Do stupid things attract you?"

"Ooh, you have a mouth. You think reading books makes you smart, but it just fills you with so much stupidness."

"Yes," he said again. "It's an interesting habit you have. What do you call it when you scrawl out the words of a book? You must have a name for it. Desecration? Doodling?"

"Course not. It's called *studying*."

"Ah. Studying, of course. And why do you start from the end and study your way backward?"

She sucked her teeth. "Tch! To keep from reading, of course. The words worm their way in. Even if you don't know what they say, they speak to you in your head and you hear it."

Senlin sighed at the idiocy of this but filed the information away for later consideration. At the moment he had to focus on the task at hand, which began with getting her out of his office. He set aside the ruined book. "What do you want?"

"You don't remember me," she said with sinister coyness, her chin dropping to her neck. She had a pretty, pert face, and her bosom bunched against an overtightened corset, but there was nothing appealing about her. She radiated vanity and cruelty. "But I remember you."

"You were on the barge," Senlin interjected. "And at the Steam Pipe. I remember."

"Ooh, no, no, no. Before that. On the piano. You looked at my legs. And I showed you a little more, and then you looked all offended, like I was some sort of floozy. Remember? Then you made such a scene with all your sneezing. The commissioner put on his rubber mask and took you out onto the porch, and you, Mr. Sneezy, had some words with him. Then, not three days later, you're on the floozy barge with your nose in the air, flying to the Boudoir with all the whores you're too good for. It's funny. How does a man go from big talk with the commissioner to the floozy barge in a few days? Maybe he's running away from something, I think. Maybe he's gotten into someone else's honey, hey? What do you think? You think I'm stupid because I'm honest. Honest here," she said, waving provocatively at her décolletage. She raised a leg and put a slippered foot on the edge of his desk, her skirts spilling up about her white thigh. "And honest here." Senlin kept his stare locked with her own, refusing to acknowledge the display. "But I'm not stupid." She dropped her foot with a little stamp. "I know who you are, and I know you're in it deep."

Senlin's initial surprise at her familiarity with his past in the Baths had time to fade during her prattling speech and had now resolved into a rehearsal of the facts. She knew him. She was trying to extort money from him. She was clever enough to see an opportunity but not clever enough to know what to do with it; otherwise she would have gone to the commissioner. Instead, she had come to him, hoping that he would startle and attempt to bribe her.

But it was apparent to Senlin now that she worked for the very man who had sold him out to the commissioner. It was the only thing that made sense. Rodion had influence and was ambitious; he had steady access to news from the Baths, and he had his eyes in the port, to be sure. Rodion would not include Goll because he would not want to share the purse, and the attack had only come after Senlin's visit to the Steam Pipe. The whoremonger had been curious about Senlin's pedigree. It wouldn't have taken much to discover Senlin's past entanglements: a few questions of the lonely captains who regularly visited the Steam Pipe; a careful, tentative letter to the Customs Bureau; or perhaps an evening frittered at a gala, and everything would be revealed.

But if that was the case, why was Senlin still alive and whole and left alone? Why had the Red Hand not returned? Senlin knew that a snipped line would not be enough to detour the assassin for long, especially if he had willing accomplices running free in the Port of Goll.

Something was keeping Senlin safe, at least for the moment. Once he thought about it, the answer seemed obvious. It was the painting. No one knew where Ogier's painting was, and that was the real object, the real prize. If they killed him or dragged him off in the night, the painting might be lost forever. The commissioner would get his revenge but not his treasure back.

Perhaps all Rodion was waiting for was a definite target. If Rodion, for example, believed that the painting was about to be smuggled from the port on a particular pirate ship, he would feel compelled to retrieve the prize for the commissioner. He would be forced to act. He would storm the port with as many men as he could gather and demand to inspect the ships. And that would mean...

The plan came to Senlin fully finished in a flash. Rodion was suspicious; Finn Goll was suspicious. Both expected conspiracy, and given one, would believe it. All that remained was to set the two against each other in his favor, to his own ends.

Senlin smiled at the yellow-haired woman in a manner that he hoped appeared sufficiently nervous. "Look, I don't want my past bobbing to the surface again. I certainly don't want Rodion to know about it."

"And there's the plum, love. Quiet don't come cheap!"

"Ah. Money, yes. I have a lot of money coming to me, I'm sure, but I don't have it yet." He swallowed with affected anxiousness. "I have to move a thing of great value first. It's worth a fortune... and I'm smuggling it out tomorrow night."

She squinted at him and formed her lips into a perfect red raisin. "How dumb do you think I am? You're just going to run off with your treasure as soon as I turn around."

"No! Please don't tell Rodion. I'll give you what I have now, and then more later." Senlin opened a desk drawer, drew out a little change purse, and tipped it onto his blotter. Six pitiful shekels spilled out. It would be taken as an insult, he was sure, but he looked at her with sham hopefulness. "Take it. I'll have more after tomorrow. Just not a word to Rodion. Please."

The yellow-haired woman chewed at her lower lip, regarding him with a mean, deadened gaze. "Yeah, okay." She swept the coins into her hand and turned to leave.

"Not a word," Senlin repeated.

"Oh, you'll get what you paid for. Don't you worry. You'll get exactly what you paid for." She gave another tart purse of her lips. Sweeping from the room, she did not see Senlin roll his eyes.

Adam passed the blond woman in the hall and came into Senlin's office with a thumb pointed over his shoulder and a perplexed expression on his face. "Entertaining guests?"

Senlin motioned for him to close the door; he was having trouble containing a grin. When Adam was seated and settled, with the brow over his active eye raised in question, Senlin explained: "She is going to tell Rodion that I am up to something."

"Well, that doesn't sound good."

"No, it is very good. She recognized me from the Baths. And I just told her that I'm smuggling something very valuable out of the port tomorrow night. Rodion is not one to run off half-cocked on a rumor, so he'll need a little extra goading if he's going to empty our ship for us. And that's where you come in."

"Our ship? Wait, you found a ship?" Adam said, craning forward. "A good ship; a realistic conquest?"

"Yes. The *Stone Cloud*," Senlin said, lacing his hands behind his head. "It's a beautiful, rustic sloop, and I know the first mate, as it turns out."

"What do you mean you know the first mate?"

"I know her. We shared a prison cell for a few days."

"Of course you did," Adam said, blinking through a daze. "Wait, what do you want me to do with Rodion?"

"You're going to rat me out to him." Senlin said it as if it were the most sensible thing in the world. "You're going to lend credence to the rumoring of floozies."

Adam's confusion contorted his expression; he looked as if he'd been caught midsneeze. "Ah, Thomas, I don't think this is a very good—"

"No, it is. Everyone here expects everyone else to be treacherous. So let's give them treachery. You will tell Rodion that in exchange for the immediate liberation of your sister, you will reveal my whole conspiracy. Well, not all of it, of course. The main thing he needs to believe is that I have something of great value—you don't need to say what; he'll know—which I am frantically trying to smuggle out of the port, and that the whole debacle is taking place tomorrow night. Then you—"

Adam interrupted. "Why would he know what you're smuggling?"

"Because I am certain that he is the one who first contacted the commissioner and brought the Red Hand down upon me. He knows all about the painting, and I'm sure he's just waiting for it to come into the open. Tell him I am smuggling out something worth a fortune, and let him travel to the conclusion himself. The less you seem to know, the safer you'll be. What matters most is that you come with him to the port, and you insist that Voleta come, too. Don't let him dissuade you from that point. Talk Rodion into letting you both come. I think he'll want to do it; he'll want to confront me with your betrayal. He'll enjoy that."

"So, you do have the painting."

"It doesn't matter if I have the painting."

"What do you mean it doesn't matter? Nothing matters more than that fact. Either you have it, and we can bargain for our lives, or you don't, and we will be strung up from the yardarms. What are you going to do when Rodion doesn't find the bait we used to draw him out?"

"A very good point, which brings me to the next chore on your list. After you've gone to betray me to Rodion, you will send a message to Finn Goll and tell him that Rodion is going to conduct an unauthorized seizure of goods in the Port of Goll tomorrow night. Tell Goll that Rodion is using his hold on Voleta to force you into scouting for treasure ships."

"For treasure ships? Are you mad?"

"Well, whatever. Tell him that Rodion is using you to find a vulnerable, valuable ship to plunder. Whatever you do, don't mention the commissioner or the painting."

Adam shook his head like a man who'd just suffered a blow to it. "This is your plan?"

"Calm down, calm down," Senlin said, easing his friend back from his rising mania with a softened tone. "I know it sounds a little ragged. But our best chance of escape is to set the egos against each other." He brought his fists together in demonstration. "If Rodion and Goll are fighting, they will be weakened and distracted. They won't think of us. We can slip away. Trust me, Adam. This could work. An empty ship, your sister at the port, all of us ready to go."

Adam brooded over this for a moment and then said, "But you do have the painting?"

"I have, at least, a very compelling painting-sized crate," Senlin said with a wink.

The chair feet squealed upon the floor as Adam stood. He pulled his shirt straight. His face reflected the grim resolve of one who has been asked to walk to his own execution. He nodded once and said, "Aye aye, Captain," then strode from the room.

Chapter Thirteen

Mirrors are not so honest as one might think. They can be mugged at, bargained with, and one can always ferret out a flattering angle. Really, there is nothing like the expression of a long-lost friend to reflect the honest state of your affairs.

—*Every Man's Tower, One Man's Travails*
by T. Senlin

e resisted the urge to change his clothes, or polish his boots, or oil his hair, or otherwise preen himself before calling on Edith at her ship. The buttons on his coat had long since been torn loose and lost. His lapels were frayed, and his hair was long and unmanaged. Worse, his face was a rainbow of bruises. Other than the daily ritual of shaving, which seemed like the useless bailing of a sinking ship, his old fastidiousness had vanished. But now, for the first time in months, he felt acutely aware of the fact. He had let himself go. There had been good reason, of course, but now he felt the old compulsion to present himself as a gentleman.

But, no, this was no time for gentlemen. And if he was very honest with himself, there was something else keeping him from primping now. If he polished his boots and oiled his hair, it would imply a social visit. And he was not a man calling on a woman for tea. Certainly not. He was a married man, for one thing. If he'd once had an uncomfortable or unbecoming thought about Edith, it had been only in passing and during the most extreme circumstances. There was nothing between them but friendly admiration.

It was night, and the port was deserted. The *Sally Quick* and the *Cornelius* had departed, and the remaining crews of the *Gold Finch* and the *Stone Cloud* were either asleep belowdecks or reveling in the Boudoir. The stars looked timid behind the intense moonlight. Senlin paused amid the cranes and bollards of the skyport to admire the natural gloom of the cosmos. His heart swelled at the thought of being finally free of the stench of smokestacks and the jangle of autowagons. Before him lay the promise of no more eight o'clock reports, no more dickering with captains over every last shekel, no more irascible Finn Goll...

"Hi-ho, Port Master," Edith called at his approach. He found her leaning over the clumsy rail of her sloop. "The captain and half the crew are out whoring. The rest are sleeping below. You can come aboard if you promise not to beat your cane on my deck. If you wake Antsy Jack or Bobbit or Keller, you have to rock them back to sleep yourself." She extended her mechanical arm over the narrow, bowed gangplank.

He hesitated only a moment. She had brushed out her hair. The moonlight cast her face in the flawless blue light of glacier ice. What a ridiculous thing to notice! Here was a woman with a dynamo for an arm, and he was waxing lyrical about her complexion. He rebuked himself silently and grasped her clockwork palm. Despite being accustomed to the height, he was still careful to keep his eyes trained on hers and away from the great, hypnotic drop he crossed over.

Being aboard a ship, even a docked one, always filled Senlin with a powerful thrill. The envelope rippled overhead, that silk thinner than skin, while the hull bobbed and shifted in sympathy with the gentle evening currents. As calm as it was at port, Senlin knew that a few hundred feet out, the desert winds ran like river rapids.

"You have an aeronaut's stance," she said approvingly, nodding down at the boots he had refused to polish. "You don't look like you're going to pitch your dinner."

"I'm fine. I like ships," Senlin said, trying not to be offended.

"Well, the ships like you, too. You also look like you've been bunking with a cyclone," she said, making a show of surveying his bruised face. "You are a sight."

Now he was offended. He brushed at the bruises on his face as if they might be swept off and pulled at his ratty collar. None of it helped, of course, and his attempts at prettying himself only amused Edith. He dropped his hands and cleared his throat. "What about a tour?"

"As you like. Welcome aboard the *Stone Cloud*!" she said with a sweeping, theatrical bow. "The most fearsome aircraft in the immediate vicinity, excluding that one over there and any large birds that might be nesting nearby." Senlin chuckled, despite himself. "Here's the burner," she said, patting the side of the cylindrical tank that stood middeck. "Hot as slag, once it gets going. This heats the coil inside the envelope—"

Senlin interjected here: "Causing the hydrogen to expand and lift to increase." Senlin's eyes followed the flexible duct that ran from the furnace to the base of the balloon, some fifteen or twenty feet overhead. "This is the umbilical."

"Very good. Maybe you're not such a hopeless wharfie after all," Edith said with an approving, one-shouldered shrug. "The heating element can be throttled from the helm, when everything's firing right." She led Senlin up the short stairs to the quarterdeck where, in place of a traditional captain's wheel, five rust-encrusted levers jutted from a weathered console. "This one throttles the element; this one injects more hydrogen, if we have a spare tank on hand, which we usually don't," Edith said, gripping the two throttles in turn. "This one releases water from the ballast hold. That swell under the bow holds two hundred gallons of water. I can jettison the ballast slowly, for a gentle ascent, or in an emergency, I can dump it all. That'll make your stomach fall through the deck."

"And the other two throttles?"

"Are broken."

"How large is the crew?"

"Thirteen, plus the captain and myself. My cabin is under the poop deck. It was the chart room before I came along. Now it looks like someone tried to stuff a library into a woman's closet." She smiled, leaning back against the raised platform of the quarterdeck. "You'll just have to take my word for it; the tour doesn't include the lady's chamber."

"And the crew, they are capable and . . . loyal?" Senlin asked, trying to sound light.

Her smile curdled, and a new line appeared on her brow. "That's a strange question, Tom. Do you mean to ask whether I have my men in hand, or whether they are opportunists at heart whose loyalty can be bought?"

Senlin waved her on, pretending to have no preference for her answer.

"To both questions: yes. Emphatically, yes. Though——" Without warning, her clockwork arm chugged like a stalling engine, heaved a great sigh of steam from every joint, and then dropped heavily to her side.

Slouching awkwardly around the lifeless weight of the arm, Edith swore under her breath. "The mudded thing always runs down at the worst time." She dug her flesh-and-blood hand into a vest pocket and pulled out a glowing red vial. Under the blue moonlight, the glass cylinder glowed like a crucible. The image of the Red Hand's metal cuff, with its tuning pegs and red vials, leapt to Senlin's mind.

"The damnedest deals . . ." Edith muttered distractedly. She pressed upon a discreet outline in her shoulder, and a little drawer came open. An empty vial fell into her hand. Inserting the luminous replacement, she pushed the drawer closed, and it sealed with a click. Immediately, the valves down the length of her mechanical arm hissed, and the cogs revved back to life. She flexed it experimentally.

"I've seen this before," Senlin said, managing his nerves well enough to keep them from rattling his voice. "That glowing serum . . . I've seen a man inject it into his veins. It makes him monstrously strong and quick and, I think, more than a little insane. It's dangerous, isn't it?"

"I don't want to talk about it," she said without a trace of uncertainty. She closed the subject by crushing the empty vial in her clockwork hand. "I am not my arm." Shaking the pulverized glass from her palm, she said, "Besides, the real question is, what are you plotting, Tom?"

"P-plotting?" The stutter had given him away, but he pressed on with the charade. "Well, I did have a small point of business I wanted to discuss..."

She interrupted with a flurry of her hand. "I know you well enough. You're honorable, you're faithful, and you have just as much reason to hate this two-faced Tower as I do. I like you. But you're awful at lying. If you're not going to talk straight, then you can get off my ship right now." Her breath puffed in the frigid air between them with the calm regularity of an engine.

Senlin stepped away from her and leaned over the starboard rail, facing the nearly full moon. Beneath him, a set of anchors fastened the ship to the iron prongs of the slip. He wondered how difficult it would be to cut all the lines and set the ship adrift right then and there. How far would they float before they were missed, before the rest of the crew woke up and the mutiny commenced? Then he thought of Adam and Voleta, the twins of opposites, and Iren who, despite the brutishness of her business, still held a good measure of conscience. He felt ashamed. "I'm not so honorable," he said.

Edith sidled up beside him on the rail. He could feel the resting vibrations of her clockwork arm travel through the wood of the balustrade. "Well, I don't know. But I haven't met many men who wouldn't take advantage of a woman they shared a cage with."

Senlin waved the point away, as if it were underserving of consideration. "I hope it hasn't come to that. We shouldn't have to go around congratulating each other for behaving with basic human dignity." Before she could say anything further on the subject, he continued on in a lower tone. "The truth is there are a few of us who want to take a ship and escape."

"You want to take my ship?" Though whispered, the question was sharp.

"No. I actually had been planning to have a go at the *Gold Finch*. But then I saw you..."

"Oh, so it's a rescue?" she said, sniffing cynically.

"A rescue!" Senlin reflected her despairing snicker. "Months ago I had these occasional fancies in which the parishioners of my old village sent out a search party to find me and Marya and bring us home. I imagined them scrabbling through the mall, picking their way up the Tower, unified by a single goal: to rescue their gawky headmaster and his undeserved wife. But"—he sighed, shaking his head—"no one came. And no one is coming. There are no rescues, Edith; there are just the collaborations and commiserations of friends."

Silently, she stewed over this. After a moment, Senlin began to worry that he had just recklessly confided in someone who needed no escape, someone who was quite content with her lot in life, thank you very much. Had he just given the whole game away? He had the urge to swallow but found that he could not move the lump in his throat.

Then she said, "My debts are complicated. They're not the sort of thing I can just run away from. And it's not the sort of burden I would want to heap on my friends, if I had any."

"That's the point. We're all burdened with something—a loss, a debt, an enemy, or all three." He laughed wearily. "It's too much for anyone. But, if we share each other's burdens, we may be able to move them, or find a way around them if they're intractable. Whatever comes, we wouldn't have to face it alone, at least."

"And who's going to be in charge of this crew of friends?" she asked, her voice pitching with curiosity, though she still seemed unconvinced.

"You could be captain. I'm sure you're more than qualified."

"You're joking!" she said in a louder blurt. "Captaining is the worst. Everything's always your fault. When things go well, it's to the crew's credit, and when things go horribly, the captain did it." She shook her head as if a horsefly had just settled on her nose. "No! I'd rather be a scullery maid than a captain. Well, not really. But being first mate suits me. I like bossing people around. Besides, Headmaster–Port Master, doesn't it follow that you would be captain?"

"I've considered it," he admitted.

"That doesn't sound very captainly."

"Yes, I would like to do it," he said, correcting his posture. "I will be captain."

"I wouldn't say that to Billy Lee."

"Who's Billy Lee?"

"Captain of the ship, of course," she said, a little archly, then quickly sobered and added, "He's hot-headed, treacherous, free with his hands, and trigger-happy, but underneath all that gentility beats the heart of a rabid dog."

"Oh," Senlin said. He'd been so busy thinking of ways to extract the crew, he'd neglected to consider how difficult it might be to unseat the captain.

"But, here, before we worry about Captain Lee, tell me what you have in mind. How do you mean to do it, and who is this 'we' you keep talking about?"

Senlin recited a brief history, and as is so often the case with history, the whole tangled ordeal sounded simple and tidy in summary: the tyrannical commissioner, the obsessed painter, and the stolen masterpiece that had won Senlin some grim news of his wife; the Boudoir, and the reemergence of Finn Goll, the mastermind, and Adam, the sympathetic thief who had become such a friend to him; and Rodion's Steam Pipe, which was a sugar trap for men and a gulag for women like Voleta. Senlin spared Edith many details and instead hurried to explain how all of this muddling misery and drudgery laid the way for his plan. He got as far as explaining how Adam would betray him, telling Rodion that Senlin was smuggling the commissioner's painting through the port in exchange for Voleta's freedom, when Edith finally interrupted.

"But, wait, why would the painting be on my ship?"

"Because I'm going to hire you, or Billy Lee, to smuggle it out for me. Rodion cannot pass up an opportunity at such influence and fortune. He will come with...twenty men at least. Maybe twice that. Your captain should feel sufficiently overwhelmed. I've seen more than a few ships searched in my time as port master. There's a standard procedure. The cargo hold is unloaded to port and gone through with the manifest, box by box, piece by piece, while the crew stands in detention. It can take hours."

She balked at this. "You think that Billy Lee will give up his ship without a fight?"

"He's not surrendering his ship," Senlin reasoned, and then saw the absurdity of it. "At least, not so far as he knows. His ship is just being searched. I'm sure it won't be the first time for that. Hopefully, the first mate will be able to smooth the way."

"Oh, sure." She regarded him as one might a lunatic who has climbed onto a roof with a pair of paper wings. "A port authority strips a private vessel by force and rifles through its cargo while the crew stands on the dock with hands neatly folded. Is that it?"

"I'm glad you share my confidence," Senlin said, forging on through her sarcasm. "Then, Finn Goll shows up to catch Rodion midsearch, which he can only interpret as a prelude to larceny and conspiracy. A great commotion will follow, and a lot of fingers will be pointed, and amid the fracas, we will board and launch the ship."

"That is a terrible idea! What's to keep them from firing on the ship?"

"They'll be distracted for one, and then the cargo will stay them. It's very precious, this painting, apparently. I realize Billy Lee won't appreciate that, but I don't think he'll try to shoot down his own ship. And Finn Goll will be afraid to because he doesn't want to attract the commissioner's attention. We just have to make sure the painting goes with us. It's like a shield, you see? They'll try to catch us, of course. But as long as we have the painting, they won't shoot us down. I think. I hope. And I have an escape route." Senlin pointed to the Tower face at a hardly visible indentation in the facade. "There. If we blow all the ballast at once, and unmoor at the last moment, we should jump to that undiscovered current." He made a guttural sound of equivocation. "Eh...probably."

Edith didn't even make a show of following his finger to look. "So, to be clear, your plan is to strike one hornet's nest, rattle a second, throw it at the first nest, and then run away amid the madness." She made a motion like she was picking a cherry from a tree. "This is your plan. You expect every one of those hornets to fly right on course, just as you like."

"I'm only planning for each to act according to their nature," Senlin said levelly, not backing down from the point. "I'm counting on greed and egotism, forces that are as reliable as gravity in the Tower. It is a gamble, but not a hopeless one." He placed his hands on her shoulders in that ancient gesture of desperate arguments and earnest pleas. He lowered his voice and said, "The real question is, will you be my first mate?"

The gangplank groaned behind them, followed by a tittering laugh that slid into a snort. Wobbling across the moon-washed deck came a woman dressed in a puff of skirt and a keyhole blouse that framed her cleavage. Behind her, swatting her backside with a bottle, came a youthful, brown-bearded man wearing a bright green tabard, emblazoned with a gold pyramid. It was an absurd outfit, more suited to a king's guard than a pirate.

"Captain Billy," Edith called, surprising the canoodling pair. Billy Lee came to a staggering, squinting stop. He swung his head from Edith to Senlin and back again, taking in the lanky figure that loomed beside his first mate.

"Who's the lurker, Eddy?"

"Man wants to buy our services," she explained easily and without a hint of the anxiety that was presently electrifying Senlin's spine. "Has a small package that needs a pocket."

"Is it legal?" Billy asked, his neck jerking like a goose, spittle flying.

"No," Edith said.

"Is it dangerous?"

"Ah. So-so. He said eight minas now, and when we deliver it to the Port of Orland, which is on our way, Captain, we get sixteen more from the recipient."

"That's a lot of money for so-so danger."

"I'm paying for discretion," Senlin said, speaking for the first time and glad to find his voice firm.

"I'm as discreet as a mustache on a two-bit whore." More spit flew out and caught in Billy Lee's beard. The woman with the locket of cleavage snorted. "Now, come on, come on, fork over my money."

"I'll send it along tomorrow with the parcel," Senlin said. "When will you disembark?"

"Tomorrow night. See that you send my money. Now, get off my ship! I need the whole deck tonight!" he said, goosing the woman.

Edith escorted Senlin back onto the skyport, where he whispered, "He doesn't seem like such a monstrous chap."

Behind her a bottle crashed, followed by a thunderous laugh. She flinched and mouthed the words: "Rabid dog."

Senlin found himself hesitating again. "The package I send in the morning, please make sure no one opens it," he said, and she nodded. The gloom that had felt cosmic before now seemed intimate. "Thank you, Edith."

"Oh, no, don't thank me. I'm first mate. I'm going to pin every mistake, every empty belly, every extra duty and flaccid wind on you. You are going to hate me."

Chapter Fourteen

Every important journey I have undertaken has
begun the same: with crushed sheets, a balled pillow,
flung open books, and not a wink of sleep. Tonight,
I added a new sort of frittering to the ritual: sewing.
I have at least solved the question of where to hide
the painting, though I mangled my coat's lining in the
process.

—*Every Man's Tower, One Man's Travails*
by T. Senlin

When Adam came to the port master's office the next morning, he found Senlin with his sleeves rolled up, leaning over
a small pine crate on his desktop. The dingy handkerchief
tied over the bottom half of his face made Senlin look like a field sur-
geon. His shoulders heaved as if he'd just been relieved of some great
tension.

"Ah, good! Just in time," Senlin said, pulling down the makeshift
mask and clapping his hands. A hammer, nails, and tufts of packing
straw littered his desktop, seeming out of place amid the papers and
ledgers. "Close the door, close the door. Today is the day! And since I
can't very well be seen walking about with a packed bag, I have transformed myself into a piece of luggage. I am wearing three shirts and all
my undergarments," he said, patting his somewhat plumper chest. "I
could hardly get my boots on. For the first time in months, I am actually a little warm. I have enough pockets for four books, but oh, which

books! It's kept me up half the night..." He was prattling, and Adam was quick to interrupt when he took a breath.

"What are you doing?"

"Ah! Well, I've just finished booby-trapping this crate."

"You've what? What for?"

"For you to deliver." Senlin gave the wooden cube on his desk two quick knocks. "Don't worry; it's only dangerous if you open it."

"The commissioner's painting is in there?"

"No, it's a decoy." Senlin pressed a finger on the side of his nose. "A booby-trapped decoy! How's that for treachery? You're going to take this to Edith on the *Stone Cloud*. Be sure to tell her not to open it, not to let anyone open it. Now, here's the eight minas I promised Captain Billy Lee. Don't lose it. It's every last shekel I have."

Untouched by Senlin's enthusiasm, Adam looked unhappily at the envelope he'd been passed; it was heavy with coins. "Who is this woman, Tom? Is she really deserving of so much trust?" He shook his head in a quick, almost shivering fashion. "Whoever she was before, she's spent the past half year cavorting with pirates. That changes a person. She might betray you without so much as a second thought."

"Of course! Anyone could. But I think she is sympathetic to our plight; she's in the same spot as us: indentured and in debt. Yes, she has lived among pirates, but we have lived among smugglers and whoremongers and thieves. We don't have to become the company we keep. We can hope for better and cling to those who share our hope." Senlin tried to project a cheerful calm, though he was not untroubled. Edith and Adam weren't wrong to question his scheme. It was daring, to say the least, and if the plan failed, he would have led them all to their deaths. It was not a burden he carried lightly. But what else could they do? Wait for rescue? Work until their concocted debts were repaid to men who could always concoct more debt? "We just have to survive the day."

Adam's broad lips thinned and disappeared into a rigid smile. "All right. But Tom, please, for my peace of mind, tell me you have the painting. If your gamble goes bad, it's our last chip."

Senlin smiled. "Of course I have it."

"Then why won't you tell me where it is? What if you are conked on the head, or thrown from the pier..."

"Thank you very much," Senlin said, drolly.

"I'm serious! Where would that leave Voleta and I? We'd be defenseless."

"Do you know what the Red Hand did to the only other person who knew where the painting was? He tortured him to death. He told me so. The painter, Ogier, died because he knew. The same almost happened to me. It isn't safe to know, Adam. I won't tell you because...it isn't safe." Senlin's voice dropped, and he had to stretch his neck to recover it. "All you need to worry about is Voleta. Keep her close. Get her on the ship, and do whatever you can to ready the ship for launch. I may be preoccupied. And, Adam, if I am"—he searched for a diplomatic way of saying it, then smiled at the ready answer—"if I am conked on the head, you should not hesitate to cast off. I don't know if you can fly the ship without a crew, but it's better to risk it than to stay."

Adam seemed ready to argue, but he pulled up short. His hearing was keener than Senlin's, and he appeared now to be listening. "Iren's on the stairs."

"Ah, my final eight o'clock report," Senlin said in a rush. "Take the crate. Careful, now. Go, go, go. If not before, I'll see you at the port at nine tonight." Senlin shooed Adam with the handkerchief he'd pulled from his neck.

The amazon passed Adam in the hall and soon dominated the doorway. She could've passed for a door herself. Senlin whisked a hand at the straw on his desk, fussing to cover the excitement that roiled inside him. "Iren, don't look so perturbed! I don't hold a grudge—"

She spoke over him. "You have to come with me."

"Oh. Well, let me just get the report..."

"Leave it," she said.

"All right," he replied slowly. He cocked his head to one side, reassessing her demeanor, trying to detect some hint of why their morning ritual was not going as usual. Her broad brow and smooth, uncreased eyelids betrayed nothing; she was unreadable. "Going on a picnic?" he said, picking up his aerorod.

"Leave it," she repeated more sharply, her eyes flashing.

Senlin froze under her glower, which contained none of the familiarity they had built during the recent weeks. It was not his sparring teacher, nor his student of letters who stood before him. This was Finn Goll's enforcer blocking the only exit to the room.

He gently lowered the aerorod to his desk and began the deliberate process of unrolling his sleeves. "Can I take my coat, at least?" he asked, and when she made no reply, he pulled it from the rack in the corner. Though it was invisible to her, he could feel the slight stiffness in the back of his coat where he'd sewn in Ogier's painting.

"Empty the pockets."

Senlin dutifully extracted the books he'd so carefully chosen: a guide to aeronautics, an engineering primer, a book on ship repair, and of course his private journal. He stacked the treasures on his desk. He hoped he'd have the chance to return for them. He also pulled out the jailor's key to show her. "Can I take my key?" She gave a slight shrug, and he smiled back with all the magnanimity he could muster. "Lead on," he said.

Finn Goll's carriage idled in the glum, yellow light of the station yard. It was the only running engine in the blister-shaped cavern, and it reverberated like a rough heartbeat. The porters, already soaked in chilling sweat from their morning work, stood quiet, frozen amid their labor. They eyed their port master, who seemed a little naked without his rod, stoically preceding the giantess toward the open door of the carriage. Goll's aged driver on his high bench looked like a scarecrow. Some of the gawking porters smirked meanly, but others watched with pitying expressions. It made Senlin wonder what they suspected or knew.

He was surprised to discover that Goll was not inside the coach. Since arriving in New Babel, Senlin had not once seen his diminutive boss outside his hearse. He had half assumed that Goll lived in it, bizarre as that seemed, and so it felt a little like he was trespassing upon a man's private chambers by entering the carriage alone. Though of course, he was not alone. Feeling the looming presence of

Iren behind him, Senlin hiked himself quickly into the coach. She followed on his heels and hardly had the door closed before the carriage lurched softly forward.

It occurred to him that Finn Goll might not take the news of Rodion's impending betrayal without comment. Goll might reasonably assume that Senlin was somehow embroiled in the plot. Or perhaps, in an inspired fit of unrelated treachery, Goll had contacted the commissioner and decided that he'd rather have a bounty than a bookkeeper. Perhaps Senlin was about to discover firsthand the grim fate of his predecessor. Really, a hundred things might have—and probably should have—gone wrong. Weighing each possibility was exhausting, so he turned his attention to the carriage window and refused to fret any further. Wherever he was going, whatever was going to happen, anticipation wouldn't change it.

They emerged from the port tunnel into an ecstatic display of lightning. The wire dome atop the central monolith spat sparks over the bleak citadels of New Babel. Fingers of electricity scratched the hewn-rock ceiling, leapt down to the flat tops of the taller cinder buildings, and tapered out into the frigid air where a colony of bats fled from the ghastly light.

Iren reached over and lowered the blind, ending the show. Senlin gave a little indignant huff and turned his attention to her. Her knees, jutting out from under her leather apron, were each as large as a child's skull. She was too large for the seat or for the carriage, and so had been forced into the humiliated posture of a big dog hiding under a small table. She stared glumly at the dark paneling of Senlin's headboard, which made him feel as if she was looking through him. He tried to reconcile this vision with the tireless, merciless martial instructor who'd hurled and swatted him about the station yard in weeks past. She seemed so lifeless now.

"I've been working on a theory for a while that you might find interesting," Senlin said affably.

"No," she said.

Senlin was undeterred. "Yes, indeed. It was born, my little theory, out of a glancing curiosity with the steam engine. The steam engine is

345

so ubiquitous here—I mean to say, they're everywhere, and not just on rails or on wheels. I've seen a mechanical hippopotamus fired on steam, and the pipe organ at the Steam Pipe is steam fed. It's a marvelous thing, steam."

"Stop saying steam," Iren said, though with little force. "Shut up."

"Sorry. I don't mean to lecture. But, it really is not an ideal energy. It's bulky and difficult to regulate. If you want to energize something that is small or portable or delicately calibrated, steam won't do. You need electricity. Now, electricity is relatively unheard of where I come from. It was sort of a parlor trick. We could make a person's hair stand on end with a simple static machine, but there was far too little of the stuff to do anything practical with it."

"Shut up or I'll put a gag on you," she said, glancing at him finally.

"If I shut up, I might as well be gagged," he quipped, hardly breaking the stride of what had indeed become a lecture. "Steam is a crude energy that can be refined into a superior form. Which is what is happening here; inside that fierce turbine that looms over our city, steam is being transformed into electricity. But it takes a lot of steam. And this brings me to my theory."

"I'm trying to be nice," Iren said, rolling her head and squeezing her eyes shut.

"Well, thank you. To my point! There are many men in the Basement who spend all day pumping water on these machines called beer-me-go-rounds. The name says it all, really; the men pump and are paid a pitiful amount of bad beer. Even so, there is never a shortage of men willing to pump, and there are dozens of beer-mes, so amounts of water are being drawn every hour from the deep wells under the valley."

"I don't care," Iren said.

"In the Parlor, people pay to roam around in costumes, acting important, and bickering, sometimes with swords. For this privilege, they must do two things: pay, which is diabolical, and work. The real task of the 'visitor' is to keep the fires stoked. The whole thing is an elaborate means of making and maintaining fires to produce heat, and cheaply so. The pumped water is heated inside the chimneys through what must be the most esoteric system of plumbing in the history of the world. The heated pipes run all throughout the Parlor, up to the Baths, where they converge into a single source. The Baths act as both a regulator of heat and pressure. Excess steam is vented, and tourists pay to romp in the byproduct of this immense engine."

Iren scowled now, though he recognized it as her thinking scowl. "Spit it out."

"We think of the Tower as an attraction or a market, but it's neither. It is an engine. The whole bottom four ringdoms are just a single, immense dynamo. Water, fire, steam, and then it turns into spark here, in New Babel!" Senlin held up his hands, as if to receive applause. Iren continued to hunker before him like an implacable toad. He dropped his hands in exasperation. "Where does all that energy go? A small amount trickles out locally to gross, dim bulbs and static overflows, yes, but think of it: Hundreds of thousands, perhaps millions, of men and women are working tirelessly to produce an energy that is not for them. So, who built it? Who is it for? What are they doing with all this power? Why are we paying for it and suffering to make something that does not help us—that in fact enslaves us?"

Iren's eyes scanned back and forth as she considered this. Though uneducated, she was far from unthinking, and Senlin knew she was capable of grasping the intrinsic injustice of what he'd revealed. He was disappointed by her conclusion, which began with a full-chested sigh. "So what?" she said at last. "It's unfair. The Tower is crooked. The sky is black. So what?"

"So we stop acting like it's not," Senlin said, and in a rush of foolhardy earnestness, reached across the carpeted foot well and set his hand on her thick wrist. She could've easily broken his hand, but she let it lay where it was. "We run away."

She gave a silent toothy leer at this, the expression suggesting she'd just recollected a private joke. Senlin felt the coach jostle onto rougher cobble and turn first one way then quickly another. "I like you," she said. "You don't give up, even when you should. I don't think you're wrong about the Tower. I like your theory. It's funny. It's maybe true. But"—and here, she leaned back and squared her shoulders, causing

347

the lustrous paneling to creak behind her—"the last time I took this ride, I strangled a port master and threw his body from the port."

A slight tremor awoke in Senlin's arm, and he felt the flesh pimple up and grate against his sleeve. "Is that what happens next?"

"Next, you talk to Goll about the money you've been stealing. I really hope you can charm him. If anyone can talk their way out, it's probably you. But I wouldn't tell him about your theory. He likes to be the one telling theories."

"Well. Thank you for that and for your honesty. For what it's worth, I think you'll do a fine job strangling me." His delivery did not quite match his cavalier pronouncement.

"If it comes to that, I hope you fight back. You've learned a lot. You were getting better. You don't lunge about as much. Lunging is bad. Keep your feet under you as long as you can. Be patient when you fight. Stand your ground."

"I will," Senlin said with rediscovered calm. He looked at his hand, and the tremor in his arm ceased as if it were a blown-out candle.

The carriage rocked to a stop, and when Iren opened the door, Senlin saw only darkness outside. The city had vanished: its coal stink and mechanical racket; its fog, thick as dreams; and its horde of lonely hearts—all gone. Iren exited the carriage and cracked her back. The driver passed an oil lantern down to her that was hardly brighter than a match. It occurred to him that he did not know where he was. If she planned to murder him, she could hardly have chosen a more private and obscure place to do it.

"Come on, Thomas Senlin," Iren said. "It's a short walk."

Chapter Fifteen

I can't stop thinking about that cocky, yellow-haired woman who tried to blackmail me. She must've felt so very clever. She really believed she'd make a fortune off of me and redeem her life. It wasn't a bad plan. But she was doomed by insignificance and ignorance and hope. And it may be no different for me.

—*Every Man's Tower, One Man's Travails*
by T. Senlin

Senlin could see nothing beyond the bubble of orange light. An impatient echo answered the clomp of their boots. He felt buried in the dark and miles away from anything familiar. Fifty paces in, they came upon a wall that was smooth as wet sand and set with a black iron door. Iren hung her lamp on a peg and pulled a ring of skeleton keys from under her leather apron. She cycled through, found and fitted a key, and then pushed the slab open.

The expanse on the other side could've held the entire station yard. The building may have been a factory or a warehouse once, though no machines or shelves were present now. It was empty except for the house.

An idyllic stone cottage stood in the middle of the floor, proud and serene, as if it had every natural right to be there. But what a feat of wealth and will to conjure such a thing! Other than the chimney, which was an odd, tenuous piece of brickwork that stretched to the warehouse ceiling, the house was quite picturesque. The gables had been recently painted, and the grout between stones stood out, white as meringue. Every window beamed warmly. Figures moved behind the curtains, which curled and kinked to make room for peering eyes. The shutters and gutters were immaculately fitted, though why a house, inside a warehouse, inside a ringdom, inside a Tower needed such things was beyond him. It was as if he'd finally arrived at the smallest doll in a set of nesting dolls.

Senlin hardly had time to absorb the surprise before Iren hustled him nearer to it. The front door was decorated with an evergreen wreath, a trifle that could not have been cheap to import. The door flew open under Iren's first knock, and she was beset by a pack of children. They threw themselves at her. They climbed her legs and pulled upon her chain belt, squealing all the while. She bent down and, speaking in a gentle falsetto, greeted each of them by name. The children, who seemed to range from three to eleven years of age, were boisterous and smartly dressed in colorful frocks. Not a one was more than four-and-a-half-feet tall, and they all were crowned with familiar tangles of dark hair.

Finn Goll stood behind them inside his home, hands buried proudly in the pockets of a corduroy housecoat. The children recovered their manners and made a path for the guests. Fresh bread and a hardwood fire perfumed the foyer. A plump, pretty woman restlessly folded and refolded a decorative towel in the doorway to Senlin's left, which appeared to lead to a dining room. To his right, there was an inviting den. The fire in the hearth cheered a set of plush chairs. Goll introduced the woman, who blushed all the way down to her throat, as Mrs. Abigail Goll. This began a round of bows and curtsies, which the children picked up and began to mimic with increasing hilarity, until their silly court was abruptly adjourned by the clapped hands of Mrs. Goll.

The lady of the house excused herself to look after lunch, and Finn Goll waved Senlin toward the fireside. Iren prattled a little more with the children, and then, despite their reluctance, separated herself. She stood by the mantel as if it were a guard post. As soon as Goll sat down across from Senlin, the children fled the room.

"Well, that wound them up. We don't have a lot of guests. Except for Iren, of course. They love her," Goll said, and something about his ease sharpened Senlin's anxiety. He did not trust this new facet of Goll's character. Senlin had not forgotten that Goll had appeared in the Basement as a harmless merchant. Perhaps this was another act. The children, the woman, and the gingerbread house—all could've been staged. But if it was an elaborate charade, what was the point of it?

"They seem wonderful," Senlin said politely. He glanced at Iren for some clue of what he had blundered into here, but she was determined to ignore him. She had said something about an accusation of stealing, which was a joke, of course. Senlin was the only honest man in the port.

"Their mother is to credit for that. I would spoil them rotten if it were up to me." Goll took up a horn pipe from a pedestal ashtray and began tamping tobacco into the bowl. "You don't have children, do you?"

"No, my nuptials were a little too brief for that." Senlin could hardly keep the bitterness from his voice. He wanted to vent his grievances, but he recalled Iren's advice to let Goll talk, and so said no more.

"I have six children. My oldest boy is away at school. I live and die for family, Tom. They give me purpose." He set a match to the bowl and drew on the stem. "So many people come to the Tower to fritter a fortune. Very few make one. They get fat in lounge chairs, roll around in the dark with tarts, and can't imagine a better waste of time or wealth. The Parlor, the Baths, the Boudoir—they're all tourist traps. It's dreadful down here." The pipe gurgled gently as Goll paused to smoke. Senlin's gaze roamed over the little cameos and dented baby cups on the mantel. Painted china, obviously done by a child's hand, and decorative tankards completed the effect: This was no sham; this was Goll's home. Senlin's attention returned to his host when the man's voice developed a passionate lilt. "But all these tourists and pilgrims don't realize what's just overhead. Wonderful, prosperous, peaceful lands are in the bowers. The trouble with mudbugs, Tom, is they get one foot off the ground and think they've mounted heaven." He laughed, his breath ruining a pretty ribbon of smoke. "You have to go much higher, past all the traps and slums. There are ringdoms up there worthy of children. But it's not a cheap neighborhood. It takes a fortune and savvy and a hundred other things to get there and stay there. You have to be leery of imposters, and overcome your greed, and make peace with your sacrifices. There will always be more than you prepared for."

"Indeed," Senlin said, trying to appear agreeable and attentive. Really, he felt baffled and worried. Why had Goll brought him into his inner sanctum? Was this some sort of an exit interview for a failed employee who would never see the light of day again?

"I worked in the Steam Pipe before I bought it, back when I was a poor lad. It's a good business for knocking the dew off a boy. It showed me the world as it was, not as one hopes it to be. It was shocking, of course. Many people never get over that shock." Goll seemed to chase a memory, appeared to not like where it led, and returned again to the present with a wry little smile. "But I did."

He leaned forward, setting aside his pipe. "I spent years wringing shekels out of wretches. I pulled gold threads from the coattails of rich men. I have thieved and saved for years, all in preparation of my ascent out of this cesspool. When I get discouraged, I think of my children and the lives I will give them. And, Tom, this is why you are here today. You have discouraged me and made me think of my children. It seems you've been going around handing out money to the men." He rounded his chest, and his voice rose to possess the room. "My money! My men!"

Senlin stiffened against the soft padding. So that was his crime: He'd given a raise to the porters. It had been a paltry sum that had no effect on the bottom line, but, apparently, it was the same as theft to Goll.

"You have complicated a simple job," Goll continued. "Collect my money. Don't educate, don't reform, don't teach the porters ballet.

Collect my money!" He beat the armrest fiercely, his sudden anger flushing across his face.

"When I began, you were losing ten, twenty minas a week to theft and rot and inefficiency," Senlin replied. "My errors, as you conceive of them, only increased your profit."

"You misunderstand the arrangement." Goll began an exaggerated pantomime of the sort one might use when training a dog or disciplining a child. "If the port makes more money because you're doing your job, that money isn't yours. It's mine. It's always mine. And there are other ways, more frugal ways, to inspire men to work."

"Oh, I have been very inspired by my beatings," Senlin said. His hand drifted into his pocket. The iron of the jailor's key was warm. At this intimate range, the little pistol would be quite effective. Using it would ruin any chance of escape, of course, but perhaps the chance was already ruined. Senlin wondered whether he would find any consolation in revenge. "You accuse the tourists of being shortsighted, but you are no better. You whip your men toward theft and conspiracy and revolt, and then punish them for it."

"What did I tell you before? There is no shortage of desperate men. They have no power because they have no value, and I pay them an according wage. If you pay them more, they just throw it at whores, drink, and White Chrom."

"That is not always the case. They have lovers and pasts, and they were all children once themselves." Senlin's fingertip rested on the scalloped trigger of the key, and he tilted the barrel up inside his pocket, guessing at the line of fire. "You are not alone in the Tower, Mr. Goll, much as you would like to think so, much as you have tried to hide yourself away." He wondered how quickly Iren would snap his neck after he fired. Would she thank him first?

"You really are a fool, Tom, and I pity you."

"Isn't that why you have brought me here? To exercise your pity? Or was it to show off your family and to convince yourself of your noble character before you have me killed?" Senlin felt a weight on his shoulder, and glancing over, he saw the walnut-like knuckles of Iren's hand. The pressure pressed his pocket into the chair, making the shot impossible for the moment. "Or do you expect everyone to be friends to your family?"

"Nobility and friendship are nothing but snake oil sold to old mothers and dumb farmers. I expect you to look out for yourself. You're so determined to make friends and to be fair and noble that you've sabotaged yourself again and again. Then you turn your nose up at me for looking after my interests. It's a joke!" Goll fumed. "You're in ruin and you will stay ruined until you recognize there is only one family in the world, one man, one Tower to climb."

"Yet, you told me to give up on Marya."

"Because it's in my best interest that you do, you loblolly idiot!" Goll kneaded his fleshy face until it glowed red. He motioned vaguely at the fire, and Iren released Senlin's shoulder to add another log. With the pressure of her hand gone, he could aim the pistol again. "I am telling you two things: work selfishly, and give me my due. That's it. I don't want to have to find a new port master, and you don't want to have your neck wrung." Goll pulled a ledger from his coat pocket and flipped through it. Iren stirred the fire, her back momentarily turned. If Senlin was going to fire, it had to be now. "By my count"—Goll licked his thumb and turned a page—"your raise cost me three minas, seven and a half shekels. That is the amount I will deduct from your wages. You will remit the raise, and if the men complain, you will choose an example from the ranks and hang him from the port. If you do all this, we can carry on together. If not, I'll carry on alone. Which will it be?"

Senlin pictured Goll's surprise at being shot: the startled wound, bloodless for a moment; the smoking hole amid the wales of his housecoat; and the last inventory that flies behind the eyes of a dying man.

A storm of little feet thundered overhead. The children were running through the halls. Their drumming turned something in Senlin's chest, and the rage drained from him. He was ashamed of what he'd almost done. It would've been suicide twice over. Even if he'd gotten away with it, which was hardly likely, shooting an unarmed man in his home while his children played upstairs would've made an end of the old, decent headmaster. The last vestige of the man who married Marya would be lost. And what sort of monster would remain? No, if he ever surrendered his conscience, even in the pursuit of dear, sweet Marya, he would become unrecognizable to himself and to her. Then there could be no reunion, and it would all have been for nothing.

"We'll carry on together," Senlin said, aware of the irony, though he hid it.

"That's good to hear," Goll said.

Senlin was glad, of course, to discover that he wasn't about to be strangled, but he still wanted to know whether Goll believed Adam's story about Rodion's intention to invade the port. Did Goll intend to do anything about it? Senlin needed to turn the conversation toward an answer. "Well, if there's nothing else, I have to get back to sign a ship's manifest before they run off with who knows what." Senlin leaned forward and patted his knees, preparing to rise and go.

"What ship?"

Senlin settled back. "The *Stone Cloud*. A disreputable little sloop with an abrasive captain. Pirates, probably."

"What's her export?" Goll tried to make the question seem casual, but Senlin saw through the effort and knew at once that Adam had succeeded in raising Goll's suspicions.

"Nothing unusual. A few tanks of gas, a bit of coal, and some private parcels for delivery. She'll be running light."

"You imagine any reason Rodion would be interested in her?" Goll's pretense at disinterest was slipping quickly.

"The whoremonger?" Senlin gave a noncommittal shrug. "Well, the first mate is a woman. Maybe he wants to have a look at her. I'm only joking. She has a false arm. She's probably not right for the stage. I only met Rodion the once, but he seemed...pleasant."

"Oh, he's just as jolly as a grave robber. He's a treacherous, paranoid, short-tempered pimp, and I haven't turned my back on him since I handed over the reins of the Steam Pipe six years ago. But he's usually predictable. He lays low; he hardly ever leaves the Pipe. I can't figure why, but he seems to be interested in this ship's cargo. You said private parcels. What's inside of those?"

"I don't know." Senlin deliberated a moment, and then said, "Do you want me to open them?"

"No, no. That's bad for business. If we start riffling through the mail, we'll lose half our business. We're supposed to be the discreet port." Goll looked troubled. "Do me a favor, Tom. Keep the men in tonight. Iren will come around with arms for the men, just in case."

"I don't understand. What do you think is going to happen?"

"Nothing, I'm sure," Goll said, and then more sharply: "That back-stabbing mudbugger." Senlin could see that Goll was working himself into a proper rage, and he was glad to not be the focus of his wrath a second time. "If Rodion does come to the port tonight, and if he brings his little troop of whore-smitten doormen, you'd do well to stay out of the way." Goll stood abruptly. "Don't you say a word to Rodion. I want to catch him in the act so he can't deny it. Who knows, maybe tomorrow you'll be port master and whoremonger. Wouldn't that be a turn? I don't suppose you can play the organ?"

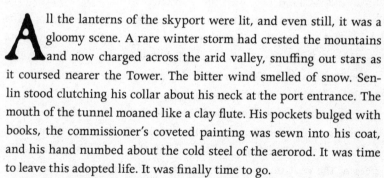

Chapter Sixteen

When teaching me to load a gun, Adam warned that an overloaded barrel does not fire faster or farther; it merely explodes in one's face. So it may be in the port this evening when Rodion and Finn Goll collide.

—Every Man's Tower, One Man's Travails
by T. Senlin

All the lanterns of the skyport were lit, and even still, it was a gloomy scene. A rare winter storm had crested the mountains and now charged across the arid valley, snuffing out stars as it coursed nearer the Tower. The bitter wind smelled of snow. Senlin stood clutching his collar about his neck at the port entrance. The mouth of the tunnel moaned like a clay flute. His pockets bulged with books, the commissioner's coveted painting was sewn into his coat, and his hand numbed about the cold steel of the aerorod. It was time to leave this adopted life. It was finally time to go.

He'd spent the afternoon with Iren, handing out aged sabers and flintlock pistols to the porters. The blades were so old and chipped that they resembled saws more than swords. Most of the porters were more perturbed by the cancellation of their evening liberty than the possibility of violence. Some elder porters took the occasion to brag about bygone battles full of near deaths and harrowing kills, though most were obvious myths. Iren gave the men direction: They were to let Rodion and his troop pass through the yard unmolested. Once the interlopers were past, the porters would follow Iren into the tunnel, where they would flank Rodion and confront him in the port. They were not to reveal themselves until ordered to do so.

Senlin had decided to delay the announcement of the canceled pay raise. Tomorrow, he would be gone, leaving Finn Goll holding the bag. If Goll wanted to trim wages in the middle of a turf war, that was his prerogative, and he could tell the men himself. Though *war* was not quite the right word for the coming scuffle. It would be a standoff, Senlin was sure. He expected saber-rattling, some bark and spittle, perhaps a little fencing, but neither Rodion nor Goll would want the threat to escalate. There was nothing to gain from killing one's coworkers or from damaging the port through which all wealth flowed. No, Rodion would be put in his place, and Goll would get his due.

The platform, from crane to bollard, was a symphony of groaning: Timbers and ropes shifted under the pressures of the approaching storm. Even the great iron struts added their bass complaints to the song. The graceful profile of the merchant ship the *Gold Finch* was lit up like a chandelier. Her crew worked hastily to batten down the hatches and redouble the tethers of the lozenge-shaped balloon. The ship's lookout, hardly more than a boy, clung to the bowsprit like a figurehead, watching the snow clouds billow nearer. Senlin marveled at the composure the Tower required of even the youngest souls; Babel aged its population with equal cruelty.

If the *Finch* evoked a chandelier, the *Stone Cloud* docked catty-corner from it resembled a lard candle. The scotched and buckshot hull, with its bulbous fore and tapered aft, knocked against the bumpers of the port ungracefully. Its ashen balloon bulged through the matrix of rigging like fat through fishnet. Not a single kind phrase came to mind when Senlin gazed upon the *Stone Cloud*, and yet, despite its homely face, he loved it to its bones. It was his ship. He only had to take it.

Edith met him at the gangplank that sawed back and forth over the drop. Her expression was grim. Behind her, a ramshackle crew of a dozen men hustled to clear the deck, inspected knots, and shoveled pans of coal into the furnace. The gusting wind made a discreet exchange impossible between them, but in response to Senlin's tentative smile, Edith gave a short, almost desperate shake of her head, then she was abruptly forced to one side by Billy Lee. The captain gave Senlin his arm and half jerked him over the gulf onto his ship. Senlin hit the deck awkwardly, and had to stagger until he found a surer stance. The ship pitched beneath him.

"I'm here to sign your manifest," Senlin said with admirable composure.

"You're a curious sot. You never said you were port master when I caught you fondling my first mate," Captain Billy Lee bellowed. His emerald smock flapped against his puffed chest, and his hand rested on the cupped guard of the cutlass at his hip. "But then, you're much more than you look."

"I was hardly fondling her," Senlin said indignantly and turned to Edith for support. She had an entirely unfamiliar face on now: Her teeth showed and her dark eyes caught no light. Disturbed, and a little confused, he turned again to find the tip of Lee's sword leveled at his nose. Instinctively, Senlin raised his hands.

"A girl at the Pipe told me all about you this morning," Billy Lee said and animated his speech with a cursive flourish of his sword. "This sweet little tart said that you were a marked man. I could hardly believe my luck."

"A fair-haired woman?" Senlin asked, knowing the answer already.

"I got the impression she was yapping to anything with a spare shekel and an ear-shaped hole. Everyone else took it for pillow talk, but me, I knew there was something to it." Billy Lee called over his shoulder, "Bring it out." A mutt-faced man in a skullcap carried over a small crate. Senlin immediately recognized it. "You're wanted by the commissioner. I wonder if this little box doesn't have something to do with it."

Senlin dropped his hands in disgust, which inspired the encircled crew to draw their swords. He'd never seen so much gleaming steel—and certainly had never been the focus of it. He felt like a pincushion. Even Edith had leveled her single-shot pistol at his head; she stood scowling behind the bead. She had warned him of Billy Lee's treachery, and yet Senlin was more surprised by her aggressive show of loyalty than Lee's wolfish revelation. At least, he hoped it was only a show. He supposed Edith had little choice but to appear his enemy until the last possible moment.

"I am the master of the Port of Goll," Senlin said, biting the words. "My employer is powerful, influential, and jealous of my time. You are accusing me based on the testimony of a prostitute and the evidence that I have engaged your services to deliver my mail. Is that the size of it?"

"Of course you would deny it," Captain Lee said, glancing briefly to one side. His sparse brown beard now seemed to have been pasted on, his uncertainty making him appear young and boastful. The flinch was enough to spur Senlin on.

"And on this damning proof, you are willing to poison your welcome at this port forever." Senlin moved his daggering gaze over the rest of the motley and haggard crew. "Do you really think that your lot, this ship, would be allowed to dock at Ginside Port or Erstmeer? Where will you take on fuel in the future? I'm sure a spit-shined dandy like you is probably clutched to the bosom of every port master from the Baths to the bell tower."

Immediately, Senlin sensed he had gone too far; he had pricked the young captain's pride. "All right. Then we'll settle it here." Billy Lee put his curled-up boot toe on Senlin's crate. "Open the box, show us what's in there. If it has nothing to do with the business of the commissioner, I'll say my sorrys, and you can go."

It was Senlin's turn to flinch, though he tried to hide it with outrage. "Are you mad? I am not going to open my private affairs for you to nose through. If this is how you operate, then I will collect my parcel and go."

"Oh no, you won't," Billy said, straightening his cutlass again to Senlin's throat. "If it hurts your feelings so much, Bobbit will open it for you." The dog-faced crewman in the skullcap drew a fat-bladed dagger from his hip. He knelt and began working the point under the lid of the crate. Senlin held his breath.

The creak of the gangplank startled everyone aboard. Before anyone could recover from their surprise, a dozen of Rodion's men swarmed onto the ship. They were dressed in the plain breeches and wool coats of stagehands and ushers, though all had flamboyant touches to their clothes: wigs, feathers, scarves, and strings of beads. Where primitive tribes might favor war paint, these men preferred costume jewelry. The effect was bizarre. Regardless of their appearance, their purpose was plain enough: They came with sabers and pistols drawn. The invaders fairly swamped the portside of the ship. Another dozen of Rodion's men waited on the dock with long guns level and ready.

Senlin was relieved by the interruption; he could only hope now that the rest of his plan would unfold peacefully. The ship would be unloaded and the cargo searched, and while everyone was engaged in that tedious business, he and his conspirators, his crew, would make off with the vacated ship. He glanced about for signs of Adam or Voleta but saw none.

The ship, now overcrowded, began to sink under the new weight. The hull knocked jarringly against the cradle of the slip. Even amid the stand-off, everyone had the sense to allow one of Lee's crew to fire the furnace. The ship lurched back to port level.

With the ship secured, Rodion boarded, pompous as a duke. He wore a full-length cape, trimmed abundantly in matching black fur. The ivory stocks of twin pistols stood prominently at his belt. Rodion squared his shoulders toward Billy Lee, who seemed amused when he said, "I saw you on stage! You're the whoreganist."

"A comedian. If only I'd prepared a joke," Rodion said, glancing around disdainfully at the weathered fixtures: the chocks, cleats, and hatch rings. "But I haven't come for you." The ostentatious pimp turned to Senlin. "I've been having the most fascinating conversation, Thomas. Bring them out." He signaled one of his men stationed by the gangplank. Two figures were escorted aboard into the swinging, drunk light of the hurricane lamps.

Senlin made a concerted effort to appear dismayed at Adam's appearance. Adam, playing his part, was unable to meet Senlin's gaze. At his side, Voleta's wild black hair and large features were fairly buried under a shawl that appeared as heavy as a rug. She stared up at Senlin with unblinking, violet eyes.

"Adam, what have you done?" Senlin blurted.

Captain Lee interrupted the awkward reunion with gruff indignation. "This is my ship, not a theater. Take your penny opera elsewhere. I've changed my mind. I want nothing to do with any of this." And yet he scooted Senlin's crate nearer to himself with the heel of his boot.

Ignoring Billy Lee, Rodion continued with obvious pleasure. "I have had my ears filled with such inspiring rumors about you. I hear you are a fugitive. I hear there may be some reward. I hear you are smuggling treasure." Rodion put his hand on Adam's shoulder confidently. "At least, I hope you are, for Adamos's sake. I've promised him that if he delivers me a fortune and proof that you have abused your station and swindled our kind employer, I will release his sister from her contract, though promises aren't as expensive as little girls," Rodion said, and pinched Voleta's cheek. She smiled and giggled gamely, and then with one dart of her neck, bit his finger. Rodion recoiled, raised his gloved hand to strike her, but stopped short. "I would miss you so much, Voleta. I need a new bed warmer."

Though he'd been standing in glum defeat a moment before, Adam's head now snapped around at this. "You will keep your promise, Rodion!"

"Of course, of course." He inspected the teeth marks Voleta had left on his leather glove. "But we must finish the play! Too many dramatic questions remain: What is this treasure, and where is it now?"

"You should know," Senlin said before he thought the utterance through.

"Why on earth should I know?"

"Because you're conspiring with Commissioner Pound," Senlin replied, seeing no reason for Rodion to conceal this obvious fact now.

"No one conspires with the commissioner! He doesn't collaborate. He crushes and he takes. No, I'd sooner tell the devil my address than bring myself to the commissioner's attention." Rodion scoffed, and his surrounding men took to the signal and laughed in a chorus. "When I turn you over to Pound, it'll be from a great distance and without negotiation. Let him send along whatever compensation seems fair to him; he'll get no argument from me." Senlin was unsettled: If it hadn't been Rodion who called the Red Hand down on him, then who? Finn Goll must've exaggerated his dread of the tyrant.

His patience at an abrupt end, Captain Billy Lee barked at his crew, "Get these yappers off my ship!"

"Indeed," Rodion said, and pivoted about nonchalantly. He drew his pistol in the same casual gesture and shot Billy Lee just above the pyramid on his tabard. All watched as the cocksure young captain staggered back three steps and struck the bulwark. He flipped backward into the open air, leaving one boot standing empty on the deck.

Edith had scarcely opened her mouth and drawn a breath before Rodion wheeled at her and fired his second pistol. The bullet ricocheted off her brass shoulder and struck one of Rodion's men in the forehead, knocking the feather from his ear and his brains from the back of his head.

Edith recovered her voice before the man hit the floor. "For Billy!" Her cry cracked with rage. She drew the pistol from a comrade's belt and leveled it at Rodion. He threw one of his own men in front of her barrel, and the surprised man caught the full blow. The powder flash set his fur stole on fire. Edith drew her sword and charged Rodion. The whoremonger snatched the cutlass from the hand of the burning man and lifted the blade in time to receive Edith's first attack.

Senlin found himself in the middle of a melee. The two sides did not come together neatly like dance partners or the teeth of two gears, as his sparring lessons had suggested they would. Instead, many fled and crashed together; others fought in pairs and gangs, overwhelming and changing targets as randomly as a swarm of bees. Some of Lee's crew began to fire at the bank of Rodion's riflemen who stood on the port, and they replied in dreadful kind. The volley of shots shattered the bulwark, severing lines and limbs as they passed over the deck. Wood and gore sprayed the air and caked the floor. A man cried out like a kicked dog. A shot pinged off the furnace and shattered a cabin window. A water barrel burst on deck, and its surf ran everywhere underfoot. It was madness.

Voleta buffeted against her brother's back as he retreated from a berserk crewman, the one called Bobbit, who was swinging a fire iron in wild, wide strokes. Adam, though strong from years of hard labor, was having trouble deflecting the heavy fire iron. The rod struck the back of a dueling stagehand, sending him sprawling headfirst into the grate of the ship's furnace. The stagehand screamed as his hair caught fire, and he leapt up to run guttering over the starboard side. His torched head vanished like a shaken-out match.

Seeing Voleta's distress, Senlin pulled her from the thick of the battle and up the four stairs to the empty forecastle. Though a deal quieter than the main deck, the forecastle was a dead end, backed only by open air and curdling clouds full of snow. Senlin regretted the tactical decision almost at once, but he could see no safe path to the port. A new burst of gunfire sent them both diving to the floor.

Rodion's fur-trimmed cape swelled and fell like a great bellows as he fought with Edith. They were evenly matched: Each attack was repaid with an equal riposte. Their battling spanned the deck, though their stage was littered with fallen men and the grim confetti of bullets. Rodion's saber rang against Edith's steel rapidly, like a butcher sharpening his knife. Even amid his frenzy, Rodion did not forget the precious investment he'd carried to battle. He called to his men, "Catch the girl! Three pieces to the man who catches her alive, and death to the man that slays her."

One of Rodion's stagehands, a keg-chested man in a corn-silk wig, dislodged his saber from a dead man's back and locked his eyes on Senlin, who stood hunkered atop the forecastle.

Though he felt like a flimsy partition, Senlin held Voleta behind him and his aerorod before him. He sorted through every piece of advice Iren had given him during their sparring lessons. He felt overly conscious of his feet: Were they too far apart? Was he standing pigeon-toed? The way he gripped the aerorod felt all wrong. Would he forget his lessons and swing it like an axe, leaving his center open to any half-hearted lunge? It was too much to hold in his head. It was like the old panic he'd suffered before an exam. All his thorough studying turned to stuffing in his head, and a nervous paralysis descended upon him. He had lost already.

But then, close behind him and almost into his ear, Voleta said,

"Don't try to reason with him. Just tap him on the head." This simple advice called to mind Iren's essential lesson: Don't think about it too much.

The bull in the wig was looking determinedly at Senlin's legs from the bottom of the stairs, his sword already recoiling to strike at his knees. As soon as the brute touched the bottom step and was in reach, Senlin crowned him, knocking the man's wig askew.

The brute reeled back and spit a mass of blood—that included half a tooth—onto the deck. He pulled the white-blond wig from his bald head and used it to wipe his mouth. When he reseated the wig, it was disheveled and shocked with gore. He looked up, no longer focused on Senlin's knees. The bull-chested man charged the stairs, his sword aimed at Senlin's nose.

Senlin managed to turn the blade aside, but he could not deflect the man. The brute bowled into him, and he was thrown against Voleta. She half leapt and was half hurled over the cannon on the bowsprit. She caught the barrel with hooped arms, leaving her feet dangling over the abyss. Senlin could not help her. He was trapped beneath his attacker. The wigged man was slobbering blood on him and struggling to bring his sword to a useful angle. Before he could shift his blade, Senlin chopped at the man's throat with the heel of his hand and pulled his legs under him. He kicked the gasping brute back down the stairs, where he collided with another man and fell to the ground in a tangle.

When Senlin got to his knees and then his feet, he turned to find Voleta standing perfectly balanced on the cannon barrel, holding the taut rigging that bound the ship to her balloon. Her shawl was gone, lost over the edge, which left her wearing only the blue leotard she performed in. He knew she must've been freezing, but she smiled even still and said, "Aren't you the scrapper. They must've teased you in the schoolyard!"

"You have no idea," Senlin said dryly. He quickly moved the jailor's key from his coat to his pants' pocket and then pulled his arms from the coat. He helped her put it on; the coat hung on her shoulders, loose as a shroud.

"Why are you carrying bricks around in your pockets?" she asked.

"They're books. Drop them if you have to. You should climb into the rigging and stay there until the ship is clear. Soon as it's safe to come down, start undoing the portside lines. Leave the crib anchors for last." He gripped her shoulder and said, "Don't lose the coat, whatever you do. It is very important that you keep it safe."

"Don't worry, whatever happens to me, your coat will survive. Long live fashion!" she said, and Senlin could only roll his eyes. She climbed the rigging toward the belly of the balloon, quickly, quietly, like a billowing black flag.

On the main deck, Adam had waited Bobbit out. The skullcapped crewman, increasingly exhausted from hauling the fire iron back and forth, now swung with more enthusiasm than he had strength to control. When the iron clipped a balustrade and snagged there, Adam drove his sword between the man's ribs. Bobbit collapsed into a writhing ball and hissed in agony.

Adam searched for Senlin and found the port master coming down from the forecastle. Anxiously, Adam asked after his sister, and Senlin said where he'd sent her. They were interrupted by a stagehand in a bowler attempting to broadside them, but Adam deftly parried the man's thrust, and Senlin used his aerorod to bat the man into the riser of the forecastle.

"It's turned into a slaughterhouse," Senlin said. "If Goll doesn't arrive soon, we'll be lost." He'd been taken by surprise when Rodion dispatched Captain Lee and could only hope now that Goll would restore some measure of sanity to the scene.

The wind and the agitation of bodies made the moored vessel swing and twist on its anchors. The water that had spilled on the deck was rapidly turning to ice. Between crossed swords and the flail of limbs, Senlin spied Edith, still sparring with Rodion. She executed a well-timed advance: a sudden leap forward followed by a rapid lunge, and Rodion was driven back against the starboard rail. His sword wagged weakly as he fumbled to steady himself. Edith pursued the advantage and grabbed the whoremonger's blade with her mechanical hand. With an effortless flick of the wrist, she snapped the blade near the hilt.

But just as it seemed she had disarmed the villain, Rodion twisted about, and using the stump of his blade, severed the line to one of the starboard anchors.

The ship bucked wildly as the remaining moorings and the balloon fought for a new equilibrium. Raiders and crew alike were sent skidding down the tilted deck toward the gap between ship and port. Half a dozen corpses and three live men were thrown overboard in an instant, their passage made more hopeless and swift by the ice on the deck. Thrown to his back, Senlin was fortunate enough to slide against the stairs of the quarterdeck. Adam also had caught a foothold on the lip of a hatch. But Edith was not so lucky. Senlin watched in mute horror as she skated on her side, arms grasping after some handle. Helplessly, fluidly, she passed through a gap in the railing and vanished into the breach with a choked scream.

The image of Edith tumbling through the emptiness overran every other thought. Senlin smashed his hands to his ears to cover the echo of her strangled cry, but the scream did not diminish. Suddenly, his plan seemed worse than foolhardy; it was murderous. He alone was responsible for this bloodshed; he was the arrogant engineer of all this confusion and death. It was not fair that she, who'd already suffered so much, be punished a second time for keeping his company. It was not fair, but neither was it a surprise. Not if he was honest. Obsession made him dangerous to his friends. They fell so he could climb.

He knew action was required. He must do something! But there wasn't a ploy left in his head.

Rodion, who had held on to the high rail when the ship pitched, knew exactly how to respond. He gave quick orders for his men to disarm the crew of the *Stone Cloud*. Leaderless and few, they put up little resistance. Senlin felt the aerorod yanked from his hand. He was hauled roughly to his feet. A new gangplank was set to the listing ship, and he and Adam were escorted across. He rolled his head back to keep from looking down at the terrible chasm Edith had just fallen into—and by chance caught a glimpse of Voleta, hiding at the limit of the lamplight, high in the rigging. At least she had escaped detection. Perhaps Rodion would presume she had fallen overboard amid the chaos. Perhaps someone would survive this folly.

The sight of Voleta stirred him from his shock. He could not give up just because he had failed Edith. There were other lives at stake, and there was hope yet.

Rodion salvaged Senlin's crate from a pile of debris at the port railing and carried it onto the pier with an air of triumph. Senlin and Adam were forced to their knees before Rodion. Senlin watched as his aerorod was handed to the whoremonger. He bandied it about experimentally.

"I think it's funny that a bookworm like you should carry about such a crude club. At least that monstrous woman could swing a sword. She was fun." He tossed the rod over his shoulder, and it went clanking across the timbers of the port. Rodion began the process of reloading his pistols, feeding a pinch of black powder into the pan of one. "Where's the girl? Where's Voleta?" Rodion asked a stagehand with a bent nose and a feather boa looped about his neck. The man gave a doubtful shrug and shook his head. "Thank you, Harold." Rodion looked down at Adam, who craned up, a bloom of rage reddening his eyes. "I hereby release your sister from her contract. Consider it a bereavement gift."

A gunshot startled Senlin. He cast his head toward the sound in time to see one of Rodion's men shoot a second of the *Stone Cloud*'s crew in the back. The shot man tumbled forward over the edge of the port, and the executioner moved on to the next in a row of four remaining men. In the Skirts, the dead were raining. Senlin quickly looked away.

Rodion was speaking again, though he was regularly interrupted by another shot. "Now, where were we?" He packed a square of wadding and a ball into the barrel of his pistol. "Ah, yes. What's in the box, Thomas?"

"Why don't you open it and find out?"

"I must have misphrased the question." Rodion pulled back the hammer and lowered the pistol to Senlin's head. "What's in the box?"

"What have we here?" a voice called from behind. Goll emerged from the port tunnel with Iren towering at his side, forty armed men at their backs. "Some heady conspiracy, I'm sure."

Surprised, Rodion raised his hands in a gesture of helplessness and welcome, the pistol lolling from one finger. "Goll, you're just in time to see the execution of a pitiful mastermind. He meant to smuggle—"

"Did you do that?" Goll interrupted, pointing at the horribly listing *Stone Cloud*. Surprised, Rodion was too slow to form an elegant answer, which was just as good as a confession to Goll. "So, you've ransacked my port, wrecked a ship, which, according to every law of safe harbor, was under our protection, and apparently executed Tom, Dick, and Harry between here and Thursday, to punish this man for passing a little contraband?"

Rodion found his smile. "Well, of course, that makes it all sound a little rash." The whoremonger was keeping one eye on Iren, who stood with a bland, almost bored expression on her broad face. "But, Finn, this man—"

"Get up, Thomas. I can't talk with you crouching there like a scolded dog. You too, Adamos." Goll again interrupted the whoremonger.

"This man," Rodion resumed, "is wanted by Commissioner Pound of the Baths. And I'm very certain it has something to do with this box, which he was trying to sneak out on that ship. I only found all this out yesterday, and I wanted to confirm it before I involved you, Finn."

"Look, here's the flat of it, Rodion. You shouldn't be here," Goll said. "I know all about this idiot's troubled past. But if the commissioner wants him, he can come collect him. No one's stopping him. The fact that Tom is still alive suggests that either he's paid his debts or they weren't very grand to begin with."

All were surprised when Adam spoke up. "No, he was waiting for the painting to come out in the open."

"What?" Goll said, expressing everyone's puzzlement. "What painting?"

"He didn't know what happened to the painting Senlin stole from him, but he wanted it back very badly. Very badly."

Senlin looked at his friend, his expression wrinkled with confusion. "What are you saying?"

"I brought this on you. When you told me that the commissioner would pay a fortune to get back what you'd stolen, I wrote him to see how much a fortune was." Adam's tone was so flat his confession seemed to rise from a hypnotic state. "I agreed to find the painting. I agreed to steal back what you'd stolen. It never occurred to me that Pound didn't know where you were. I didn't know I was drawing a target on your head. I tied the grappling line to the Baths. I was going to use it to send the painting down. I didn't know I was giving that madman a way up. When the Red Hand came to torture a confession out of you, I knew I'd made a mistake. I wrote to Pound and told him that he could keep his fortune. I was done."

Adam shivered, and once he began, he could hardly stop the tremor. "But, Rodion is right, you don't conspire with the commissioner. He crushes and he takes. I'd gotten his attention. He knew who I was, and he quickly found out about Voleta." Adam's face was as pale as wax. The first glint of snow arrived, the crystals so small they made the air twinkle. "I'd never heard such threats, never imagined such cruelties as what he promised for me and my sister. I had to produce the painting." Adam looked wounded when he finally met Senlin's unbelieving gaze. "But you wouldn't tell me where it was. I searched your room and your office, and I begged you to tell me."

"I was trying to protect you," Senlin murmured. The snow clouds reflected the light of the port lamps and glowed orange like smoke from wet firewood. A moment before, he had not thought that he could feel more alone. His wife was lost, perhaps irretrievably so. Edith was dead and Ogier with her. Tarrou was buried in slavery. Adam's betrayal seemed the crowning defeat. He had no friends.

Yet, even as he thought it, his heart bucked. He was succumbing to self-pity. True, Adam had made a grave mistake, but it had been a mistake of desperation and naivety. Senlin had made plenty of those since his arrival. And hadn't Adam rescued him from the Red Hand, at great risk to himself? Hadn't Adam gone along with Senlin's plan, though it seemed—and proved to be—the height of folly? Really, was Senlin any better of a friend?

Perhaps not. But then, could any of these arguments, sanguine as they were, ever restore his trust in Adam? Senlin was unsure, but he decided, with only minutes remaining to his life, that he would try to forgive Adam at least.

Rodion, smiling like a man vindicated by the ruling of a court, lowered his ivory-stocked cannon at the desolate and shivering Adam. "And there you have it," he said. "The conspiracy undressed."

Finn Goll held up a staying hand. "This boy's blunders don't do any service to your own, Rodion. Put the gun up. Adam, what's the last thing you told the commissioner?"

"That the painting was coming into the open. I told him that it would be on the humblest ship in port tonight and easily picked. That's what I'm trying to tell you. I'm confessing now because he's coming. He's coming here tonight."

As suspicious as they'd all been of one another a moment before, they shared a single spasm of fear now. Each one in the uncomfortable, hostile assembly took a silent stock of their chances. Senlin suppressed a morbid urge to laugh: Here he thought he'd overloaded the gun, had set too many cocks loose in the yard. The commissioner would overshadow them all.

"Where's the painting?" Goll asked, and it took Senlin a moment to realize he was the object of the question. When he looked, Goll was glaring at him hotly. "No lies, Tom. I'm in no mood."

"In the crate," Senlin said, gesturing at the box that had naturally, inexplicably migrated to the center of their gathering.

"Open it up, Iren," Goll directed, and the hulking woman obediently took a knee, stooping close to the small crate.

What came over Rodion was not exactly clear. Perhaps he'd calculated his odds of surviving the evening and not liked the results, or perhaps he saw opportunity in this moment of discovery to change the focus of power. And it could just as easily have been a spasm of wrath or terror that made him set his pistol to the back of Iren's ear.

Senlin didn't think. He just moved his arm, his hand bursting from his pocket like a startled bird from a bush. The modest pop of powder sounded like a champagne cork. A red tear stood out under Rodion's eye, and the fur-lined whoremonger reached up to brush it a way. But the tear swelled when he touched it, then like an opened faucet, began raining down his face. Rodion let loose an awful rattling snore and then fell dead amid a fine powder of snow.

Senlin lowered the jailor's key when he realized he was being stared at, not least of all by Iren, who raised herself up amid a great creak of leather and rasp of chain.

"Well, that's one riddle answered," Goll said. Senlin brimmed with disgust, though not regret. When Goll spoke again, there was no malice to his announcement, but neither was there any uncertainty. "While we're hurrying through the uncomfortable consequences, Iren would you please deliver Adam to the eternal bosom of the earth? Quick as you can."

The amazon's usual iron mask seemed to warp at the corners, and her expression became so anguished that for a moment Senlin thought she might be stifling a violent sneeze. Then she reached, halting more than once, for the chain that encircled her.

A chorus of gasps from the forty men spared Adam his eulogy. They turned as one and were all transfixed by the vision of three black moons rising over the horizon of the platform's end. The dawning silhouette was unmistakable: The hull was like an uprooted coliseum. It was the *Ararat*, the commissioner's flying fortress, the most feared airship in his fleet.

No sooner had the cannon hatches cleared the limb of the port than they began to fire. Their target was immediately apparent: the tethered *Gold Finch*, the regal merchant's ship. A dozen holes perforated the hull, delicate where they entered and jagged where they left. The artfully carved flourishes of balustrades and bulwarks burst into puffs of plaster. The *Finch*'s crew, who'd gone belowdecks to weather the storm, came pouring from the galley hatch in a frenzy, but before any could get to port, the centermost of the ship's furnaces was struck by the ricochet of a cannonball. The devastated furnace ignited the umbilical, which fled like a fuse to the mass of hydrogen gas contained above. Ignited, the gas inside blossomed into orange flame. The fire

devoured the long, silk envelope spreading with the surreal deliberation of a burning page. The ship did not drop so much as rapidly sink,
the withering flames glowing and falling as the moorings were torn
from the port, and the hull rolled, screeching, from its insufficient
cradle.

A moment later, there was nothing left of the *Gold Finch* but embers
glowing in the dark like the candles of a vigil.

Chapter Seventeen

I still recall a line from that feckless *Everyman's Guide*. It said something like, "the Tower's real trade is in whimsy, adventure, and romance." I cannot imagine a less accurate trio. Though, who in their right minds would've come if the editors had said, "the Tower's true trade is in tyranny, dismemberment, and heartbreak"?

—*Every Man's Tower, One Man's Travails*
by T. Senlin

The snow revealed the shape of the wind. Senlin watched as distinct gusts pulled at the fire that had leapt from the *Gold Finch* to the port. Feeding on the coal dust that coated the dock, the flames flashed toward the Tower. The blaze soon divided the porters: half flew back to the tunnel before the fire cut them off from escape; the other half, whether out of courage or surprise, remained outside in the pall of the commissioner's warship.

The deck guns of the *Ararat* fired a volley of harpoons at the platform, and for a moment it looked as if a monstrous nautilus was grasping for the port with its mass of tentacles. Then the grappling spears bit into the wood beams, and the trailing lines were pulled taut.

A bevy of blue-coated agents zipped down the lines, clinging to pulleys that piled at the end of the line like the beads of an abacus. The men drew their sabers the moment their boots hit the ground, and in seconds, the commissioner had a platoon standing on the Port of Goll.

The agents, in stark contrast to the natives of the port, were uniformly arrayed in epaulets and gold braids; they appeared professional and calm in a manner that unnerved Rodion's remaining stagehands and Goll's porters. These ragtag defenders would've likely broken and run, even into the fire, had it not been for Iren. Swinging her hook and chain at her side, she rallied the men from behind, chasing them into battle.

Goll had vanished. It was no surprise to Senlin that the diminutive boss had fled. He had survived the Tower on the merit of his wits rather than his fists. And anyway, it took a very small helping of wits to recognize just how dire the situation was.

Momentarily forgotten amid the new war, Senlin gripped Adam by the arm and said, "I'll rake you over the coals later; there's no time for it now. Get to the ship. Feed the furnace. Be ready to launch the moment we're aboard."

"What are you going to do?"

"I'm going to make sure Iren is coming with us."

Adam, who moments before had been convinced the amazon was ready to strike him dead, was not thrilled by the announcement. "Leave her. She's a beast."

Senlin grabbed Adam up by the shirtfront and pulled him near enough that the young man could feel the force of Senlin's breath when he said, "Say 'aye aye,' Adam."

Adam's eyes were wide and bright with alarm; he had not seen this side of Senlin before. Senlin knew he could no longer afford to negotiate and explain every point and action to Adam. Either Adam would follow his orders now, or he never would. The sooner that was established, the better.

Their noses hovered nearly together a moment longer, then Adam repeated the phrase and added a word he'd used before but never meant, not until now. "Aye aye, Captain."

By the time Senlin located his aerorod in the piling snow and joined the fight, it was apparent he was on the wrong side of a rout. Rodion's men, already wounded and spent from grappling with the crew of the *Stone Cloud* and demoralized by the loss of their leader, fell quickly before the commissioner's agents. The porters fared little better. What heart they had was torn apart by the organization of their enemy. The porters were used to scrapping in the yard or charging as a mob— both useless tactics against a force of superior numbers and training.

Only Iren gave them hope against the onslaught. She by herself was more devastating than a bank of riflemen. Her leather apron flared as her thick arms snapped life into her chain. The agents caught in the path of her hook looked as if they had fallen under a buzz saw. They attempted to swarm her, but she refused to stand still for the dog-piling. She leapt about, mad as a top and nearly as nimble as Voleta. Twice an agent fired at her, and twice the bullet was late: cutting at her blur, passing through the air, and finding a fellow agent to burrow into.

Senlin couldn't reach her. Every time he thought he might've beaten a path through, the way would clog with retreating agents, clutching ruined limbs and gushing wounds. They were desperate to get away from Iren and her great mauling propeller. Even amid the chaos, Senlin could not help but to admire her grace, gruesome as it was. In her warring, he saw all the lessons she'd drummed into him, here combined into a single, fluid reflex. He'd long suspected that she had been overly hard on him when they'd sparred, but now he knew just how gingerly she had handled him. He'd been a cub in the mouth of a lion.

She was a master of violence. She was indomitable, and she was winning the war.

Then a familiar, ungainly figure climbed over the rampart of the *Ararat*. The bulbous middle and spindly arms, the broad straw hat and white linen clothes were unmistakable. The specter released the zip line while he still hung twenty feet from the ground. He landed in a crouch in the clearing Iren had cut through the ranks of men. The agents opened the circle even farther, like a snake's mouth widening to make room for the appearance of the fangs. The Red Hand straightened and said, "Did you know that this is only the third time it has snowed in the Valley of Babel this century? It's quite rare. I'm so glad you got to experience it."

The snow was driving now and had begun to snuff the fires that lapped futilely against the Tower's stony face. Though Senlin wanted to believe that this opened the door for reinforcements, it seemed more likely that it opened the door for retreat. For the moment at least, the few porters still on their feet appeared intent on watching the coming contest between the champion of the port and the commissioner's dog. Even they were not immune to local pride.

The two gladiators could not have been more different. Iren swung her chain above her head until, tightened by velocity, its ringing became a clear musical chord. The Red Hand tweaked the pegs on his brass cuff. The vials of red, luminous serum flared as they sloshed and drained into his arm. He appeared no more anxious than a man winding an old, fine watch. Iren scuffed elegant figures out in the snow as she circled. The Red Hand clasped his hands behind his back and seemed to glow a little more brightly.

If the Red Hand was trying to lull her into thinking he was not a fierce and worthy rival, it didn't work. Iren whipped the chain out at the level of his hips, meaning to break the assassin in half.

The Red Hand flattened himself, collapsed as if he'd been sucked to the ground, and her chain whizzed harmlessly over him. He had popped back to his feet before the hook had snapped back to her hand.

"We are on the leeward side of the mountains," he said. "Iron ore is more easily mined on the lee side because of a historical dearth of vegetation turning to soil and burying the rock. Not to mention, of course, the lack of rain and snow."

Again she paced. Again she swung the chain, forcing it around faster and faster until the veins stood out on the raised pillar of her arm and the sinews in her jaw bulged like a welded joint. She heaved it at the assassin with an explosive grunt, and it sliced at an angle, intent on the notch between his shoulder and neck.

He leaned back, a subtle but sufficient dodge, and snatched the slowing chain from the air once it had passed him. He yanked it sharply, and Iren, unbraced, fell into him. He caught her chin with what seemed a simple uppercut, though the result was dramatic. The blow raised her off her feet. She arched backward, bounced once on her shoulder blades, and slid ten feet in the snow flat on her back.

She hardly had time to lower her chin to her chest before the Red Hand had leapt on her. She was quick to move before he could pinch his knees into her ribs. Twisting her legs around his, she flipped him under her. She grabbed him by the neck and began to beat him ruthlessly about the head. It was a pure drubbing, like a blacksmith hurrying to hammer a rod before it's had time to cool. His hat torn from his head, exposing his blond infantile hair, the Red Hand seemed momentarily dazed, vulnerable. The detached smirk was gone, his lips now bunching to preserve his teeth.

But her advantage did not last long, and the blows that would've killed another man only stirred this one's blood. The Red Hand wriggled one arm from where Iren had pinned it under her knee and latched onto her wrist with all the determination of a shackle. He twisted his hold with such violence Iren was thrown from her perch on his chest, though she managed to funnel her momentum into a defensive roll.

Separated, they bounced to their feet. Iren pulled a spike from her belt and threw it at the villain. It stuck, quivering, two inches into the man's flesh just beneath the sternum. The surrounding agents shared a communal gasp. Senlin's heart leapt to his throat as he stood craning over the wall of gawkers. She had done it! Surely this was a fatal blow. They all waited for him to collapse. But he did not. The Red Hand snorted, like a man shaken from a shallow nap, and reached up to pluck the spike from his chest. It came out as easily as a thorn.

The wound seeped with luminous blood, but bled only a little. "Iron ore can be tempered into steel, or it can be filed and transformed into the lightest of gases: hydrogen. This illustrates the paradox of consciousness: We are vapor in rigid form."

Reflexively, Iren swiveled out of the way when the Red Hand returned the spike to her in the same manner he'd received it. The missile narrowly missed her head.

The Red Hand leapt like a man launched from a catapult. Flying over her head, he grabbed her by the shoulders and flipped over her back. He pulled her along with him as if she were little more than a cape. When he came down on his feet, she was hurled over his head, high into the air. She struck the smoking scaffolding of a scorched crane upside down and flat on her back. Already weakened from the fire, the whole structure collapsed on top of her. She surely would've been burned alive if the snow had not recently doused the blaze. Senlin could only see her boots jutting lifelessly from the haystack of charred wood.

Senlin turned to run to her but was caught immediately from behind by a pair of agents, a man on each of his arms. With Iren dispatched, there was nothing left to distract them from him. The agents wheeled him around and frog-marched him toward the *Ararat*. The Red Hand brushed with annoyance at the bloody gouge that marred his shirt. He found his hat, which was rumpled but not torn, and returned it to his head.

A drawbridge opened near the base of the floating fortress. The lip of the bridge dragged unsteadily back and forth across the pier as the immense vessel wrestled to hold firm amid the storm. Commissioner Pound, dressed in a severe black suit and wearing his monstrous gas mask, crossed the bridge briskly. Senlin was forced to face the hypochondriac tyrant, who stood casually tightening the fingers of his gloves and surveying the battleground.

"Scour the port. Bring me any cargo that you find!" he ordered his men, and then turning to Senlin, said, "If you only knew whom you have troubled with this idiotic caper." His voice buzzed through the blunt silver tusks of his mask. "I'm not even allowed to kill you, because there is a long and illustrious line of men who want to contribute to your demise. They will have to hold a lottery, I suppose, or draw straws for the pleasure of dissecting you."

Senlin shrugged almost demurely, as if he were pleasantly surprised by all this attention. "Perhaps you could hold an auction. I know how you art collectors love auctions. What quicker way is there to inflate the price of some poor artist's work?" Senlin stared into the smoked glass lenses of the gas mask as if he could see the man's high forehead, womanish skin, and colorless eyes. Senlin wanted the commissioner to know he was not afraid. "My crime is that I returned a creation to its creator."

A sound like a rook's cry burst from the mask, then repeated three more times. The commissioner was laughing at him. The man bent at the waist and rolled his head. "You're talking about that horrible humpbacked amateur! He didn't paint that masterpiece."

"Of course he did. It was signed. And I saw his other works. His name was Ogier, or was that some wild coincidence?"

"He was an imposter and a forger who fell in love with his charade! He even went so far as to recreate the real Ogier's studio above that blasted perfumery so all of his paintings would reek just as badly as the originals." The commissioner was still in good humor, plainly reveling in Senlin's confusion. "The painting you stole is a hundred years old."

"So why did he ask me to steal it?" Senlin asked, his confidence curling into bewilderment.

"Ah," the commissioner said, drawing close. He patted Senlin flatly on the chest, as if he were an old horse. His confidence shaken, Senlin could no longer imagine Pound's hidden expression. He only saw his own reflection, doubled, in the commissioner's lenses. He looked no larger than a picture in a locket. "That is the question: Why did he ask you to steal it? And why did he not keep it? Why did he give it to you?"

Senlin recovered his slipping self-possession and said, "You should've asked him."

The commissioner stepped back. "Oh, I wanted to, though I have a pretty good idea what he would've said. This is an old feud. Still, I would've liked to converse with the painter, but you know how it is, Mr. Senlin. Sometimes a falconer can't keep his falcon from tearing up the hare." The commissioner nodded at the Red Hand, who was at that moment appearing through the snow.

The Red Hand carried Senlin's crate under his arm. He set the box at the commissioner's feet with great care. "This was the center of a lot of attention: There was a circle of tracks and a body."

"Open it," the commissioner said.

Senlin was confounded by the revelation that Ogier was a fraud, but he had no time to consider it now. All of his attention fell upon the booby-trapped crate and the Red Hand hovering over it.

The Red Hand, hardly needing tools to pry free the nailed lid, delicately wrenched the top off. A thicket of straw packing stared back at him, and he began to pluck the stuffing from the box until the edge of a canvas was revealed. As the Red Hand worked, puffs of white powder were shaken free of the straw. The powder swirled in the air, the clouds mingling with the snow. No one seemed to notice its presence except for Senlin, who was looking for it. He had laced the packing straw with enough White Chrom to drug a hundred men. He held his breath.

The Red Hand pulled the painting free, turning it toward the commissioner. Pound's voice cracked with anger. "What is this?" He snatched the painting and thrust it into Senlin's face. Senlin, who thought he was about to be struck, gasped. A familiar tingling sensation instantly bloomed in his sinuses and ran down his throat. He cringed. He'd meant to use the Crumb as a last-ditch attack on the senses and faculties of his enemies. His own exposure to the powerful narcotic had, of course, not been part of his plan.

Before the commissioner could interrogate Senlin further, the Red Hand abruptly reeled back with a wild snort, startling everyone. "Who's there?" he cried. His eyes glazed as they tracked unseen specters. The Red Hand flinched and swatted at the air, recoiling from some sound no one else could hear. The commissioner tried to bark his assassin back to his senses, but the Red Hand's mind had wandered beyond reach. He backed into an agent, who stood frozen in terror. The Red Hand startled, spun about, and snapped the man's head around until his chin hung over his spine. The man dropped like a wet towel.

The scene quickly descended into chaos. The Red Hand tore into the ranks of his compatriots, his uncanny strength heightened by his frenzy. He used the men like clubs, beating one against another, until both were lifeless husks. He flung men from the port as if they were boneless and weightless. The snow blushed red as the warmth that leaked from the maimed and the fallen turned the powder into slush. The Red Hand cried, "Who's there?" again and again, though no one dared to answer him. Shots were fired and swords were swung, but these just extended the gore as panic led to crossfire and wild strikes.

The men holding Senlin did not release him, but they did retreat a few paces, holding him as a helpless shield between them and the berserk assassin. Senlin, craning his neck about for some sign of help or escape, caught sight of something that would have made his heart swell if he hadn't been sure it was a hallucination brought on by the Crumb. What he saw was impossible. Edith was running toward him, dashing the commissioner's men aside, her elbow raised like the wedge of a plow. It was a wonderful vision, but this was the Tower, he reminded himself. No one was coming to the rescue.

The Red Hand, having devastated the commissioner's force, now turned to Senlin, still pinned up by his arms. The assassin's veins shone so brightly that they radiated through his skin: He was webbed with fire. The Red Hand leapt at them behind an arm that jutted like a battering ram. Senlin threw all of his weight to his right, pulling the agent on his left into the line of attack. The blow landed on the man's ear. The struck man stiffened and fell, pulling Senlin and the other agent into a flailing pile. Sandwiched between the two men, one unconscious, perhaps dead, the other terrified and cursing, Senlin tried to pull himself out. The weight on top of him vanished as the Red Hand plucked up the profanely babbling agent by the neck, pinching off the flow of words and holding him like a farmer holds a chicken for the block. The Red Hand squeezed the man's neck until it made a sudden wet cracking sound, like an egg dropped on the floor.

Rocking like a crab on its back, helplessly caught on the soft fulcrum of the agent beneath him, Senlin gaped up at the haunted executioner. There was no cruelty or malevolence in his expression. The Red Hand twitched and blinked almost childishly. He said, "Who's there?" but weakly. His intelligence had fled, his docent manner reduced to a mere primitive instinct. He reached for Senlin almost in boredom, though his hand was a radiant star.

Edith's fist struck the assassin's temple with the speed of a train running downhill. The blow sent the Red Hand sprawling across the snowy planks on his side.

"How?" Senlin asked, disbelieving her presence even now. Only later would Edith explain how she'd caught the rope of an anchor and swung into the trestlework under the platform. She'd caromed about like a billiard ball and nearly fallen to her death. But she had caught a handful of snagged silk: a tangled remnant of the fallen *Finch*. She then spent the next half hour shinnying up frozen iron crosses amid a centurial blizzard.

Edith yanked Senlin to his feet, saying, "We must get to the ship!" Even as she spoke, the Red Hand had come again to his feet. One of his eyes bulged out of its socket, cocked at a wild, blind angle. Red light poured through the gap. The blow seemed to have blunted his drug-induced mania. What remained of his gaze was clearer now and trained chillingly upon Edith.

He flew at her, and she caught him by the hands. They grappled on unsteady footing, careening about in the deepening snow. Senlin drew the sword from the scabbard of an agent who would have no further use of it. He was about to go to Edith's aid when a saber flashed between them, quick as a guillotine. The commissioner recoiled with his sword, giving Senlin only a moment to bring up a defense before Pound slashed at him again. Senlin stumbled under the attack. The cup guard of the commissioner's sword was arrayed with silver spikes, the purpose of which was immediately evident when he struck Senlin in the cheek.

Warmth streamed down Senlin's neck. He shoved the commissioner back on his heels and took up the fighting stance Iren had taught him. Senlin parried the commissioner's thrusts, hoping that his muscles would recall the reflexes he'd tried so hard to beat into them.

But before he could develop any confidence in his approach, before any semblance of rhythm could soften his puppetlike and jerking limbs, Marya walked out from behind the commissioner as if she had walked around a corner in their old cottage. She wore a long white nightgown with a crocheted hem. Her feet were bare. She was drinking tea from one of her beloved and chipped china cups. Her expression was soft and unaware; it was a look that could not outlast the first hour of the morning, an expression only her lover would see.

Senlin paid a painful price for his lapse in concentration: A lancing pressure shocked the nerves in his arm. He looked down to find the commissioner had skewered his shoulder. The sword was withdrawn, and the burst of pain became a thrumming ache.

"That was so rewarding," the commissioner said. "You can't imagine how I have been chided for letting you get away." He attacked again, but Senlin was quick to deflect the stroke. "Where is my painting?"

Trying now to ignore the upright piano that had appeared behind the commissioner, Senlin said, "Safe."

"There is no such word," the commissioner quipped.

Marya seemed unaware that her husband was embroiled in a sword fight. She set her teacup on the sidearm of her piano. She fanned her nightgown like a concert pianist on stage before sitting on the bench. She looked over her shoulder at Senlin. "What should I play?" she asked, brushing the hair from her face. The familiar gaiety of her smile made Senlin's heart ache.

"Play what you like," Senlin said. The commissioner, briefly confused by the non sequitur, soon took it as an invitation to advance.

As their battling resumed, Marya commenced playing in her characteristic explosive style. She played an old, frenetic reel—a popular clap-along in the pub back home. He could almost hear the clapping now. No, he could in fact hear it, and the tankards clanking on the tables, and the chair legs dragging on the pub floor. As Senlin listened, he felt his muscles loosen. His movements became more fluid. Then he was struck again, a glancing blow on the back of the hand, but it felt indistinct and painless, as if someone had only caressed the hair. Pound seemed distant, like a man standing at the end of a tunnel, waving his arms. The lid of Marya's piano burst open, and sunlight streamed out like a golden diadem. The light flickered in time with the song. A school of kites joined the light, flying out of the piano case on piano wires, each cord vibrating madly with color and sound.

Senlin stumbled over one of the harpooned lines that held the *Ararat* to the port. Marya and her piano vanished. He had to twist and skid in the snow to keep from losing his feet, and he flailed perilously near the port edge. The commissioner, overeager and misjudging the distance, slashed at Senlin, but struck only the rope that had tripped him, severing it. The winds pulled fiercely at the commissioner's flying fortress, trying to draw it out from the Tower into the churning storm. The loss of this one anchor started a chain reaction. The nearest harpoon line twanged under the additional pressure, then promptly snapped. The *Ararat* cantilevered from the port, and its drawbridge, once level, now stood at a sharp incline.

The commissioner, realizing that his ship was about to be blown off its moorings, ran for the drawbridge as it scraped wildly along the end of the pier. Behind him, one of the anchoring harpoons ripped loose, then another, and another, until one tenuous line remained. Pound leapt at the bridge just as a vertical shear of wind drove the *Ararat* down. The last line snapped. The commissioner hung in the open air for a moment: His limbs gyrated like a falling cat's, and the drawbridge clapped loosely at the end of its chains. Then the wind shifted again, and the portal seemed to swallow him up. He tumbled into the bowels of his ship. The *Ararat* reared back from the port and was engulfed by the snow.

Clearheaded for the moment, Senlin cast about for signs of Edith and found her standing dangerously near the precipice of the platform. She held the Red Hand at arm's length by the back of his neck as one might hold a venomous snake. The assassin flailed, but she had his feet off the ground and his arms could not bend back far enough to reach her. Her clockwork arm, engraved with ringlets and darts like vines about a trunk, glowed in the red light of her prisoner. She dangled him over the precipice. It was miraculous that she had caught the man, and Senlin couldn't understand why she hesitated, why she didn't just release the Red Hand to his fate.

Still some strides away, Senlin heard the Red Hand speaking in a gargling, mangled voice. He said, "Wait, sister, wait! What will you say to the Sphinx? You cannot!"

The bizarre nature of his appeal, this allusion to some familial connection, made Senlin shudder. Surely she wasn't considering this monstrosity's plea! Edith hadn't a jot in common with this murderer.

And still, impossible as it was, she hesitated. Senlin could not see her face in that stretched second in which she considered the Red

Hand's fate. Then her hand opened, and her arm dropped, and he was gone.

Senlin reached her side, feeling a burst of relief. Surely, he thought, it was only natural to hesitate before killing a fellow human being, no matter how vile and perverse. She had only deliberated a moment, allowing her conscience time to catch up with the conclusions of common sense and justice. She would never have let him live.

Then Senlin saw that the little drawer in her shoulder plate was jutting out, offering its exhausted battery of red glowing serum for replacement. Her mighty brass arm hung dead at her side.

She gave him a look that was both rueful and relieved. "And sometimes it runs out of steam at the exact right moment," she said, echoing the conversation they'd had the night before. Senlin could think of nothing to say.

Thunder sounded in the thick clouds of snow, then the thunder developed a whistle, and the whistle became an explosion against the face of the Tower. "They're firing their cannons blind!" Senlin said, feeling almost glad; he'd rather be shot at than continue this unsettling moment. "We have to go before they get off a lucky shot. But first we have to get Iren."

Senlin collected his aerorod and Ogier's painting of Marya, now scoured clean of the drug by the blasting snow, and then hurried with Edith to the collapsed crane. They found Iren half buried under a snowdrift and charred wood, unconscious but groaning. "Are you sure she wants to come with us? Did you recruit her or is this a kidnapping?" Edith asked. Senlin deliberated momentarily, then a cannonball struck the edge of the port where they had recently stood, raising a geyser of splinters.

"Does it matter?" he said. They pulled her from the wreckage, Edith helping as best she could with one arm. They dragged the amazon like a sled to the gangplank of the *Stone Cloud*. It took everyone to help get her aboard. Adam reported the state of the ship as they worked to pass her over the gap. All was ready for launch.

The cannon fire was more regular now but no less wild. The *Ararat* still hung, veiled by the clouds, not far from the port. Senlin had no interest in being swept in that direction. He could only trust that his escape draft had not been disrupted by the storm.

Edith, naturally taking up the duties of first mate, orchestrated the launch. She stood at the helm, directing Voleta and Adam to release the mooring lines on her word. She cried, "Now!" in a voice that cut through wind and cannon blasts. As soon as the tethers were loose, she threw the lever, and the ballast hatch burst open, dropping its entire burden of salt water in an instant.

The ship surged upward at a sickening pace. The wind bullied them back nearer the Tower, tail first. It seemed for a moment that they would be dashed against the impervious stone blocks, but then they slid into the current Senlin had discovered, and their deadly careening ceased. In the bat of an eye, the Port of Goll fell behind the curtain of the storm. The guns of the *Ararat* retreated. They had escaped.

But there was no time for a moment of triumph. They had no ballast and their course was set beyond their control. They were barreling up through the black into the bursting heart of the storm.

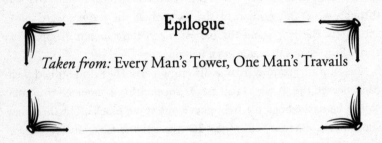

Epilogue

Taken from: Every Man's Tower, One Man's Travails

My old moniker has spoiled, much like a cracked egg, from exposure to air. *Thomas Senlin* has been too often on the lips of the imperious and the dangerous. Uttering it, even in alien lands, may ring bells that I'd rather leave unrung. So, I require a new name, and I have chosen one that is a ubiquitous curse: I am Tom Mudd, captain of the *Stone Cloud*.

As we set out, a frank assessment is required of our present state and stock. The ship is airworthy but wounded, and her crew is similarly imperfect. My first mate is a woman of infinite character and strength, but Edith, I suspect, is still tortured, despite the elaborate binding of her wounds. Her recent past is a riddle, and I fear she is concealing something vital and perhaps dangerous from all of us.

I believe Adam, who must become our engineer, will be a loyal friend right until the well-being of his sister is in question. I don't begrudge him this, but his inability to trust makes his devotion to her particularly treacherous. He will not share his deliberations or divulge his decisions where she is involved. He would betray the world to save her from harm.

If there is a bright and reliable spark on this ship, it is Voleta. She is braver and more capable than her brother admits. She will live, I think, up in the rigging. Already, she has climbed and shinnied across every surface of the ship like a squirrel; she has dangled from the anchor and surmounted the silk hill of the balloon. She is a born lookout, if ever there was one. Iren, of course, is our master-at-arms. She is the only one I'd trust with the cannon, and I think of her as our primary defender and tactician. I'm not wholly certain if she meant to come with us, or if she was merely swept into our pan by fate. However it was, I am glad to have her along.

Our immediate problem is one of supplies. The ship was stripped before we wrenched her from the port. We are underequipped for any mission and are poor as paupers to boot. Our fuel is low, and we have had nothing to eat but squab since we left. In many ways, our desperation has increased since our escape, which goes a long way toward explaining why so few attempt it. With subjugation comes certainty. Liberty is full of gambles. But I meant what I said to Edith the evening before our odyssey began: We must share our burdens if we are to survive.

As soon as we are bandaged and fed and our survival is no longer in doubt, I mean to proceed to the Ringdom of Pelphia, Seat of the Pells. Marya is waiting there; I am sure of it.

The dose of White Chrom has yet to drain from my system, though I'm hopeful it will subside soon. I must admit that I am writing this in the presence of Marya's ghost, which appears now with some regularity. She is dressed as she was on the train in her white blouse and red pith helmet. She is sitting with her hand upon mine; her skin is as pristine as a lily. It is terribly distracting and dangerously nostalgic. I must remind myself that Marya will not have gone unchanged by the Tower. I only need to look in the mirror to convince myself of that. She may be posing as another man's wife, or she may have been ruined, as Voleta was so nearly ruined, or she might be mangled, like poor Edith.

Whatever Marya's state, whatever mine, I will find her, and I will carry her home.

—Tom Mudd, captain of the *Stone Cloud*

The story continues in . . .

ARM OF THE SPHINX

Book Two of the Books of Babel

Acknowledgments

If you know anything about my books, chances are you have Mark Lawrence to thank for it. Were it not for him, and his wonderful Self-Published Fantasy Blog-Off, my books would've likely been consigned to the oblivion of the unread. Thank you, Mark.

I have my agent, Ian Drury, and indeed all of the people at Sheil Land Associates, to thank for finding such a wonderful publisher in Orbit Books for me to partner with.

I wish to thank all the people who have taken the time to write reviews, including Jared at *Pornokitsch*, who first attracted Mark Lawrence's attention, Adam Whitehead at *The Wertzone*, who fanned the flames of interest, and Emily May, who helped to spread awareness of the series to the *Goodreads* community. I'd also like to thank the thriving and welcoming subreddit "r/fantasy," for providing me with a much-needed online community.

I'd like to thank the community of writers who participated in the 2016 Self-Published Fantasy Blog-Off: Dyrk Ashton, Phil Tucker, Timandra Whitecastle, Benedict Patrick, and David Benem (among many others), all of whom are incredibly talented and hard-working and deserving of your attention.

Thank you to all of my friends who supported the writing and editing process: Monica Zaleski, Allison and Dave Symonds, Renee Wolcott, and Kevin Wisniewski. Thank you to Nicholas Reading and Ivan Fehrenbach for reading the first drafts of this adventure (*Cavete Idibus Martiis*). Thank you to Benjamin and Will Viss for supporting me with advice, encouragement, and loud music.

Thank you to my parents, Josiah and Barbara Bancroft, for teaching me to love writing and reading, for supplying me with every opportunity to pursue my passion, and for supporting me through my many false-starts in life.

I owe Ian Leino more gratitude than can be expressed in a few lines. Of course, he supplied the series with its striking cover art, which has attracted many, many readers, but he also taught me how to survive and succeed as an independent artist. He commiserated when I was discouraged, counseled me when I would listen to no one else, and kicked me in the pants when my pants needed kicking. A man has never had a better friend.

Finally, I wish to thank my wife, Sharon, who supported me emotionally, creatively, and financially through so many ill-conceived creative projects, and who, despite my best efforts to dissuade her, never lost faith in me. Were it not for her love and support, I would not have had the confidence, focus, or opportunity to write these books.

extras

orbit

extras

meet the author

Photo Credit: Kim Bricker

JOSIAH BANCROFT started writing novels when he was twelve, and by the time he finished his first, he was an addict. Eventually, the writing of *Senlin Ascends* began, a fantasy adventure, not so unlike the stories that got him addicted to words in the first place. He wanted to do for others what his favorite writers had done for him: namely, to pick them up and to carry them to a wonderful and perilous world that is spinning very fast. If he's done that with this book, then he's happy.

Josiah lives in Philadelphia with his wife, Sharon, and their two rabbits, Mabel and Chaplin.

Interview

When did you first start writing?

I started writing my first fantasy novel, *The Quest for Mortoangus*, when I was twelve years old with the help of my best friend, Ian Leino. The story is about a couple of teenage boys who are swept away to a foreign land full of magic, elves, orcs, a dragon with a Latinate name, and (most unlikely of all) girlfriends. The heroes bore a striking resemblance to Ian and me, but with long hair and pecs like dinner plates. It was essentially *The Hobbit* with hormones. Soon after we started, Ian decided he was more interested in illustrating the story while I decided the book needed to be a 250,000-word treatise on the value of friendship, personal growth, and heavy smooching. Twenty years later, Ian was still an artist, and I was still writing. When I told him I was going to take another crack at writing fantasy and asked if he would be interested in illustrating the covers, he agreed straight away. *Senlin Ascends* isn't as epic as *The Quest for Mortoangus*, and there aren't any scenes featuring wet tunics and woodland elves, but I like to think our boyhood selves would still be pleased with how things turned out.

And fun fact: one of the main characters in *The Quest for Mortoangus* was a halfling thief named Fingol, which was the direct inspiration for Finn Goll. I have to credit Ian for the name.

extras

Where did the idea for* Senlin Ascends *come from and how did the plot begin to take shape in your mind?

The original idea for *Senlin Ascends* came from reading Italo Calvino's *Invisible Cities*, which is a beautifully written travelogue of fantastic, unreal destinations. It is a perfect specimen of literary accomplishment. So, naturally, I decided to rip it off.

At the time, I was trying to become a professional poet, which is sort of like trying to become a unicorn. The Books of Babel was going to be a collection of prose poems. The collection was going to be a fabulist pastiche, an impressionistic olio, a book of surreal psalms. In short, it was going to be dreadful, and no one was going to read it.

Then I woke up one morning and realized it was over. I was living a lie. I didn't love poetry anymore. We had to break up. It wasn't an amicable split. I called poetry some awful names, and poetry changed the locks. Lonely and bereft, I started hitting up my old flames—Jules Verne, H. G. Wells, Robert Louis Stevenson—just to see what they were up to. Turns out, they were saying awful things about women and minorities. But once I got past their startling bigotry, I remembered what it was that I had loved so much about those musty old scribblers. I remembered why I had begun writing in the first place: because I liked adventure and mystery and romance. I wrote because I liked to be surprised and delighted, liked to gasp and laugh, and wanted to share the whole mad experience with someone else.

The plot came later. The story began with disillusionment.

Senlin Ascends *is set in a mythical tower which feels both ancient and alive. Were there any challenges with creating the history of the Tower and the settings of each ringdom?*

I think the main challenge to writing lore is knowing when to stop. Creating a world is an intoxicating process, and I've known talented writers who've gotten so lost in their lore, they never found their story. So, while I have the broad history of the Tower in mind, I've let the story direct how and where I build the myth of the Tower. That was Senlin's original purpose: to reveal the Tower, to uncover its machinations and mysteries, to make the monolith human and knowable. Senlin is my lamp in the dark, and so only the path before him is well-lit.

The characters in Senlin Ascends *really jump off the page. If you had to pick one, who would you say is your favorite? Which character was the most difficult to write?*

Finn Goll was a joy to write. It's fun to write roguish characters who are quick-witted and unencumbered by human decency. But I didn't want Finn Goll to just be an uncomplicated baddie. Pure evil is boring, just like perfect darkness is boring. Shadows, on the other hand, are interesting. I don't think Finn Goll is evil; he just conceives of the Tower in a way that the guidebooks, and Senlin, and the oligarchs don't. He sees the Tower not for what it represents, but for how it works. He's pragmatic, unsympathetic, and a monstrous capitalist, but he's also insightful and can be truthful when it's to his advantage.

I struggled to understand Edith when she first appeared in the Parlor. I liked that she was surprising, but I didn't understand her. She was all brashness and bluster. I had her tell Senlin her history while they were locked in the cage together so I could figure out who she was. She tells him about her doting father, her farm, her reluctantly accepted husband, the loss of her raison d'être, and her decision to squander her money on the Parlor, all of which was news to me. By the time I started writing *Arm of the Sphinx*, Edith had become one of the most defined and tangible characters in my mind. She still surprises me, but I think I understand her when she does.

Senlin undergoes drastic changes throughout the course of the novel. How did you approach this development from unassuming headmaster to the man he is at the end of the book?

I've never been able to connect to characters who suffer some personal tragedy, and then immediately emerge from the disaster toughened and prepared for the journey ahead. It just feels disingenuous. When I've experienced setbacks, I don't rise from the ashes with all the answers. I flail about. I fall over. I take a step back and fall over again. I think that developing strength and wisdom takes time and practice.

Senlin is not a hero. He's a human. Which means he's a bit of an idiot. And he doesn't really know himself, which is the cause of so much of his misfortune. He is slow to let go of his illusions because they're so essential to him. When he encounters a problem, he proudly learns a lesson, but it's often the wrong lesson. He rushes when he should linger, and he is patient when he should insist. He does learn, but slowly; he grows, but not in a straight line. Senlin's strength, ultimately, is his adaptability. His education and his determination make him a capable chameleon. But otherwise, he's a small man on a big adventure, which means he makes a lot of mistakes.

It's clear that Marya is undergoing a dramatic journey of her own. Will the reader get to learn more about her adventures through the Tower in future books?

Marya embodies the many ways that the Tower conspires to obscure a person. The Tower doesn't just erase people all at once; it overwrites them; it duplicates and forges them; it shuffles the genuine and the untrue together. In the first book, we see Marya mostly through the lens of Senlin's memory and Ogier's secondhand account. While the reader is able to get some sense of her from these refracted narratives, she seems vague, jumbled, and idealized. That obfuscation continues in the second book, but in a different way as Senlin begins to confront his illusions, his assumptions, and his guilt. I don't want to give too much away, but Marya will get the chance to tell her story eventually.

Do you have a favorite scene in Senlin Ascends? *If so, why?*

My favorite scene is probably when Senlin gives Marya the piano as a wedding present, and he struggles to articulate his feelings. I'm a sucker for romance. I've always loved rom-com films. I know they're invariably clichéd and sappy, but those moments of long-awaited intimacy, when the sense of bubbling affection and swelling desire get undercut by self-doubt and general bumbling, and then the audience feels that unique feeling of frisson when the two unlikely lovers finally kiss and tumble onto the bed...yeah, I'm a sucker for all that stuff. The scene where Senlin gives Marya a piano is probably the closest I've come to capturing that feeling. If I were less squeamish, I'd be writing romance. But I'm better at writing the bumbling than the tumbling.

Who are some of your favorite writers and how have they influenced your work?

I'm old enough to have had more than a few love affairs with writers. When I was young, I loved C. S. Lewis, Terry Pratchett, and Douglas Adams. They taught me that writing about principles can still be entertaining. In college, I discovered the weirdos: J. G. Ballard, Philip K. Dick, and Kurt Vonnegut, who showed me that normalcy and sanity are tenuous states, at best. Post college, I fell into the usual existential slump: I swooned over Jean-Paul Sartre, Franz Kafka, and Vladimir Nabokov, who made alienation seem sexy. Then as I began to mount the slow, nearly invisible slope toward middle age, I fell in love with the story-telling humanists: Hermann Hesse, Italo Calvino, Gabriel García Márquez, and Salman Rushdie, who taught me that folklore is often more useful than philosophy.

When you're not writing, what do you like to do in your spare time?

I'm probably the happiest when I'm playing with my band, Dirt Dirt. The band is comprised of my wife, Sharon, and Benjamin and Will, who are brothers I've known since I was sixteen. We've been playing, recording, and performing originals for six years, now. I hope we do it for sixty more. Really, everyone should be in a band. It's like meditation but with more screaming and beer.

I've always enjoyed art. There was a period in my life when I was convinced I would be a graphic novel artist. I was going through some old files recently, and found a rejection letter from Marvel Comics from 1999. I was a terrible art student for about a year. I drew a comic strip with a friend for a local rag in Richmond, Virginia, for a little while. Nothing came of any of it, and soon I decided to grow up and do something more sensible with my life, like writing poetry. I still like to draw, though mostly I just scrawl on flyleafs and my office wall, which I converted to a blackboard.

I love cooking: the spices, the aromas, the snap of hot oil, the knives, the chopping, the blood, the Band-Aids, all of it.

My favorite dish is pub-style curry, though I don't think I've ever made it the same way twice.

Senlin Ascends *is the first book of four. Without giving too much away, can you tell us a bit about what we can expect from book two,* Arm of the Sphinx?

Arm of the Sphinx is more of a swashbuckling adventure, I think. While Senlin's search for Marya continues, we get to spend more time with the crew of the *Stone Cloud:* Edith, Iren, Voleta, and Adam, each of whom have their own stories to tell. They discover that life in the clouds is not as carefree as they had hoped. Their journey takes them to pirate coves and taunts them with treasure maps. They encounter monsters, some of whom are human. They make a new enemy and get caught up in a conflict that none of them want. And they learn more about the person who created the Tower's many wonders and gave Edith her arm: the mysterious Sphinx.

Finally, we have to ask, if you had the choice to visit one of the ringdoms, which would it be?

I would like to visit the Basement. Not for the bull snails, parrots, and pickpockets, but to ride the beer-me-go-round. If my local gym had one of those, I'd be a member.

if you enjoyed
SENLIN ASCENDS

look out for

ARM OF THE SPHINX
The Books of Babel: Book Two

by

Josiah Bancroft

*The second book in the stunning and strange debut fantasy
series that's receiving major praise from some of fantasy's
biggest authors such as Mark Lawrence and Django Wexler.*

*The Tower of Babel is proving to be as difficult to reenter
as it was to break out of. Forced into a life of piracy, Senlin
and his eclectic crew are struggling to survive aboard
their stolen airship as the hunt to rescue
Senlin's lost wife continues.*

407

Hopeless and desolate, they turn to a legend of the Tower, the mysterious Sphinx. But help from the Sphinx never comes cheaply, and as Senlin knows, debts aren't always what they seem in the Tower of Babel.

Time is running out, and now Senlin must choose between his friends, his freedom, and his wife.

Does anyone truly escape the Tower?

Chapter One

The difficulty with a disguise is that it must be worn for some time before it hangs credibly upon the shoulders. But if worn for too long, a costume becomes comfortable, natural. A man always in disguise must take care lest he become the disguise.

—The *Stone Cloud*'s Logbook, Captain Tom Mudd

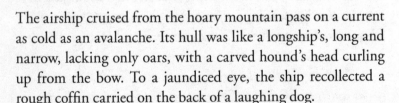

The airship cruised from the hoary mountain pass on a current as cold as an avalanche. Its hull was like a longship's, long and narrow, lacking only oars, with a carved hound's head curling up from the bow. To a jaundiced eye, the ship recollected a rough coffin carried on the back of a laughing dog.

To the crew, it was but a frozen raft.

Swaddled in long furs, they stamped about the deck like disgruntled bears. Wind strummed the rigging. The men said nothing. Forty barrels of rum sloshed in the main hold beneath their feet, seeping and sweetening the air with sugar cane and new oak.

The *Cairo Hound* was bound for the Baths, where rum fetched ten times the price it did in the capitals of Ur. In a few short hours, each of them would have half a year's wages in their pockets and all the Baths to fritter it upon. But despite the coming payday and liberty, the crew was anxious. They were afraid to speak because, once begun, idle talk turned easily into nervous rambling, and then terror was sure to follow.

Pirates prowled these skies. Violent wind shears were not uncommon. Then there were the whims of the Tower ports to fret over. A safe harbor one voyage might be a shooting gallery the next. Only a few months earlier, cannonballs and fire had demolished one of New Babel's more reliable ports. A crew could never be sure what sort of welcome the Tower would offer them.

And where was their captain during all of this worry? Drunk again, still drunk, always exquisitely drunk.

No, it was better not to talk. Better to stay stoic.

Far below, rough slopes gave way to a suburb of tents and then a shantytown of canvas and tar-paper roofs. Trains cut through the dense Market on tracks that ran from the Tower like the rays of a compass rose. The Tower did not look like it had been built, brick by brick, by human hands. Rather, it looked like something the world had begun to birth—a new crescent moon, perhaps—before surrendering the effort. The Tower loomed over the encircling mountain range. An imperturbable fog enshrouded its peak. Some romantics called this haze the "Collar of Heaven," believing it marked the point where the Tower passed from blue sky into bleak, black space.

The captain always woke up mean.

He stayed mean, too, but there was an excess of meanness in his waking. Drunk or not, mean or not, the captain would still have to sign the manifest and dicker with the port master over the price of rum. He still had a job to do. They would have to draw straws for who would wake him. The boatswain trimmed straws from a broom and measured them on his palm.

Then the girl appeared.

She seemed to just materialize in the air near the grumbling furnace and the biscuit barrels. One of her arms snaked about the rope that held her; one toe of her boot touched the deck ever so lightly, like a bather testing a bath. She was beautiful—but not garish like those harlots in the pub who sat on your lap if you bought them a drink. Nor was she voluptuous like the sketches in the gentlemen's books, nor handsome like the marble statues with robes no thicker than spilled milk.

She was beautiful like a doe in a glen: lithe, alert, and distant. Her hair was wild, her face small, her eyes bright. Her yellow frock had been hacked off at the waist, and her overlarge gloves looked like something a blacksmith might wear.

They did not all see her in the same instant. She mesmerized them one by one.

The bear-skinned crew of the *Cairo Hound* began to close on her with the slow deliberate steps of men in a trance. With each step they took, she inched her way back up the rope and toward the gas envelope above. She did not seem nervous at all. The men found her poise captivating. They found it maddening.

When they could stand it no longer, they lunged after her.

She darted into the high netting, quick as a flash, and they crashed together beneath her, toppling the barrels and knocking one another against the singeing furnace as they grappled for the rope. As soon as one man began to climb, the others pulled him down. She tugged at her ears and stuck out her tongue. One crewman threw the water ladle at her. She nimbly caught it and threw it back at him.

They began to quarrel about who had seen her first, and who should go wake the captain, because now he definitely had to be awakened, and somebody had to do it, and where were the straws?

Their lively debate was interrupted by the tattoo of unfamiliar boots behind them.

The crew of the *Cairo Hound* turned to discover they had been boarded.

Captain Padraic DeFord had crawled into a barrel of rum on the first day of the voyage and stayed there. A fleshy man with the mottled complexion of a newborn infant, he was at the point in his career where all other men were fools, the business was foolish, and the pay fit only for imbeciles. His men thought him tyrannical, but in truth he spoiled them. When he was a cabin boy, if he'd once made the sort of blunder his crew did on a daily basis, he would have been whipped till he bled. He wasn't a tyrant; he was a parent stuck with a brood of dunces. And rather than improve, rather than rise to the challenge of his leadership, his men grew sullen and resentful. They slouched toward mutiny.

How the world had changed.

In the face of this, would any man of character blame him for indulging in a drink? He found that if he drank enough, he slept deeply and dreamt little. He could fall into bed the same as into his grave. Every morning was a resurrection; every evening was a death. It was such a pretty thing to come and go into the dark as one pleased.

This morning, he was rudely roused from his grave by something like an anchor chain wrapping about his neck and wrenching him from his cot and out of the wonderful dark.

Having long ago trained himself to nap with a pistol in hand, DeFord was quick to sight the figure behind the chain. He had just put his finger to the trigger when a thick arm knocked the barrel up, and the gun discharged into the cabin ceiling with an earsplitting bang. Wood dust and smoke stung his eyes. Sun beamed through the bullet hole, brightening the dark and giving DeFord his first glimpse of the man behind the iron noose.

But it was not a man. It was a gargantuan woman with short silver hair lying close to a square, stony face. He felt like he was looking up at an ox that was standing on its hind legs.

Captain DeFord gave the amazon a speculative kick, and in return, she picked him up by his arms and thumped him twice against the ceiling. The blows made the chain clang about his ears. When the pounding stopped, his spine felt a little shorter. Docile now with pain and shock, DeFord didn't fight as he was dragged above deck, wearing nothing but his breeches and a tangled white bedsheet.

He was disappointed but not surprised to see his useless crew standing under raised hands. A girl in a ripped dress and a woman with brass plumbing for an arm held them at gunpoint, and confidently so. The realization caused DeFord physical pain: A trio of women had taken his ship. What further proof could one ask for? His men were conspiring against him. They hadn't even put up a fight.

There was one other stranger: a lanky man in a long black coat. He looked as sturdy as a scarecrow. Yet, there was a coolness and a gravity to his expression.

"Ah, there you are," said the scarecrow. "Captain DeFord, is it?" The man offered his hand. DeFord numbly shook it. "I'm Captain Tom Mudd. This is my crew. We have, as you've probably gathered, boarded your ship for the purpose of lightening it."

412

"Don't talk like you've come for tea," DeFord said, his speech thick with sleep and the lingering vapor of rum. "Give me a sword, and we can settle this like men." They were bold words for a man whose neck was in a chain.

"We're not that sort of pirate," Captain Mudd said. He leaned on his polished aerorod as if it were a cane and not a sacred tool of navigation. This lack of respect for the instruments of the profession told DeFord all he needed to know about this invader. He was not a seasoned airman. His crew of women suggested his last career had been as a pimp or a wifemonger. He was probably the sort of man who never worked very hard, never strove. He was lazy, cowardly, and smug. In short, this Mudd represented everything that was wrong with a generation.

"Oh, don't pretend that you're some sort of rare genius," DeFord said. "A herd of cows wearing bells could've snuck past this lot." DeFord scowled at his crew. They scowled right back at him. He knew it was dangerous to humiliate them in this moment of vulnerability, but he didn't care. They were such a disappointment. "You got no one to blame but yourselves for this gutting!" DeFord told them.

"Come now, there's really no reason to shout," Captain Mudd said. "I'm sure your men are very hardy. In fact, in a fair fight, I have no doubt they would've given us quite a run of it. And we're not going to bleed you dry. We just need a little of your... of your..." The scarecrow trailed off, his brow wrinkling and his gaze glassing over. He seemed entirely distracted, like a man listening to a distant strain of music. DeFord wondered just what sort of lunatic had gotten aboard his ship.

"Rum, sir," the woman with the clockwork arm said. "They're carrying rum." The filigree that decorated the gleaming brass shell of her limb was fine enough for a woman's locket, though the machinery that showed between plates resembled nothing so much as the black workings of a locomotive.

"Yes. We just need a little of your rum," Mudd said, his attention recovered. "We'll also take whatever food you have. Then you can be on your way. By this evening, you'll be in port, paid and drunk, and this whole unfortunate business will be a dimming memory."

"Don't any of you think you're going to be paid! I don't care what this mudbug says—" DeFord stopped, squinting as a thought occurred to him. "Mudd. I've heard that name before. Aye. Aye, I met one of your victims once. I bought him a drink because his story about you was so entertaining. He had the whole pub in stitches. Mudd the half-a-pirate. Mudd the clown. He said you came in under a cloud of gulls and fish guts, and then you, reeking like a chum bucket in July and covered in feathers, demanded a tenth of his cargo. A tenth! What sort of parsimonious pirate are you?"

The woman with the brass arm snorted.

"Thank you, Mister Winters," Captain Mudd said. "Now, we'll take two barrels of your rum, your pantry, and any black powder you have."

"You didn't say anything about powder before," DeFord said.

"That was before you complained about my generosity," Mudd said.

A harpoon crashed into the deck behind them. At the aft, an airship descended past the curvature of the *Cairo Hound*'s balloon. The emerging ship was encrusted with the warts of battle, age, and repair.

A pulley zipped down the harpoon's cable and clunked against the deck. Captain Mudd turned to the crew of the *Cairo Hound* and said, "Gentlemen, the sooner you load my ship, the sooner I'll be off of yours."

The bear-skinned crew looked to their captain with black expressions.

The amazon pulled her chain from DeFord's neck, and he gathered the white sheet about his shoulders and raised himself to as dignified a pose as he could muster, though the wind made him shiver, and he was still drunk. He addressed his men. "You wanted to humiliate me? Well, you've done it. But I am not humiliated because I stand here in a sheet on a ship given to a mudbug and his harem. No, I am humiliated to stand alongside of you. You will be a laughing stock if you indulge this man, if you give him one single drop of rum, of *my rum!*" DeFord beat his half-bare chest. "If there be one atom of self-respect or loyalty left in you, you will not aid this man. You will stand by me, your captain. You will refuse this injustice, or you will look for other work."

Captain Mudd said nothing in his defense. He smiled at the berated crewmen, awaiting their decision. He hadn't long to wait.

Pirates were as common as pigeons in the airstreams that circled the Tower. Many an honorable captain had been forced by a grim turn of fortune to stoop to piracy at one time or another. Some recovered their scruples as soon as their accounts were leveled. Of course, others who dabbled developed either a taste for the life or an inability to escape it. And then there were those shameless entrepreneurs who chose the bloody work willingly. They considered themselves a sort of ecological necessity: They were the wolves that thinned out the weak and old to the benefit of the herd.

Regardless of the cause, the life of a pirate was dangerous. The wealthy and powerful ringdoms regularly sent gunships to patrol the desert air. Infamy made the work of a pirate captain easier to undertake but more difficult to maintain. A wolfish reputation might soften a target, but it also attracted unwanted attention from military men eager to improve their own name. As often as not, as soon as a captain became the subject of a song or a limerick, he was welcomed to immortality with a mortal wound. One could try to maintain an innocuous or sympathetic profile, as Captain Mudd did, but subtlety was often lost on the sort of men who made their living at the end of a rope, lashed to a sack of combustible gas.

Truth be told, Captain Mudd and his motley crew were, for the most part, a toothless wolf. Their ship, the *Stone Cloud*, was a relic. What firearms they had were unreliable on their best days and decorative on their worst. The ship had one harpoon cannon on the bow that was incapable of launching a ball. If another ship decided to engage them, the *Stone Cloud*'s only reasonable recourse was to run. And run they had on more than one occasion.

According to Mister Winters, the ship's first mate and the only seasoned aeronaut among them, the *Stone Cloud*'s previous captain conducted his piracy purely by boarding party. Captain Billy Lee's crew of a dozen cutthroats would surprise a plump merchant ship, skewer her with a harpoon, draw her in, and overwhelm her while the startled crew was still tugging on their boots. It was a dicey business, and Captain Lee had lost and replaced many airmen during his command.

Under Mudd, the *Stone Cloud* boasted a crew of only five, including the captain. They were too few to swarm a deck, so they had adapted to survive. What they lacked in brute force, they made up for with ingenuity.

Captain Mudd had a talent for devising unorthodox ways to raid a ship. His crew, to their credit, followed his outlandish direction with hardly a squint.

extras

On one occasion, they had snuck onto a merchant ship under the cover of fog and opened a barrel of cooking oil on the deck. The natural sway of the ship distributed the slick evenly, and the next morning they invaded on spiked cleats while the unsuspecting crew skated helplessly about, trying very hard not to impale themselves on their own swords. On another occasion, Mudd's crew had dropped several pounds of rotting fish onto a ship's envelope and then boarded amid a horde of frenzied seagulls. They had once resorted to posing as a wounded vessel full of collapsed damsels. Their would-be princes, who rode in on a barge of cured tobacco, helpfully lashed the two ships together and came aboard armed with decanters of brandy to revive the ladies from their swoon. The rescuers rushed to the sides of the fallen women only to be greeted by gun barrels drawn from under skirts.

"The rules of engagement," Captain Tom Mudd explained to the irate captain who'd been duped by this ruse, "were invented by men who would benefit most from them."

This philosophical pronouncement might've commanded more respect had it not been delivered by a man wearing a frilly bonnet.

The taking of the *Cairo Hound* had been simple in comparison. They had shadowed the ship since dawn. Once convinced their approach had gone undetected, they crossed to the *Hound*'s balloon by a rope ladder and used the netting to climb down to the gondola. Voleta distracted the crew while the captain and the others got into a favorable position. The rest was just talking, which the captain was quite good at.

With their supplies moved from the *Cairo Hound*, the mated ships decoupled and drifted apart.

Edith called to Adam at the helm on the quarterdeck, "Hard burn, please. Let's see if we can't find that southwestward

417

current we came by." Adam repeated the order and plied the lever that opened the flue to the heating element in the ship's envelope. It didn't seem likely that the *Cairo Hound* would follow them, but if they did, Edith wanted them to be the ones squinting into the sun.

Voleta watched the retreating ship for any change in course. Though she had recently baited and eluded a mob, she showed no sign that anything very remarkable had occurred. She balanced atop a rail and leaned over the vast drop, casually gripping a tether in a manner that made her brother Adam quite nervous. A grackle flew into view, and she marked the subtle turn of its wings. "The current's shifted due west now," Voleta said.

"It'll do," Edith said. She turned to Captain Mudd. He stood, straight as a stovepipe, staring at the Tower that dominated the sky. "Captain," she called to him twice, the second time more sharply, but neither disrupted the intensity of his trance.

"Tom," she said with a little softness. Concern had turned her dark eyebrows into a single, severe line. Thomas Senlin refocused on her face and smiled. "Where to, Captain?"

He was still uncomfortable with the formalities that Edith insisted upon. She would call him "Tom" only in private and asked that he call her "Mister Winters" in front of the crew. "Mister" was the title that first mates were due and was only reasonable, but "Winters" was the name of her estranged husband who had edged her out of managing her family's farm and then refused to give her a divorce when she asked for one. Senlin couldn't imagine why she would want to be constantly reminded of such a man.

In quiet moments, Senlin recalled the hours they'd once shared in a cage that was bolted to the face of the Tower. They had been frightened by the unexpected cruelty of the Parlor and confused by the abrupt camaraderie the ordeal inspired. But they had also been only "Tom" and "Edith" to each other.

It seemed a long time ago. That was before she had lost her arm and joined a pirate crew, before he had missed a reunion with his wife by a matter of hours and stolen first a painting and then a ship.

Standing before Edith now, Senlin couldn't help but marvel at how, despite it all, their friendship had survived.

"I think we shall make for the Windsock, Mister Winters," he said. "We have some rum to sell." Really, they had little choice of where to go. The Windsock was the only cove that hadn't turned them away.

"Aye, sir." She nearly turned to spread the order but stopped short. She drew in close to keep her voice from carrying in the serene silence. Unlike the sea, with its crashes, howls, and tattooing waves, the air seemed quite a tranquil medium. "You were doing it again, Tom. You were staring off at the distance." When his only response was a pinched frown, she went on: "If I can see that you're distracted, the crew can see it, too. That worries me. Are you sure you're all right?" Her clockwork arm, beautifully doused in sun, illuminated her face with a golden light.

"Yes, yes, of course." He put a hand on her shoulder. "I was only—"

"Man overboard!" Voleta called from the balustrade. They turned in time to see a flailing figure in a white sheet plummet from the *Cairo Hound*. They were too distant to hear a cry if one was uttered, but the silence of the spectacle only made it grimmer.

No one doubted who it was.

Iren broke the moment of quiet reflection. "He was a bad captain."

"But a worse bird," Voleta said.

419

if you enjoyed
SENLIN ASCENDS

look out for

SOUL OF THE WORLD
The Ascension Cycle

by

David Mealing

Three lines of magic must be conquered and three heroes must rise in the first book of this epic fantasy trilogy.

It is a time of revolution. In the cities, food shortages stir citizens to riots against the crown. In the wilds, new magic threatens the dominance of the tribes. And on the battlefields, even the most brilliant commanders struggle in the shadow of total war. Three lines of magic must be mastered in order to usher in a new age, and three heroes must emerge.

Sarine is an artist on the streets of New Sarresant whose secret familiar helps her uncover bloodlust and madness where she expected only revolutionary fervor.

Arak'Jur wields the power of beasts to keep his people safe, but his strength cannot protect them from war amongst themselves.

Erris is a brilliant cavalry officer trying to defend New Sarresant from an enemy general armed with magic she barely understands.

Each must learn the secrets of their power in time to guide their people through ruin. But a greater evil may be trying to stop them.

Start reading this gripping, vibrant, and imaginative addition to the epic fantasy canon for readers of Brandon Sanderson, Brian McClellan, and Miles Cameron.

1

Sarine

Fontcadeu Green
The Royal Palace, Rasailles

"Throw!" came the command from the green.

A bushel of fresh-cut blossoms sailed into the air, chased by darts and the tittering laughter of lookers-on throughout the gardens.

It took quick work with her charcoals to capture the flowing lines as they moved, all feathers and flares. Ostentatious dress was the fashion this spring; her drab grays and browns would have stood out as quite peculiar had the young nobles taken notice of her as she worked.

Just as well they didn't. Her leyline connection to a source of *Faith* beneath the palace chapel saw to that.

Sarine smirked, imagining the commotion were she to sever her bindings, to appear plain as day sitting in the middle of the green. Rasailles was a short journey southwest of New Sarresant but may as well have been half a world apart. A public park, but no mistaking for whom among the public the green was intended. The guardsmen ringing the receiving ground made clear the requirement for a certain pedigree, or at least a certain display of wealth, and she fell far short of either.

She gave her leyline tethers a quick mental check, pleased to find them holding strong. No sense being careless. It was a risk coming here, but Zi seemed to relish these trips, and sketches of the nobles were among the easiest to sell. Zi had only just materialized in front of her, stretching like a cat. He made a show of it, arching his back, blue and purple iridescent scales glittering as he twisted in the sun.

She paused midway through reaching into her pack for a fresh sheet of paper, offering him a slow clap. Zi snorted and cozied up to her feet.

It's cold. Zi's voice sounded in her head. *I'll take all the sunlight I can get.*

"Yes, but still, quite a show," she said in a hushed voice, satisfied none of the nobles were close enough to hear.

What game is it today?

"The new one. With the flowers and darts. Difficult to follow, but I believe Lord Revellion is winning."

Mmm.

A warm glow radiated through her mind. Zi was pleased. And so for that matter were the young ladies watching Lord Revellion saunter up to take his turn at the line. She returned to a cross-legged pose, beginning a quick sketch of the nobles' repartee, aiming to capture Lord Revellion's simple confidence as he charmed the ladies on the green. He was the picture of an eligible Sarresant noble: crisp-fitting blue cavalry uniform, free-flowing coal-black hair, and neatly chiseled features, enough to remind her that life was not fair. Not that a child raised on the streets of the Maw needed reminding on that point.

He called to a group of young men nearby, the ones holding the flowers. They gathered their baskets, preparing to heave, and Revellion turned, flourishing the darts he held in each hand, earning himself titters and giggles from the fops on the green. She worked to capture the moment, her charcoal pen tracing the lines of his coat as he stepped forward, ready to throw. Quick strokes for his hair, pushed back by the breeze. One simple line to suggest the concentrated poise in his face.

The crowd gasped and cheered as the flowers were tossed. Lord Revellion sprang like a cat, snapping his darts one by one in quick succession. *Thunk. Thunk. Thunk. Thunk.* More cheering. Even at this distance it was clear he had hit more than he missed, a rare enough feat for this game.

You like this one, the voice in her head sounded. Zi uncoiled, his scales flashing a burnished gold before returning to blue and purple. He cocked his head up toward her with an inquisitive look. *You could help him win, you know.*

"Hush. He does fine without my help."

She darted glances back and forth between her sketch paper and the green, trying to include as much detail as she could.

The patterns of the blankets spread for the ladies as they reclined on the grass, the carefree way they laughed. Their practiced movements as they sampled fruits and cheeses, and the bowed heads of servants holding the trays on bended knees. The black charcoal medium wouldn't capture the vibrant colors of the flowers, but she could do their forms justice, soft petals scattering to the wind as they were tossed into the air.

It was more detail than was required to sell her sketches. But details made it real, for her as much as her customers. If she hadn't seen and drawn them from life, she might never have believed such abundance possible: dances in the grass, food and wine at a snap of their fingers, a practiced poise in every movement. She gave a bitter laugh, imagining the absurdity of practicing sipping your wine just so, the better to project the perfect image of a highborn lady.

Zi nibbled her toe, startling her. *They live the only lives they know,* he thought to her. His scales had taken on a deep green hue.

She frowned. She was never quite sure whether he could actually read her thoughts.

"Maybe," she said after a moment. "But it wouldn't kill them to share some of those grapes and cheeses once in a while."

She gave the sketch a last look. A decent likeness; it might fetch a half mark, perhaps, from the right buyer. She reached into her pack for a jar of sediment, applying the yellow flakes with care to avoid smudging her work. When it was done she set the paper on the grass, reclining on her hands to watch another round of darts. The next thrower fared poorly, landing only a single *thunk*. Groans from some of the onlookers, but just as many whoops and cheers. It appeared Revellion had won. The young lord pranced forward to take a deep bow, earning polite applause from across the green as servants dashed out to collect the darts and flowers for another round.

She retrieved the sketch, sliding it into her pack and withdrawing a fresh sheet. This time she'd sketch the ladies, perhaps, a show of the latest fashions for—

She froze.

Across the green a trio of men made way toward her, drawing curious eyes from the nobles as they crossed the gardens. The three of them stood out among the nobles' finery as sure as she would have done: two men in the blue and gold leather of the palace guard, one in simple brown robes. A priest.

Not all among the priesthood could touch the leylines, but she wouldn't have wagered a copper against this one having the talent, even if she wasn't close enough to see the scars on the backs of his hands to confirm it. Binder's marks, the byproduct of the test administered to every child the crown could get its hands on. If this priest had the gift, he could follow her tethers whether he could see her or no.

She scrambled to return the fresh page and stow her charcoals, slinging the pack on her shoulder and springing to her feet.

Time to go? Zi asked in her thoughts.

She didn't bother to answer. Zi would keep up. At the edge of the green, the guardsmen patrolling the outer gardens turned to watch the priest and his fellows closing in. Damn. Her *Faith* would hold long enough to get her over the wall, but there wouldn't be any stores to draw on once she left the green. She'd been hoping for another hour at least, time for half a dozen more sketches and another round of games. Instead there was a damned priest on watch. She'd be lucky to escape with no more than a chase through the woods, and thank the Gods they didn't seem to have hounds or horses in tow to investigate her errant binding.

Better to move quickly, no?

426

She slowed mid-stride. "Zi, you know I hate—"

Shh.

Zi appeared a few paces ahead of her, his scales flushed a deep, sour red, the color of bottled wine. Without further warning her heart leapt in her chest, a red haze coloring her vision. Blood seemed to pound in her ears. Her muscles surged with raw energy, carrying her forward with a springing step that left the priest and his guardsmen behind as if they were mired in tar.

Her stomach roiled, but she made for the wall as fast as her feet could carry her. Zi was right, even if his gifts made her want to sick up the bread she'd scrounged for breakfast. The sooner she could get over the wall, the sooner she could drop her *Faith* tether and stop the priest tracking her binding. Maybe he'd think it no more than a curiosity, an errant cloud of ley-energy mistaken for something more.

She reached the vines and propelled herself up the wall in a smooth motion, vaulting the top and landing with a cat's poise on the far side. *Faith* released as soon as she hit the ground, but she kept running until her heartbeat calmed, and the red haze faded from her sight.

The sounds and smells of the city reached her before the trees cleared enough to see it. A minor miracle for there to be trees at all; the northern and southern reaches had been cut to grassland, from the trade roads to the Great Barrier between the colonies and the wildlands beyond. But the Duc-Governor had ordered a wood maintained around the palace at Rasailles, and so the axes looked elsewhere for their fodder. It made for peaceful walks, when she wasn't waiting for priests and guards to swoop down looking for signs she'd been trespassing on the green.

She'd spent the better part of the way back in relative safety. Zi's gifts were strong, and thank the Gods they didn't seem to register on the leylines. The priest gave up the chase with time enough for her to ponder the morning's games: the decadence, a hidden world of wealth and beauty, all of it a stark contrast to the sullen eyes and sunken faces of the cityfolk. Her uncle would tell her it was part of the Gods' plan, all the usual Trithetic dogma. A hard story to swallow, watching the nobles eating, laughing, and playing at their games when half the city couldn't be certain where they'd find tomorrow's meals. This was supposed to be a land of promise, a land of freedom and purpose—a New World. Remembering the opulence of Rasailles palace, it looked a lot like the old one to her. Not that she'd ever been across the sea, or anywhere in the colonies but here in New Sarresant. Still.

There was a certain allure to it, though.

It kept her coming back, and kept her patrons buying sketches whenever she set up shop in the markets. The fashions, the finery, the dream of something otherworldly almost close enough to touch. And Lord Revellion. She had to admit he was handsome, even far away. He seemed so confident, so prepared for the life he lived. What would he think of her? One thing to use her gifts and skulk her way onto the green, but that was a pale shadow of a real invitation. And that was where she fell short. Her gifts set her apart, but underneath it all she was still *her*. Not for the first time she wondered if that was enough. Could it be? Could it be enough to end up somewhere like Rasailles, with someone like Lord Revellion?

Zi pecked at her neck as he settled onto her shoulder, giving her a start. She smiled when she recovered, flicking his head.

We approach.

"Yes. Though I'm not sure I should take you to the market after you shushed me back there."

Don't sulk. It was for your protection.

"Oh, of course," she said. "Still, Uncle could doubtless use my help in the chapel, and it *is* almost midday..."

Zi raised his head sharply, his eyes flaring like a pair of hot pokers, scales flushed to match.

"Okay, okay, the market it is."

Zi cocked his head as if to confirm she was serious, then nestled down for a nap as she walked. She kept a brisk pace, taking care to avoid prying eyes that might be wondering what a lone girl was doing coming in from the woods. Soon she was back among the crowds of Southgate district, making her way toward the markets at the center of the city. Zi flushed a deep blue as she walked past the bustle of city life, weaving through the press.

Back on the cobblestone streets of New Sarresant, the lush greens and floral brightness of the royal gardens seemed like another world, foreign and strange. This was home: the sullen grays, worn wooden and brick buildings, the downcast eyes of the cityfolk as they went about the day's business. Here a gilded coach drew eyes and whispers, and not always from a place as benign as envy. She knew better than to court the attention of that sort—the hot-eyed men who glared at the nobles' backs, so long as no city watch could see.

She held her pack close, shoving past a pair of rough-looking pedestrians who'd stopped in the middle of the crowd. They gave her a dark look, and Zi raised himself up on her shoulders, giving them a snort. She rolled her eyes, as much for his bravado as theirs. Sometimes it was a good thing she was the only one who could see Zi.

As she approached the city center, she had to shove her way past another pocket of lookers-on, then another. Finally the press became too heavy and she came to a halt just outside the central square. A low rumble of whispers rolled through the crowds ahead, enough for her to know what was going on.

An execution.

She retreated a few paces, listening to the exchanges in the crowd. Not just one execution—three. Deserters from the army, which made them traitors, given the crown had declared war on the Gandsmen two seasons past. A glorious affair, meant to check a tyrant's expansion, or so they'd proclaimed in the colonial papers. All it meant in her quarters of the city was food carts diverted southward, when the Gods knew there was little enough to spare.

Voices buzzed behind her as she ducked down an alley, with a glance up and down the street to ensure she was alone. Zi swelled up, his scales pulsing as his head darted about, eyes wide and hungering.

"What do you think?" she whispered to him. "Want to have a look?"

Yes. The thought dripped with anticipation.

Well, that settled that. But this time it was her choice to empower herself, and she'd do it without Zi making her heart beat in her throat.

She took a deep breath, sliding her eyes shut.

In the darkness behind her eyelids, lines of power emanated from the ground in all directions, a grid of interconnecting strands of light. Colors and shapes surrounded the lines, fed by energy from the shops, the houses, the people of the city. Overwhelmingly she saw the green pods of *Life*, abundant wherever people lived and worked. But at the edge of her vision she saw the red motes of *Body*, a relic of a bar fight or something of that sort. And, in the center of the city square, a shallow pool of *Faith*. Nothing like an execution to bring out belief and hope in the Gods and the unknown.

She opened herself to the leylines, binding strands of light between her body and the sources of the energy she needed.

Her eyes snapped open as *Body* energy surged through her. Her muscles became more responsive, her pack light as a feather. At the same time, she twisted a *Faith* tether around herself, fading from view.

By reflex she checked her stores. Plenty of *Faith*. Not much *Body*. She'd have to be quick. She took a step back, then bounded forward, leaping onto the side of the building. She twisted away as she kicked off the wall, spiraling out toward the roof's overhang. Grabbing hold of the edge, she vaulted herself up onto the top of the tavern in one smooth motion.

Very nice, Zi thought to her. She bowed her head in a flourish, ignoring his sarcasm.

Now, can we go?

Urgency flooded her mind. Best not to keep Zi waiting when he got like this. She let *Body* dissipate but maintained her shroud of *Faith* as she walked along the roof of the tavern. Reaching the edge, she lowered herself to have a seat atop a window's overhang as she looked down into the square. With luck she'd avoid catching the attention of any more priests or other binders in the area, and that meant she'd have the best seat in the house for these grisly proceedings.

She set her pack down beside her and pulled out her sketching materials. Might as well make a few silvers for her time.